FOR THE LOVE OF ANGEL

Losing love, devastating, then there's the journey back

PETER L. HARDING

It should be understood, this novel is a work of fiction. The events and characters described herein are imaginary and any association to real people, living or dead should be construed as coincidental. Where applicable historically names and places depicted are real. The opinions expressed in this manuscript are solely the opinions of the author and do not represent the opinions or thoughts of others.

The author has represented and warranted full ownership and/or legal rights to publish all the material in this book. No part of this publication may be reproduced, stored in a retrieval system, or transmitted in any form or by any means, electronic, mechanical, photocopying, recording, or otherwise, without the written permission of the author.

Author photo: Chrystina Lammers
Paparazzi Productions
Cover Photo: Robert 'Rob' Rose - Brisbane

ISBN-13: 978-0615904344
Publisher: Big Thumb Publishing
First published 2013

Printed in the USA

Dedicated to my wife, Lynne, a most beautiful lady in every way. An inspiration for this fictional manuscript

To my children, Justin and Lisa
Grandchildren, Max and Lulu
You enrich my life ten-fold

Also to
David and Kerry, Chrystina and Danielle

CHAPTER ONE

Twenty-eight years old, when he first saw Angelic Taylor across the room, while his heart did a no holds barred double-back flip spin, his mind chimed in simultaneously telling him to take a second look, then, uncontrolled, exhausting a third look, casual as he tried to be, there was no question, he had never, ever, in his life, seen anyone quite like her before. Having lit up the room like a bolt of lightning brightens the night sky, she radiated a glow that riveted him to the very spot he stood. Even his legs felt wobbly! Talking to fellow attendees at the New Orleans Convention they were both registered for, this unknown woman to him, then, had not moved an inch in five minutes, caught up, it seemed, in a very intense conversation. Only her arms moved every now and then as if to make a point in whatever the topic was that had four people's attention. Instantly, Steve Frankston knew there was no choice. Win, lose or draw, he had to meet her. His only problem was – how? The convention, attended by some 1,500 people, the declared official count meant finding a valid, credible reason. Maybe, he considered, through surreptitious means by him they could accidentally on purpose bump into one another, or, he could register to a designated group session choosing one for no reason other than this delightful lady had, or, or…undaunted in his mission, he'd find one. His courage…he'd find that, too!

"You're a very persistent man, and yes, you wore me down, but it was nice," Ms. Taylor shared over a cocktail they were enjoying in the bar of the Chateau LeMoyne down in the French Quarter where she had elected to stay. "However, I might add, had you not mentioned your links to Central Florida, I doubt I might have responded favorably to join you for dinner, so maybe you should thank basic geography and not me, personally for tonight. Our commonality of Volusia County was the lynch pin to me sitting here and to dispel your immediate curiosity of that connection, if you are wondering, I will explain it all better over dinner, although, it's all really quite simple?"

Steve Frankston was stunned. So it wasn't his charm, his conversation, his good looks, or his elegant newly bought suit and tie that had attracted her to him, favorably - it was Florida, the Sunshine State. *'Why Florida, but I'll find out soon enough, I guess'* he surmised silently, not that he wanted to labor the issue. For now, though, just to be with her was good enough, and thankfully, they were hitting it off as natural as two people should; fortuitously, they both seemed to have plenty in common. He could thank their related profession for openers but also, music, travel and, of course, as she had said, Florida, the bigger mysterious bonding connection. How glad he was, albeit, not easy, that he'd managed to find and meet this delightful lady. Tough as the mission was, initially, tenacity had paid off, it had been worth every ounce of the relentless effort he'd put in to attract her attention. Oblivious in real terms, he had learned the harder, and sometimes more disheartening way, just how difficult it was to physically meet someone in natural day-to-day settings, or simple and social ways, rather than the well known *'pick-up-joints'*; bars, clubs, events and the like. A convention, though, was not a place he'd *ever* have considered when it came to matters of the heart, but it didn't matter, the large hall gathering was the perfect start, just as their opening conversation was in the place they were sitting now, a restaurant bar, enjoying a pre-dinner drink. Warming socially to each other, it was time to release a little more of his SF charm, he decided.

Angelic Taylor turned out to be a more than interesting woman. Extremely down to earth, she was obviously well educated and apart from being very attractive, a blonde-hair blue eyed instant head-turner, she was both dynamic and confident in every way, too. She also had a soft side, one that showed every so often, especially when she spoke of her family. Steve Frankston had no doubt she would be highly successful in her chosen career, the same one as his, for now - Real Estate. Personality, everyone knew, in selling real estate, was a no-brainer. If you couldn't talk the talk as well as walk the walk in a field as highly competitive as property you were destined to be an *'also ran'* failure. Clients in the market of buying or selling houses liked to be well informed, to believe they were dealing with trustworthy people who knew their industry and who would protect their dealings honestly when it came to the most valuable, expensive item they would ever, in their life-time, invest hard earned money in. Angelic Taylor had that air about her. She was capable, indeed, a skilled veteran of all the necessary traits, hands down! From small talk to better-defined subjects; she was a natural.

Never short of conversation, their dinner provided ample opportunity to cover a myriad of subjects, not the least, backgrounds. Angelic's parents, he learned, were Florida loyalists, hence, the Volusia County connection; her Father, a self-declared Cracker, was born and raised in New Smyrna Beach, while her Mother, originally from Fort Lauderdale, grew up mostly in neighboring Daytona Beach. Borne out of a mutual love of all things, NASCAR, through the motor sport was how they both met and as if destined to be, fell in love. For years, they smiled about the moment, sharing it with all and any who cared to listen or know. In the spectator stands of the speedway track, located near the famous mound and a mere eight seats away from each other, returning from buying drinks, her Mother spilled the full contents of four large cups of Coca-Cola over her Father as she tried to step around his long legs. She had *'accidentally'* tripped - the rest became history! Within four months they were married…and their first years – blissful. Not to plan, what came naturally to her parents, followed. Extracting themselves from a friendly BBQ one afternoon, ahead of the well-touted day of debut, two days hence, unexpected, their baby, Angelic, began her slow grand entrance into the world in the nearby small inland town of DeLeon Springs. Famous today for its popular State Park and tourist trappings, historically, Native Americans used the springs as far back as 6,000 years ago, while in the 1800's, the earliest settlers built sugar and cotton plantations that were processed by the Seminole Indians. Folklore; many claimed *'a fountain of youth'* existed. Maybe, Angelic added with a recollected smile, it was why her parents always looked so young and certainly younger than the well into their seventies in years when they passed. Although never having actually lived there, DeLeon Springs and the neighboring city of DeLand, site of the hospital in which she would finally be actually delivered, her childhood links to Florida still meant something to her, although, she admitted; it had been a long while since she was last in the State. Anecdotally chatty and reminiscent as she'd become, she proffered a thought, that someday she would seek out once again, not only from whence she came and where she spent some younger, memory filled years, but to visit what would then become the first time, the origins of her physical birth, acknowledging, *'it would be interesting to see what the place down there was really all about?'* Finally, she concluded, from settling in Orlando where her Father worked, she still a child, he having risen to the top of his profession as a civil engineer, and having been promoted, it required their transfer out of State, to of all places, Memphis, Tennessee. The city would remain where he saw out his workdays. On retirement, her Father took himself and her Mother immediately back to Florida, to New Smyrna Beach. *'I gotta get back to my roots'* Angelic mimicked in the southern accent of her Father before adding that she, by then, had grown to love Memphis, and being in the work force, and happy, couldn't see herself leaving anytime soon.

Sitting, listening with delightful interest of the life and times of Angelic Taylor, the night of what became a million stories between them, wore on. Then, before either could even begin to believe it, nine-thirty rolled around. Sadly, it was almost time to call it a night. The final day of the Convention was due to start at 7.45am and a big day was planned with many guest speakers, one motivational speaker particularly. No one wanted to miss Troy Hazelwood. He knew his subject, he knew his game – he was a must see and hear. First up on the agenda, if one wanted to be seated within the first five rows, it would mean an early morning wake-up call. A nightcap drink, a brief chat about the convention so far and a light hug in the hotel foyer – it was time to part. Agreement had been made to *'catch up'* tomorrow night, before the fateful next day when everyone would be heading back to where one came from originally. While Steve Frankston would be leisurely driving to nearby Florida, Angelic Taylor would be on an already solid booked no cancel 7am flight to Memphis. *'Duty calls, I have appointments,'* she told him, he having already asked, more than once, if he could visit her sometime in the Volunteer State. With a nonchalant nod of her head she had quietly said *'yes'*, not expecting to have to repeat it more than once. One daunting piece of valuable information he had gleaned along the way, not wanting to hear it at all, while not married, yet, Angelic admitted to be seeing someone, although she was careful to qualify, nothing serious, while annoyingly adding, *'he's nice, I like him.'* Again undaunted, Steve maintained his hope!

Irrational, as he wondered if he might have become, or was being, eight plane trips later with four months gone, the ninth trip for Steve Frankston by car, pulling a U-Haul to Memphis Tennessee, was definitely going to be the last. When Angelic, earlier, had agreed, he had jumped for joy, the suburban township of Whitehaven would become their new shared home. All he knew specifically about the area of Memphis she had chosen was that the famed singer Elvis Presley once lived there, and his home, Graceland, was a shrine to the performer, still loved and visited by millions the world over. His recollected thought; *'Graceland, in Whitehaven, historically has to be good to attract as many people as it does, three times a year; his birthdate, January 8th, the anniversary of his death, August 16th and Christmas.'* Mildly familiar with Elvis' music, regardless of age, who wasn't? And could well understand why such adulation could last so long as over and over, it was forever claimed, Elvis was the revered, original, King of Rock and Roll. Although his birthplace was Tupelo, Mississippi, the family moved while he was still young. In his teens, Elvis quickly found his feet going on to ultimately find his success from Memphis, something gladly accepted he was now going to have imitate vocationally. Deep South Southern in both style and living, and hot, muggy and humid as it gets, he could embrace Memphis, likewise, if it meant having Angelic Taylor by his side, and soon, hopefully, as his wife, not that she knew that, then!

Their whirlwind romance had been pure storybook. Love at first sight, for Steve, Angelic quickly warmed to his exuberance of life, his romantic side, his quirky sense of humor, his interesting, somewhat sad background, but above all, his penchant for hard, honest work. From visiting as often as he did, as he promised back in New Orleans, and then undertook, flitting between his home in Ormond Beach, Florida to Memphis, getting to know one another, they soon found a very similar mutual relationship that became the proverbial *'two peas in a pod.'* Giving back in enthusiasm, no stone was left unturned to share with Steve, the city Angelic had adopted and then settled into, knowing, it had been by choice that she had stayed long after her parents retired back to Florida, to finally, having no qualms over time to inevitably call Memphis home, period. Together, love and laughter prevailed as they shared many sightseeing *'getting to know you'* places; The Orpheum Theater, The Memphis Zoo and Botanic Gardens, the architectural Cotton Exchange Building, the Mud Island River Park and Walkway, Sun Studios and Stax Museum of American Soul Music, and that was just for starters! And when any day was done, Beale Street downtown never failed to wrap up any night for restaurants, music and an atmosphere that spelt joy…their joy of simply being together. Time, it seemed, moved so quickly, soon, they began to realize, there would be no turning back.

"I love you Angelic, like no other I've known, but…" he told her the night before it was time to go, again, his eighth trip concluding. She hated the word *'but'* spoken in the context he'd used it, somehow, it seemed to conjure up bad things and for a split second, a doubt consumed her. He continued. "…But, I *can't* keep doing this," he shared, honestly. "And truth of the matter is, I've made a decision."

She looked at him, almost scared at what he was about to say. It *couldn't* be that he didn't want to see her anymore. It *couldn't* be that he wasn't able to come back to Memphis anymore, and it *couldn't* be that he had a life back in Florida he needed to get back to, that he'd let too much slip over these past four months, and he had to stop being a fool and realize, time and distance, even money, was becoming prohibitive to their relationship, happy as he appeared to be, loving their relationship as he did. *Didn't* he? Angelic dreaded what she was about to hear as he took her hands in his. Looking deep into her eyes; she felt the faint hint of tears forming.

"I don't like the sound of this Steve. You're much too serious and after the day we've had so far, in fact, the four days this trip, something seems ominous, out of character for you and although I'm listening, I'm not sure I want to hear what you're going to tell me. It's that word, *but*...it always seems to..."

He squeezed her hands a little tighter. Gentle enough, but just firm enough to dispel her fears, as he interrupted her words, her train of thought.

"*Angelic*! I didn't realize I emanated such a vibe. I never *meant* to, but, and while I'm using that word again, let me tell you, *assure* you, the but, as a word, means *nothing* as all I have to say is not actually bad. It's just that..."

"What do you mean, *all* you have to say is not actually *bad?* Does that mean maybe *some* of it is?"

She shuddered a little as she spoke.

"*No* sweetheart, *no*. Of *course* not! *My*, you're sounding *so* sensitive tonight."

Ready to jump in again, stop his course of news, good or bad, or whatever it might be, Angelic was about to speak when he withdrew his hands from hers, holding one in the air as if a summons to cease all conversation completely. Obviously, he had procrastinated a little too long with his news. It was time to get straight to the point, to end the doubt, the fear, which was clear on her face. He couldn't stand the agony of what was, no doubt, her inner pain.

"I'm moving to Memphis," he blurted out. "Moving, *here,* to Memphis," he repeated. "I'm actually *leaving* Florida. I can't *take* it anymore. There, I've said it. Your turn!"

Stopping abruptly, he leaned back in his chair, heaving a sigh as he did, waiting for the response. It came quicker than anticipated and the words spoken were not quite what he thought he might hear.

"Oh dear, I didn't expect that or see that coming..." she began to say.

"You didn't?" he exclaimed, interrupting her. "You don't *like* that idea? *Me, Memphis!* Well, I thought..."

He was surprised. He'd expected a much different reaction, in fact, a bigger, more positive one. But then, obviously, he had reacted faster than he should have

"*Like* it?" she answered. "Of *course* I like it you klutz. I *love* it, I *love* it and I can't wait, but what made you decide to do it and are you *sure,* I mean, *really* sure?"

She had shocked him again, however, this time, in all the right ways.

"Of *course* I'm sure you *big* klutz back. I've thought about it for a while and frankly, I just don't want to be apart from you anymore. I miss you every time I leave and the only way I know how to fix it is to come *here*. Come to Memphis, to you, unless you want to come back to Florida" he threw back as an idea.

"Oh, Steve, you know I can't do that, yet, anyway. It's not to say that someday maybe, but for now, I couldn't, but anyway, you've said you'll come here, so that's it. Please, do it. Yes, yes. We'll make it work, we will, I promise."

Angelic meant every word. She loved Steve and everything about him. He had made such a difference in her life, short as the time might have appeared, or actually been. Ever since the conference, their meeting in New Orleans, when it was over and she'd left that final morning to fly home, she had done nothing but think about him, wishing many times she could see him again, wanting to spend time with him. Believing it might never happen, wondering if they were simply words at the time, or if he really meant that he would come and visit her in Memphis, when he'd asked and she'd said yes, his turning up that first time, it was as if it were the 4th of July. Sparks, bubbles, butterflies and smiles were all she could remember. Her heart fluttered; she even felt scared inside. And yet, had no idea why, really? Was it all a wishful dream, an aberration of life? It was true – in reality, they hardly knew one another except what they had shared over staggered conversations, limited as they had been! What was it; she often challenged herself, that made her say *'yes'*, that opened the door for a new adventure? Happy enough in Memphis, doing things her way, she loved her life, simple but rewarding as it was, and certainly had no problems in her social life when it came to men seeking her company. What, then, could it have ever been, that this stranger, Floridian or otherwise, captured her attention, then her heart? The only thing Angelic could believe, in the why and whatever, whirlwind or not, their love had to be for a reason. Unquestionably, choosing Steve Frankston, for her, would be right in *every* way. She *wasn't* wrong!

Fortunately, Steve had really liked Tennessee, and especially Memphis. Successful as he currently was, and hoped to be with the Company he was contracted to in Holly Hill, when he told them he was leaving, that he had no choice but to ask for a release, that he'd fallen in love and it was all their fault for demanding that he attend the New Orleans conference in the first place, they took it way better than he could have believed or expected. Initially they said *'No'*, then, reconsidering, given their many branch offices throughout the South; they chose instead to re-post him, to also help in his relocation, thereby, keeping the investment already made in him, intact. And when he headed to Tennessee, it was with the best of wishes, and a farewell gathering that concluded with the Branch Manager, Willis Rogers, saying *'Do us proud Steve, do us proud, and if you both ever decide to come back to Florida where real estate is gaining momentum, our doors will always be open, you'd be more than welcome.'* It was quite the compliment for a dynamic up and coming Sales Executive and Rogers' words were meaningful, taken to heart. Grateful, he could not have anticipated the changes coming.

Within the week, Steve Frankston headed north, determined to not only continue to build a successful career for himself in a big city, but also, in anticipation of broadening his relatively personal more mundane life to dizzying heights of the unknown, he wanted it to include, in tandem, being a good husband and hopefully, someday, an even better Father. He *knew* what he wanted in life, and if this was stage two, with gusto, he was on his way to achieving it.

Angelic, of course, then, knew nothing of his enthusiasm of settling down as quickly as he had envisaged, or of marriage, or of children, however, that small fact didn't deter him at all. He had no doubts about his future; all he had to do was secure the missing link; Angelic was it! There was a life to live and he wanted to live it in every way possible, with no stone left unturned, or missed, and he knew that could only ever be with Angelic Taylor. She had captured his heart, now he wanted to make sure she took it, and held it, so they could forge, together, his plans, his dreams, that hopefully, would fast become hers, too. With so much to do, to see, accepting time stands still for no one, it was time to harness life, and never let a second ever get away. It was a challenge. He would meet it. Angelic Taylor would agree, he believed?

Two months later, they married, in a small civil ceremony without pomp or splendor. Their home in Whitehaven, two blocks off the still posted U.S. Highway 52, re-named Elvis Presley Boulevard, was a four bedroom, three-bathroom, ranch style bungalow. They considered themselves, middle-class *'doing okay'* folk, with a dream ahead. Honorable as he was and after repaying transfer fees, forsaking real estate, Steve Frankston opted instead to pursue his preferred well-entrenched first love and hobby, Graphic-Design, in to which he immersed himself with renewed vigor. Angelic meanwhile, exceled selling prestige properties.

Thirteen months into their marriage, on official announcement of her pregnancy, Angelic slowed down sufficiently to glow and enjoy the impending new challenge of motherhood. Life was sweet. Months later, blessed with a child, a little girl, Josephine Lisa, the Lisa being Angelic's mothers name, happiness abounded, their lives now more complete, and their home - full of love.

~~~~~~~~~~
~~~~~~~~~~

CHAPTER TWO

Josephine was such a joy. Happy, bright, always smiling, rarely tearful, she enriched immensely the life of Steve and Angelic as if she were sent from heaven. And as the months passed, from crawling to walking, making unknown sounds to real words, being spoon fed to sitting up at the table with them eating solid foods, Josey captured their hearts in so many indescribable ways. They couldn't believe it had all been seen, shared, or done before, by anyone. With such magnitudes of blessed contentment with everything they were enjoying in a baby all being so new, surely, they thought, they must be blazing new trails in human behavior. A model child going everywhere with them, it didn't matter what time of the day or night, Josey was always by their side, snug and safe. She was their little piece of heaven, truly loved. With business thriving and the down time plentiful enough, the big wide world Steve Frankston had promised and said would be captured and shared, was slowly being checked off. Life really was for the living! Angelic couldn't believe his energy.

"Where this time Steve?" she asked.

"New York, the Big Apple," he told her.

"Well, I must admit, we haven't been there, together that is, but I thought you said California would be the next part of America we'd explore," she queried, not that she cared, she would go anywhere in life with the man she loved as he'd already enriched it ten-fold, another ten was always welcomed.

Josey had just turned three and as much as she'd never remember any of it, she was quite the traveler. From baby to small child, she actually like planes, although the car gained her attention more, only because it meant greater freedom to do what she wanted whenever the whim took her, especially staring at DVD's or being able to get out anytime they stopped for gas, a meal, a break, to sight-see. Little Josey loved being spoiled at gas stations, with a big ice cream. They didn't have those on planes.

Counting down, documenting, sharing the remembered photos and video, life together had been all Steve and Angelic expected. Their sequence of travel was impressive; the French culture of Montreal, Canada, snow and skiing in the Colorado Rockies, the magnificence of Sedona and the Grand Canyon in Arizona, Tex-Mex and the Riverwalk in San Antonio, San Francisco and the Bay and of course, a return trip to The Big Easy and New Orleans, to finally, outside the USA, so far, London in England; they were all forming a pattern, the way they might like to live their life. So much so, Steve, lately, had become a little more comfort driven, adventurous even, in wanting to buy a Fifth Wheel or an RV, but that was something, an output of money Angelic baulked at declaring, *'too expensive for now'* and she was right! The Ford Expedition they drove most places performed well and served their purposes perfectly when it came to comfort and style, and when they didn't drive, they flew. It was a win, win and as a two-some with a little one, life was feeling mighty good.

Driving back from spending a magnificent week in Pensacola, a region Floridians and many others call the *'Redneck Riviera,'* citing as reference, magnificent wide and white sandy beaches and the clear crystal waters of the Gulf of Mexico, while cruising initially, the back roads up through Mississippi, it was Angelic who chose the subject and for some reason, known only to her, finally, after all this time, she had to know what was going through his mind, then, and whatever had possessed him to be so hasty in choosing her and especially the way he pursued her. It was actually a series of questions, rolled in to one. Steve shrugged his shoulders, the seat belt rising effortlessly with his body action.

"Oh, that's simple, real simple,' he replied. "One look and I was a gone, and yes, given it was immediate, I couldn't believe my good fortune, but of course, I'm the only one who knew it. Yeah, I know it was quick..." he enthusiastically qualified, "...but when we started talking after that first really brief encounter of a simple hello, when I took the high road, the pulling no punches, nothing to lose cavalier attitude, right there and then, dumbfounded as you were, from your reactions, your carefree responses and your willingness to share and enjoy approach, a chatty dialogue simply flowed between us. Interested or not, you at least showed conversational compassion and let's face it, you could have blown me off easy and may have had every right to do so. But you didn't. I prevailed, with you, *because* of you, and believe me; I was floored!

"Frankly, I had never met anyone like you, ever, and every time I asked you something, be it simple or with a little more depth, you seemed to know the answer or at the least, exactly what to say. It was like, to me, you were an encyclopedia, a scholar, a learned individual who had, or must have embraced an insatiable appetite to learn, I mean, how can you, anyone, have known so much, I wondered. What I'm saying is, you were sooooo interesting, and back then, you captured not only my mind with your ways of the world thinking, but I have to add, the way you enunciated, qualified yourself…it was like music, pure verbal music, with a lilt that belongs to only you. That's what captured me first, then, when we finally ventured into personal chat, family, friends and significant others along the way, none if it bothered you, none of it. Honesty prevailed and that's a rare commodity, pre-relationship these days, dare I say! Anyway, how's that for openers?" he queried, knowing his reply had been certainly long-winded.

From momentary silence, then an added comment.

"I could go on you know, and will, if you want, because I realize I haven't answered all of your questions, loaded as they were, are."

Inwardly, he glowed inside. He had expressed accurately, exactly all he felt and believed about the lady by his side, his wife; and he had meant every word spoken!

Josey was sound asleep. The drone of the wheels, the moving motion of the car, the soft chatter of two people talking about matters that were foreign to a child, all worked, sending her into a dream world of her own. With her little head falling from side to side every now and then, or bobbing up and down, and her eyes closed in gentle rest, the peaceful innocence that let her drift away to wherever her little mind took her, conjured up a wish; that her life be as calm and happy, relaxed and bountiful, as it was here in the immediate and onward for the future, for all it could ever be, and that never a moment of hardship, of grief or pain, ever comes her way. Wishing was okay.

Angelic, meanwhile, responded to his welcomed lengthy answer of explanation.

"*My, that's* a speech. You over credit me I feel, Steve, and I have to believe it can't *all* be so cut and dried, however, I'll *take* it, I'll *take* it," she double confirmed, while adding, she doubted she could *ever* live up to such expectations, that he was overstating his case and his evaluation of her in those first couple of meetings back in New Orleans.

"Not at all and in no way would I have said it if I didn't mean it, Angelic," he told her. "There's *so* much about you that you don't give *yourself* credit for I'm *amazed,* and maybe, sometimes, it takes another to lead the way. I mean, let me give you an example of what I'm trying to say, okay?"

He proceeded to enlighten her as to why he had so much adoration and admiration for her, reminding her of their second meeting, their lunch together, following the appearance of the motivational speaker, Troy Hazelwood, who had spoken that morning of *'taking chances'*, and of being acutely aware of the part *'trust and honesty'* played, as opposed to *'not knowing or ignorance'* in business, but also, and especially, in personal human relationships. Hazelwood had implored it being paramount to any real success in life, accepting immediately and unfortunately, that it is sometimes extremely hard to come by. Failure *'in trust, incorporating honesty'*, he had emphasized, before adding the words too often exercised instead, *'cheat, scheme, cover-up'*, then, if that is one's modus operandi, when least expected, in life, expect to lose all, to fail. And you will, he had confidently suggested, offering to give examples if needed given he had them readily available! No one took up the call. Too many failures in all arenas had been sensationalized in the media over the past many months. Speaker Hazelwood's point had been made!

"And so, from how I saw and heard, in everything about you, it was as if this *Troy* character had struck a huge personal connect with you. Your family, your life, your work, your moving from here to there, and then some guy you were seeing off and on, now and then and that you liked him, my goodness Angelic, there wasn't a thing left out and then…and then…with me, without batting an eye-lid, without offering an excuse and without even a mild sense of hesitation, you said to me, *'I have no idea what it is, none whatsoever, but Steve Frankston, you are a piece of work and I mean that in the very nicest of ways. Whatever has possessed you about me, I don't know, but yes, if you want to come to Memphis and see me, if you're prepared to do that, then I'd love to spend more time with you. Strangely, I admit, you also intrigue me a little, too.'* Those were your almost exact words. Do you remember that at all?" he asked, wondering if she did.

"I *do*," she admitted. "And I *also* remember saying to you that I was deeply touched by your sharing with me, firstly about your Mother and her passing, to then, how your Father turned on you, I was so devastated for you, I couldn't imagine it, at all. It was heart wrenching to hear you tell it. But no sooner had you emotionally shared the story, *then* you *really* touched me, because immediately after the revelation of your life, you added very quickly, how important it was that you learned from it and made something of yourself, and that it inspired you to become motivated to be an achiever, someone who didn't want adversity to affect your life ahead, and I couldn't help thinking at the time how you had already started that part, the where you were going, quickly adding, love and the right woman would complete your life, and of course, a child, too. You mightn't have realized it at the time, but you were so passionate about what you were saying, so positive and so in touch with yourself and what was required of you, I couldn't help but think of the most wonderful qualities I saw in you, to believing, here was a good man. And another thing, you were *right,* Troy Hazelwood *did* reach me, *did* motivate me, especially with his impassioned plea about *'trust, honesty and getting a grip on life',* especially one's own, it was all so true. Then, lo and behold, when we were together, chatting, knowing it was the last time as we understood it might have been, then, that we might actually never see each other again, for all you had parlayed to me, *guess what,* it seemed we were both sailing in the same boat. I truly liked, loved might be the better word, all you portrayed and the character you put forth which was you and you alone. Unwittingly, or maybe not and it didn't really matter, but you had laid yourself bare, no blustering, self-aggrandizement, or the like; it was simply you being you. I truly liked that, a lot! So you see, similar to you, I had a reason and now, here we are, today, together, and all I can say to that, thank God we are. I *love* our life, and you, too, my dear sweet Steve Frankston."

For both, it had been a delayed moment of truth, confession, even. Finally, with time getting away from them, they moved from being on the secondary roads to the freeway joining Interstate 55 just past Jackson, Mississippi. Now making good time, there were still about three hours to go before they'd make it home to Memphis. Enjoying the ride and their own company, their conversation continued to flow and while not counting, the miles had flown by. Before they knew it, in between laughing, smiling and remembering, by unanimous agreement, in their jocularity, they self-inducted each other into their very own MAS - Mutual Admiration Society. Not done with it all, yet, to endorse her induction, Angelic had a final question of her husband. It was true; he hadn't answered all her questions. There was one she still had to know.

"So when you arrived in Memphis from Florida, *dragging* that U-Haul behind you, it seems to me, as I recall, vividly, *after* you'd unloaded, showered and we went out, back to what had become your favorite little haunt on Beale Street, you had no sooner finished your first course, then, as if a light bulb went off in your head, your words, correct me if I'm wrong, your very next question was *'Angelic, I don't have to think about it, and I hope you don't have to either, but darling, will you marry me, be my wife forever and always.'* Was that about right? Did I capture it exactly as you said it?"

"*Yep!* Exactly right, *every* word," he gladly confirmed. She continued.

"What was it Steve? What *was* it that made you move so fast, asking me to marry you, because as much as I wanted us to be together, to see if we had a chance at life and to be sure we were even right for each other, you circumvented the normal course so fast, I wondered if you weren't being hasty for a reason, or was it that you really loved me, as you said, *'love at first sight, no doubt about it.'* Not that I had any hesitation, or regret a single thing, but what was it? I've always been quite curious about that."

Steve Frankston had never had a doubt about Angelic Taylor. He knew it in New Orleans, he knew it back in Florida, he knew it over his growing number of trips to Memphis and he knew it now, driving his SUV with her and their baby girl beside him.

"You mightn't ever believe this Angelic, and it might sound odd, or even in the broader concept of life, perceptive, but do you know something, sometimes one simply *gets* it, and that for no explainable reason, there's a deep down underlying unknown force that compels you to act a certain way, do something *extraordinary,* believing you're doing it because it was right, that it *had* to be, that it was waiting for you and you alone. Now, if any of that makes any sense, it happened to me, with you. Deep within my mind, I knew instantly you were meant for me, that I was drawn to you for a reason, it being the one I wanted it to be – for love. You, it, me, love; all hit me like a sledgehammer, a force I'd never known before and probably in my lifetime never will again. *Now,* accepting that, somehow, within those unknown brain portals that exist, that harbor our inner strength and understanding, when you least expect it, they open up, which meant, in our joint cases, I knew that you would find me, too, and *why,* because we were destined for each other, *believe* it! And not to leave it there, strangely, there was always a good reason why, and that goes for both of us. We simply don't know the why of it yet only time will answer that part. Anyway, with that aside, we're sure off to a great start, huh?"

"*Wow!* How do I answer that, Steve, *that's* deep, *profound* even, but whatever, you obviously believed it."

"I do, I do and what's more, when I asked you to marry me, I actually *knew* you would say yes. There was never a doubt in my mind and of course, I was right! You not only said yes, immediately, you also posed another question, your own question which was - *'When, I can't wait'*, do you remember that?"

"Of course I do, and this is what you said back to me. *'Tonight, if you want'*, so how about that?"

"And I meant that, too. It mightn't have been practical but from where we were that night, I bet we could have found a preacher if we wanted one. And *hey,* if we *had,* in the park across the street with that big statue of W.C. Handy in it, I *bet* also we could have found a stray Memphis blues band that would have gladly played our wedding song, albeit, their way. Now wouldn't *that* have been the coolest thing? Mr. Handy would have been impressed, had we actually *done* it!"

"Well, Steve, all I can say is, you've excelled yourself. And to end it, let me share this, and may God be my witness; there's not a single thing I'd change about us. I love us, and all we've become, and continue to be. Josephine has been my, *our,* pride and joy and you're a marvelous Daddy to her. My life is so much richer for having found you and every day I thank that same God that you were so *persistent* in your pursuit and *love* for me. I *am,* a *very* lucky girl. Being Mrs. Angelic Frankston, I feel blessed, and whatever about all the driving forces you speak of, and whatever the deep underlying reasons you claim exist, and are the reasons for you and me, I'm *glad* you knew them, I'm *glad* you saw them. And Steve, truly, I love you in every way possible."

"You're welcome, sweetheart and I love you back, and right now, I'm ready for home, dinner, and you. I can't wait."

~~~~~~~~~~
~~~~~~~~~~

CHAPTER THREE

Through and through, Josephine Frankston was a girl's girl, and from the get-go, most everyone called her *'little Josey.'* With a mop of blonde hair, a wardrobe full of colorful dresses she loved to wear, and a heart as big as could be when it came to her most favorite person in the whole wide world – Daddy, whenever possible, she was always by his side taking in every moment she could to spend with him, doing the things she loved to do best, writing, drawing, making things like cardboard cutouts, people or animals, or putting together plastic buildings, Lego, but especially listening to him when he read her a book, as they did regularly. Anytime Josey was with Daddy, she was the world's happiest little camper. Unashamedly, she was no tomboy, unlike many of her friends who wanted to ride bikes, scooter ride up and down the streets after school, or climb trees, all Josephine, *'little Josey'* wanted to do was go home where she felt secure, safe, and sit in her room, or around the house doing what she always thought as *'normal things.'* Was that so bad? Thankfully, Daddy didn't think so. He knew she'd find her own level and in occupying herself in ways that pleased her most, for now, if that meant staying a girl's girl that much longer, then he was never going to impede the natural progress of what came effortlessly. He loved his baby, his beautiful girl just the way she was. She'd grow up fast enough, and for now, at eight years of age, he'd let her do what she wanted, when she wanted and how she wanted. In his mind, there was no doubt already she would grow up to be *'somebody'* someday – she was way too creative, too dog-minded to achieve, and he loved the way she took to all projects, large or small, and made them come to life. Was that the artist in her, a budding future entrepreneur, a writer, a painter…for now, it wasn't a priority. A fine attribute, a wonderful quality, when his daughter put her mind to something, she saw it through, right to the end.

It was nine o'clock, Josey had turned in earlier than normal for a Friday night when she could normally stay up a little later if she chose to, but tonight, it wasn't the case. She was completely worn out, not only from her afternoon sporting activity, a rival netball game against a neighboring school in which she had scored the winning goal, and the celebratory gathering they held immediately after, but also, the time she had spent, after a later than normal dinner putting the finishing touches to the wooden doll house she was constructing, with Dad's artistic help, of course. Josey was the greatest love of his life; he'd do anything for her, just as he and Angelic had shared together, when they were a family. But that was then! Too often, most times late at night, all Steve, Daddy, could wonder would be; why did God see a need to take her Mommy, his wife, Angelic, the love of their lives away from them, just when they needed her most. And oh how he wished he hadn't been left alone to raise Josey, to becoming the wonderful daughter she is, before He called her home. There was never a doubt, many times Josey would miss her as much as he did, and every day, for some reason or another, there would always be a moment, a reason, that seemed to trigger their need to bring Angelic into their lives, and when they spoke of her, the room would seem to light up that little bit brighter, as if she were standing right there with them. And tonight had been no different. As the last piece of furniture was placed inside the doll house they had taken almost three months to put together, it was Josey who posed the question, *'Mommy would have loved this doll house Daddy, wouldn't she, because Mommy loved dolls, and I think this would have been special for her, do you think so, too?'* Daddy had no problem agreeing with his baby girl, as it was true; her Mom did love dolls and had collected a few over the years, but none was ever more special than the one she gave Josey on her birthday, when she was five years old, the last one they would ever share together. It was the same doll that was *her* treasure; the birthday present Angelic's Mother had wanted her to have when she had turned five, all those years ago. On this occasion, for Angelic, symbolically, she had a personal need to match the timing, knowing, someday, she would give Josey her doll, anyway.

Coinciding the gift to mirror their ages at the time, in her eyes, it made the day and event all the more special. Unspoken, there was also a secondary reason, why. Regardless, with all the love in the world, when handing the doll over, wrapped in a little pink blanket with a note attached to her wrist, ironically, at Josey's behest, together, they would name her, Angel, a direct connection to Mom's given birth name, Angelic. At the time, Mom, was touched deeply at her daughter's choice of names and had no trouble agreeing, in fact, she was ecstatic, a reaction that delighted Josey no end. Her smile said it all! Unknowing to her, though, the naming suggestion would forever remain a deep-seated question - was that prophetic, then? If so, how could Josey ever have known? It didn't matter. Mom and Dad looked at each other before sharing a kiss – their seal of approval to their little girl. As a family, it had been a momentous occasion and clearly, Josey was deliriously happy. She read the note out loud. *'Josephine - once my little baby doll, she's now yours. Love her forever won't you, just as I did. She is special, like you. Love to you both, always, Angelic - Mommy XX.'*

Looking innocently pretty, Angel, at a mere fifteen inches tall, had been as cute as could be and the smile on her faintly painted lips was just enough to make you want to smile back, while her eyes...when yours met hers, nothing much else mattered; light blue, they seemed to gaze directly back at you with love. And her hair; it was blonde in color…but it wasn't real. Long enough to be short, or short enough to be long, it was known as molded and settled beautifully in a slight curl, a little above her shoulders. Complementing her visual beauty, her rosy cheeks were cute, blushed to perfection. Angel was actually quite captivating, and no matter wherever she might be in a room, you couldn't help but want to pick her up and give her a little hug. Unquestionably, she had the ability to capture a little girl's heart, and did. There was something very different about her. Unique in her own way yes, but also, she was uncharacteristic in an intriguing way, and maybe that's what really drew one to her in the first place – or not! Made of composition material, the doll was a child of the fifties, forties, even.

Unfortunately, today, due to her current condition she was held more secure being dressed in a body-hugging onesey undergarment, and for that, there was a valid reason. About three to four months ago, as far as Steve Frankston knew; from being well loved, played with and tended for, she had developed a problem. Her head had become floppy, falling forward, backward, sideways, left, right, also, her arms and legs dangled loosely by her side. She gave the appearance of being broken, literally, or maybe it was just something simple inside needing a little attention that would correct the problem. But how did one get to find out without damaging her further? It was an unanswered question posing quite the dilemma to an eight-year-old, and there were no quick answers, either. She had told her Daddy but not even he knew how to correct it, and he knew everything, that was a well known fact…well, almost everything, however, on this occasion, all this Daddy could say was *'I don't know, sweetheart, I really don't know what's wrong but believe me, I'll find out, I promise.'* Josey knew he would. When her Daddy said he'd do something, especially for her, he always did it. He'd never forget and although many times it might take a few days, ultimately, he'd always be true to his word, then, when least expected, whatever the problem, it was done, fixed, good as new! This time, though, with her precious Angel, it was taking a little longer than usual. All Josey could do was wait. Daddy must be real busy these days, she surmised. And that was okay; her little doll wasn't in pain as such, that much she knew. With expert knowledge and a little TLC to get her little body put back together, made strong again, the way she once was, maybe then they could start playing, spending time together as they often did before. Josey had accepted, probably, it wouldn't be long now?

Ritual, Steve Frankston had gone to double-check his daughter. Standing quietly at Josey's bedroom door, watching her, a smile on his face taking in her peaceful innocence as she slept, suddenly, it hit him – hard! For no reason, casually glancing to his left he saw Angel, lying snug in her basket, the original small pink blanket covering her. Immediately, guilt overtook him, still, he hadn't done a thing about repairing her, and yes, Josey would no doubt be quietly disappointed, but then…? He knew nothing about dolls, except they belonged to little girls, and grown women too – yes, Angelic. He shook his head, inwardly angry with himself, accepting; he had to make sure he paid more attention and not adopt the *'out of sight out of mind'* mentality that had clearly existed here! The task of fixing the doll, or arranging for it to be fixed, had gotten away from him, and shouldn't have. Chastising himself even more, beyond the shadow of any doubt, had Angelic been with them, sharing their lives still, she would have had the doll repaired long ago and her namesake, Josey's absolute tribute to her, would not be lying face up looking sad, forlorn, next to her favorite Barbie Doll, who, by contrast, looked all shiny and new, still in her box. Now feeling like a *'non-caring'* Daddy, he was remorsefully annoyed at himself!

~~~~~~~~~~
~~~~~~~~~~

CHAPTER FOUR

Daddy, what happened, if you remember, what happened to Mommy, and why was she so sick all the time? And Daddy, you fix so many things for me, how come you couldn't help Mommy? Why did you let her go away, or didn't you know what to do to make her better?"

The heart inside Steve Frankston about stopped. Whatever had possessed his little girl to ask such a question, out of the blue one afternoon, he wondered. Time had healed some wounds but there were, still, it seemed, many that lay dormant. This was clearly one of them. Now eight, Josey was only five at the time when Angelic passed, and to her, too much happened, or changed over the past three years, leaving now an obviously growing blank in her young, ever expanding and growing mind. Unexpected, she had caught her Daddy off guard, big time! Never before had such a question been posed to him, and for all the people that knew him, for all the people that supported him, for all the people that wanted to help, then, Doctors, Nurses, care-givers, neighbors, friends – *none,* could have posed a question so impactive, so heart wrenching, so truthfully, as an eight year old who still innocently wondered, but knew, her Mommy was never coming home again. Not that she had brought the subject up, or mentioned it over the past…too long - what hurt even more; her doll, Angel, her Mom's namesake, still lay in her bedroom, broken, as if she too, were lifeless. From the tears that welled in his eyes, to the sadness he felt for not being able to do more, and for the heart that beat inside him that was feeling so heavy…it was all he could do, as a Daddy, to not want to whisk his little girl up in his arms and hug, love and hold her forever, until all the hurt went away, never to return. Try as he had over time, he had done his best to keep the memories of such a beautiful lady etched, to be seen anytime, anywhere, as if she still stood in their very midst. But, it couldn't be, would never be, however, it was not a crime to dream, to wish, to want.

Josey's question of *'what happened'* had turned back time, more than he ever wanted, but still, she needed an answer, indeed, was old enough to expect one. Carefully, Steve, Daddy, cast his mind back, seeking a way to frame how best to tell her more about her Mom. There was so much she would want to know, be it now, or at a later time. Now, he decided, was as good as any might ever be, to start. Josey had opened the door; it was time to step up. He did!

Angelic was in a melancholy mood, reminiscing, sharing with Steve some anecdotal stories of her family. Why, again, he had no idea? Some he'd heard before. They were sitting on the back patio, cooling off from the sultry day that had seen the temperature reach a seasonal high of 99 degrees. The humidity was still stifling.

"My father loved Elvis Presley, his movies and his music. His favorite song was It's Now Or Never and I can remember him singing it all the time. Mom was the same although she claimed one called Love Me Tender, but it wouldn't matter, they'd play his records, sometimes way too loud, and I'd be in my room trying to study, wishing they would turn it down, but now, as I think about those days, those times, I'd wish them back a million times. How I'd love to hear them all over again."

"But you *can,*" Steve reminded his wife. "Grab the iPod, an mp3, a CD even and put it in the player, or the USB in the car and we can *all* sing along, anytime we want. That would do it, it's easy!" Angelic smiled. He never changed. He loved his electronic toys, today's modern marvels.

"I remember their stories," she continued, "and my Dad telling me that when he got the word about being transferred to Memphis, all he kept saying to Mom was *'Why did Elvis have to pass so young? Here I am, moving to the same city he lived in, and now he's no longer there. Now I can never meet him.'* He was like a big kid apparently, and Mom, she told me she would smile and say, *'yes darling, but don't forget, he was a big star, everyone wanted to meet him, so why would he have taken time out for you?'* But he didn't care. Important as he was and what he did, Dad that is, he hadn't forgotten his childhood hero, just like we all had them, but anyway, now, all those years later, there we were, all of us, heading to Memphis. So I guess he had his idiosyncrasies, his dreams and wishes, too."

Nights together, sharing each other, planning their next adventure, chatting, cooking a BBQ, to sometimes, even, sitting in silence, reading a book, they were the best times ever. There was one night when it had been no different.

"You know, Angelic, like your Dad, I get it, I think, about Elvis and all! I know *you* were entrenched in Memphis when we met, but for *me,* it was simply another big city, however, since being here, listening and learning so much from you, I've become a bit of a pseudo aficionado, especially hearing your Father's stories about the guy, and now I get it in the bigger picture stance. Elvis Presley was never my kind of guy, or my kind of singer, even, and that's not being disrespectful, facts are, he was just *way* ahead of my time, I mean, *neither* of us were even born when he died. But what is *undeniable,* there's a ghost of the guy everywhere you go. Anyone who lives in Memphis knows that and it's eerie, really. One thing I do remember pretty good and more from *our* time as kids was that song *Walking In Memphis* by Marc Cohen, Cher also did a great video clip of it, too. And that's what I mean about it all, 'cause that was *quite* the song, *spiritual,* even, which is the sense I get of it all now. Do you know what I'm talking about, even?"

She did, and had heard it all before. The best part, though, any Elvis chat always reminded her of her Dad, and there was always another story, Presley related.

"There was a guy, a family, actually." She started to share another one. "They came into the office looking to buy a house and do you know, fanatic as he was, he insisted it had to be on one of the neighboring streets with a property that backs up to Graceland, which meant the odds were small to zero. He said they'd wait. Can you believe that? The houses on the Graceland perimeter are limited in number at the best of times, but more to the point, *what* was the point, except the obvious? They were from Texas and moving to Memphis and living there, in that vicinity became their dream, their need, their absolute only place to buy. Needless to say, I couldn't help them, but that's not to say they might not have found one since then; that was about two years ago. Elvis may be long gone, but his lights haven't gone out. Strange, isn't it?"

"Someone should have reminded them, *'Elvis has left the building'*, Graceland that is," Steve was compelled to say in reply. It brought a smile despite the number of times the line was used, especially in Angelic's line of business.

Leaving Florida and all her friends back then was hard, Angelic recalled another night, explaining, Dad said they had to go if he was to move further ahead with the Company, while Mom said, it was a big adventure, and we'll all come back one day. Angelic didn't believe them, asking, why couldn't she stay behind? None of it had made any sense to her, at the time. Reality was, being much younger, she hated Memphis initially, and then, in relating another incident, that no sooner had they arrived and settled there, a small student riot took place at her new school forcing the teachers to lock them all in their classrooms until Police could quell the mêlée outside. Known *'troublemakers'* who demanded more sports time started it. They also wanted less phys-ed. Scarred from the incident and scared for her young life that day; she begged to be sent back to Florida where she had always felt safer - all to no avail. And so the stories went.

Oddly, Angelic's melancholy lingered, as did, equally, many growing conversations that had turned far too much to reminiscing the past, of family and childhood stories. Mildly confused, one day, Steve Frankston decided to ask - *'Why are you always looking backwards?'* Her response, unusual, it was almost confrontational. *'Don't you* ***like*** *hearing my stories? I always thought you did, I'm sorry!'* She didn't mean to be hurtful in her reply; it was, to her, simply, how she felt at the time. Steve understood, or tried to, however, it was more that he was worried there might be something deeper to it, an underlying reason. Wisely, he didn't dwell on it! Regardless, in her own time, Angelic heeded what she considered might be a cryptic call, triggering a personal reaction of her own.

Quietly, prophetically, consulting her Doctor, she sought the reason, any reason, if there was one? Two weeks later, totally unrelated to the original question, the probable, never to be suspected real reason, reared its head! Haunting him for the longest time, he wished he had never said anything, then, maybe, she, they, would never have known, but then again…?

From the routine Doctor's check, blood tests were called for followed by a Cat (Computer Axial Tomography) Scan. An abnormality was clearly evident; the dark shadow of a tumor existed in her breast causing grave concern. Exhaustive examinations and biopsy brought forth worsening news; cancer was active in her body. Angelic was devastated. From the specialist, soul destroying, unexpected, and unnecessary, adding to the devastation, the shattering diagnosis was delivered without heart or sensitivity; it was, as if, it were a common occurrence, an every day event, imparted with the words - *'we'll deal with it, not a problem!'* How wrong the Doctor was, and how could he have acted that way? His so-called verbal *'bedside manner'* was cold, and callous, not what the medical profession was known for. Medicine and its dispensation is one thing, doctors' who treat and save lives, another. For Angelic, both left a deep psychological scar; *'what now of my baby girl, my husband, and my life? I have so much to do and share,'* she cried.

Instantly, Steve Frankston stepped up, he knew no other way; a dedicated unselfish loving duty was called for; both his girls would need him now – he'd be there, unquestionably.

Was this the reason that destiny called him that day, that wonderful day, when across the convention hall room he saw the most beautiful girl in the world? He hoped so. If there were a way for Angelic to win the fight, he would be there for her, by her side, every day, always. He vowed to never falter.

That night, as if all alone in the world, with Josey asleep in her bed, they cried together. Also, that night, Angelic doggedly assured her husband she would fight. Come hell or high water, devoid of the odds, no matter what they threw at her, operations, IV's, pain, drugs, counsel, *nothing,* she declared, *nothing,* would stop her from winning the battle for life. And on that first night, Steve hugged and held his wife closer than ever, he kissed her, talked to her, reassuring her he would be there, with her, all the way, pledging his very life to help her, regardless of the odds. And that same night, while Angelic prayed for help in her journey, he rallied his forces to stand beside her. Now, they were both ready. It turned out to be a battle royal!

As the days, weeks and months wore on, collecting prescription drugs and administering them, to preparing meals and drinks to keep a body going, Angelic began to slip a little. *'Oh, it's probably the chemo, or radiation'* she would declare, always with a smile. It was then, Steve recalled, just how brave she really was and had been throughout that period. Nighttime, though, was always the worst. Tossing and turning, trying to sleep when sleep wouldn't come, the mind would race in a such a dizzying whirl not knowing if any of the never ending thoughts rushing through the brain, deciphering all of life's problems, worries and heartache, would make any sense - it all took a toll. Remembering all the good times, reminiscing the way it all was, still, there remained a why…the old saying *'life wasn't meant to be easy'* was well and good, however, for Steve Frankston and their little girl, life was factually quite hard, hard, hard! Sadly, finally, almost thankfully considering those last few weeks of a long eighteen months period, one day, as she lay in his arms, Angelic, his wife, Josey's Mommy – left them.

Stark realization hit; they'd never again see her smiling face, or hear her laughter, or share the loving home they'd built together, again – and Angelic's last words as he remembered them, *'I love you Steve, and thank you for my life, and our life together, but now, God needs me.'* He heard them over and over again, *'He needs me in His Angel Band',* became her added words of simplified justification of why, and her journey ahead, alone. Steve wanted to scream out loud, because many times, those last words wouldn't stop, they would echo over and over in his brain almost tormenting him.

"Well, God,' he would finally cry out in open reply, "***we*** needed her too. Didn't you *understand* that? Josey and me, ***we*** needed her too, and ***why*** did you take her so young, when she was so vibrant, so full of life, and God, a question for you – *'why don't you intervene, find a cure for cancer and save so many more of your children?'* Surely you don't need a band *so* big that you call on so *many,* and if you do – why, that's selfish."

There were never any answers…and the nights still remained the hardest period of time to endure. Then there were many memories. And they forever flooded back. Someday, the many assuring repeated, someday, his mind wouldn't torment as much, and he'd begin to see a new day for the reality of its beauty and glory. All Steve could do was listen, with grace. While Angelic may have released him, he doubted he could ever release her, doubting further, there could ever be a life and love as strong as the short one they had enjoyed. And yes, he shed his tears of sorrow, his loss of such a wonderful partner. Through Josey, he would love her always, and for her, he would be a strong, devoted and loving father, always. Again, he vowed his mission, never to default.

Angelic, wife and mother, who both dearly loved, had lost her hard fought battle to breast cancer, triple negative carcinoma; a newer aggressive strain with an astonishingly high failure rate of 70%. She had fallen victim to the numbers. At just thirty-two, she was far too young to have contracted the dreaded disease, another one for which there was still no real cure…and with no cure, there could only ever be - hope! Angelic, as demonstrated often, had had plenty of that, and then some. Full of confidence, belief, and a driving will to join the 30% survival-rate group, she had striven valiantly to overcome her plight, however, the debilitating treatments, chemotherapy, radiation, and medications ravaged her, wearying her more and more, day by day, and with God calling her, finally, with no choice but to let go, bravely, she reconciled in her mind that her time had come – His Angel Band, beckoned. Every day, it seemed, there was always a reason for Steve to ask questions. The strides made in modern medicine, the growing technology, the drugs now available, the newer cyber knife surgery, the money spent on research, the Doctor's, the Oncologists, the Radiologists who all specialized in cancer treatment; wherever you turned or looked, it was top of mind, on every list available as being the number one disease to meet, to conquer, forever. And yet, for all the never-ending efforts, the fund-raisers, the marathons, the telethons, the prayers - every day, another person is lost to the dastardly, dreaded disease…and then, another family mourns their loss. Steve, who had been at Angelic's side from the beginning, mastering every challenge put in front of him to work with and help Angelic beat it, had been a sworn member of that *'never-want-to-be-in'* 70% failure fraternity; until, reluctantly, vehemently opposed, with kicking and screaming no choice, on the saddest, darkest day of his life, he was forced to join.

That was three years ago – today, he clung tightly to his memories…his beautiful, his marvelous, his wonderful, memories. And he cherished every one, fresh, each new day, as if they were real - only yesterday. Angelic was embedded forever in his mind – no one could ever take that away from him. He wouldn't let them!

For just the shortest of time, while part of Steve Frankston had struggled with his reminiscent answer to Josey's question, he had relived some of the happiest, and saddest, moments of his life. Such was the love he had for Angelic. And he knew only too well, there would always be another story to tell, that Josey would ask about, or he would volunteer. Lovingly, he expected it. For now, though, his story, his thoughts, and the many anecdotal moments had been shared, and from it…he hoped he had answered her original question, as innocently as she had asked.

~~~~~~~~~~
~~~~~~~~~~

CHAPTER FIVE

For all the right reasons, a team excellence emerged. Life might not have been the same anymore, having been dealt the severest of blows, however, it wasn't going to change Steve and Josey's will to gain control of their much-changed lives. Work and school became their respective challenges. They had needed to prove to each other they could handle adversity, regardless. And they did!

Now, at eight and thirty-five, the younger, Josey, had graduated to Grade 4 in school, while Daddy, the elder, had elevated to CEO of Visual Communication; Graphic Designs - Web and Software, incorporating Entertainment and Film. Josey excelled her grades and marks topping the class each term. Steve also excelled. Delegated with strong personal overview on all projects; the Company prospered.

Unlike anything they had ever done before, this year, as Christmas approached, their joint decision was easy to make; both needed *'time-out'*, a vacation. Too much in life over too many months had changed, and apart from the house being in need of a good scrub from top to bottom, a chore they many times shared, this time, on conclusion, sitting around talking and thinking, it was time to *'chill'*. With no pun intended, it was winter; Memphis was down around forty degrees, with the nights even chillier. What they needed, they felt, was warmth and sunshine.

"We could go to Hawaii," her Father offered, "*that* would be different, for you." Josey didn't respond.

Then, he suddenly remembered, he and Angelic had been there once, pre-Josey, staying in Waikiki, they'd loved it. The visuals flooded back momentarily – bad call!

"*Nah!*" he suggested, "Maybe not!" To his surprise, Josey agreed. She had other thoughts.

"Daddy, let's forget going away. We don't have to. It'll be nice here, too."

Steve didn't get it. Confused, he wondered why she wouldn't want to spend time away this year; Christmas's were never the same without her Mom. They had agreed not to have a Christmas tree, they agreed not to share presents the way they used to, except maybe just one, and they had agreed, being someplace new, different, would be exactly what they wanted. To be alone, time for themselves, and yes, they would still, as always, share a special moment, for Mommy, but not in the house, where she wouldn't be.

"Why sweetheart, why, we agreed? Tell me what's changed, tell me what's on your mind?"

Happily, her Dad was used to spending many nights and weekends together with her and no matter what they did, their time was always precious. Bonding ever tighter, slowly, as best he could manage, he helped Josey understand why, the loss of her Mom, except, sometimes, when least expected, she'd go to bed sad, wishing things could have been different. It would be during these tender moments, Steve knew, Daddy's hugs and reassurances were paramount to make her feel better, to accepting that they, together, could keep going and get by. Yes, he shared, he missed her Mom as much, and yes, he loved her, too. It was a fine line to walk and at times, emotionally difficult. And then, in complete contrast, when least expected, out of the blue and for no reason, sometimes, on the weekends or holidays, Josey would walk into his bedroom with a tray loaded with pancakes smothered in Maple Syrup and a big mug of coffee. *'Wake up, Daddy. Here's your breakfast.'* What a treat, what a moment, what a girl! And Daddy loved mornings such as that secretly wishing for more, truth was, selfishly - he never wanted her to grow up.

"Daddy, can I be honest with you?"

"*What,* of *course,* Josey, of *course* you can be honest, how could you *ever* think you shouldn't be? Nothing is more important to me than you and if something ever bothers you, if you ever need to talk, or want to tell me something, *anything,* don't ever believe you can't, and as for being honest with me, I'd *expect* that, *always*! Now, the big question is, *what's* on your mind? Please, tell me, I'm listening."

"Well…" she started to say, hesitating a little.

"Tell me, baby, don't hold back."

"Well, Daddy, I *know* it's Christmas, and I *know* we have agreements, and I *know* things cost money, and I *know* we're on our own, you 'n me, and I *know* you're the only one that, that…"

"Josey, what is it?" her Father asked, almost demanded, but in a pleasant way. He couldn't stand where her *'I know'* line was going and what the real problem was, except, he was fast becoming aware that something pretty big must be on her mind, and now, he had to know *what*?

"Is it *pocket* money? Do you want *more,* am I not *giving* you enough, or is there something for Christmas you really want deep down and it cost a lot and you don't want to tell me what it is, or the *trip* we've yet to decide on?"

"No, Daddy, it's *none* of those things, the trip a little maybe, but yes, it *does* mean money, I'm just not sure *how* much or even if it can be done."

"Then tell me straight out. *Don't* beat around corners. I *need* to know and when I do, *then,* maybe, I can help you, okay?" It had been time to get to the real point.

"Okay, Daddy," she said, all enthusiastic, yet serious. For Christmas, I'd like to have Angel back, all mended. I'd feel closer to Mommy with Angel, and Daddy, it hurts me to see her in that basket, broken. I *know* we have to find a way, a place to fix her, but if we don't *look* then she'll *never* be fixed, she'll just lay in the basket, and it's been too long already. So, *that's* what I would like for Christmas, Angel, all better."

Again, Steve Frankston felt a renewed heart jolting inner regret. His Josey, growing up taller, smarter, every day, had just shared how she had a heart that pined for something special in her life, her Angel, her Mother's namesake. How could he have let this all get away from him, again? *How*? And *why*? It wasn't the first time! What ever possessed him to forget – was it out of sight, out of mind? Angelic would be furious with him, he knew it! He felt his body almost begin to tremble. His first reaction was take his little girl in his arms and hug her, hold her, comfort her; she had, he was sure, built up so much courage to say what she just had. And he knew he should have taken care of Angel long ago. Obviously, he hadn't been paying enough attention.

"Whatever it cost, whatever we have to do, that's *all* I want this Christmas. Nothing much else matters, and especially not a trip!"

Josey had said all she wanted. Now it was up to her Father. Going somewhere, anywhere, wherever, wasn't important. She could stand the winter blast if she had to, but Angel couldn't anymore, she'd reasoned; the money that would be spent on going away could be saved, Angel could be mended. That would be, to her, the greatest gift of all.

Christmas, without Angelic, Mommy, birthdays, too, were always the hardest. This time, though, there was a set in cement concrete plan. Angel would be taken care of, that was a promise, and they were still going to *'chill-out.'* With a two-week break that would take them into the beginning of January, they branded themselves 'The Duo', Josey explaining the night before they simply had to have a nickname; otherwise it would not be *'cool'*. Different, her Dad had thought, however, whatever made her happy made him happy too, so, 'The Duo' they became.

Finally, all packed and ready to go, their adventure mapped out together, Steve and Josey Frankston headed out for places unknown. Earlier, her Father had comforted Josey with all the compassion he could muster, assuring her in every way imaginable, that as fast as their shared Christmas-New Year break was over, that as soon as they returned home, and as fast as he could possibly find the solution - promise, promise, promise – he, they, would find where, or a way, to have her precious Angel back together and as good as new again. Somebody had to know of a place; or maybe the Internet would provide the answer. As fast as he had said it, he knew he should have gone down that path long before now. However, it didn't matter; when they returned home he'd find the answer, someone, anyone, who knew how to fix dolls; a doll hospital, even. Josey smiled at her Father, wondering, in her fertile mind, if there really was such a place; like, a real Doll Hospital. *That* suggestion sounded a little far-fetched.

Places unknown became a de'ja'vu of the way Angelic and Steve had set out to live their lives, traveling. Now it was Dad and Daughter and what a feeling. Steve Frankston loved every minute of it, knowing it wouldn't, couldn't last. Eight would become ten, ten would become teenager, and from there, who knew? He decided to take what he could, as he could, accepting time would be the arbiter of how he might succeed of he and Josey and their being a one-parent family. Heading south, chasing sunshine, Tupelo came up first, then Atlanta, and from there it was on down to Tallahassee and finally, Panama City and Destin, both part of the Florida Panhandle. Christmas and New Year that first time out, couldn't have been more different, or better! Stopping here, there and everywhere, sightseeing, beaches, restaurants, wonderful hotels, select tourist rides, some historic spots highlighting the nation's growth, it was memorable, rewarding and above all, loving. Then, while homeward bound, as if it were meant to be, something happened! Fate, of a special kind, entered their lives when they least expected it. It was called, Dunbridge. Steve Frankston, knowledgeable as he was, had never heard of it!

He and Josey were in the food court area of the gas station after refueling to pick up a snack. McDonald's had an outlet in the facility that he knew would take care of them both, Josey especially. She settled for a simple cheeseburger and coke, he ordered a coffee and a premium grilled chicken wrap. They sat down to eat. Trying to eat and drive, he knew, was way too cumbersome, and anyway, he'd probably spill half of it all over him, to say nothing of the fact, it was also dangerous and the last thing he would ever want would be to put Josey in peril, ever! Dining in was much easier. It turned out to be an excellent call. Halfway through her meal, Josey noticed a girl, about her age, sitting four tables across. In her arms she was holding a doll, a little bigger than her doll, Angel, except hers was complete, and from what she could decipher; her arms and legs were able to be posed, her head, movable, sturdy and firm, too. The doll was wearing a light mauve dress edged with frills, also a pair of shiny black shoes. From Josey's vantage point she looked very pretty. It was her first reminder of Angel since being away from home in Memphis, causing her to think about her. Her Father, not missing a beat, noticed.

"I *haven't* forgotten the promise, sweetheart, I want you to know that!"

"I know, Daddy, I know. I was just looking. It's a pretty doll, though, isn't it?"

Not so discreetly, again, they both looked in the direction of the table and the family of four, and this time, as they did, the younger girl noticed. She lifted her doll higher for Josey to see better and as she did, they smiled at each other. Her Father caught the interaction. The young girl with the doll then said something to her Mother, who nodded her head in reply. Sliding back the chair she was sitting in, she then moved away from the table heading straight for Josey. As she approached their table, her words were not only friendly, but touching, too. She motioned her doll forward.

'I saw you looking at her, would you like to hold her? Her name is Charmaine."

"That's a beautiful name," Josey shared. "*My* doll's name is Angel, it's named after my mother who died and my doll always reminds me of her, except she's broken."

"*Broken*?" the young girl asked, as if a question. "Oh dear, that happened to mine once but I had her fixed and now she's fine again."

Steve raised an eyebrow to no one as he took in the words. Again, he felt guilty. Josey, meanwhile, took the doll in her arms and gave her a small cuddle before lifting her up in both hands to look directly into her face. She thought she was beautiful.

"So *how* did you fix it?" she asked, innocently, happy to make conversation with the little stranger who must have liked dolls as much as she did.

"My Mother took her to the doll hospital over in Dunbridge and although it took longer than I thought, the lady in there still fixed it and when I went back to pick her up, she was like the way she was before. I was happier than I'd been in a long time because before that, I didn't know what to do and my Dad was no help, he couldn't fix her."

Steve Frankston gulped, wondering as he did, were all us Dad's the same? Their problem had been eerily similar.

"So was that a hospital for dolls you took her to, like a *real* one?" Josey asked the girl. "I've never heard of a doll hospital before."

Surprised she didn't know, the girl nodded a simple *'yes'* in reply. Josey's face immediately lit up. She turned toward her Father having heard the good news.

"My Daddy's going to have mine fixed when we get home, *aren't* you, Daddy?" she reminded him before continuing, "And then I'll be able to play with her again, like you and take her places, just like you do. Oh, and I love your Charmaine, she's really nice, thank you so much for showing her to me, for bringing her over."

With a broad smile she handed her back.

"That's okay, but you should take your doll to the lady we did, she's nice and she's got so many other dolls and things in her store, you'll really like it. Maybe you can find yours a sister there, too, I did" her newfound friend of the moment suggested.

Listening to the interaction, now intrigued, Steve had an idea.

"Excuse me little girl." She looked his way.

"If you don't mind, what's your name?"

"Cammie." She stared straight at him.

"Well, Cammie," Steve began. "Your Daddy, is that him over there at the table where you were sitting?"

"Yes," she replied a little sheepishly, almost coy. "He's with my Mom and my brother. My brother's name is Rhys."

"Rhys, that's a nice name, you both have nice names, I like them, but I'd also like to talk with your Father," he told her, "Have you all finished your meal yet?"

Cammie beamed a broad smile, happy to share the news of where they were heading next.

"*Yep!* And from here, we're going to the movies, what about you?" she asked direct to Josey who had been distracted by her Father, wondering why he wanted to talk to the girl's Father, thinking, hoping; maybe it had to do with the doll hospital Cammie had mentioned.

"Stay here, both of you, until I get back, okay?" He slid out from the table.

Josey was right! No more than a couple of minutes later, her Father returned. Cammie said good-bye to Josey then headed back to her family who were beginning to move out. As they all waved to each other on exit, Steve Frankston, now firmly ensconced back in his seat, had a smile on his face that spoke volumes.

"Guess where we're going from here?" he asked his daughter.

Josey remained silent, looking at him, still hoping. She wasn't disappointed.

"To Dunbridge. It's not that far from here it seems, an hour or so, maybe, but we've got time, and here's the better news. We're going to see this lady Cammie mentioned along with her doll hospital. And who knows, maybe we'll find out from her all we need to know about Angel, and what to do, how good is that?"

"But Daddy," Josey interrupted, "Angel's not with us, how would we get her there, to the hospital?"

"Well, let's see if we have the solution to Angel first, because, remember, we may not!" he added. "So be prepared, either way. Right now, there's only one way to find out, and we will. We've got nothing to lose but time, so, let's go little girl. Next stop, Dunbridge."

~~~~~~~~~~
~~~~~~~~~~

CHAPTER SIX

The town was bigger than Steve Frankston thought. On the outskirts driving in, all the name chain stores and restaurants were present; Sears, TJ Maxx, Office Depot, Burger King, UPS, Arby's, Payless and more, however, on approaching the downtown area of the city, it all changed. No chain names, only small, independently owned establishments existed. Dunbridge was certainly quaint, one could have suggested, even historic, and it was certainly clean! Eyeing each store name as they passed by, they were only interested in one. Slowly, checking them off out loud, finally, there it was, The Dunbridge Doll Store. 'The Duo' had read the name off together, in unexpected unison. Josey couldn't hold her enthusiasm any longer.

"Daddy, Daddy, this is it," she almost shouted. *"This* is the place, the hospital for dolls. *Wow!* Can we go in? It looks like it's open, I *hope* it is!"

To hear the excitement in his little girl's voice, to see the smile on her face, to share the moment of what might be the answer to his prayers, it was worth a million dollars. His only hope; that it *was* open and that someone was there. Somehow, glaringly, both had missed the neon *'OPEN'* sign hanging in the window. Conveniently, Steve managed to park his SUV right out from the front door in a bay that must have been earmarked especially for him. The omen pleased him. This day, now late in the afternoon, had all the potential to be all he hoped for, and as for Josey, this stop may even turn out to be the highlight of all the days and the much traveling they had done, rolled in to one.

Safe on the sidewalk, they stood together, admiring the front window. It was staggering. Picturesque, with so much to see, everything looked so magical. Was this a little girl's heaven on earth? There were two dollhouses, one a double-story full of the tiniest but nicest doll furniture. It was marvelous. Standing next to it was a beautiful doll that seemed to be peering into the second dollhouse, her hand leaning against one of the walls. She had long blonde curly hair that hung down behind her back accenting her beautiful blue dress. Staring at her, Josey seemed enthralled. Then, peering harder through the large plate glass window, there were dolls everywhere. Josey had never seen so many. In fact, she had never walked into a fully stocked traditional doll store before, or for that matter, even seen one, or had any idea they existed, believing only, that dolls came from Toys R Us or Wal-Mart or, or…wherever? Memphis certainly didn't have a doll store like this, or anything even remotely close!

There was truth in everything she felt. Doll stores don't exist much anymore. What once was a thriving industry, a mecca for girls and women alike, was today, a dying art, a disappearing proposition in retail, except through the conglomerates who provide only the latest, most fashionable and many times, outrageous of dolls and dress styles! The glory days of making dolls, of doll stores, was fading rapidly. And as the years go by, they become less and less, until one day, only what China or wherever want to thrust upon the young girls will be seen and then, unlike generations before them, doubtfully, any will be collected. The Dunbridge Doll

Store, incorporating a hospital as displayed on the colorful 'A' frame sign, defied the odds. The visuals of the exterior were like a magnet, the inside; Steve and Josey Frankston were about to find out.

The eyes said it all. As Dad watched daughter, his smile, and her shocked absolute amazement should have been captured on film. It was a magnificent scene. Josey's hands went up to her face where she seemed to hold them for the longest time. She was rendered momentarily speechless! Steve, a graphic design artist, knowing photography and special effects, visual and so much more, remembered the clichéd line, *'a Kodak moment'*, and old as it was, and gone as Kodak were, what he witnessed would remain forever stenciled in his mind - *'a very Kodak moment'*. Oh, for a camera. He, too, was mildly shocked at all he was witnessing, in both his daughter, and the store itself. Josey turned to look at him; all he could do was blankly look back and then smile at her. And as they stood together, in awe, a voice seemed to come out of nowhere. They both turned in tandem.

"*Hello,* I thought I heard someone in the store. *Welcome,* so nice to see you both, although I don't think I've seen you in here before, would that be right?"

Steve Frankston remained awe-struck, now, twice. If the store and all it represented wasn't enough, then admiring the woman that came toward them certainly was. She was beautiful. Tallish, about five seven-eight, the first thing he noticed was her long flowing red hair that seemed to shine in the light as it came to rest just above her shoulders. She also had a smile that captivated one immediately, and hers, certainly did, him! A fair complexion with rosy tinged cheeks that matched her hair almost to perfection, she wore a stylized deep green V-neck top that accentuated her virtual perfectly shaped figure. It was worn loosely over cream-colored slacks. If first impressions counted for anything, Steve Frankston was pleasantly, stunned. This woman, in his eyes, was simply gorgeous! As if unable to, although not intended, he never said a word. Josey, meanwhile, picked up on the question and spoke for both of them.

"Yes, we don't live here, we were on our way home, but we were told about you from a little girl we met so we came to visit, and she was right, it's *lovely* in here."

"Why *thank* you, that was *quite* a compliment, but anyway, who might *you* be if you don't mind my asking, or more importantly, if Daddy, this *is* your Daddy, isn't it, if he doesn't mind that is?"

"Not at all," Steve finally managed to get out, "Not at all, and yes, I *am* her Daddy, and she's right, you have a *wonderful* store, but how in the tarnation do you manage to keep it so well stocked and presented? Oh, by the way, this is Josey, my daughter, say hello Josey, its okay."

Responding, easing the moment, the store lady spoke first. She had also loved the verbal compliment offered.

"Why, *hello* Josey, I'm Margaret McConnell, but everyone calls me either *'the doll lady'* or Maggie, and you can as well if that's okay, again, by your Daddy, I won't mind at all." She had looked at him as she spoke.

Steve nodded his head in approval. If friendly was the word, this lady oozed it! And her voice, to his ears, sounded so melodic. Her eyes glanced away from him as she lowered her look downward toward Josey, a most beautiful little girl, she thought, as she did.

"And may I ask, is Josey your *given* name or is shortened from something else like Jocelyn or, or…?" Maggie asked as her hand lightly touched her shoulder.

"Oh *no,* my *real* name is Josephine but everyone calls me Josey which I like and it's easier to say don't you think? But I like Josephine, too, though."

"Well I think I'll call you Josey, if you approve."

Nodding her head in the affirmative, *'the doll lady'* continued. It was time to go to work.

"Right, with that settled, where do you want to start, Josey, or maybe I should just give you a tour first?"

For the next few minutes, Maggie McConnell began to show her around asking question after question as they walked, making lots of small talk, doll talk mainly, however, she did include dresses and doll houses along with many other items that were on the decorative well lit shelves packed full of some of the most marvelous items with not a speck of room to add any more.

"So *there,* did you enjoy that?" the doll lady, Maggie, asked as they headed back toward Steve who had wandered aimlessly in the aisles looking at – nothing!

"I loved it, but now I have a question, too," Josey replied, anxious to know about fixing Angel.

"Then go ahead young lady, go ahead and ask me, and if I can, I'll answer it."

Josey looked at her Father. As if routine now, it seemed, he nodded his head. Sheepishly, she looked at *'doll lady Maggie'* who looked back at her, waiting, wondering just what it was that she might have missed on their mini tour of the store. She thought she'd shown her everything.

"The sign says this is a hospital. Does that mean you fix broken dolls here?"

Maggie, feeling all the more proud as the store owner, who loved little children, especially those who loved dolls, knew what was coming. She'd seen it all before, heard it all before, but somehow, for whatever reason, this little girl was strangely, nicely, different in framing her query. She saw the slight anguish on her face, sensed the concern in her voice and noticed an apparent overall anxiety, anticipating, that there might be a problem in the answer she was about to give. Would it be a yes, or no? She sensed, deeply, a no would mean some degree of probable devastation. Regardless, she could say only what was a fact. Happily, her answer was all Josey wanted to hear.

"Yes, I do," quickly followed up by, "Do you have a broken doll that needs a Doll Doctor, maybe?

Excitedly, Josey spun around, again looking at her Father. He knew what was coming.

"*Daddy,* Angel can be fixed, we can bring her here, we can have her put back together again, oh thank *goodness,* I *can't* wait. When can we do it?"

The enthusiasm that followed her answer, the small jump for joy and the absolute spirited tone that rang in Josey's voice was the reason Maggie did what she did. Nothing pleased her more than to see the new breed, the young, especially the very young, react so naturally when it came to dolls and their love of them. It was the very reason why she was determined to make sure everyone and anyone who enjoyed dolls would never be let down in her store. She never wanted to see the love of dolls die to modern technology in the making of them, churned out as they are in this more modern day and age by machines, against, and as opposed to, the masterful craftsmanship that went into many of the most beautiful dolls ever made, over many decades, centuries even, out of the doll capitals of Europe, Germany and France, as she reminded herself often. Maggie was dedicated in her quest, evidenced by all that surrounded her – her most delightful, welcoming, mesmerizing, every cliché one could think of - heart-warming store.

With a hint of delight, Steve Frankston looked at Maggie, then at his daughter and then heaved a sigh. There was a problem and he knew it, having unwittingly walked into it blindly, without thinking. Overwhelmed on one hand, as they had both been, loved what they were seeing on the other, he was now boxed in with the dilemma of, *yes* to finding someone who could bring Angel back to life, but *no, maybe,* in practicality because they lived so far away. He had walked into his own jeopardy. Dunbridge to Memphis he guessed, was about 450 miles away and maybe 7 hours driving, therefore, solving one problem, fixing the doll, had created another, logistically. He needed a moment to think. Aware he was being watched while pondering an achievable action, fortuitously, when two other shoppers entered the store, Maggie, this doll lady, walked toward them, allowing him unfettered time to, maybe, come up with a plan. Josey watched her retreat, as did Steve. Looking at Josey it was glaringly obvious. Clearly, his daughter had taken an instant shine to this most delightful store-owner, noticing her as he did, watch her every move as she looked at, or picked up, many attention-grabbing dolls, interacting warmly with her customers. Josey had not taken her eyes off her! Questions, then answers he could hear were running thick and fast, and it appeared to be no problem in customers being given treated with service par excellence, just as they had when they first entered; a very professional approach. One he loved. Pleasurable as all the in-store activity was, there was no escaping a very silent thought, this Maggie, quite the attention getter, her beauty and personality had garnered his equally and big time. *That* bothered him a little more than a little! He had never wanted to notice anyone else; his thoughts, love, would only ever be, forever, for one person.

Attentive as they had been, to business and visiting, the hour got away from them and extracting Josey out of the doll store and its built in hospital was harder than Steve believed could ever have been. Aided and abetted by the most hospitable, knowledgeable, and *only* doll lady he'd ever met, Margaret McConnell elected to chastise him, playfully, when he had respectfully called her Miss McConnell along the way. She repeated, with a smile, *'everyone calls me Maggie, so it's Maggie, okay?'* Did he, he wondered, sense chemistry in that moment, or was that more, unwanted, wishful thinking? Regardless, he smiled a boyish grin, which Maggie noticed. She, in turn, thought, *'cute, and my, he's handsome!'* Josey, meanwhile, oblivious to adult interaction had no problem chiming in, as once she knew her name, and was then allowed to call her by her first name, it quickly became, *'Maggie this, Maggie that, and Maggie said this, or Maggie thinks that, or knows this'*, and so it went. Steve Frankston could do nothing except go along with it all, happy, as he was to let his little girl enjoy herself. Josey had found, it seemed, not only a latent, and probable, after this visit, *new* passion that had captured her completely, along with spontaneous and natural laughter and incessant questions, but something else was happening, too, and it didn't go unnoticed; she had become extremely comfortable around Margaret 'Maggie' McConnell. Quickly, he began to wonder, what next? It didn't take long to find out.

There was no option; Dunbridge became their unintended overnight stay on their way back home to Memphis. Fortunately, time was on their side before it was back to school and work, and Dunbridge had nice facilities. Checking in the nearby and recommended namesake motel worked well for them and the rooms, as they had mostly been so far on their journey, were comfortable enough. That was the all-to-easy bit. However, obviously, and too late now for sure, in his head, Steve Frankston kept asking himself *'why?'* and repeated it many times over. Why did he say *'yes'* when Josey asked him back at the doll store, just before they were leaving, and given they had decided to stay the night in Dunbridge, to then agreeing that maybe Maggie could have dinner with them? Spontaneously, without a second thought, he had said *'yes'*, realizing almost immediately he had somehow been talked into sharing a social moment in what would probably be a never-ending discussion about dolls. The doll lady, Maggie, to his Josey, had something in common with her that clearly touched her deeply. That part he liked, the rest, bothered him, more than slightly. Dinner with a stranger was the last thing he wanted. And the other last thing he wanted was to share time, socially, with another woman. He wasn't ready to explain his life; such as it was, as would surely happen in some form or another. He wasn't ready to talk about Angelic, explain how he had lost a wife and Josey, a mother. He hated the thought of bringing up the word 'cancer' and sharing the battle that followed, and how they had lost! What must he have been thinking, he wondered? For just the shortest moment it had become the recurring question of why, why, why? Then, conceding to the moment, allowing the feeling, the emotion, the memories, to drift away, to then casting negative thoughts aside, as he knew he should, the plus side from all that was happening in Dunbridge; Josey was springing back to life, her transformation, incredible. She had become noticeably, naturally happy, loving her surrounds and talking endlessly, to another adult, a female, albeit about dolls or not! Taking the high road in his thinking, analyzing the position and situation at hand, maybe, he deduced, Margaret 'Maggie' McConnell might achieve the one thing, he felt, probably wrongly, that he had been unable to do – bring Josey, through a repaired doll, Angel, back into the fold of embracing the feeling of well-being, of good fortune and of realizing that life goes on, and that things in life always get better in time. Another major point worth considering, he admitted to no one, maybe it was also a leaf from the same book that he himself might consider embracing more. Angelic would appreciate that and of course, not to forget, he did also make a promise, one he was hell-bent on keeping!

A Sprite, two glasses of wine and a table for three, dinner was delightful. There was something about smaller towns, their service and friendship, and the restaurant owner couldn't have been more hospitable. Aptly called The Dunbridge Diner, the menu was a mixture of, whatever you wanted, it seemed. Fixed as the menu appeared in print, the owner, Johnny Scott, everyone called him *'Big John'* according to Maggie who knew him well, announced, proudly, if there was something else one craved, given the ingredients, he could make it, or at the worst, at least try and if he failed, no charge! Different as that may have been, strange as it sounded, or, typical of a small town, Steve Frankston wondered if the call sounded way too cavalier. However, as it turned out, he didn't have to worry or put *'Big John'* to the test. Coming to his rescue, Maggie McConnell made a suggestion. All three ran with it. Dinner was delicious.

Josey was in her element. All evening long she was a little chatterbox, however, not to Dad, but to Maggie. They talked about everything, and interestingly, Maggie, in her own inimitable way, seemed to know when to listen, when to answer and when to pose a question of her own, and always on a subject Josey had at least some familiarity of. Female intuition, mindful perception, or simply good luck given she dealt with children on a virtual everyday basis, none of it would be important, Josey responded in a way her Dad hadn't witnessed in a while. He began to guess his earlier thoughts had been exactly right! Watching them interact, he felt, was actually therapeutic, something Josey could do with a lot more of. Also, luckily, he was aware that their time spent, their chatting, and their enjoying each other's company, meant he didn't have to worry about being taken in areas of conversation he didn't want to, especially at a, probable, personal level. Josey had helped spare him of that, and he was grateful, although, silently, Maggie did intrigue him. The more he watched them both, and listened to them, concentrating on every word spoken, every action taken, the more he began to understand some things he was clearly missing along the way, even and especially with his own child. And with due consideration of it all, it was important!

Angelic had left them when Josey was just five, and now, at eight, soon to be nine, even though it was only three years, she was a different child altogether. Denied loving, caring, female tutoring from a mother, listening and learning primarily from a male, her father, there were elements of natural understanding he was seeing much clearer for the first time, all in a casual, easy-style setting. It was marvelous and a real learning curve. Somehow, he thought, he would need to, in the future, find ways to be sure Josey shared much more female interaction and attention, apart from school.

Then; the expected inevitable?

"So what about your Angel?" Maggie asked direct to Josey. "You'll have to tell me what's wrong because until I know the problem, I can't know whether we can put her back together, so, explain what you *think* it is and we'll go from there. Does that work for you?"

With the hint of a smile, as if for approval of the question, Maggie glanced at Steve who raised his eyebrows and as was certainly the trend in the past many hours, tipped his head to one side, offering her a smile in return before glancing across at Josey as if suggesting, *'tell her, she's listening'*. Josey, meanwhile, had looked at her Father thinking that he, not her, would tell the doll lady the problem. He didn't! He remained silent. Instantly, Josey read the sign and realized, it was her explanation to make.

"Well, Maggie," she started, "it's all quite simple really, because her head is falling all over the place and her arms, well, they fall all over the place too, and every time I try to make them stay together, they won't. And if I push her head in tight into her neck it just falls out again and with her legs, well, there isn't anything I can do with them either because it's the same thing. She seems to be broken. It's probably something inside but I can't see inside so I don't know what to do and that's the problem, and Maggie, it's annoying me, lots! And it makes me sad, too."

Josey had hardly come up for a breath as she articulated in her very own concise detailed way, all that she felt was wrong with Angel.

"*My*, that's *quite* an explanation and I understood it all," Maggie told her.

Steve was amazed. Confident in every way, his little girl had verbally rattled off all she knew about the problem with her doll, never missing a beat. He doubted he could have explained it any better, in fact, he believed, he would have pontificated it in a way that would have sounded more technical, suggesting one thing that might have turned out to be quite the opposite. He was proud of Josey, extremely proud and he wanted her to know it.

"*Hear, hear,*" he added to Maggie's response. "Well done, Josey, you're *exactly* right!"

"And, echoing that," Maggie began, "I think, from your accurate description I know just *what* the problem is. In explaining it so well I have absolutely no doubt what needs to be done, and I might add, I can probably fix it while you wait, in the morning, if you and Daddy bring her back to me, at the store. How would *that* be, does that work for you?"

Instantly, Steve's pre-determined conundrum had surfaced, as he knew it would, and it was about to become a problem of gargantuan proportions. Josey realized the same thing, her look said it all as she glanced up at him, expecting the news to be broken about where her doll was and then…and then? She was confused. Maggie McConnell recognized it all. Neither of them had to tell her what the problem was.

"Angel is not with you, is she?" she asked of Josey.

"No, Maggie, she's at *home,* in Memphis."

"Memphis!" she exclaimed. "Well I'll be, but isn't that funny because given all the talking we've shared, it never occurred to me that you didn't live somewhere a little more close by, but *Memphis,* well, that's quite the journey."

Learning that bitterly disappointed her.

"Yes it is," Steve concurred, "And it poses quite the challenge, I fear, however, let me think about it, because I'm sure we can solve it, *can't we Josey*?"

Josey looked back at him with a vacant stare, as if, confused. Too young, she had absolutely no idea her Father was seeking an opinion from her, as if it might be her suggestion as to how they could get Angel back to Maggie. Steve, meanwhile, thought it was do-able and was quite prepared to consider getting back to Dunbridge sometime, especially over a weekend, and…who knows…maybe?

"I don't know, Daddy," Josey replied, her face now more forlorn, the smile gone from her lips. "I don't know, but maybe you can…" she paused, as if thinking. A mere three seconds later, as if it were a revelation, she changed tact. "Maggie, what do *you* think?" she asked looking toward her, "Angel can't go anywhere until she's fixed so…so…" she paused again, her mind still seemingly, everywhere. The idea in her head was sound, saying it came harder.

Both adults stayed silent. Prophetic as she wanted to be, Maggie felt she knew why, and then hoped she was right. Josey continued her pondering. Moments later she went to speak, then paused again. It must have been agony for her to think of a way to get her doll back to her. Then, suddenly, it hit her. Anxious, now with a smile, she was ready to offer what she considered a concrete solution. Looking at her Father, who, on giving his predictable nod of go ahead, she blurted it all out.

"Daddy, I've got it, and it's *simple,* I think!" He waited with baited breath. So did Maggie. She continued. "We can come back again, come back with Angel. It's not that far. She can ride with us in her basket when we do, Maggie said she would fix her while we wait. Oh, Daddy, that'd be so awesome Can we do that, can we come back sometime, can we…*please, please*?"

Coherent, or sensible, impractical, or a great solution, none of it mattered. While Maggie McConnell's' heart fluttered, violently, it felt, Steve Frankston sighed, soft enough not to be obvious. Rushing wildly, his mind swirled silently.

'How unwittingly perceptive of adults is this little girl of mine. That's what I thought, but why am I saying this, why am I thinking this? Coming back to Dunbridge could also be a bad idea. But Josey's doll, she has to be fixed, I promised. And what about Maggie? If we do return, could that be tempting fate? No, there's no fate here, it's just a doll store that has a doll doctor as Maggie calls herself and, well yes, she's nice, but then…we could get here on a Saturday morning by noon I'd guess, and then we'd be gone again, by about two o'clock, although I might have to buy Maggie lunch as a thank you, however, with the mission complete, and Angel fixed, we'd be on our way, on the road again, back to Memphis after which we'd never have to be in Dunbridge again. Up and back in one day, easy, it's only time. Right, that's it, that's what Josey and I will do, it is for Josey of course, although I admit, seeing Maggie one more

time would be pleasant, too. Hey now, what the hell am I thinking, it's not about Maggie, it isn't!'

After what seemed minutes, an eternity in his head, but in fact a mere second or two, thoughts aside, he finally answered her question.

"I believe we can, sweetheart, that's a great suggestion, we'll do it!"

Maggie McConnell, too, was not immune to the power of the moment, Josey's request. Immediately, her mind had begun to race. Who, what, why…whatever - it didn't matter. Incredibly confused, she couldn't begin to imagine what had overcome her. Was it more about Steve Frankston or…what was it? Her silent bewilderment became; *'I hardly know these people, this man, this little girl, and yet?'* Echoing in her head; *'how sad if I never saw Josey again, or Steve, especially Steve, maybe. What, did I really think that?'* Nothing was making any sense. A mere some twenty-four hours ago, two strangers, who she never knew existed in this world, to a now – *'what's happened to me'* rolled over in her mind? In reconciling, Maggie's only thought, one she really hoped might turn out to be mutual; did Josey propose a wonderful suggestion, or…? As fast as the thoughts had been processed, immediately, a realistic doubt existed, dampening any thoughts of ever seeing them again. Sometimes, words are just words of the moment; they appease, and close the issue at hand. In the situation just tabled by a little girl for her doll, time and distance reared as a fierce enemy.

~~~~~~~~~~
~~~~~~~~~~

CHAPTER SEVEN

Safely back home in Memphis, tucked into her warm, snug bed, just before closing her eyes to go to sleep, Josey lifted her head up from her pillow to glance at 'Angel', in her basket, the small pink blanket covering her to keep her warm from any outside elements. There hadn't been any snow yet, but it sure felt like it was coming, that's what she told Angel giving Daddy credit for the information, adding that he had told her it might snow, reminding her, Daddy always seemed to be right. The bearer of bad news, she also wanted to share some good news, too. Quietly, she told Angel about Dunbridge and all that happened while she was there.

"You'll really like Maggie," she forewarned Angel as she finished her story. "She's very nice and knows so much about dolls, and being a doll doctor, I can tell you, she promised me she'll take extra special care of you when you're in the hospital, so don't worry, everything will work out you'll see and anyway, I'll be there with you all the way to make sure you're all right, and safe."

The soft glow of her night-light allowed her to see Angel. Lightly, she patted her composition body, then turned her over, closing her eyes. Her little mind wandered. What a wonderful trip she had shared with her Daddy this Christmas season, traveling everywhere, and to make the trip special, *extra* special, they, 'The Duo', had found Dunbridge, and a lovely lady, a doll doctor called Margaret 'Maggie' McConnell. And now, because of her, soon, Angel will be all new again. Can life get any better than this for an eight-year old, soon to be nine. *'Night-night Angel,'* she whispered. Her thoughts, beautiful as they were, lulled her to sleep, even to dream. Daddy's promise was coming true, that he would find a way to *'fix'* Angel. Meeting Maggie came back, clear as it had all unfolded, and to think, it was a chance meeting.

"Oh hi, nice to hear from you, Steve. So you made it back okay, all safe and sound? I'm glad, I was a little worried, not meaning to critique your driving skills, of course."

Maggie McConnell was thrilled when her cell-phone rang and the caller ID showed Steve Frankston. Expecting to hear from him, only because he promised, yet not expecting a call at all because, well, he didn't really have to, after all, they'd only met yesterday. Saying one will was one thing, expecting it to happen was another thing completely, however, not knowing why, Maggie believed Steve would, for no other reason than he promised to bring Josey's doll back to her. He also promised Josey they would stay in touch, at least until the *'job was done'* and Angel was all new again. That being the catalyst of their brief but impactive association, their dinner aside, their meeting each other again next morning at the doll hospital aside, too, and then exchanging phone numbers, Maggie's once quiet, even staid world had been elevated tremendously, and she felt unbelievably invigorated, new again. For some reason, she shocked even herself having never felt so attracted so fast to someone before, or attached and interested in another, a child, thereby making it two people at once. And yet, it had all unfolded so easy, so effortlessly and so instinctively. Josey might have won her heart, and she hers, but Steve Frankston, he was so…so…finding the word, or words didn't come easy. Maggie searched in her mind but that one specific word wouldn't materialize. She rattled off a few anyway; interesting, affable, alluring, strong-minded, gentle and more, but not the one that described him best. It would come to her, she assumed. One thing she did like on picking up the phone, he was at least true to his word and therefore, immediately, caring, resonated. For now, she would take caring as part of his persona, plus the other words she had conjured up, accepting, the more, the merrier.

He responded to her opening kind words and her added opening critique.

"The driving was easy but the more important thing is, thank you for being so kind to Josey and for being so available to her in offering to mend her doll. You have no idea how *that* simple project, I assume it is, has plagued me over these past…well, too long, for sure. I promised Josey and then didn't deliver, however, you have come on the scene like…to coin the actual word, *'angel'* from above and now I can breath easy, so Maggie, again, I just wanted to say thank you, and *yes,* I meant to mention at the outset, of course we arrived home safe, and Josey right now, well, she's dead to the world, sound asleep, and if you can believe it, the house is all quiet so for just a little while, I'll put my feet up."

Maggie McConnell had hung on every word. Articulate, she would now add to her earlier list. Everything Steve Frankston had briefly shared with her was music to her ears, and my, she thought, so complimentary of her in the process. And his tone, friendly, warm.

"My pleasure, Steve, she's a beautiful girl, you should be proud of her and so caring is a way I would describe her, too. Angel must be some doll and I am really looking forward to bringing her back into her life, so don't leave it too long will you?"

'Perfect,' she thought. Not planned, unintentional and yet, open-ended; she had invited him and Josey back to Dunbridge as if they had known each other forever. The truth was, she couldn't wait to see him, make that both of them, again. Time wouldn't pass quickly enough.

"You *truly* do have a beautiful store, Maggie. I hadn't ever thought much about your line of product, or the importance of what you do and provide, and of course, why would I, in real terms, however, I see it now and especially through the eyes of Josey. You are *quite* the lady and I'd hope you're appreciated by your customers?"

'Was that a question,' she wondered? *'And I'm quite the lady!'* Unquestionably, this man has class. There, another word! And he certainly knows how to throw a compliment.

"Thank you Steve. I know what I do is a dying art and that there are so few doll stores left in the USA anymore, and you know, it's sad really. Too many children, girls especially, many like Josey, although there are millions of women who still love and collect dolls, they will all miss out on understanding them the way previous generations have, but anyway, without laboring the issue, my point is, someday, one day, it'll be left up to a mere handful to protect the art, the skill and the diminishing numbers of dolls in this world, and that's a tragedy in real terms."

Not meaning to pontificate, she still felt the need to qualify her statement. And her point was valid!

"Seriously, what I am in many ways is a keeper of history, and that's incredibly important in this throw away world that can openly dismiss another form of art as if it isn't important. My store is a destination, you and Josey are living proof of that, and I like that, however, what will happen, I wonder, to the magnificent collections that still exist out there? Will they finish up in the trash, unwanted, in flea-markets, swap meets, sold for pennies or discarded because they take up too much space…?" She could have gone on and on but quickly realized, she was on a form of soapbox, unintended. "…But enough of that, it's not where I meant to go with your call so I'll quit while I'm still ahead, hopefully?"

"No, no, Maggie, I *hear* you and it's *true* and clearly, you are passionate about it all. And if I may, I'll concur with you admitting, I've actually learned something important. You are so *right,* and I see it more now, understand it better and *especially* since wandering around your store, and it's sad to think that not too many people can see or can buy what you stock. Josey was in awe, me too, so don't *ever* give up on something so important. America needs entrepreneurs' like you, that's for sure. I'm a supporter. Put me in on the Maggie McConnell bandwagon. You do the doll collectors of this nation and your industry a service, I believe."

Steve Frankston had meant every word spoken.

"My, *oh* my, you *flatter* me, Steve, you *really* do. I think I might actually be blushing, thank *goodness* you can't see me, that's all I can say."

"Well, I never meant to, but anyway, Maggie, short and sweet, again, I simply wanted to say thank you and we, Josey and me, look forward to seeing you, soon and on that note, I'll bid you a good night. It's been a long day."

Seconds later, two cell phones canceled out. At both ends, there was a smile.

Maggie McConnell was in bed already. It had been a long day for her, too. Doll hospital work had again claimed too many hours to say nothing of deadlines and what could then mean, slightly annoyed customers. She lay back into the soft pillow to look blankly at the ceiling. Josey came to mind first, then Steve. She saw his face clearly. Although nothing of their private lives had been shared, except, both were single, Josey telling her openly, *'Mommy died'*, and she having no qualms admitting, she was divorced some six years now, nevertheless, Maggie guessed Steve to be about thirty-five…well, she juggled it a little, maybe thirty-six, but maybe also, thirty-four…or maybe? She shook her head, who's counting, especially considering she was thirty-two. Whatever the number, they were virtual equals. Josey was her biggest clue. At eight, and if Steve was married in his mid to later twenties, then thirty-five, six would be about right. Finally, Maggie claimed they were both the same age. She added to her thoughts; that he was incredibly handsome, his face so…well…he was beautiful, his chin and nose that looked so perfectly sculpt, they set off his rugged overall looks. Completing his visuals, thick, dark-brown hair, always combed neat and tidy giving him an air of sophistication. Her mind awash in thought, sleep came easy. Dreams, too, came easy. Meeting Josey, and Steve, came back.

Unfolding clearly, it was yesterday once more.

"Hello, *Josey*. Welcome back again to my store. I hope you slept well last night, did you?"

"Yes, Maggie, I did, but I was so excited, I couldn't wait to wake up, to come back to see you again and to see everything in here again *and* I wanted to see your hospital too, can I, will that be all right?"

She looked toward her Father who glanced at Maggie. He then proffered his arms forward as if to say *'go ahead, take all the time you need.'* Maggie took the cue.

"Of course. And today, for as long as need be you will have my undivided attention, or at least until your Daddy tells me you have to go because I know time is limited, but until then, my time is your time. Now, let's start by you walking around the store with me, looking at everything that is here until we find the doll that is either the same as yours that needs attention, or one as close as can be to yours. That will help me understand exactly *who* Angel is, okay?"

Steve Frankston left them to it. Having agreed last night, and now again this morning, leaving Josey in the capable hands of Ms. Margaret 'Maggie' McConnell, he left to see what Dunbridge was all about. Giving in to Josey who had begged to see the store one more time before they had to end their *'adventure trip'* to head back to Memphis, he had no problem with that, or with her *'guardian'* who had offered to protect her. Left to his own devices, he'd walk the streets of this town called Dunbridge.

The girls extended grand tour began. While they searched for Angel, Josey's type of doll, she in turn listened intently to Maggie, thrilled to become so aware, and to see and share so many different types of dolls.

First - the newer style and name; Ashton Drake, Lee Middleton, Adora, Madame Alexander, Marie Osmond, Zapf, Berenguer, Franklin Mint, Seymour Mann, handling a few as she went, singling out especially the incredible Obitsu Ball-Jointed Dolls and then one of the most expensive of that caliber and range, Annette Himstedt.

Next, she showed her the vintage, the collectible, and also expensive dolls; Simon Halbig, Steiner, Sonnenberg and Armand Marseille. From there, the stylized names, familiar to the generations to whom they applied; Patty Play Pal, Barbie, Terri Lee, Shirley Temple, Bratz, Raggedy Ann, Cabbage Patch, Kewpie, American Girl, Tootles and so many more, not forgetting the Bears of course; Steiff, Reiker, Harley Davidson.

Finally, she sampled by touch, the many different materials dolls were made of; porcelain, celluloid, vinyl, plastic, rubber, silicone, composition and bisque.

Clearly, almost all of what Josey had come to understand in the world of dolls were totally foreign to one so young, and yet, she never once showed any sign of boredom, propelling Maggie, at the completion of her allotted, about two-hours, feeling the need to end on a high and different note. Unbeknown to Josey, her Father had already sanctioned her plan, a gift. Simple enough in the bigger picture, it was designed to be a memory of her visit to Dunbridge, to one of, if not the, finest doll stores in the country – a well known, touted fact. Maggie McConnell catered to the world. Whether a bricks and mortar visit, or surfing the Internet's World Wide Web, nothing could ever change the dedication she gave when it came to service. Maggie preached it, her staff adhered to it, and the public, from the avid doll collector, to the *'on a whim'* buyer who wanted nothing more than to suit and serve the moment, it would never matter, all, were important. However, on this very day, at this very moment, none more so than the eight-year old who graced her premises. Maggie McConnell had taken an extreme liking to this girl – and, if her inner thought, then tremble, was attributable - her Dad, too! That fact scared her a little. But nicely!

Amazing Maggie, but then again *'why'*, she thought, given the circumstances of where she was coming from about her doll, as a parting gift, Josey chose a bear. With access to anything in the store to an up-front agreed value, of course – oddly, she gravitated toward and quickly chose a bear, a small huggable bear. For now, she didn't want another doll, something Maggie fully understood, not minding at all. Further, she never sought the reason why, believing it was probably quite obvious. As it turned out, she would be right, without qualifying. For Josey, until her Angel was fixed, until Angel was whole again, until she could take Angel anywhere she wanted, when she wanted, or not at all, Angel had to be whole again. Never intending for it to be a reason why, that's what Josey would voluntarily share with Maggie in acceptance of the bear. What Josey hadn't shared; Angel was once her Mother's doll, they had named her together, and she was therefore more than special in her life. There had been no reason for her silence about it; it was more that it hadn't occurred to her, yet. Maggie, meanwhile, saw it, as portrayed, a child's first and therefore, very precious doll. One that would take precedence over all others, and bears too!

The time had slipped by. Unexpectedly, when Steve walked back through the door, both Maggie and Josey looked up as if they had another any number of hours to go to spend together. He smiled, acknowledged that he, too, had enjoyed his day while reminding Josey it was a long drive home. Then, all too soon, Steve, after sharing a very light hug, and Josey, hugging Maggie as if she were a long lost relative, after closing the door, walked around his vehicle positioning himself to start the journey back to Memphis. With s friendly wave, seconds later, they were gone.

Maggie woke next morning with a smile on her face, the night had been…perfect, and she wondered…why? *That* hadn't happened before! Steve Frankston sprang to mind.

'No, it couldn't be…' she thought.

~~~~~~~~~~
~~~~~~~~~~

CHAPTER EIGHT

The school in West Whitehaven went into lockdown immediately. On direct orders, children had been extricated from the playgrounds, the sports field and front general entrance area into either designated classrooms or the school gymnasium. Teachers bellowed orders to stragglers for their own protection, to hasten their retreat and flee to the safety zones now well under their control. Regular mandatory basic fire drills had worked almost to perfection. Meanwhile, with police, ambulance and fire sirens wailing loudly from all directions, the blue, red and clear lights flashing incessantly, first responders took every protective stance they could to keep not only the immediate area clear but also a three block radius around the school, to end what they understood to be, not only a multiple bomb threat, but also, to apprehend the dastardly perpetrators, two men wearing partial face masks, who threatened to detonate the devices if their demands weren't met. The only problem; authorities had no idea just where the *'so-called'* bombs were? Best information gleaned so far; they were in key positions on the school property. Question was; where exactly, and what represented *'key positions?'* With two hundred and fifty-five students on the grounds, plus a staff contingency of forty, they were at a loss as to where they might begin. A highly trained negotiator from the Memphis Police Department was on site, also a SWAT tactical team, select military personnel and a team of Doctors and Nurses from nearby hospitals, the latter, all on *'precautionary worse case scenario'* standby. Authorities could take no chances. It had already been almost two-hours with little progress. What they did know; where the perpetrators had positioned themselves. What they didn't know, yet – why they had perpetrated the act and what was it exactly that they wanted? None, of all that was happening, especially to a school, made any sense! It became a waiting game. Fear, tension and degrees of anger were mounting.

Steve Frankston was horrified when he heard the news. Working diligently with, of all organizations, the Red Cross, on a new and expanded national web site they were in desperate need of to help better coordinate national emergencies, on being drawn to the television like many staff members, he couldn't believe the visual images he saw, all of them, in and around the school his daughter, Josephine, attended. If Memphis was shocked, rapidly, so was the country at large. From Los Angeles to Chicago, New York to Houston and all points anywhere and everywhere in between, the USA was on edge. Could there be copycats, was there a cell network gathering or in place elsewhere? In Memphis, if the *'so-called'* bombs were detonated, if the perpetrators, whoever they were, activated their payload as they had vociferously declared they would if their demands were not met, the mayhem, death and destruction that could follow would place the city on the same page as Connecticut, Colorado, Boston, even 9-11, and *'believe me'*, one had allegedly said, *'you won't want that!'* He was right, which placed the authorities in a very precarious position. Surely these men knew that America never gave in to threats or demands, and if so, then why make such a statement, as in the end, they would surely perish and then the reasons might never be fully realized. Such was the dilemma, Chief Lieutenant Michael Nelson the Head of Operations had, aware also, that martyrs looking forward to heavenly rewards were commonplace in most terror activity. Why would these two be any different?

"So how do we open up meaningful negotiations to get these radical idiots to agree to allow the children be taken to safety before we consider any demand they might place on us, regardless of what the hell they want, money, transport, Lord knows?" he asked, politely demanded of Bill Williams, an expert in negotiating and human relations. A veteran of two tours of duty in Iraq, two in Afghanistan, and prior to coming to Memphis to join the force, a four-year stint with the NYPD, Williams had declared, many times, Memphis was a great city, that he loved the more layback way of life here, and certainly, his wife and two children who gave him great joy, grounded him in the everyday of well-being. Right now, though, he hated the situation he was in, again. He was tired of this kind of human scum! If he had his way, what he was about to undertake would be brought to an end in an instant, if he could only find the way, the right moment. The Middle East had taught him that. This kind of violence, threat and above all, abhorrent abuse and use of children as a means to an end; he had seen it all before, however, not quite on the level and scale, in numbers, that currently confronted him at the Whitehaven School.

Josephine Frankston, together with her friends Amy Quartermane, Mary Johnston and Tiffany Robertson were all sitting on the floor huddled together in Classroom 12 along with the rest of her class, including two others, bringing the room to near full capacity. The weekly planned drill emergencies had worked to perfection. Their teacher, Mr. Jones urged silence, assuring them confidently, it would all be over soon. Remarkably, the children remained incredibly calm, doing exactly as they were told, keeping any talking they did to a mere whisper. Not that talking was encouraged.

"Daddy will come and get me," Josey whispered to Amy. "I know he will."

"Mine, too" Tiffany chimed in. "He's not afraid, he was in the war once."

"My father is a policeman," added Mary Johnston. "He's probably outside at the moment getting ready to come and rescue us," she hoped

"Quiet! No talking," Teacher Jones asked in a soft voice. "*Please,* I know you're probably scared but remember, we have to remain strong. We know help is on the way, but for now, we have to be patient and very quiet."

Josey glanced at Tiffany who smiled. Smiling back, she mouthed, *'We **are** being quiet.'*

'I know,' Josey silently responded before covering her mouth with her hands.

Outside, at the three-block cordoned off perimeter of the school there was elevating chaos; frantic parents demanded something be done. All the police could offer in response was the obvious; *'we are doing all we can believe me. We'll end the drama as fast as we can but for now, please, you have to work with us. We're on your side.'* For many, it wasn't good enough, for others, they supported the authorities urging calm in the face of what must be terrified children inside the school. Meanwhile, the media swarmed on the area, adding to the growing frantic situation and for many, inflaming the restless crowd. Regardless, cameras were set up as journalists took to the streets hypothesizing, editorializing and interviewing willing parents, any one who had an opinion or pontificated a thought, especially about terrorism or who the major players might be or represented. An audience of the nation at large grew as every second, minute, hour passed. America, the world too, in this day and age, was riveted.

Steve Frankston, like everyone in Whitehaven, and any parents who had a child at the school, was distraught, bewildered, and devastated. Nothing sounded good, all news reports were negative, and police could offer no real confidence as to the outcome, it was; soul destroying. *'What can my little Josey be going through?'* he asked himself over and over. *'And I'm helpless to help her'* he cried inside. *'Please don't let her die'* he prayed to God. *'Don't let any of the children die, please, don't let anyone die'* he added, silently, alone, and yet, standing among what seemed, hundreds of people. And then he remembered. Angelic had told him of a time, not long after her family moved to Memphis, she, too, was locked down in a school. She expressed how it affected her, and how she pleaded with her folks, then, to let her go back to Florida, where she was happier. Recalling vividly that story, he then wondered what might happen with Josey. Eerily, the fact that bothered him most would be, Mother, now Daughter; caught in the exact same childhood predicament, school lockdown, separated only by years. It was a chilling reminder! Angelic's, though, ended well. Today, now, still unknown for Josey?

Bill Williams was ready. Dressed casually and more every day civilian, not police, military or authority, he wore a pair of dark brown slacks with tan shoes to match, also a coffee colored open neck shirt with the sleeves neatly rolled up, and yet oddly, not tucked in. Underneath it, not conspicuous, he had donned a tight fitting bulletproof vest. A black ball cap with the city's namesake Memphis completed his ensemble. He was ready to go, prepared to move in for what many deemed, *'the tough task ahead'*.

"And you really don't want us to back you up, to give you armed support, I mean, Bill, you *have* to be kidding me, surely?" Lieutenant Nelson asked.

"Nope! It's the way I want it, I'll take my chances but you *can* wish me well," he replied, about to walk into the proverbial *'lion's den'* of terror.

"But that seems like potential suicide to me," Nelson suggested, adding "Look, Bill, we have hundreds of people here, all trained. We have the weaponry, a proven precision sniper, plenty of police, I mean, come on now, you can't expect to just walk up to these thugs blindly and believe a simple chat, a heart to heart or whatever you're thinking is going to have them lay down their arms and come waltzing out with you whistling a tune. *Or do you?"*

"Nope, but we've got to start somewhere. They're not answering our calls, phone or loud-speaker and they're not going to sit there all day, or night for that matter so, we have one choice, to start with I'd reckon, and I'm happy to get the ball rolling."

"But what if…" the Lieutenant never got to finish.

"What if, *nothing* Mike." He always called the Lieutenant, Mike and never Michael, although on official occasions, then, it was always, Lieutenant Nelson.

"Frankly," he continued, "we don't have much of a choice and if there's one thing I've learned over many years of doing this ridiculous giving in to this lot, it would be, catch them early in dialog, walk the walk with them verbally and make them feel important, even for a little while. Somewhere down the line, Mike, like everyone who is desperate, they make a mistake or, or…"

"*Or what*?" the Lieutenant wanted to know, anxious to find out what makes a guy like Bill Williams tick in situations such as they were facing. His current tactic was an all-new one to him. Sure, over the years, he, too, had been in tense situations before, and mostly won, sometimes, though, there had been loss of life, but mostly, he'd concluded, law enforcement prevails, however, this time, negotiating in a style such as Williams was about to walk into was unexpected. He didn't like the idea one little bit!

"Or we give them what they want," Williams answered, "albeit, not sincerely, but when we offer it, we then have a chance to lure them away from where they feel secure and in control, we get them more out into the open where we can see them better, have better access to them, maybe, or at least have a chance to get a hold of any weapons, particularly cell phones that might be linked to bombs and bomb detonation. *That*, I learned the hard way, was very much an Iraq procedure and who knows, it might be in play here, right now. Sadly, we still don't know but, as I say, there's one way to find out and the first rule of thumb is, in my book, act confident, be seemingly open and importantly, let them see your face. When they do, remember, on most occasions, then you get to see theirs and *that* could go on to provide us with artist sketches, computer match ups, background ID checks or whatever we can get, *anything* to get us started. And on that note, Mike, I've gotta go. Terrorists or whoever are waiting. They're expecting me."

"Okay, Bill, but know this, we've got your back, *and* got you covered no matter what happens, old friend. That said, I can only add one thing, good luck, you're gonna need plenty of it. And by the way, *stay focused*."

"Thanks, Mike. I'll see you back here, God willing."

He had no idea if he ever would. As always in a negotiating situation, you have to get as close to the bad guy as you can. It was never easy, as people, the likes of whom he was about to deal with, were cowards. They hid behind walls, doors, buildings, or if they weren't readily available they would resort to women and children, and in this case, there were already too many children involved given they'd chosen a school. Bill Williams shook his head as he began the slow trek forward; toward the school air conditioning building that housed also school maintenance equipment. The large glass window on one side had a perfect view of the sports field, the school playground area complete with swings, trampoline, even a large sandbox that many of the younger kids loved to gravitate to after their day was done, waiting for parents. Surveillance had already told authorities; this building was the location where the demands and threats originated. Williams sucked in a huge gulp of air as he approached. He was also aware his heart rate had begun to pick up.

~~~~~~~~~~
~~~~~~~~~~

CHAPTER NINE

Unexpected, and almost frightening him, Steve Frankston's cell phone rang. Sliding it from his side pocket he glanced down at the screen; 'Maggie McC.' He instantly knew why, but felt he wasn't sure he wanted to talk right now. Why, he didn't really know? Maggie, friendly and caring, would only be calling to check on Josey, and him, of course. Memphis was the center of the world at the moment; even Dunbridge would know what was going on and anyone who knew anyone in Memphis was probably on the phone right now asking the same questions; *'are you all right, is so and so okay, is there anything I can do, it must be frightening, do you want me to come there?'* And so all the concerns would all go. It was human nature, and to be fair; it was a good thing, in every possible way! Steve pushed down on 'Accept'.

"Oh, Steve, it's Maggie. *Please* tell me everything is all right, *please,* because I...'

It was as far as she got. He understood.

"Everything's all right, Maggie, or as right as it can be right now, however, the bad news is, Josey's *still* in the school. The better news might be, apparently, they are trying to negotiate a settlement but to be honest with you, calm as I'm trying to be, I'm kind of scared and I'm dying a little inside, too. This whole mess just needs to be *over,* that's all I can say. I'm sure you're watching it on television, and in fact, you may know more than me right now."

To Maggie, Steve sounded awful. As he admitted, he also sounded scared, very scared. It was all she could do but pour her heart out to him in sympathy, but she knew, instinct told her, that would be the last thing he would want. Like all parents, all he really wanted was his little girl back, safe and sound. She was torn in which way to approach the delicate subject of hostages and the peril they were in as Josey and many others realistically were.

"I wish I knew what to say Steve, but I don't…"

"You don't have to say anything Maggie. I know you care, as does everyone, but we're dealing with terrorists here, it seems, or something *damn* near close to it, and tell me, what low life takes a school down, children, teachers, everything that spells good in this world. *Who could do such a thing?* It's despicable and all I can think is, if I lose my little Josey to them, if I, if we, *all* of Memphis, if we lose *one* life and heaven forbid, a whole school, there will be an outcry and a vengeance unseen or unheard of before. This is simply incomprehensible, outrageous and yet, all we can do right now, all any of us can do right now, is pray, and pray hard. I hope Maggie, *Lord I* ***hope*** *we prevail* with sanity, common sense and a peaceful ending."

Maggie McConnell could not believe the desperation she was hearing in Steve Frankston's voice. She may not have known him long, in fact, brief as their time had been, it didn't change a thing. She had spent enough time to clearly see, Josey was his world, Josey was all he lived for and he would give his own life, she was sure, if it meant she could be spared from being held captive by unscrupulous people. *'What has this world come to,'* she wondered. However, at this moment in time, on the phone, there was little she could do. What she did know, believed, the love she had seen in the eyes of Steve Frankston for his child would be embedded in her mind forever. From an unplanned side trip to Dunbridge, a visit to her doll store, an inquiry about her doll hospital, a surprise invite to dinner, and a mere two-hours explaining the world of dolls to an eight year old, miraculously, had transformed Margaret 'Maggie' McConnell and her once well accepted dwindling belief of romance and men, into a new found revelation, that the world might still be a truly wonderful place and that wonderful, good-hearted people still existed and love, shown in many ways, was around every corner, if one chose to make the turn. The only downside of her momentary feeling was; the world right now, in Memphis, was showing a really dark side. Dark enough that the man she had been slowly drawn to was hurting. And his beloved precious daughter, hurting probably even more.

"Steve, I can't *begin* to say that I know what you're going through or that I understand your fear, your heartbreak of the moment for Josey, but *please,* believe me when I tell you, if you *need* me there, if along the way I might be able to ease any pain or be a comfort to Josey, *please know,* I'll come to you, I'll come to Memphis. Of course, I'll pray for you both in the meantime, and for *everyone,* in the hope it'll all end soon, and peacefully, but again, in the immediate, I'm here for you, I'll be on standby for you."

"That's very sweet, Maggie, really, and I hear it and just so you know, I take your words kindly and to heart. It's a great comfort, and maybe I will, but for now, I'll do what I have to and I'll wait, wait for the outcome and see what happens over the next hour or two, or more. Again, though, thank you. I'm glad you called me it means a lot."

Maggie looked at her phone. Before the screen went black she saw the word *'End.'* An omen? No, she knew it meant end of the call. It didn't matter. Uncontrolled, she immediately burst into tears.

It had already been four hours. Right about now, the school bells should have chimed and the first of the students, who had concluded their learning for the day, should have been leaving the school grounds heading for busses and home. Instead, not a soul was seen anywhere. Eerily, everything around the grounds was silent and still. Surrounded by every imaginable source available in law enforcement to bring the hostage crisis to an end, and with it, the potential of bombs being detonated capable of bringing down school buildings and sending billows of fire and smoke into the air, to the sad, horrendous thought of men, women and children being sacrificed for a cause no one might ever understand; the scene playing out in Memphis was, as if, straight out of a Hollywood horror movie.

Josey Frankston, showing obvious worry on her face, looked up at her friend to whisper a simple question.

"Do you think we're going to die Amy, do you think we're going to die, here in this school?"

"*No,* Josey, but I *am* scared, I'm *really* scared now, but I'm glad, too, that I'm here with you. If I die, if any of us die, I would want to be with you most. You're my bestest friend and I've always liked you, you know that."

"And you're *my* bestest friend, Amy, but I wish Daddy would come and get me" was all Josey could say in response.

"I bet he's out there, outside near the school and he'd be so worried, I know it, he would."

"I want mine to come, too," Amy shared. "But I'm glad the teacher, Mr. Jones, is still with us here. He keeps telling us everything will be all right, and I believe him. And Josey, we know one thing, as long as we stay where we are, and as long as we follow the orders and do the right thing, in the end, we'll be safe and we'll get out of here."

"I hope you're right, Amy, because I hate it here, but I wonder, too, what's really happening, why we're locked down? I wish we *really* knew."

"I don't. I'd rather *not* know. But *hey*, maybe the teacher knows, Josey. He has a cell phone. He has to know. Should we try and ask him?"

"I don't think so, Amy. He would have told us, I'm sure, and anyway, we don't want him to get mad!

Josey and Amy continued whispering and while others could hear them, hardly anyone said a word or joined in, they had all been told to stay quiet and most adhered to the orders. Their friend, Tiffany Robertson, not one to be left out, finally chimed in, but not about the locked down situation they were in. Unintended, but with degrees of comic outcome, she confessed, if they don't, or *she* doesn't get out of the classroom soon, she was probably going to *'pee her pants'*. Josey and Amy could only offer the faintest of laughter, agreeing, a potty break would be a great idea!

For no reason, Steve Frankston thought for a moment about Maggie McConnell; the phone call they shared. Disinterested, unfair about her coming to support him, or any other reactions he now felt he might have shown as they prepared to hang up, his real question became; *'Did I, Was I, Had I been,'* swiftly followed by, *'Why am I thinking all this,'* adding to his thoughts, *'I hardly know the woman, we barely met.'* Then he thought of Josey, the *real* connection between them. It was irrelevant. Where Josey was now, with other children, her friends, Amy, Mary, Tiffany, three who came to mind, the best he could hope for; that they were all together and not alone with strangers, for no other reason than the four of them would be great company to each other in their time of need, fighting fear. Common sense, calmness, detached, nothing resonated with him despite the actions and reactions, and at times, unruly crowd he was forced to share time and associate with. Angry, he was, yes, but not with the authorities, the first and always courageous first responders who, lately, seemed to have been called upon far too much. *'We live in a growing, sickening world'* he believed, *'and to hurt children, nothing could be more despicable'* swirled in his mind, and sadly, his Josey was now amongst them, the latest in the world of hurt, of mayhem and heartbreak.

Watching the assembled crowd around him, standing on the perimeter of the school, he wished he could be someplace else, however, nothing would ever allow him to not stand vigil, to be there, to be the first to rush forward when the all the innocent children would be released, unharmed. Hating the media's frenzied attention, the way they seemed to glorify the moment, the way they scrambled for anyone who would stand in front of a camera lens, he watched one journalist after another seem to pressure people to react, and the more vocal one was, the more angry they appeared to be, then all the better! When one came his way, as if to single him out, a likely candidate, he told the journalist exactly what he thought of his actions, his intentions. With microphone in hand, the reporter had his cameraman record the outburst. Why, he didn't really know?

"You all *feed* their ego," Steve Frankston told the unknown audience. "Television provides *every* bit of the fodder they seek, notoriety, fame and if need be, glory and martyrdom, and believe me, it's *not* worth it, *none of it.* Why do you people in TV, the media at large, think you have a God given right to be the arbiter, the judge and many times, even, the jury? And I have any number of questions to the perpetrators who think they also have a right to inflict what they do on the innocent. What *is* it that drives you to such hatred, such violence, and such scorn for a society that on one hand welcomes you, one that believes and gives you freedom, dreams, peace and a way of life that suggests harmony, well being and at the least, a better way of life that ever was, from whence one came? And yet on the other, *why* is it that you choose to decide that it wasn't *good* enough? Weren't you suppressed enough before you came here, and wasn't *that* the reason you did, or was there always another purpose, sinister and set up, one that you needed to be here for, to achieve such dastardly goals?

"Whoever these people are, that have my daughter, and many other fellow citizens' sons and daughters, the same question prevails, what is it that drives them to such hatred? Heaven forbid, we give them everything, even American citizenship and *this,* all that we're witnessing at our school right here in Memphis, becomes our payback? Right now, *angry* as I am, *scared* and *fearful* for my daughter as I am, all I can say to them is, walk away, accept whatever your failings are, and reconsider what it is that has angered you, in whatever honest belief, because right now, you are so cornered, so caught in a situation you can never gain control of, *it can't end well*. Know also, though, under our system here in the USA, you will be treated fair. *Please,* I beg of you, *stop and consider the children.* I am *sure* you never really intended to hurt them, but then again, sadly, if you did, if they were your *only* means to gain attention, notoriety, *then God help you,* because be assured, nothing else ever will. *Hell* will be your destiny when it's over, *not* what you all think it will be with your misguided belief of that after life you're promised."

The cameraman switched off his camera, placed it on the ground and without compunction, applauded him. The gathered crowd joined in. The journalist reporter shrugged his shoulders: *'I was simply doing my job folks, you be the judge when you see it back'.* He moved quickly, tapping Steve Frankston on the back. He turned.

"*Man,* you *believe* it don't you?" he asked, off the record. Unresponsive, he walked away. *'Another stupid question,'* his only thought.

Moments later, he had an epiphany! His hands moved to his pocket from which he withdrew his cell phone. He had an urge to call Maggie McConnell. He scrolled her number.

~~~~~~~~~~
~~~~~~~~~~

CHAPTER TEN

In living memory of such dire circumstances, it was the boldest move ever made in a hostage negotiation situation anyone could ever remember. A first, a last, time would tell. Bill Williams had stunned the hardened of law enforcement, defying the odds of common sense, and managing to bewilder Lieutenant Nelson to a level he could not comprehend. Why Nelson had ever agreed, why he had not ordered *'no such action'* and why he had succumbed to a veteran, who not only had the *'gift of the gab'* but also seemed to know exactly what he was doing, indeed, about to do, he had absolutely no idea! The Lieutenant had watched him bravely, yet brazenly; walk into the *'hands of fate'*, maybe, probably, to his ultimate demise. But it was too late to make changes. Whatever, and why, at this very moment in time, there was no turning back. Williams was almost at his designated point of contact. Shocked, Lieutenant Michael Nelson and his protective force at large were about to witness an unbelievable, and what they collectively believed might be, surely, a suicidal act. With bated breath, they watched *'one of their own'*, both hands held high in the air, slowly, cautiously and yet, casually, walk up to the darkened plate glass window to stand about five feet away, motionless, where, behind it, he could now make out two obviously evil looking characters standing rigid, monitoring, in every direction possible, any outside activity. They were fully aware of the large contingency of law enforcement, anxious to bring them to justice, to end, what was termed, the futile effort to bargain their way to *'spoils of compensation'* and freedom. Realistically, from Memphis to a world, a location country beyond the USA, was virtually, physically impossible, except by plane, probably, but nevertheless, a long shot for success. So far, one had not been requested, however, one million dollars in cash had, but why? Whether that was the start of protracted additional benefit had not, yet, been ascertained. Overture had been made, more benefit was being determined, but so far, monetary gain was their sole request. It was expected, Bill Williams, in negotiation, would realize the real end result motive. He suspected release of prisoners from somewhere, either in USA jails, or, Guantanamo, or what would be outside of American jurisdiction, overseas jails. Harrowingly, as both sides of the stand off watched his every move, the taller of the two gentlemen inside shouted his question.

"You're a fool! Why have you come so close? I could have shot you, maybe I will."

Bill Williams always knew that was a distinct, immediate possibility, originally, but now, seeing the men, the odds were stacked against them. *'Shoot me accurately, through a window'* he thought. He now figured them as rank amateurs out for glory. Regardless, from the outset he had taken his chances of the danger, now, he believed, things might be going his way, not theirs, except, he could see that one did have a cell phone in his hand. Could that be the detonating instrument for any bomb? Still standing, with no action, phase one was achieved, they had not acted, yet, which led him to believe, a conversation was highly possible. Phase two, his, he had deduced, was now well within reach.

"As you can see, all I want to do is talk" became his truthful opening remark.

Eyed suspiciously, the second of the evil men asked another question.

"We have a specific request we need to know. Are you in authority to grant it? If not, we're wasting valuable time."

"Yes! I do. Whatever your demands, we will meet them, within reason…" he blatantly lied in reply, "…however; the children in the school *have* to be released first before we agree to anything. There is nothing we hate more than watching innocent children suffer, I am sure, or hopeful, that you understand. If you don't, I have nothing more to say to you. I will walk away and you will be on your own and the chips will fall where they may."

"Who are you to be so demanding?" the perceived leader challenged, angrily, "*we* hold the keys, we hold the path to what will happen, and if it means blowing the school to smithereens, then we'll do it, and that applies to the children and anyone else who is in there. We don't *care* about people, *or* children. We don't care who dies, us, too, maybe. Do I make myself clear, or do I blow the place up, now?"

On both sides of the negotiating window, it had been a bold move. Williams had no clear idea of what next except play for time and emotion. Whatever the missing piece was to their demands, he had yet to find out. Unquestionably, it had become a more than a delicate balance as his earlier bluff about walking, hadn't worked. The men were adamant, and clearly agitated. Referencing the children and their fate was now a hot button issue. He had to try another tactic.

"Alright, I hear you, so let me suggest instead that you allow me in, allow me to sit with you, allow me to work with you, that way I believe we can access what you want and need rather quickly. Not wanting to pontificate, I'd much prefer to understand what's at stake and reach a settlement quickly, and we can, I know it. I'm sure you feel the same way and look, the reason is, I care about what's happening out there more than anything. Lives, anyone's lives, are more precious than the money and whatever else you want, *that* would be the easy part. So let's talk! I'll work with you in every way, believe me, we'll reach an agreement."

He had lied again.

Attempting to gain more confidence, Bill Williams had kept his arms held high in the air as he spoke. Standing, staring at the window, the two men interacted with each other, not that he could hear a word they were saying, and even if he could he'd expect it to be *'foreign'* to him, anyway. Suddenly, he had another idea. He'd concede it a little risky, yes, however, from where he stood, it was worth it.

"Say…" he shouted, "…I'm *not* asking you release any people here, but *please,* give me two minutes, two minutes, that's all I ask. It'll help me understand what you want and from there we have a chance of making sure that whatever happens here, that so far is not getting us anywhere, was for the right reasons. We have to at least try, after all you didn't set this all up and do it all for nothing, I doubt!"

Seemingly reacting, the two men spoke together again. Finally, as one nodded his head, as if an affirmative to the request, within seconds, the other moved slowly toward the door located just to the left of the window. Assuming it to be locked and bolted, Bill Williams watched him. Apart from wearing a thick, black beard all over his face, the other thing he noticed, he had a limp. He saw that as a good sign, that he would not be overly agile. The other man stood firm, not budging an inch. Instinctively aware, their eyes on each other, from a motion with a nod of the head, Williams edged toward the door, his arms still held above his waist for all to see, however, as he moved closer, he lowered them slightly and by the time he reached the door, they were virtually fully down by his side. As the door opened, it was as if friends were about to greet each other, but without the smile. That was the first mistake made. The second was instantaneous.

Maggie grabbed the phone, *"Steve!"*

"I don't know if you're watching TV live, or if they even showed it live, but I was just interviewed on Channel 9 which is ABC here, and unfortunately, I let loose with my feelings, never meaning to be so explicit in my thoughts. I walked away thinking, I hope I didn't do or say anything wrong, anything that these bad dudes are doing here because it never occurred to me, until I'd said it, they might have been monitoring TV, too, a lot of that crowd can and do. Did *you* see it? Did it look or sound bad, Maggie, because I so worry for Josey and all the children still locked in that school?"

"Yes, I did see it, Steve, I mean who *wouldn't* have? Me, Dunbridge, millions out there I'm sure would be glued to it. This story is everywhere let me tell you, and I've been so scared, so worried. More important, though, how are you, are you okay, are you holding up all right?"

"I'm okay, Maggie, I'm okay. It's more about Josey, the kids. What the hell must they be going through? We all feel so helpless, all of us, parent's and all, I mean, the cops won't let us anywhere near the school grounds, it's like we are so far out of the loop and don't know much except what's being beamed in the media and for us, that's only the radio. What if something happens? What if they blow up the scho…"

"They *won't*, Steve, they *won't*. We *have* to believe that. From what I'm seeing here, and they've interviewed everybody, especially the people on the front line and while some of it is marred by speculation, one thing's for sure, they said, they have one of the best negotiators in the country going in. He's going to try and work a deal, or a way out of it all so we have to believe it will work, Steve, we have to."

He knew Maggie was right. He also learned for the first time that negotiations were underway to end the crisis. Being so close to the scene, the watching, the waiting, accurate news information was harder to come by. Within the huge crowd that had gathered, everyone had different reports to share, radio particularly, however, none would have been as accurate as the one he had just heard.

"I *believe* it. Maggie, I *want* to and thanks. What you've just told me about the negotiator has given me added hope for a better outcome. I've been so tense and worried about Josey. How do you think she'll come out of this when it's all over, though? She'll have to be traumatized, even not wanting to go back to school again, *that* one anyway."

"She's a strong willed girl, Steve, I learned and saw that when you were both here. Don't underestimate her. Children have iron constitutions when they need it and hopefully, that'll be the way for Josey, but remember, I will come to help if you feel you need me. Your call and no pressure, but I *am* here and *will* help."

"Thanks, Maggie. You're a gem and a great source of information to me, especially with some news updates. If anything big happens, it's okay to call me, in fact, I'd appreciate it a lot, okay? And by the way, if I sounded short before, I apologize, but I'm just a bit uptight, I know it!"

"Oh, that's okay, Steve, I understand, *more* than understand, and yes, if I get to hear anything big, I'll let you know immediately, meanwhile, though, stay strong, Josey's gonna need you when she gets out of there."

Once again the cell phones went quiet. Maggie had loved receiving the call, however, again, she wasn't happy with the way it ended. She had hoped Steve would have asked her to come to Memphis. He didn't, hadn't! Heaving a huge sigh, her head turned back to the television and the never-ending flow of *'Breaking News Updates'*. The latest one, she knew, confirming an apparent dialog had started between what the reporters and news anchor people were now officially labeling *'the terrorist group'* and the Memphis Police Department. In the background, the Whitehaven School grounds were being shown at a time when normalcy prevailed. They clearly avoided any pictures that contained children in the file footage.

Steve Frankston prayed for Josey, as he did for all the children, and teachers, too.

~~~~~~~~~~
~~~~~~~~~~

CHAPTER ELEVEN

Restless as the children were in the locked down class where Josey was, and fidgety as they were clearly now becoming, the teacher, Mr. Jones, in a softened tone, offered praise to them for having, and still maintaining, adherence to every order given and every task, so far, expected of them. Aware that the situation had become tense on the outside, that the school grounds were totally *'off-limits'* to any and all, parent's especially, he had monitored the constantly up dated news bulletins on his cell phone. With a building anxiety beginning to enter his thoughts, coupled inwardly of being emotionally torn to shreds, he knew he had a continuing job to do of holding the children in his charge, together. He was acutely aware it was also his job to remain strong, vigilant and above all confident. Watching the children, looking into their eyes, either one by one, or collectively as a group, an inner strength re-emerged. How could he buckle under the strain, if they didn't? It was approaching three thirty-five, almost four hours into the lockdown. He decided to share what he knew with the classroom. All children were asked to sit cross-legged on the floor and face him, at the front of the room, near the door. He took his chances standing up, motioning them all at the same time to remain calm and above all quiet. They did! In his softest voice, yet audible, he shared the news.

"It's not as bad as we think…" Teacher Jones imparted, untruthfully, "…and apparently, the Police know who came to the school and they know what they want. It's not you and me, and it's not to do us any harm, thank goodness, it's just that these people have friends who are in a jail somewhere, and amongst other things, they want them out."

So far, his flirting with the truth sounded more than plausible. Some of the children sighed, as if, relieved.

"What's going to happen is,' he continued, "the Police are going to talk with the people and if they can, reach an agreement to work with them and get their friends out of jail, but they will have to let us all walk off the school grounds in an orderly fashion to do it. So kids, if we hold on a little longer, if you can remain quiet and strong, as we are, a little longer, soon, we'll all be on our way and we can get back to going home again and be with your parent's, okay. If we can do it, together, raise your hands."

A sea of hands raised swiftly, many of the children with more satisfied smiles. Teacher Jones hated doing and saying what he did, however, he was aware, there were no other options. He knew the fear that would have followed if he had told them the truth, exactly what was transpiring on their school grounds, in their school, a place they all, mostly, loved to come each day. And to think, friends with each other as so many were, the angst and anguish that would have flooded their minds if they knew Whitehaven was in danger of being blown sky-high, that they might die, that their friends might die with them. Teacher Jones knew he could not inflict such hurt on children so young, despite knowing, he, too, might die, and that he, too, might never see his wife and child again. Fortunately, Tracy, his wife and their one-year old little boy were at home, but he was aware she would know the danger he was in, and that he may never come home again, either. He wanted to cry, for himself, for all the children in the room, for Tracy, and Thomas, his first-born young son he called, *'Little Tom-Tom.'*

Josey, Tiffany, Mary, Amy, all had stayed together; they were a foursome, fierce friends. When Teacher Jones had spoken, they held each other's hands.

"There, we'll be out of here soon. Mr. Jones said so." Josey Frankston was sure, now, that all would be well. "Our Dad's will be here to get us, I know it. Mine will, anyway, and I hope he's not too mad about what's happened."

"I still need a pee, Josey…" Tiffany reminded them, "…and I don't know if I can hold on much longer. What can I do, this is terrible. I wonder if anyone else needs to pee. Should I go and ask Mr. Jones what to do, he'll know. Maybe he needs to pee, too!"

Concerned as Tiffany was, all three girls giggled at her remark, dreading the thought, thankful that her situation was not their personal immediate plight.

"I'll come with you," Josey said in full support, trying to make her feel better. "I'd go, too, if we could get to the bathroom. But I don't think he'll let us."

Odd as it was, crucial as the situation had become, tense and dangerous out on the school grounds, Josey, Tiffany and Amy had found humor in their predicament. They guessed many others were in the same situation. Elected leader of the gang of four to find an answer, Josey edged over to Mr. Jones and asked the question. The other two saw a smile form across his face, while at the same time, he began to nod *'no.'* Tiffany immediately became more desperate! She looked at Amy who animated, *'cross your legs, tightly'*. When Josey made it back she shared, *'Mr. Jones said we should be out of here in about another fifteen minutes, and to hold on.'* Together, the girls held hands, again, and with nothing else they could do, even if they wanted or could do, they began to stare blankly at each other. Seconds later, Tiffany burst out with a muffled laugh. Meanwhile, Teacher Jones thrashed around in his head, all he had said to the students, moments ago. He, too, had his own needs, many of them! His thoughts again went back to Tracy and *'Little Tom-Tom.'* While he and the class remained, *'as directed'* ', silent, elsewhere, outside in the school grounds, the pace had picked up dramatically.

When Bill Williams stepped into the building the two self-proclaimed terrorists had taken up as command post to their operation, and from where they had a wide vision of the school building and the grounds, he was already aware that the one with the limp who had approached the door, was seemingly, empty handed. A bad miscalculation! The other, who maintained an eagle eye on him, was very slightly side-turned as if trying to see two things at once. One reason, Williams figured, he was endeavoring to make sure no one else was anywhere near the structure, behind him, when he first approached them with his arms held high in the air, but specifically, to when he moved toward the door to join them inside. The next reason, probably, to be absolutely certain he was not carrying any weapons. Clearly, he must have believed, he wasn't! The second bad mistake! The man with the limp, meanwhile, cautiously eased the door open, and while watching him closely, allowed him to walk through the door. Neglecting to immediately frisk him as a safeguard measure, became the third, and costly, *really* bad mistake!

Bill Williams moved with the speed of lightning, as fast as the Japanese bullet train, or a car approaching the finish line at the Indianapolis 500 - all three rolled into one! Without the hint of impending movement, his right hand went for the Glock pistol tucked in his belt and with one pull of the trigger; the second man keeping watch over the Whitehaven school grounds hit the floor with an instant thud! His partner, the one with the limp, realizing the predicament, screamed a jihadist style cry while clumsily moving to retrieve his weapon, any weapon. But it was too late! A bullet from Williams's second pull went straight through his temple with precision accuracy. It was all over in a split second. Both men lay dead on the floor, in a growing pool of blood. Looking down at his weapon, Williams let out a huge sigh of welcomed relief, immediately slowing down the adrenalin rushing through his body. Then, leaning for a moment to gather his thoughts on a close by stool, heaving another huge sigh but this time with a smile on his face, he pondered the last probable two to seven seconds of what could also have been, his own life. Regardless, he didn't care. The school was now safe. Lieutenant Nelson, meanwhile, hearing shots, specifically, he thought, two, ordered an immediate surround of the small maintenance building, unsure of what had had happened, satisfied nevertheless, through instinct, if Williams had acted in any way that upset or compromised the terrorists, they would have blown at least one bomb, or more, if they had ever existed! Nothing else, beyond two gunshots, remained the result. An odd silence prevailed everywhere. Momentary confusion reigned. Time being of the essence, Bill Williams knew he couldn't sit where he was, knowing he had to signal a rapid *'all-clear'*. He did so by making one simple cell phone call. Lieutenant Nelson, who was given the good and bad news of what had transpired and the action Williams had taken, was not aware he was even carrying a cell phone, or, for that matter, was also packing a 4th generation, compact version of a Glock 19. He smiled to himself; he hadn't asked, expecting, naturally, as a negotiator he would have gone in unarmed. That's a first, he accepted, understanding, *'heaven forbid'*, if there was ever another occasion, he would be sure to be more vigilant in the way his men conducted themselves. He was aware of repercussions, and public opinion. Swiftly, he and his men entered the building to find Bill Williams.

Authorities had long recognized, and practiced, in schools, colleges and Universities particularly, teachers had huge responsibilities; therefore, calls went out to all to the recorded cell phone numbers; the lockdown in Whitehaven had ended. Except for the immediate area of the school that required it to be considered *'a crime scene'*, one specific area on the grounds was lifted for parents to retrieve their loved ones, the children, frightened and traumatized as they expected them to be. Mostly, though, it was not the case. The time factor, an approximate five hours, and the speed at which the school had exercised their due diligence of immediate reaction to a potential threat, the children, students, had accepted all that had been required of them as a natural reaction to such a circumstance. Television, laptops, iPads, tablets, cell phones and video games were steeling new generations of youth to embrace and respond to what might be; *'the digital age, the new norm!'* Parents hated it, shuddered, however, in light of the Memphis threats, somehow, breathed a sigh of relief of at least, understanding. Now the children could come home.

Steve Frankston's cell phone rang He knew it would be Maggie.

"Steve. Steve, it's over! Do you *know* that yet?" she asked, excitedly, wanting to be first to alert him.

"*No* Maggie, are you *sure*? We heard something over at the school, and it sounded like gunshots, but no, *what* do you know, *please,* tell me, I'm glued to the phone!"

Maggie was thrilled to be the bearer of good news, great news. She had been glued to the TV, scanning channel after channel, searching for any news that was genuinely new, not repetitive. The Fox Network had been the first she tuned in to that *'broke'* the latest, that the siege had ended, that the perpetrators had been killed, adding quickly, the school was about to freed from the lockdown of students, and that all of the children, soon, would be back in the arms of their loved one's. Steve Frankston, and the many parent's surrounding him didn't know any of it. The earlier sound of gunfire freaked all who were gathered where he was and mild panic struck a few, however, within seconds of what they all believed might have been catastrophic, the worst, the police, on megaphones, were announcing, *'good news at Whitehaven, but bear with us folks, we don't have the full picture yet, except, we have prevailed, the people that threatened us have been overtaken…'* There had been nothing else?

Steve's heart skipped a beat. Maggie had been a proverbial news lifesaver, and now, officially, he knew, Josey was safe, Josey was fine, and Josey would come back to him. Soon, the absolute love of his life would be in his arms again. He wanted to shout, he wanted to cry; he wanted to…be somewhere, anywhere, no matter where except, other than

Memphis...with his little girl.

"Thank you, Maggie, thank you, thank you, thank you. My heart has lifted, my mind can rest a little and my life can start again, *God, if you only knew."*

Maggie felt she did. And yet, she didn't really. She didn't have children, a child. Always wanting one somehow, none of her relationships, so far, had been the kind she wanted to share and bring into this world, a child. Her first and only marriage had ended in disaster, the likes of she never wanted to encounter again. For too long, instead, she had been content to be the mistress of her own destiny. The doll store, the doll hospital and her most wonderful of clientele had provided what joy and happiness she might, or could ever have asked for...until...Steve Frankston and a little girl by the name of Josephine, 'Josey', came into her life. And to think, for no reason other than her profession, her livelihood...and a doll hospital. Another little doll, broken, needed to be brought back to life again. Oh, how she needed to see this doll, this very special doll, and oh, how she longed to be the Doctor in charge!

"It's *really* over, Steve. Josey will be with you soon and I'm so happy for you, for you both. I'd say it's only a matter of time before you go to her and believe me, I so wish I could have shared the moment, and be with you, but..." Maggie McConnell never meant to say it. Thrilled, happy, relieved that the standoff had ended, it hadn't been her intention to reference again her coming to Memphis if he needed her as the offer was already out there. She had told him once, twice, maybe three times, but he had never asked it of her. She knew instinctively, he would have spoken up if he did - he hadn't!

Annoyed for what she had enthusiastically imparted, frustrated within, and emotionally drained, it was time to go, to hang up and let him do what he had to, what he needed to…without her.

"Anyway, Steve, that's the update for now, and despite your distance from the school, at least you know all is well, but please, tell me later how it all worked out, okay. For now, though, I'll let you go."

"Will do, Maggie, and thanks, thanks a million. What a relief, I couldn't have survived it all without you. Thank you, I'll call, promise."

Again, their cell phones went quiet. *'Story of my life'* Maggie thought, frowning, her only consolation, the promise of a call. He'd delivered on a promise before; maybe he will again became her new hope. Staring at the television screen, with children emerging from their traumatic captivity, she stared hard, searching for Josey. She knew it was a hopeless task, though. Smiles, laughter, hugging and crying; all she could think; *'I **so** want to be there.'* But she was in Dunbridge, in Florida. Steve and Josey were in Memphis, in Tennessee, together. That very thought became her realistic feeling of happiness, of sadness, of sole, and only, consolation.

~~~~~~~~~~
~~~~~~~~~~

CHAPTER TWELVE

The negotiator, who didn't, knew he was probably in big trouble for one reason or another, and yet, to him, it didn't matter one iota. Emerging from the building, to the fury of Lieutenant Michael 'Mike' Nelson, all Bill Williams could do, by natural instinct, was lift his arms partially in the air and accept his fate, regardless. Much else was too late already. They'd do what they had to, regardless.

"Whatever you want to yell at me for, whatever you think I did wrong, and whatever discipline you might want to suggest for me, frankly, Mike, in the words of Clark Gable, *'I don't give a damn!'* Say it, scream all you like and when you're done, maybe, just maybe, you might want to thank me, too."

"Thank you, thank you…for what? For *killing* two people in an instant without asking even *one* question, I assume. Is that the way it went down Bill, *is it?"*

Mike Nelson was furious!

"Pretty much, Sir, yep, pretty much."

"*Why*, Bill, *why*? That's all I wanna know. Why couldn't you have at least tried for a reason, at least that might have answered a few questions, I mean, we don't even know, yet, if there *were* any bombs planted anywhere in or around the school. Did that cross your mind at all?"

"It's not the way I saw it, Mike, as the first thing on my mind going in were the children. The kids and their teachers, aren't *they* worth something, weren't *their* lives worth saving against the backdrop of a couple of thugs, terrorists, creeps, jihadist's, call them what you will, but to me, our biggest and best assets are the kids in the school there. I didn't say it, I didn't imply it, I didn't want to compromise anyone up front, *especially* you, but when I was called in, when I heard the facts and when I saw the danger, I had no choice. I believed we had one chance and I was the chance, so I took it. And anyway, Mike, I'm the one that'll have to explain, not you, because you had *no* idea which means you're off the hook. That said, I'll take my punishment with not only what I have to face now, but also with the American people, and believe me, when they're done with analyzing this threat, this danger and their children whose lives were at risk, I think they'll side with me. Regardless, even if America didn't side with me, *I'm done.* I don't *want* this crap anymore, negotiating with the likes of the sleazebags that were in there. Take this as a fact, *now* if you like given where you might be coming from, but I'm going to hand in my badge anyway, effective immediately, and on that note, *you* tell me the next move."

Lieutenant Nelson was astonished. He hadn't expected such a tirade, outburst, or a resignation right outside the door of the building where two men lay dead, gunned down by one of his men before even asking any questions. He was painfully aware, as of this second; he had a huge conundrum to deal with. Deep within his mind and soul, he sided with Bill Williams, actually agreeing with the actions he took believing there was, probably, little choice, however, there was protocol, too. With the mashing of the mind he was going through, his silent, inner self wanted to embrace him with a slap on the back and a *'well done', good job,* but he couldn't. The law was the law, an action was an action, and the media, he was sure, were about to have a field day when they learn the truth, of the end, and how it came about. It was not something he was looking forward to, at all.

Bill Williams and Mike Nelson, man to man, stood facing each other; the look on their faces said it all, anger on one hand, emotion on the other. With three officers inside the building assessing the outcome, checking the victims and generally doing a fast recognizance of what clues they might be able to find of where bombs, or incendiary devices, if any, might be placed on the school grounds, Nelson wanted to assess quickly, officially, on the record, finite detail of Williams's entry and what transpired, all before he called in the rest of his squad to take over and secure the inner area of the school and do the search.

"Bill, listen to me. There's going to be questions, answers will be demanded, and fair enough, but look, this is how I see it, maybe, how you see it, let's go down the…"

Five minutes later, Nelson motioned his department to move in and assist with the release the children, and to be sure to keep them all confined to one small perimeter of the school until every last child and teacher were evacuated, back to their loved ones. Meanwhile, the three blocks restricted zone was partially lifted and parents, too, were allowed back to the school area, and as with the children, confined to one section, one pathway only, the location where the children would be directed.

Josey, Amy, Tiffany, Mary and the rest of the locked down classroom cheered when teacher Jones gave them all the news *'we're going home kids, we're going home, I've just been given the all clear.'* The girls all hugged each other, and many other classmates, as they readied themselves to be directed down the corridor, out into the school grounds and fresh open air. Standing, waiting, anxious to be gone, the teacher asked for quiet. Immediate silence prevailed. Tiffany looked at Amy with a frown that suggested bewilderment, wondering, was it a mistake that they're not really leaving? Teacher Jones, a pillar of outer calm throughout the crisis, allayed the fear.

"Children, all I want to say is, thank you. Each and every one of you behaved and performed in an exemplary manner, which, as you know, in circumstances of emergency, it's what we expect, however, really, you were all quite amazing and I want you to know, we as your teachers more than appreciate your best cooperation's. And on that note, let's get ready to move, it's our turn, I believe. I'll see you back in class in a couple of days."

Delighted, Josey whispered; *'we must be getting a couple of days off, how cool!'* Amy quickly butted in, *'Josey, it's Friday, remember?'* They all smiled at each other. Of course, Saturday and Sunday, the weekend, are no school days anyway!

When Steve Frankston saw his daughter exiting the school gate at the far end of the grounds, it was all he could do not to run toward her and swoop her up in his arms, to hold her forever and never let her go, or ever out of his sight again. He was overjoyed, as was every parent who witnessed and shared in the same reunion.

"Baby, baby, tell me *all* about it," he urged from her immediately after he'd finally ended his embrace and able to look into her eyes, to see the happy glow on her face, the smile on her lips. And then she laughed. Did that mean no

trauma, no inner fear? He'd expected the worst.

"Daddy, it was *pretty* frightening although we never really did know what happened and why we were kept locked down. Do *you*, you must?"

It didn't surprise Steve that the children weren't given the total facts, the bigger picture of why. He assumed it was probably policy to calm down a delicate situation, an emergency and not frighten children. And he had no problem with that.

"It was all about some bad guys…" he confessed to her as they began to walk away from the school and the rather large crowd, "…they meant harm to whoever they could get at because they had a personal agenda. It's a bad guy thing and they don't ever care who they hurt, or upset, only this time, it was you all and the school. But let me tell you also, as always, they *never* got away with it, they *never* do and we, the public at large, *you, me, everyone,* are always left wondering why they do it in the first place. Anyway, the main thing is, for you and all of your friends, and the school, all is okay again, so we'll get on with our lives and the bad guys, they pay for their sins, and this time, did. But enough of them and all that, let's go home, huh, or do you want to head out some place and we'll sit and share some outside dinner time, how about that? Does that work for you?"

The last thing he wanted to do was mention bombs, guns, death, the word terrorists and the like to an eight year old, a child. They needed calm, peace, tranquility and the nicer side of life and living. And that's exactly what Steve Frankston had in mind as they headed for the Josey selected, family styled, Cracker Barrel Restaurant.

"Did you talk to Maggie about what happened today Daddy, or did she call you, maybe? I bet she knew how bad it was because I saw TV cameras at the school."

It was an innocent question, not unexpected, or was it? Steve Frankston had a small problem processing the answer knowing they had both spoken along the way, but Josey? He wondered whatever brought Maggie McConnell to her mind so quickly. The connection between the two ran deep.

"Yes, we did talk, in fact, we talked a couple of times."

"Was she worried about me Daddy, did she ask you about me at all?"

"She did, for sure, because she knew it was here in Memphis, right near where we live so naturally she wanted to know everything, and I mean, *everything* and to ease your mind, yes, she was worried a whole lot about you, too, how about that?"

"That's nice, Daddy, because I like her, so I'm glad she thought of me."

Mystified, a little, he glanced at her She was in the middle of placing a huge helping of meatloaf on to her fork. As she readied it to eat she noticed him looking.

"What's up, Daddy? That's an odd look."

"Nothing, Josey, except, I was wondering. What made you ask about Maggie? What's the fascination?"

The meatloaf was placed back down on the plate.

"Well, Daddy, she *is* going to fix my doll and you *said* she could, but truthfully, I was really wondering because when we were in the classroom, waiting and sitting inside there, forever it seemed, I wasn't sure for a little while if we might ever get out and if we didn't, *then* what would happen to Angel? She'd never be fixed and you wouldn't know what to do with her, would you? And Maggie would never have got to see here, either."

Steve Frankston was quite taken aback! His little girl, wise beyond her years, for sure, it seemed, must have thought about not getting out of the school alive, which means she and everyone else thought they might all die right where they were. He was horrified to think that the events of the day could have gone that far in her mind, to believe, death might be her fate, her friends and classmates, too. *'She's only eight,'* he exclaimed to himself! It should never have been, he believed, in one so young.

"Josey, let me ask you a question."

"Okay, Daddy, go ahead, *what*?"

As a Father, he'd choose his words carefully, but then again, maybe he was underestimating an eight year old in this day and age; she had defied his thought process many times already. For the first time in a while he suddenly realized he thought of his wife, Angelic, Josey's mother, asking himself, *'what would she have done, or said.'* Before proceeding, oddly, he wondered why the thought, the memory of Angelic had popped into his head at such a crucial moment. First, it was Maggie, from Josey, now Angelic, from him. He shook his head to clear all the thoughts running rampant. Right now it didn't matter. There were questions and answers remaining.

"Firstly, Maggie *is* going to fix your doll, I *made* a promise and I *keep* my promises, *especially* to you, however, just for a second, let me ask you something. When you were in the classroom, wondering what was going on waiting to be let out to go home, did you ever think or doubt that you were really safe, as safe as the teacher told you? Did you talk about other things and if you did, what were they?"

Josey sat silent for a moment. The small frown on her forehead told him she was thinking. It was quite a grown up reaction.

"Safe, yes, we thought we were going to be alright, but other stuff, not really, Daddy, although Tiffany and me did wonder if we were going to die, and Amy agreed, wondering the same thing. *That's* when I thought of Angel, and then Mommy, and if we did die, or might die, I thought Mommy might wonder about Angel, too, because I am sure she knows she broken. That's it, not much else, except, I did want to see and be with you again so I told Tiffany we shouldn't think that way anymore, and anyway, the teacher had said we were all okay and would be going home soon and he's nice. And he wouldn't tell a lie about that, *would* he?"

It had been a long answer, a little confusing or muddled, even, and Steve wasn't quite sure what to make of it. He needed a moment to think it through. Meanwhile, Josey placed the last of her meatloaf and potato on her fork and proceeded to finish her dinner. She was actually looking forward to dessert, as promised, if she finished it all. Peach cobbler and ice cream was her favorite.

"No, of course not, but Josey…" it was time to be a little more truthful. "…Some of what happened today will be on the TV and will be in newspapers, but you know, for all they say and show, I don't think you were ever in any *real* danger. A little, yes, but *not* too much, I doubted. The Police all knew what was happening and they're good at catching bad guys, so to me, I think what the TV people say and what really happens, sometimes it's not always the same thing, in fact, I was on TV and I…"

"*You* were on TV Daddy, what for, what did you do?"

"Oh, nothing, Josey, not really. I just said all the same things I'm telling you now because I believe them but the main thing is, and what I said, and am saying to you, the TV and news people aren't always right. What happened at school, to you, it was scary, of course, and I hated it, knowing you were alone in there without me, but I always knew you'd get out okay, I really did. I had so much faith in you and all of your friends, the teachers, too. I knew you'd come home, so please, all I'm saying, asking, is try and stay away from what isn't the truth, and believe that all the bad guys get caught, always, and the good people stay safe, like you, do you understand?"

"Yes, Daddy, I do pretty much and I'm okay, too, about it all, truly."

"And Josey, so you know, Angel would always have been all right, I'd make sure of that and I'm sorry you had to worry about her, but not anymore. By the way, Maggie saw me on TV, too, and that's another reason she called. She thought I did fine."

"Can *we* call Maggie, Daddy, I'd like to talk to her, I think?"

"Of course we can and she'd be happy to hear your voice, count on it."

Devoid of any urgency, he picked up the menu to check his selection for dessert. There was quite a choice.

"I mean *now*, Daddy. Can we call Maggie, now?"

"Now, *why* now, we're having dinner."

"That doesn't matter. We're finished really, except for dessert and that's not here yet so why don't we call her on the cell phone, now? I'd like to talk to her anyway."

Joey's adamant request wasn't quite what he wanted. His little girl had just come off the back of a rather traumatic day, this was her time, their time, their bonding time for the normality of life and well being…but then again? In the mind of an eight year old, Maggie McConnell had figured once again. Realistically, he had no choice. From his inner jacket pocket he withdrew his phone and scrolled for Margaret McC. He pushed her name. The call was underway.

That night, after a most stressful day, with Josey sound asleep, Steve Frankston found himself nursing a three finger stiff drink, a JD. He was wondering what his life could, or would possibly look like, without, what could have been, not only his wife, Angelic gone, but also, if it had been, today, little Josey, too. What if she had suffered a fate, death, as portrayed in the media, as in the after effects of an horrific bomb blast that could have torn down not only all the buildings of the school she attended, but could have taken so many innocent lives, children, at the same time?

Tears welled in his eyes as he pictured his life without the first real true loves he had ever known. Too many times he had lay in bed, thinking of Angelic, wishing there was more that could have been done to spare her life, and why, again, did God choose her, so young. It was wrong, totally wrong! And now, as it could have been, he dreaded, had fate not played a hand at ending today's drama, an even younger life could have been taken. Accepting God had taken Angelic, if he had taken little Josey too, Steve knew, deep within his soul, he would forever have troubling accepting, that if a higher being has a cause, a needy one, that required taking from him, a second time, to satisfy that need, whatever it was, he doubted he could ever be a believer again. He would have had no choice but to turn his back on God, and go his own way. God would have forsaken him! Thankfully, mercifully, it hadn't happened. Instead, he took the higher road, thanking God for sparing Josey, and *all* the little children. And then he thanked the first responders, those who had ended the school siege of Memphis. *How* it ended, what the circumstances were, and who masterminded the terrorist's demise he had yet to learn in its totality of hard facts, but whoever and whatever, he gave added silent thanks.

From all the thoughts that had swirled through his head, suddenly, he had an urge to again look in on Josey. Peaceful, and pretty as a picture as she slept, unexpectedly, he glanced from her across to Angel. Sighing heavily, another thought rushed through his mind. Lifting his head upward, he silently uttered the same two words he had moments ago – *'thank you.'* Maybe God had played a role, through Angel, to Maggie McConnell?

Alone, philosophical in thought, he slowly began to realize a common belief; things happen for a reason, that fate plays a role in everyone's lives. And as long as they were good, it was okay to role-play. He smiled as he recollected the phone call between Maggie and Josey at the restaurant. He had loved the cheery lilt in Josey's voice, the big wide grins every now and then, and the joy that seemed to come naturally as the two of them spoke. And yet, he had no idea what they were really saying to each other. But then again, it *was* Josey's call. *He* was really an eavesdropper. It wasn't rocket science; that he knew. Those two had bonded. With that thought Steve thought of Angelic, then Maggie. He wanted to believe, or at least he hoped, Angelic wouldn't mind if he and Maggie spent some time together, and Josey too. Would she? Again, with the same thoughts spinning in his head, he fell asleep. For the briefest of moments, out there, somewhere, he saw Angelic. Standing still, upright and tall, she seemed to smile at him. She looked so beautiful, just as he always remembered her. He wanted to run to her, to hold her again, in his arms – but for some reason, powerless, he couldn't move. Angelic seemed to say something, from afar - what? He couldn't quite catch it. Her voice, it had been too soft. Could it be, as he had hoped, approval of what he was thinking, of where his life may be going? From the distance as she had remained, she nodded her head – as if answering him. She smiled again, and waved. It was the smile he always remembered. Then, as fast as she had appeared, Angelic was gone. Steve was sure; the nod of her head was a yes.

But for the love of Angel, a broken doll, something surreal was happening, something he was beginning to lose control over. And Josey, too, unwittingly, was playing her own role. A remaining question; how would it all play out?

~~~~~~~~~~
~~~~~~~~~~

CHAPTER THIRTEEN

Reactions might have been mixed, however, they were heavily skewed in Bill Williams favor. The children, the teachers, the school, and their safety, towered over and above a couple of alleged terrorist bombers who meant, real or not, to do America and American citizens harm. The media, however, would not rest on the case. Demands were made for a full inquiry, and where needed, justice to be served, if any wrongdoing was revealed, and as suspected, might be. It was a double-edged sword that one could fall on. Under a different type of attack, Bill Williams remained relentless. Two nights later, after what the media had now billed, to dramatically themed music, *'The Siege of Memphis'*, he sat with the one man who probably wielded the strongest and most powerful media stick on all of television, George Rillington, to answer, unafraid, any and every question he could throw at him. He had nothing to lose, hopefully; instead, he had a whole lot more to gain. Riveted, Steve Frankston was an audience member that night.

"So tell me Mr. Williams, are you a Police negotiator, and is it your job to go into a stand-off situation, with anyone, to try and find a peaceful solution to the problem at hand, in an effort to have them withdraw from the position they are in, and, or, give themselves up peacefully, if that were at all possible?"

"Yes!"

Silence prevailed. It had been, and remained, a one-word answer.

Noticeably, slightly chagrined, Rillington proceeded.

"Okay Mr. Williams, I get it! Now, second question. Right off the top, *did* you, or did you *not*, pull your gun immediately on entering that building, and *did* you, or did you *not*, *kill* the two men inside without asking a *single* question?"

"Yes!"

Silence again prevailed; it was still a one-word answer. Rillington pressed on.

"But you're a negotiator, an *authorized* Police negotiator, didn't you think you should at least ask a question, *any* question, *first,* instead of firing off the two shots you did without knowing *one single solitary thing about them*?"

"No! I didn't have to think, at least I doubted I did," he answered in the calmest of tone.

"*Why,* Mr. Williams, *why*? It's your *job,* isn't it?" Rillington virtually demanded.

"It's also my job, Mr. Rillington, to protect the innocent, and in this case, many, many children, and teachers, too. Further, it's my job to defend America, in this case, one of the finest schools in Memphis. That's exactly what I did!"

"Yes, Mr. Williams, *it is, you did, I grant you that,* but Sir, you didn't hold up part of your, what might be called, Police oath of office, and in this case, I can't say blindly, necessarily, but you went into a situation to *kill* people, no questions asked - *didn't you*? Is that the way you see it? Is that a *fair* interpretation of the matter?"

"No, Sir, not at all, on either charge. I would have talked to them, gladly, however, I saw them through the window, looked directly into their eyes where I saw the *anger*, the *hate*, the *distrust* of me, and *all* who were outside, backing me up. I saw the weapons in their possession, one brandished clearly for me to understand they were well armed. There was never a doubt in my mind that I was their enemy. If I had felt they wanted to talk, as I had asked them to, then I would have, as I said, *gladly*, but Mr. Rillington, facts are, and think about it, I had gone to them with my arms held high and I was alone. What I did was maybe not the smartest tactic in the book of negotiating, I admit, but, this was a desperate situation and none of us had any idea what we were in for, except, a school and many children's lives were at stake. *Was* there a bomb, we didn't really know? Were there *two* bombs or more, and if there were, *where were they*? We knew *nothing*, Sir, *nothing*! So ask yourself, and everyone can quarterback, including you, Mr. Rillington, respectfully, but ask yourself, *what* do you, *what* does the public, *what* do the authorities, *what* do the media, *all of you*, but most of all, and probably more importantly, ultimately, *what* do the American people *want*, or *expect*? An end result their way we could never live with, yet would have to accept, like it or not. Did we *really* want what could have been; mass murder, destruction of magnitude, followed by chaos, mayhem that would have fed even more sensationalism in news…all at the expense of too many lives, children's lives. Add to that, acceptance of overblown political correctness, adhering to the rule of law, or giving in to terror, I could go on and on. *Is that what is wanted here?* A pretty please of *'don't do that, don't set off that bomb, will you, we'll be nice to you.'* I don't think so, or put it this way, I didn't think so, at the time. And it was at *that* point I asked myself a question, and then answered it; this crowd, these people and the likes of this type who come here and wreak havoc on our society, for no reason, *none,* don't deserve what we give them, provide for them and we certainly *can't* afford to allow them to hold us all to such ransom, all on their personal whim. There's nothing American in *that*! And let me add a thought, what we have here is a new trend, one that's creeping into our society. I'll propose it as self-destruction. Some of these people *don't care;* it's as if they feel personally disposable, for a cause, and frankly, it's *quite* a concern, one we'll all have to address. "

While Rillington raised an eyebrow at the interpretation, Bill Williams took a sip of water before proceeding. He had a platform. He'd use it.

"Mr. Rillington, have *no* doubt about it, the two in question fit that mould, they had *no* intentions of talking to me, and believe me, *I knew it immediately,* and remember, I *had* asked them to talk at the very outset. I *also* asked that the children be released. Their retort, after my humanitarian request; who was I to be so demanding of them? Quote - *'if it means blowing the school to smithereens, then we'll do it, and that includes the children and anyone else who is in there. We don't care about children, we don't care who dies, even us',* Those words, verbatim, were their words of reply, and Sir, faced with that choice, accepting that I was in harm's way personally, and that many hundreds around me were indeed in harm's way also, I could have done one of two things. *One,* walk away and we carry on for Lord knows how long, wondering *what* might play out and *how,* and a reminder here, they had already made one set of demands for money, crass as that is in the overall picture. Or *two,* for me to stay focused and do what I had to do, to bring it all to an end, if indeed, I was able to get myself into a position to be capable of achieving such a result.

"To me, though, and with hindsight twenty-twenty right now, Mr. Rillington, I have *no* regrets, *none.* I therefore did what I needed to, questions or no questions, and Sir, they paid the price for what they did, or tried to do and that was, again, disrupt and frighten America as others before have tried to do, and there are many examples to cite, none ended well! *Frankly,* I'd had enough, so I followed my gut, and with that said, *truthfully,* I will pay whatever price America, or the justice system, the media at large, society, or anyone else, whatever judgment and penalty they choose to place on me. At face value, I will *accept* it, I'll even go to jail if need be. Those children are *safe,* and those teachers are *safe,* and *that school still stands* allowing many parents' today to breath a huge sigh of relief. I did what I thought I had to do, and that is, keep America safe, except this time, *my way,* not the molly-coddling we seem to do, too often! I was *done* with that, this time, okay?"

George Rillington hesitated for a moment, not totally sure if his guest had finished, he had wanted to give him all the time he needed. Shifting in his seat, not hard to follow the explanation offered by Williams, he stayed on script.

"So what now? What's next, because obviously, you're adamant and to me, it sounds like you're ticked off, *really ticked off,* and that you've had enough?"

"I *have* and *am,* on all points, and frankly, I've said about all I want to on the subject. I have *nothing* left to say, I mean, *what's left,* it's how I feel, and Sir, if you don't mind, to coin that well know phrase they use every time the Super Bowl ends and they ask the same old question to the fixed quote, *'I'm going to Disneyland,'* well, this time I'll give it a Memphis, Tennessee ending. Mr. Rillington, of your query, what now, what's next - *'I'm going to Graceland'*, who knows I might actually be more welcomed there, I'd hope!"

Unexpected, the interview ended on a much lighter note, including a slight smile.

"Well said, Mr. Williams, well said…" became the initial closing remarks to the much-touted Fox News Williams-Rillington television *'exclusive'*, "…and Sir, I commend you."

After leaning across the news desk to shake his guest's hand, looking directly into the camera, Rillington continued. He had a message of his own he wanted to deliver.

"Mr. Williams, from my stance, I believe you are a brave American, a patriot who has served our country well, and I thank you, and for what it's worth…" for added effect, when he paused, the camera came in even closer on his face, "…America, this man did our country a service. Those, who on one hand come here behind whatever veil, only to blend in and sponge off our most generous society while plotting evil against us, as these two did, we are well rid of them. However, allow me to add, it may apply to the born here homegrown terrorist types, too. Your fate may well have been the same. Regardless, for now, for Mr. Williams, I say, let this man go, in peace. Don't prosecute or persecute him for standing up for America, and OUR rights! And on a final note, as many believe, more than might ever be understood, there should be no charges, none. Justice was done, swiftly and with a clear message. From it, America benefits. That's my opinion."

Steve Frankston had shielded Josey, so far, quite successfully, from much of what was parlayed out in the media at large. She didn't need to hear gory details of what could have happened, might have happened, and if it happened; it was completely unnecessary and yet, there it was, hour after hour, being played out in living rooms across the USA, indeed, around the world. Instead, over that weekend, before heading back into the classroom come Monday morning, he set them both a frantic pace of a number of time consuming tasks; taking in the movies, a marvelous long riverboat ride on the Mississippi complete with lunch on board, and that was just Saturday. Next day, after church, they first rode their bikes all around Mud Island and The Riverwalk, then took a casual walk around downtown, even down to Beale Street, where as luck would have it, a small band was playing out in Handy Park, especially as the lead singer looked so cool, Josey's comment, adding, she wished Amy and Tiffany were with her. With the day wearing down, and a chocolate fudge sundae in their tummies, they headed for home; finishing their hectic schedule that Sunday night watching, together, with popcorn in hand, the get away from it all, kid rated, Disney fantastical adventure movie, called; OZ The Great and Powerful.

As it turned out, during the movie, a text came in; school on Monday was canceled. The grounds were not cleared for use and wouldn't be for a further 24 hours. While Josey was happy enough, her Father found solace in the fact that he would be able to spend another day with his baby girl, eight years old going on nine, maybe nineteen he thought, when it came to her bravery, her overall outlook on so many things! Together, no matter what, they would find as much to do tomorrow as they had in the past day or two, and for a Daddy, he saw it as a blessing, in a rude awakening of life, and of just how precious time is in sharing all you can with those you love most. Steve Frankston, with all his heart, so loved his Josephine, his little Josey. And time was against him, he knew, when the little girl would grow up…and leave him. Then what?

~~~~~~~~~~
~~~~~~~~~~

CHAPTER FOURTEEN

Work was never the same. School was never the same. Memphis could never be the same. Life, for the community, was never the same, either. Steve, Josey, in their own way, also, joined the ranks of the majority, the nervous unrest. But what had changed them – the obvious was one, however, in the bigger picture these days, probably everything?

Strange really, cognizant of the fact it had only been days since the Whitehaven incident, *'The Siege of Memphis'*, the lockdown of the school, and the nightmare that day that revealed, quickly, there were *no* bombs, there was *no* exit strategy, and the terrorists were really suicide recruits spreading primarily, on this occasion, fear to what was termed *'infidels'*, who don't understand *'our way of life, our religion'*, whatever that was supposed to mean? Did they, the believers of their religion, followers of the Quran, Islam's Holy Book, their document, want to convert the world, away from the Bible, from Christianity, our religion, to theirs?

Perplexed, Steve Frankston did not like, at all, what was happening. Too much had transpired too quickly. Psychologically, there had been changes and yet he could not put a specific finger on exactly what it was. He racked his brain, over and over, thinking, maybe, it was him! His greatest concern, though, was always, Josey. Again, for reasons that baffled him as to why, he went back to the phone conversation she'd had with Maggie McConnell, the evening of the very day it all happened, remembering, of course, it was one-sided; he could only ever hear what Josey would say in response to…whatever?

'No Maggie, of course not!'

'Yes, a little, but not too much.'

'Daddy, of course.'

'Maybe, if you could.'

'Yes, I'd love that, I would.'

'No, but I did think of Angel, and I remembered.'

'Oh yeah, lots. Well, I think so.'

'If Daddy thinks so, yes, but for now, we've got lots to do anyway.' To the closing line, he recalled, *'That'd be super. I think it's a great idea, yeah, maybe we can talk later about that.'*

And so it went, on and on and on. It was as if the conversation would never end and while it was very lopsided, the interaction the two shared and obviously enjoyed judging by Josey's body language and particularly laughter, it was clear, the two of them had a lot in common, a little girl to a grown woman, girl things. At the time, subconsciously, Steve wondered what they could possibly have been talking about, however, he didn't pursue it, mainly from feeling like he shouldn't, settling on the fact he wanted Josey to be relaxed, to feel loved, cared about, and to be as natural, independent, even, as she could be after such an ordeal. He had decided to let their interaction be *her* call; no Daddy interference. That seemed fair to him, then. Was he wrong? Now, he wondered, because in a small way, it actually bothered him a little?

'Oh, Angelic,' a voice in his head cried. *'What am I to do? Why did you have to go, why? I so need you, your answers, Josey and me, we need you, we miss you, and Angelic, I still love you so.'* He hated being so alone in a moment of personal upheaval, of despair, remembering all those years ago when he married Angelic, thinking, now I have a friend, a lover, a confidante, someone to share my life with, forever, and yet, fate…it was never to be, and fast forward time, it's back to being alone. However, from their love, now, he had the most wonderful gift given of their short time and years together, Josey, his life, and of course he'll take care of her. But oh, how much sweeter it would have been if he still had Angelic, he thought, and the help she would gladly have shared. And yet…!

Steve's mind had wandered. Far. Maggie had offered to help…should he…? He shook his head, *'why am I thinking about Maggie? Why? Is this another part of fate? Life's fate! Is this de'ja'vu?'* he wondered. He'd given up Florida, once, for Memphis, and now, the tables seemed reversed. *'Oh dear Maggie, we have a problem?'* Memphis, Florida?

Although it shouldn't be, believing she probably had no right, a slow building revelation was also overtaking Maggie McConnell. An overwhelming feeling of finally having met someone, and that something was happening, was becoming the embryo catalyst to the start of a change in her life, and yet, for some inexplicable reason she remained at complete odds with herself in trying to formulate a mindset that would allow her to believe, whatever it was, that if it was real, or if it had a purpose, might it then have - a future? Steve Frankston and daughter, Josey, had, by sheer default, placed themselves in her life, turning it upside down to the point of absolute confusion! *That* part she didn't like, at all. In a million years, never expecting to meet two people who could become so impactive in such a short period of time, in her every day, indeed, her very existence, Maggie began to despair, a little, more than she felt she should. For too long, alone, content as she had been, loving her life, her existence, her work, her friends, today, alone in her doll store, in the doll hospital section, she sat on her metal high back stool at her work bench, she called it an operating table, staring aimlessly at a Madame Alexander 'Scarlet O'Hara' doll that needed stringing. Looking so helpless in her designer plastic hospital container, Maggie called them beds; she felt the exact same way as the doll, helpless. What had Steve Frankston and daughter, Josey, done to her?

It had been a long week. The Memphis drama had slowed dramatically and there was no longer a reason for her to stay connected through news items, to Steve, on the phone, as they had done throughout the ordeal, at the height of the siege. She recalled the last words he had said, the last time they spoke, after Josey's call.

"We've had a nice time tonight, Josey and me. Dinner was great and she had quite an appetite I must say, but anyway, Maggie, all is fine now, we're back to some kind of normalcy, if you can call it that. Thanks by the way for your calls, for the caring, the news, it was very helpful, and made all the difference, to me, anyway. I guess I'll be in touch and we can set something up sometime as we've said, although I'm not sure when at the moment under the circumstances, however, I will call, I promise, okay?"

"Yes, Steve, and thank you, too. Josey's a great kid and I love chatting with her, and you're right, she's a little chatterbox sometimes but that's a good thing in children I've learned in dealing with them as often as I do in the store. Anyway, nice talking to you again and I'll look forward to next time. Stay safe and bye and thanks again."

"Yeah, Maggie, till later."

She reminisced the voice, the tone, and the words, to the final *'Yeah, Maggie, till later.'* Sadly, Steve Frankston had sounded, then, quite removed, distant, and almost disinterested. Maggie wanted to cry. She did!

When her *'Doctor-in-Training'* to the doll hospital walked in twenty minutes later, she found Maggie still perched on her metal high back stool. A workaholic, and not an uncommon sight to behold, along with her always stalwart, brave and *'never-a-problem'* demeanor whenever she came in ready to start her day, what *was* uncommon and very different on this particular occasion, Maggie had a tissue in one hand while with the other, she'd formed a clenched fist that was placed under her chin propping up her head. It did nothing to hide the deep worrisome furrows on her brow, and worse, she looked painfully sorry for herself and clearly, she had obviously been crying.

"Oh-oh my dear, what's the matter, and *please,* don't say your usual, *nothing*?"

Karen Kartney was not only a dear friend, but also a valuable help to Maggie McConnell, and if there was one thing she knew, it would be, answer the question! Karen would stop at nothing, ever, until she knew exactly what was going on, and that applied not only to specific work matters, but also, particularly, to personal matters. She was relentless, if need be, in extracting whatever details that prevailed in a problem, then, in processing the answer, together they would sit and have a *'meeting'* until the issue, the problem, was solved, albeit temporarily. *This* morning was no exception.

"If I was to make it a two-word dilemma, if we call it such, would I be right in saying - Steve Frankston?" she asked, having sensed, clearly, a no reply was likely to be the response, not that she'd leave it there!

Maggie looked at her friend. Sorry for the way she felt might have been her sensitive inner feeling, however, Karen was right! She had no option; come clean immediately because if she held back, Karen will pursue it anyway.

"Why are you *always* so smart, so clever, so astute, but then again, maybe it was obvious and I gave myself away too easy for your observation, but yes, you are absolutely right, Steve Frankston *is* the reason. He has stormed my brain, my life, too. I hate it, I think."

"I knew it, but Maggie, it's okay. All new relationships, however slight or slow they appear on start up, they have a way of testing us all, of challenging our feelings, and in many ways, bringing in a doubt, a fear. It's natural, and here, *today*, you're no different, in fact, you've joined the brigade. We women can sometimes be our own worst enemy when it comes to men because we *think* different, *act* different and seem to find more in a circumstance than there might be. You know, Maggie, I've always seen that as *'wishful thinking'*, not to say, of course, that's the situation with *you*, however, from what little you've shared along the way so far, assuming it's *everything* and not just the bits you want to share..." both had a little smile over that remark, "...but look, have a personal pity-party, that's fine, but remember the old, old, adage, *'if it's meant to be, it will.'* Simple, but mostly true, and maybe, for now, you'll even agree."

"*Damn*! Karen, why are you always so right?"

"Because I've been there, that's why!"

"You have?"

"I have."

"So tell me more, I might need to know. You've never been down that trail before."

"And I won't now, either, Maggie. You have your own problems, you don't need mine, long gone with the wind as they are now, though."

"Well I don't know if your experience back then is mine right now, but whatever, I feel so out of sorts, like, lost, *completely lost!* Steve, in fairness, hasn't done anything wrong per se, and he's never made commitments, promises or anything remotely like that, it's just me, feeling as though he's drifted somewhat, as if the Memphis thing at the school has come and gone and he's gone back to being the way he was, as if nothing happened, oh, I don't know," she rambled, "I'm just all mixed up in my head. I sooooo want to hear from him, something, *anything*, is *that* so wrong?"

"Of course not, well I don't think so, but let me ask you a question."

Maggie looked at her friend, and then at the front door, hoping customers wouldn't come in at such a crucial moment for her. Business she certainly wanted, *yes*, advice as she was about to get from Karen, probably, was more important. Fragile as she was feeling, she needed support, closure, a pep talk, even, and with Karen, she certainly could rely on her for that. With an open invitation her friend fired away, all guns were blazing.

"Do you *honestly* think, what happened this week, what happened in Memphis, what happened to his little girl, his baby, that he hasn't been affected by it all, that he has been able to take it all in stride as *'just another day'*, no biggie? Do you *really* think he hasn't soul searched, looking for answers, looking for ways to make his girl, Josey, manage what she went through, what she endured, to find ways to make her feel comforted, loved, cared for? Do you think maybe you are not necessarily, but *should* be, his number one, or equal priority at this moment in time in his life? Know you, *yes,* talked with you during it all, *yes,* and because he did, he needs you to help him find solutions, whatever they may be? Maggie, if you can *honestly* answer those questions, in a way that places you in the *absolute* front seat of where he needs to be right now, and then convince me that he has *failed* to recognize *who* you are, and how *derelict* in his duty he must be not to understand that *you* are paramount to his end result, then Steve Frankston has let you down badly. Steve Frankston has erred in *every* way in not consulting you, and in the process, Steve Frankston has done a *complete disservice* to his relationship with you in *not* calling you, *not* wanting you to come to Memphis and help him sort it all out. And last, but *certainly* not least; this devil named Steve Frankston, *because* of it all, has treated you with *utter* and *absolute* contempt in his silence. And *that,* therefore, is *shameful,* as is he! And *what* a creep he turned out to be, huh?"

Maggie McConnell could do nothing, except stare at Karen Kartney, blankly. Frankly, she didn't know what to say, or think. Her answer, but question, had been so long, it wasn't really either anymore; it was a lecture, a torrent of words that made a lot of sense, and yet, *stung* at the same time! She was also very, very right. At no time had she seriously sat and thought about what Steve Frankston must have not only gone through in physically being there the terror of it all, and what could have been a nasty outcome, but also, what he must be going through in the aftermath. Alone, sure, and she wanted to be there for him, had offered, however, it wasn't her right to have such self-claimed, selfish expectations. It was *his* crisis, with *his* daughter, in *their* lives – not hers!

"Oh, my, my, and Lordy! I can *only* agree with you Karen. Hard or harsh as it may seem, it's basically all pretty true, you nailed it and yes, I guess I have expected too much. In listening to you it's pretty obvious I need to take a backseat and cool my heels, my thinking, my *'what I want'* feeling, in the hope that he'll call me for all the right reasons, if at all, when he's ready, when he's more calm or at peace with himself and his conclusions. I can see that, I get it and I can accept it, too, so, no need to answer your questions. I'm going to heed the advice instead, however, that said, and accepted, let me ask you this, anyway."

Karen looked at her with a smirk that suggested she knew what was coming. This road had already been traveled.

"What is it with you, how come you're the Miss Smarty-Know-All who never misses, that you get all the brains in this hospital room?" she asked, picking up a doll from the bench that needed attention and was about to get it.

"I didn't, 'cause you're smart, too," she replied. "As I said before, it's not just me, and it's not rocket science either. It's called *men* and they're strange creatures at the best of times with women, and you don't need me to tell you *that*! As they say, *'can't live with them, can't live without them'*, although we all seem to spend enough time trying to do it anyway, and *you*, my dear, sweet, friend, *you* are head longing in wanting to live *with* them I sense, especially *this* one who without a doubt has a strangle hold on your heart these days, and *please*, spare me the agony and don't try and deny it!"

"I *don't*!" was the two word, instant reply. "But I'll heed your counsel, I'll wait for his call, I'll pine alone at night where not a soul knows, or can see me, okay?"

The sarcastic smirk of a smile on her face was obvious. Fortuitously, as if timed to perfection, the first customer for the day walked in the door. Maggie, ever vigilant and customer oriented went straight to her, all upbeat and bright with chatty small talk. Happily, she was a regular in the store, which made the moment more convivial, friendly. Karen, meanwhile, settled in for the day at her workstation, readying her very old European porcelain patient to replace her eyes.

Fifteen minutes later, the doll store quiet and the hospital busy, suddenly, Karen had, what she excitedly termed, *'an incredibly good idea.'* Maggie McConnell could do nothing except sit and wait for the revelation.

"Are you ready for this?" she asked.

"Why of course, why wouldn't I, Miss I-Can-Always Fix-Everything-In-Life?"

"*Three words,* well, technically four," she said. "The Nashville Doll Show."

Maggie immediately repeated them.

"The Nashville Doll Show. Okay, that's about two weeks away yet. What about it?"

"Memphis, Nashville, up the highway, what two, three hours, close anyway!"

"*Aaannd,* your point?"

"Okay, Maggie, I'll spell it out the way I might see it. Call it the Kartney recommendation." Taking a deep breath she proceeded to plant the seed already germinated.

"Steve's in Memphis, Josey loves dolls, Maggie's at the Annual Doll Show and maybe, I mean, just maybe, there's an outside chance a certain little girl can be invited to the doll show, compliments of one who is already attending, is booked to be there and one who might love to have a reason to make a call, a suggestion, offer an invite, give a little girl a respite from *'bad thoughts'* that might have been. I could go on and on, but won't. I don't really think I need to."

"*Wow!* Karen Kartney, you're a genius, a devil in disguise, a born matchmaker, do you know that?"

"*What,* Maggie? I thought you'd *love* it."

"*Love it,* I do and what an *incredible* thought, and so apropos. Why didn't I think of that?"

"Because you're not me and if I'm right, this doll show coming up could be the perfect vehicle for you to make a call, take advantage of a real proposition that makes a load of sense and maybe, at least, let's you talk with Steve, and if he likes the idea, is looking for ways to entertain and help Josey through any ordeal, this might fit the bill. It's innocent enough and let's face it, it is you, *who you are.*"

"I agree and in all honesty, I would *love* to take Josey to the show, assuming she is really into dolls, although I must say, she certainly gave me the impression she was, that morning, right here in the store. She was in awe and come to think of it, so was Steve. And you're *right;* it's the *perfect* opener for contact. I'll do it, tonight! Good call."

"Perfect, but remember, have your game plan totally worked out. How you'll handle it, the logistics of it all. Either you drive up via Memphis to make it easy on him, or, if he counteracts and says he'll drive her to Nashville and meet you there, have a basic idea of how it can be handled and be sure to make it all easy, *that's the key.* By the way, how far is Memphis from Nashville, do you know?"

"I'm not sure, however, something tells me it's not a daytrip and that fact alone right there could become a problem, I wonder? Oh dear! That alone might sink the idea right there."

On a need to know basis, Karen asked her iPad a voice-activated question. A Map Quest detailed answer filled the screen almost immediately. Cities, route and mileage, it was all there. Thankfully, Maggie had been wrong, quite wrong!

"About 220 miles, maybe three hours plus driving. Not bad, a small haul I'd say."

"It all depends on what's considered a haul. I mean, what's three hours, or four for that matter?"

Maggie had taken the high road, the positive one, and the one that spelt *'no biggie!'* Regardless, she'd still have to think of something and make it sound easy.

"The Nashville Doll Show is a three day event Karen. If I go up on Thursday as I'd planned, I'll do Friday for me, then if Steve can maybe drive up on the Saturday, I can, hopefully, take Josey to the show then, or, of course, on the Sunday, if that's the way it has to be. Mind you, I have no idea how the overnight situation might apply but that doesn't matter, I'll let him know I'm at the Downtown Renaissance, and it's walking distance to the Convention Center so maybe he'll consider staying there, too. Anyway, without pre-supposing anything, I'd guess he'd come up with something that's workable, that makes sense either way, if he likes the idea, so maybe we're off to a good start here. Bottom line, if it's meant to be, it'll all work out."

"I believe so, to me it's easy enough." Karen agreed.

"Hey, I wonder if Steve likes country music because the Grand Ole Opry might be a great suggestion for the Saturday night, you know, turn the whole weekend into an event, but if he doesn't...?" She paused, pondering an alternative. "Well, there's got to be a million things to do in Nashville, I might surf the Internet tonight and find out."

"Now you're thinking, however," Karen cautioned, wisely, "be prepared for a no. It's possible, and all the dreaming in the world won't change it. Maybe we should cool the heels for now, see how he reacts, and get a vibe or an affirmative, after that, if it's a *yes,* then Maggie, you'll have a whole lotta planning to do. Nashville's a big town, the drive from here to there is enough already, but when you're there, if he and Josey are, too, there is so much you can see, do and learn, it'll be a game changer I'm sure. Fingers crossed, toes crossed, le...*woops,* I doubt I should go *there.*"

Maggie laughed. She guessed where Karen's head might have been or going, but if not, then she had her own thought that almost made her blush!

"You're bad!" she told her.

"I'm bad, are you *kidding* me? Look at *you* girlfriend."

~~~~~~~~~~
~~~~~~~~~~

CHAPTER FIFTEEN

I'm a *wreck,* Maggie, a *wreck,* and I admit it. *What* a time it's been. It's *awful,* believe me, and *talk* about *stress*!"

Maggie McConnell could hear it in his voice. There had been no question, the billed Siege of Memphis had taken a personal toll on not only Steve Frankston, but as it turned out, many children and parents who were involved that day at the school in Whitehaven. What had aggravated him even more was the fact that the local channel that had recorded an interview with him the day of the siege, and with the subsequent deaths of the two perpetrators, they had played it over and over, to the point he was sick of watching himself on screen, pontificating his beliefs, while many analysts and anchor news people had debated it as; is that the average U.S. attitude or belief, to asking; *'what do you think?'* He felt like a puppet, a scapegoat of sorts. Even Josey had seen it, impossible, as it had been to shield her from the initial and incessant 24/7 coverage.

The first few minutes of their phone conversation were spent on an overview of the past few days since the unfortunate events that had rocked the local community; the aftermath of grief for many children, the anger of parents, the calls for stricter enforcement of laws, to finally, *why* the media onslaught in times of sorrow, and *why* the need to go to such lengths in repeating tragedy as if it were a game!

"But that said, not accepted, we're okay in general terms, Maggie," he finally acknowledged, "However, not to labor the point but I have to say, who could have believed all of this? I never expected it and the sad part is, the kids, Josey, her friends, their parents, and I've heard it all, they are *sick* of what's happening too often now in this country. We've lost some innocence, the innocence we all knew and accepted once as normal. Today's kids are growing up in a world that's fractured and I don't think it's healthy, but the bigger question or the broader picture might be in searching for answers and directions; where do we go from here? What unhealthy roads are we all being led down, politically? I sure don't know, do you, Maggie?"

She was momentarily stumped. She had not expected the *'down in the dumps'* vibe she was getting, hearing. It saddened her because the facts were, what had been pontificated vocally was all too true. But enough was enough! Time for a change of tactics, she believed, time to state her somewhat more adventurous and hopefully brighter case.

"I *don't* Steve, I *don't*, but as always, there's a light at the end of every tunnel they say, and right now, maybe I can turn one of those lights on for both of you, and brighten your day a little, Josey especially, because I have an idea spinning in my head. Of course, ultimately, it'll be your call, *that* I understand but hear me out first, won't you?" she threw in as a safeguard against a let down.

The mere mention of Josey and brighter lights gained Steve's immediate attention.

"I'm listening, Maggie, anything positive right now would be most welcome."

Boldly, Maggie outlined her proposal; the Nashville Doll Show, and truthful as it was in detail as a major event, in taking her chances on it, she added, maybe it could even be turned into a full weekend event. Then, a *'spur of the moment'* thought; that Josey could bring a friend, or friends, if she wanted. She hoped *that* idea would be the favorable finite decider? Temporarily, it was! Instantly, as fast as it had been tabled, Steve Frankston had loved the idea; *'a perfect mind blowing opportunity, that in a million years, I could never have dreamt up'* was his reaction. However, he cautioned, it would require approval from the parents, whoever Josey chose, if they were to join them, and if they were not forthcoming, for whatever the reason, he confirmed, he and Josey were joining her anyway. Maggie felt herself take a huge gulp, and then, to make her feel even better, he added, Josey will be thrilled to see her again as she had done nothing but talk about her lately, imitating, as if he were Josey, *'when will I see her again, when are we, you and me, going to see her again?'* Margaret 'Maggie' McConnell had underestimated herself, Josey and, indeed, probably, Steve Frankston, too. *'Why?'* she asked of no one, *'did I ever doubt myself, and others? My, I was a fool.'* A fool she might have silently been, but the crowning glory; not a soul knew, except Karen, who would be guardian of the Dunbridge Doll Store while Maggie was in Nashville, bonding, and spreading joy to a little girl. And maybe…?

Over the next few days, phone calls became the norm between them. Lighthearted and easy, joyful and full of laughter, happy, yet serious in the planning, slowly, the Nashville Doll Show, now a mere five days away, became the week that wouldn't end fast enough for Josey Frankston and her best friend Amy Quartermaine. Tiffany and Mary had other commitments with their parents, much to their horrified dismay. To say they were envious: Josey chose not to say too much about it when they were together. The trip was now, exclusively, hers and Amy's, and Daddy, the designated driver. They would all meet, at the Downtown Renaissance, in Nashville, on Saturday morning, 11am.

For the children, Tuesday went by as normal, Wednesday was sports day and packed with events. Thursday was the longest day of the week, and everything took, forever. Friday started with school choir practice, followed by in-class geography, then reading. Lunch time was a drag and by the time three o'clock rolled around and the bell went, two children scurried out of the classroom so quickly, and moved so fast, they ran by the SUV Josey's Dad was sitting in, waiting for them so they could get home, complete the homework they had, to be turned in Monday morning, and then settle in for the evening, ready for the next morning early start, 7.15am sharp was the call! Hearing the car horn, doubling back, Josey and Amy opened the car door, jumped in, snapped on their seatbelts and with a collective, in unison, laughing all the while, ordered; *'we're ready, Nashville, here we come!'*

"I don't think so, girls. Tomorrow. Amy, your folks dropped off your bag, plus, I've got $35.00 they gave me for you so I guess it's your treat for dinner tonight, okay? Josey, where shall we choose, your call, name the place."

"Mr. *Frankston,* you're *not* serious are you?" Amy asked, afraid it might be the case, and not really wanting an answer. $35.00 was a lot of money, and she might need it!

For the first time in the last little while, too long, the smile, the lilt of voice, and the happy tone of two girls, buoyed by huge expectation of going to a doll show, in the capital city of Tennessee, Nashville, a place neither of them had been to, ever, Steve Frankston could not have been more thrilled. *'Good choice, Maggie. No, great choice,'* he muttered to no one. *'I really owe you one.'* Within himself he was looking forward to the weekend, wondering how it might all play out.

If only...Maggie, at that very moment on the same Friday afternoon, standing at one of the larger name brand doll wholesalers booth at the Nashville Doll Show, conducting business that she was anxious to get out of the way and over with given her own expectations...if only Maggie knew, how two little girls and one special man felt – she would have never have doubted Karen's words that day when she mentioned Nashville, Tennessee and then planted a seed that grew rapidly, adding; *'if it was meant to be, it will.'* How right she was. Regardless, she could never have been happier than where she stood, looking at a brand new release doll, carefully packaged in her colorful box, ready for ordering, to become a collectors item in some little girl's already growing display. Strange, she thought, unable to concentrate, deciding instead to look away and reflect; a broken doll and a little girl was rapidly becoming the catalyst of a circumstance that was changing her life in ways she couldn't begin to fathom, one she couldn't wait to find, somehow, someway, just where it was all heading, if at all?

'I can't wait to see Angel' she thought, recalling all she had been told so far about Josey's broken doll. Shaking her head, and smiling, and certainly not concentrating, *'maybe I need a drink'* became her next thought. Putting the new doll down, she walked away. It could wait. Everything could wait. Even the Nashville Doll Show had become secondary,

superfluous. Life, right now, she accepted, is beautiful. *'But I wonder how the next day or so is going to play out?'* she thought. Two minds were in synch. Both wondered the unknown?

With the weekend arriving, Steve Frankston, finally, began to relax a little. Josey and Amy were tucked away, and as he believed, sound asleep. And for Josey, having a friend stay over was true and needed real therapy in every way, a necessary part of youthful growing up, *that*, he now knew, or could sense in play. A most glorious work in progress, raising a daughter alone, everything he was sharing was part of correcting mistakes he'd obviously, or not so, been making. Friends, happy times, dinner together and anything else that took their fancy, all were the real key to forgetting about the negative things that happen in life, and tonight, it had been a father-daughter, and friend, king size shot in the arm – the way it should be. He had loved the laughter that two little girls could bring to each other, it was infectious, something, in fact, he might be a whole lot short of, too! He had work related friends and a few fellow parents he knew, yes, but the one real thing he missed, was love, the touchy-feely of another – and maybe, especially, a woman in his life. Almost everyone he knew, or associated with, was married. And happily so! He missed Angelic, he thought of her often. Nothing will ever bring her back, but he loved her memory, the things they did and shared, the places they went, their up time, their down time, their moments of impulse, their planned and un-planned activity, like; he tried to remember a few. He racked his brain but it all seemed so long ago now, he sadly recollected. A few bounced back – Alcatraz and how scary it must have been to be in that jail; tire skiing down a slope in the Rockies or the night they skinny-dipped in Lake Okefenokee near Waycross, Georgia, never sure, always wondering if there were gators anywhere in the water, or the area. And how could he forget, in England, walking up to a high-hat policeman, a London Bobby, asking, as Angelic did, *'can I have a photo taken, wearing your hat?'* The answer was a stern *'No!'* They laughed about it anyway. Too many memories, all wonderful, and yet, slowly, they were fading.

Then, the biggest one of all; not wanting to hear it at the time, Angelic had said to him, in her final days, *'...please, go on with your life, I'll understand, because it wouldn't be right for you to not find new love, to be or to share with someone else, believe me, I would',* she tried to reassure him, as if it was a mild threat, to make him accept it was oaky, proper, fair and realistic. Steve knew; Angelic had made her point, as he would have, to her, if the roles had been reversed. He understood, and especially in their both being so young still. *'But I'm in no hurry,'* he had told himself, many times, however, slowly, as time moved on, as one became two and now three years, he was beginning to see the light of a new day, a new beginning, something he really doubted he might have if Maggie hadn't come along the way she did, quite unexpected. Never able to shake the word, it was always there. Had *'fate'* intervened, he wondered, to answer Angelic's prophetic words that day, that last night they had laid together. The memory of the moment brought tears...with love, alone, the tears fell, dampening his pillow.

~~~~~~~~~~
~~~~~~~~~~

CHAPTER SIXTEEN

The traffic on the freeway, between Memphis and Nashville, sailed like a yacht in a stiff breeze in the warm Biloxi, Mississippi waters out in the Gulf of Mexico. Linking to the Natchez Trace Parkway, it was a sight to behold, with the trees in full bloom and a plethora of colorful flowers everywhere. Making good time, Steve Frankston had chosen the much touted *'All-American Road'* so the girls could see and learn a little more of not only, Tennessee, but the beauty, charm and elegance that in his mind makes up the greatest country on earth. He explained to Josey and Amy, as they drove to their weekend adventure, that America might have its faults and might have its shortcomings, such as the one they experienced back at school during the siege, but in reality, there was so much more to offer and share, and that it was important they embrace all that was good, not the every day darker side they were too often exposed to. He implored on them, the future is theirs, that it belonged to them, their generation, and that someday they would be the policy makers, the guardians of all they were seeing and learning about. A little too deep he accepted for the trip they were all on, however, timely, he so wanted to impart his well being for America, much as he had grave doubts about certain elements in today's society!

"I *know,* Daddy, and I *know* what happened wasn't the normal," Josey said, trying to make sure he knew, that she knew, he was trying to make better the bad situation of the last few days, aware also, part of the reason they were heading to Nashville was because he wanted to make life a little nicer, easier, and to brighten up a *'bad week'* as she had heard him say, often, to whoever, on the phone. Changing the subject, she added, "Are you looking forward to seeing Maggie again, Daddy, 'cause I am?"

Her Father ignored the question, instead, he reversed the psychology of it all throwing the ball right back into her court. It wasn't a game, but he meant it anyway.

"Are you looking forward to the doll show, or did you think it was a great idea just so you could get out of the house for the weekend, and Maggie was the way out, although I do know you like her?"

"Daddy, that wasn't nice," she threw back at him, "Amy and I *love* dolls and we really *wanted* to go to the show, *so there*! We can't wait to see what it's like and what it's all about and *yes*, I'm *glad* Maggie called you, and I think you might be, too. Am I right?"

Intended, Josey had turned the tables, again. For a moment Steve was checkmated, stuck for a reply before finally admitting her observation.

"I like Maggie, as you know too well I do, I think, and yes, she's nice, however, more important, *she* thought of *you*, and this Nashville trip were *her* idea, so I hope you treat her well, you too Amy, *both* of you. Remember, do what she asks, or tells you at the show, okay? This is a pretty big deal you know and you're both very lucky little girls, and that's for sure! I hope you realize that."

"I do and I will Mr. Frankston," Amy chimed in; anxious for him to know she was grateful.

The conversation was over. And there need be no *'winners.'* Steve smiled as he drove, heading off the Parkway that was ending, knowing thicker traffic was ahead, calculating at the same time that the Nashville downtown skyline would soon be in view. He was right on both counts.

Maggie was thrilled with not only the warm and friendly hug she received from Josey, but Amy too, whom she had never met before, however, nothing was more willingly exciting than the first extended hug from Steve Frankston. He not only made her feel welcome, he made her feel *'special'* in ways only she knew. His body against hers was all she imagined it to be, especially after not seeing him for so long, and she could only hope that the weekend ahead might have all the same vibes she graciously accepted now, their initial greeting in the lobby of the Downtown Renaissance Hotel. And his smile…it was as if the embryo of the idea to invite Josey to the Nashville Doll Show had magnified to an *'event'* of proportions she could never have imagined, after all, she had been to many doll shows in a number of cities over the years, and yet, this one, so close, in Nashville, maybe, held her future in her hands, something she could never have imagined, once?

"My, you *both* look so pretty, so grown up and very colorful. *Perfect* for the doll show, that's wonderful," Maggie told both Josey and Amy.

Josey, her hair pulled back in a ponytail, was wearing a black top with big white circles on it with long black tights covered by a short grey dress. Ankle tall boots finished off her dressy yet sporty look. Amy, meanwhile, wore a patterned pink T-shirt tucked neatly into jeans and a light blue denim jacket. They had a look of twins about them, visually, as they stood side by side and more so being the same height almost exactly.

"Thank you, Maggie," Josey replied, and you look nice, too. I love your sweater, and, ya know, it's my *favorite* color." Maggie glanced immediately at Steve.

"She's right…" he openly endorsed, "…you look wonderful, but the real question is, are you ready for an afternoon with them? These two might be a bit of a handful. We can still opt out and do something else, you know."

"*No!* Daddy, we *can't*, what are you *saying*?"

"Oh, Josey, I was only fooling, of course we won't. Maggie can handle you two, I just wanted her to know that I could over-ride the worry and look at dolls with you, too."

Smiling at the father-daughter *'fun'* interaction, Maggie's mind had drifted a little. She was thinking more about what he'd said seconds ago. She loved the compliment he'd lightly given her, pleased to know he approved of the way she looked as it had worried her all morning if she was either too overdressed, or even, too casual to make a first impression. *'You look wonderful'* rang in her brain. It was enough, for now. She had, after all, bought the sweater for this very occasion. Her smile lingered.

"We'll be all right, won't we girls?"

Enthusiastically, they nodded, in unison.

Opting to the coffee-shop restaurant for both a snack and to set the wheels in motion and plan the day's activities, having heard the call of an *'all clear'* about the doll show, Steve tabled his feeling immediately as they walked; the *'girls'* could attend the show, alone, together, without him; he'd find something else close by to do. The question was, what?

Having picked up brochures in the hotel lobby it was an easy call. The choices were endless!

"Five-thirty back here, in the lobby, okay? That should give you all plenty of time, and while you're doing that, I'll start at the Old Ryman Auditorium around the corner from here. That should keep me busy for the first hour." It was his way of saying he'd find plenty to do.

Refreshed and ready, they left the coffee shop for the street. They were both within five walking minutes, thereabouts, of their respective destinations. Maggie watched as Steve first hugged Josey, tightly, all the while wondering, *'what will be my farewell feeling?'* He then turned to look at Amy giving her a smile before a light friendly hug. He then turned to Maggie. Happy, still smiling his big broad grin, he didn't disappoint.

"C'mon Maggie, you didn't thing you'd get away without a hug, did you?"

The gentle but decidedly warm embrace he shared sent unknown vibrations through her body. She thought he lingered just that little bit longer, but did he? Was that her mind running amok? It didn't really matter, the feel of his arms wrapped tantalizingly around her was all she had longed for, thought about, wanted the most over the past many days in simply thinking about this trip, her once, alone trip to Nashville for the doll show; how different it all turned out to be, magically so. Hating the thought of leaving Steve alone, wanting more to be with him, there was nevertheless a mission in play, and it was time to see it through and enjoy it all; the girls were most anxious to be on their way. A new adventure for all, it seemed, was about to begin. Enthralled, as the girls were, anticipating the unknown, they said their farewells, waving to each other as they did. *'Bye, Daddy,'* Josey shouted as distance slowly separated them.

Not that he overly indulged, listened to or talked about country music a lot, Steve Frankston was nevertheless a fan. Growing up in the South, hearing country on the radio and at times, going to a country music show that came through, mostly to Daytona, a visit to the legendary Ryman Auditorium was a bigger thrill than he might ever admit, to anyone. Opened as the Union Gospel Tabernacle in 1892, it was renamed the Ryman Auditorium in memory of the riverboat captain, Thomas Ryman who built it. A Museum, complete, with church pews, the old house of worship is as revered today as it was over too many years, still maintaining its nickname *'The Mother Church of Country Music.'*

A walk through the building, seeing in one's mind, as Steve clearly did - Marty Robbins, Jim Reeves, Patsy Cline, Dolly Parton, Alan Jackson, Reba McEntire, Charley Pride, Tim McGraw and so many more, none, in his recollection, was more idolized than The Drifting Cowboy himself, the master of song; Hank Williams. He stood for a moment, looking in each and every direction, and especially while standing in the wings of the stage where so many waited to be called to go on; imagining, even, the one time First Lady of Country Music, Tammy Wynette thrilling the packed out crowd with Stand By Your Man. If the walls could talk, what stories they could tell, most starting in Tootsie's Bar across the back alley and the fast way in to the Ryman from a *'session'* (drinking) for many of the legends, Ray Price, Waylon Jennings, Willie Nelson, Webb Pierce, Faron Young, David Houston...the list could go on an on. But it was George Jones he remembered most, a real idol of his in the older genre and according to most critics, the consummate voice of country music. He recalled the recent funeral The Grand Ole Opry held for *'The Possum'* as if it were only yesterday, Vince Gill being the emotional standout performer that day. Nashville, The Opry, the Ryman, WSM, all combined to be a country music fans fantasy, and for Steve Frankston, in his element of living and past music greats, he was no different than most. As he exited the stage area and the building, he told himself, as if a gentle reminder; *'Too many pass, way too young, but thanks for the memories.'* Stepping back out on to the street, glancing left from 5th toward Broadway, he saw the huge piano backdrop of the Country Music Hall Of Fame. There was no contest; he headed that way!

Maggie signed herself in first, then introduced the girls, her *'guests'* as they were duly noted, giving them immediate status, and in their eyes, a kind of importance which they loved. Greeted by the staff with such warm friendship and welcome, they looked at Maggie who confirmed their belief; they were in good company and in for a good time, also. Next came their official, personal, nametags - Josephine Frankston and Amy Quartermaine. Pinned on, they glanced down at them, touched them; convincing and accepting themselves, as if no one else had them, *'extra special.'* Laughter and smiles abounded. Without further ado, following orders; they commenced to follow Maggie into the Convention Hall. What came next was a sight to behold. It was, as if, the whole world had turned into a doll heaven, magical kingdom. It was awesome! The two girls stood frozen, eyes wide as saucers. They didn't know where to turn. People were everywhere, swarming the room in all directions, most holding dolls of all sizes, large, medium or small, one, even, as small as a finger on a hand. Including teddy bears, there were beautiful fairies and princesses, bride dolls so incredibly dressed they could have been from another world, also, stylized fashion dolls, and one range that caught their attention, mesmerizing them both, babies that appeared to be *'real!'* Maggie noticed. Looking at Josey, she told her, *'they're called reborn, we'll get to see some later, they're incredible, you'll love them.'* Amy asked, *'will we be able to hold one?'* Noticing they were a little overwhelmed, Maggie assured them a yes, then suggested, it was time to be moving along, there was so much more to take in yet.

The afternoon got away from everyone. A beer at Tootsie's legendary bar on Nashville's Broadway, a snack, then a visit to the Ernest Tubb Record Shop before heading for the Country Music Hall of Fame to spend the rest of the afternoon, Steve Frankston had to tear himself away to meet the deadline he had set. He thought about it, as he exited to head for the Renaissance; a quick phone call, and maybe, Maggie and the girls might need more time, too. It was too late. Ironically, Maggie had thought the same thing when it came to looking for more time, acknowledging the doll show closed at six sharp, however, she didn't feel comfortable making the call, as much as Josey and Amy begged her to. She had her instructions, Steve had set the time limits and she was not sure if he was adequately entertaining himself or not; it wasn't worth the chance, especially if he was bored, killing time, waiting anxiously for 5.30pm. It turned out they were both wrong on all accounts. Both would gladly have taken the extra half hour! Regardless, for Maggie, she couldn't wait to see Steve anyway; a silent but secret thought she kept to herself. Beaming smiles on the faces of two little girls as they met back together in the hotel lobby said it all. All, it appeared, had had a wonderful day out.

"So, tell me all about it, little one," Steve asked of Josey as she withdrew from his welcome embrace, looking up at Maggie as he did, mouthing a silent '*thank you*'. It was an easy response, *'you're welcome'*, she replied, delivered the same way. Josey couldn't wait to tell her Daddy all she and Amy had seen and done and shared, and who they talked to and, and…and. If he'd let her, she would have talked for the next ten minutes, Amy, too, who had chimed in more than once. Clearly, Maggie had scored an entertainment ten!

"Well, you both have much to thank Maggie for haven't you, after all, it was *her* show and it was all *her* clients and friends who made your day so pleasurable, I think a big thank you would not go astray."

"Oh Steve, it was my pleasure," Maggie gladly reminded him. "They were perfect and the fact they loved it all, that we even ran out of time says it all. That's fine enough to me and they're welcome, anytime."

"Thank you, Maggie," became Josey's spontaneous response as she eagerly edged toward her, arms outstretched wanting to endorse her gratitude with a hug. To Maggie, it was a thrill. If she could please Josey, be accepted willingly with open arms, hopefully, she thought, Steve might see the connection and accept her, too, as a friend, for now, and who knows in the future. It warmed her to even think of the possibility. There had been no contest; already he was having more than just a little effect on her! With that thought, timely, she wondered, *'what about me, on him?'* As it turned out, he had other things on his mind.

"Okay, for dinner, we need a plan, any ideas anyone? Who'd like, what?"

Maggie looked at Josey, who looked at Amy, who looked back at Maggie, who looked at Steve. Not a word was spoken. Suddenly, everyone burst out laughing.

"My call, huh?" Steve asked.

"Yes, Daddy, your call. We'll do what you say, won't we, Amy? We don't mind what we eat."

Amy nodded the affirmative. Steve turned toward Maggie. He was definitely looking for some help.

"You've been here before, Maggie, any suggestions?"

"One, maybe two," she replied, confidently. "Apart from any number of places downtown on and off Broadway including the somewhat different Rocketown, that's children user and friendly, but also…" Maggie listed off a couple of easy distance walking spots before suggesting her initial thought, one she believed both Josey and Amy would like while hoping Steve might see it as different and worthwhile, despite having to drive to the location. "…The General Jackson Showboat, it's a paddle steamer that cruises on the Cumberland River, and has dinner and live music, too."

"Hey, I love it, but first, what about you girls, paddle steamer on the river or downtown where we can walk and see the sights at the same time? Whatever *you* choose, we go."

The General Jackson Showboat was more than delightful. From viewing the landscape of Tennessee from the deck of a huge paddle steamer, to enjoying a southern meal they couldn't finish, coupled with entertainment grandiose that paid tribute to not only country music, but also, bluegrass, gospel and a little soul; their evening began to come to an end far too quickly. To the girls; it was a magical night out, far different from anything they had ever experienced, while for Maggie; she was in her element, singing along, laughing, partaking willingly in the frivolity of freedom and good company, and Steve; happy beyond belief to have shared such an adventure and to have seen Josey, Amy, and Maggie, doing what they all love best, enjoying each others company. *'What a night,'* he thought. *'Could this be the start of a new beginning for Josey,'* indeed, he further extended his thoughts; *'for me, maybe?'* He believed he'd like to find out. Again, Maggie's Nashville doll show suggestion had been the most wonderful of ideas, to see it all play out the way it had. He owed her a small debt of gratitude, and had to remember to make sure she knew it, that he was appreciative for her input, support and sharing. And amongst his delightful thoughts of her, he also began to worry a little, in a nice way he could be getting more attached to this Ms. Maggie than he ever believed he might, or should. Then, as always, when he felt that way, Angelic would come back to his mind and he'd see her face. Lately, though, it was always with a smile. Again, he'd think, was that her sign?

~~~~~~~~~~
~~~~~~~~~~

CHAPTER SEVENTEEN

Steve Frankston's suite at the hotel came with two bedrooms and a large separate dining lounge, traditionally used by business people who find it necessary to conduct interviews and meetings. On this occasion, it was most convenient; Josey and Amy had one room complete with a bathroom ensuite while he had the other, equally equipped. At no time would he ever have to leave the children alone, a matter of priority when arranging their accommodation. It was another fine suggestion recommended by Maggie who knew the hotel facilities having used them before.

With the girls tucked in bed, asleep, after checking in on them, Steve came back out into the lounge area of the room to continue his *'night-cap'* drink and chat with Maggie. The children had been exhausted!

"Redundant I know, but Maggie, you've done so much and shared so much with the girl's, you went above and beyond for them, *and* me, and again, a great choice, and I thank you, I'm touched by your generosity and kindness."

"I could never have done it if I truly didn't want to, Steve, believe me. I saw the chance for some happiness, and it all seemed so right and let's not forget, the main thing here is, Josey, of course. You saw it, too, so I guess, together, maybe *we* did something that made one little girl, and as luck would have it, *two*, as happy as they could ever be and especially in light of what happened and the trauma of that school lockdown. If anyone ever deserved a treat, they did and you made it happen, willingly. My part was merely mentioning it, *you* saw it through, so thank me all you like, and believe me, I gladly accept it, but *you,* and maybe *some* of me, made it work for them. And thankfully, I couldn't have been more pleased to see how the doll show played out today, I loved it as much as they did and that's the truth."

"You make it all sound so simple, Maggie, and maybe it was, for you. You've been to the shows before, however, these two, *what* a transformation, *what* a thrill to see the reaction from what they've had, and shared today. Say what you will, without you, and you had access to the whole idea, I am indebted to you. In fact, the me 'n you in all of this has made me equally happy, so I win twice, I think."

Maggie McConnell couldn't believe even half of all she had just heard. It was a thrill to hear unending compliments lauded on her, all spoken in a way that was sincere and touching. To make this man she was sitting with, in a hotel room, late at night, *'happy',* as he had declared, for something that came so easy, she wanted to move from where she was sitting, across from him directly, and kiss him as if they were lovers in a movie and that was to be the next scene. It was all she could do from acting out the fantasy that had flashed through her mind, devilish in thought, as it might have been.

"Why, that's nice of you to say, I'm pleased, which means we *both* win, Steve. And now, great as it all was, unfortunately, it's over, which leads me to raise an obvious question, what plans do you have for tomorrow, Sunday? Are you up for doing something else with the girls, or are you planning, maybe, heading back to Memphis earlier than later? Have you thought about that yet, or maybe waiting till morning, which might be more practical, maybe?"

She dearly wanted him to say they should all share the day, together, including her and not the alternative. Seconds passed. Watching him ponder the thought to then offering the hint of a smile, immediately, she felt a possible affirmative to another of her indirect ideas. She was right, again! Holding his smile, then expanding it, as he looked directly toward her he said exactly what she quietly longed to hear?

"It's a little two-way really, Maggie. Going back, of course, we have to, however, now it's *my* turn to step up, and I admit it, *this* time it's for *you* and I say that selfishly because I'm not ready to see us go our separate ways so quickly, yet. We've got at least part of tomorrow and I'd like for us all, the girls, me, you, to come up with something for sure, but with something *you personally* might like. Would that be okay, does that suit, I mean, we're not ready to go *that* quick, unless you have commitments, and I'd understand that?"

Again, Maggie wanted to shout from the hilltops, rooftops, any tops, *'I want to be with* ***you****, Steve Frankston, I don't* ***want*** *to go home to Dunbridge,* ***period****!'* Her answer came easy. His response had been music to her ears.

"I'd love that, Steve, that's very kind of you to suggest, and sweet. I'd love that, for all of us, so yes, of course, I'm truly glad you feel that way, thank you."

"Then we have a deal, huh?"

"We have a deal. Put me in, Coach!"

Maggie wondered if that was her cue to leave and head back to her room. She knew she had to at some stage, and probably sooner than later given the time of night; however, she wasn't ready, but *how* to extend her stay, even for a few more minutes, she wasn't sure. Erring on the side of caution, she took her chances.

"Well, time marches on I guess and it's getting late, however, I must say, *admit* might be the better word I think, but I do want to tell you, Steve, before we call it a night..." she paused to finish the last of the wine in her glass that had been sitting untouched longer than she realized. Placing the glass back on the coffee table, she was about to finish her sentence when Steve interrupted.

"I don't mean to stop you, Maggie, but before you continue, would you like another drink, because I will, if you do, after all, we do have half a bottle left yet?"

Maggie guessed he must have read her mind. It didn't matter if he hadn't, though.

"Why, yes, I would, 'cause *hey*, it's almost a crime to waste such a fine wine, and I really enjoyed that one. What was it by the way, and from where?"

It was an easy way to extend the conversation, mindless, as it might have been.

Moving to get the bottle, he checked the brand and from where it was bottled, enlightening her as he poured them both the rest of what was left, topping their glasses a little more than usual. He agreed; it would be a waste to have left it.

"Sorry, I never meant for you to lose your train of thought a moment ago," he told her as he sat back down, anxious to hear what had been on her mind.

"Actually, all I wanted to say was, in being open about it, meeting you and Josey when you first came into my store and then sharing your time with me back in Dunbridge, the way you did and why, in getting to know you both a little more, spending time as we did over the phone with what happened in Memphis, and then you all coming here to

Nashville, I've actually, slowly, got to see a side of you, *both* of you and dare I say it..." she hesitated momentarily, hoping she wasn't rambling with idle words, however, it was already too late anyway. She continued, "...*but,* and this is true, the love I see in you, the love you have for Josey and in going it all alone, raising her the way you have had to, I admire you immensely. You have done such a tremendous job, Steve, and Josey, she is such a nice little girl, so effervescent and bubbly and chatty and confident, I think you should be proud, very proud. I respect your skills in keeping her so grounded and there's no doubt, love abounds, on both sides. You are a remarkable man for sure, and from me, to you, my observations, you must have a side to you that is not only strong and responsible, but soft and caring, a trait not always easily come by, especially in a lot men, and I say that respectfully, Steve, however, you *exude* them all; and corny as that may all sound, seriously, to you, well done. You're quite a man and I'm really glad I've had the good fortune, the very chance to meet you, and Josey. Thank you for letting me share with you all that we have, so far."

Feeling a glow, happy to have expressed her thoughts, hopeful that he might take all she said with the true feeling of the lengthy way she had expressed herself, Maggie leaned over to take her glass, raising it to him as if it were a salute to the job she had applauded him for. He responded with a smile, an affirmative nod of his head - both, with thanks. Their glasses touched to a gentle sound before taking a sip.

Steve felt the need to respond; too many kind words had been imparted, and many, from the heart.

"She's a good girl, Maggie and she's never baulked at anything with me, especially during harder times, however, kind and nice and thoughtful as your words were, to me, I can't take all the credit, *some, yes,* but her Mother shares a lot of that, too. There was enough love in our house, then, for us all and while we both had plenty to give, not only to each other but also particularly for Josey, she *must* have felt it. I've tried to keep it all together and so far so good, and I might add, days like today help, which is back to you. Having Josey responding the way she has, with you and by that I mean an adult, a woman, it's all good grounding and helps with what will probably become, the rocky road ahead as a teenager, so I'll take all the plusses I can. Again, yours was a good call and who knows, there maybe more along the way. Now, having said all of that, there are times that I miss what we had, and I know Josey does, too, but children are more resilient, they can move ahead a little quicker than we mere adults, me included, especially, even. Josey talks about her Mother, and asks about her, but as time passes, it's harder to keep memories alive, after all, she was only five when Angelic passed."

Maggie noticed Steve begin to falter a little more as he spoke, especially as he edged further into the sensitive area of his late wife, apropos Josey. It didn't matter, though, she loved his honesty and with that, she again took a chance with her response.

"I can't speak, obviously, Steve, about your loss of a loved one, and I can only imagine the affect it must have had, however, in my getting to know Josey a little more, I'd love to hear a little about Angelic also, unless it's too painful, and if so, I'd be the first to understand. I can hear in your voice how much you loved her and the hurt in losing her, but I'd love to know *who* she was, *how* you met, even, because she was, unquestionably, a wonderful lady from all you say, and such a joy, yet loss to Josey. I hope you don't mind. If it's too sensitive a question, believe me, I more than understand."

Steve didn't! In fact, there was something therapeutic in actually talking about Angelic, to a stranger, and yet, not a stranger, in Maggie. Thoughtful, kind and sweet, especially to Josey, accepting it might even help, he began to open up a little more.

"Angelic was a gentle lady, and in fact, I see a little of that side of her in you, Maggie," he started out telling her, expressing his true feelings. "Losing her, the way it happened, and in the end, so suddenly, hurt. Actually, it made me ask more questions, and mostly, all without answers. Cancer is such an awful disease, one we all can relate to somehow given the inroads made on one hand to combat it, and yet, seemingly, breast cancer is still an epidemic in women. But you know, Maggie; I'm learning to live with it a little better these days. Sure, I have my moments and yet, oddly, coming here to Nashville, the home of country music, it puts me in mind, as it did today, I confess, of Angelic's more than passive interest in country, and by that, I mean, of an older breed and style, Glen Campbell and John Denver of all people but she really liked Martina McBride, Shania Twain, the Eagles, you know, that sort of pop country, and especially Garth Brooks. In fact…" now on a thought processed role, he reminisced openly, with a smile, even, "…it was Angelic who invited me to a Garth Brooks concert not that long after we met and I can remember sitting in the audience singing along to Shameless, Two Piña Coladas or Friends In Low Places, catchy as they were, then. And being here in Nashville, I thought of those days, although *this* time, and from a straight out country music point of view, it was *you* who got me here and reminded me of so many good times and for that I…"

"Oh, *Steve,* I never meant for that to…" Maggie was about to qualify her intentions, however, he never let her finish. He understood.

"*No, Maggie,* I *know* that, *believe* me! All I'm saying is, what it all means, and this is my important point, things happen for reasons and being here was meant to be, it *was*! In a really nice sort of way, *there's* the quirky link with you and Angelic and because of that, it makes it all good, for real and wonderful reasons. Don't get me wrong; if I could be here with Angelic, if she and I had shared this experience, the one you and I have today, I'd have welcomed it with open arms and would have loved it as much, but it's *not* the way it was, and it can *never* happen. I've had to accept that Angelic has gone and she's not coming back. I can wish all I want but it won't happen. I loved her, I loved our life, and with that said, I can also accept, fate plays its role, intervenes and then makes other things happen for reasons. Think about it, *look* how the country music connection has brought you into Josey's and my life, today, tonight, and believe me, I'm mighty pleased it happened that way. *Your* unselfish actions have brought *so* much joy to us both; I have much to be thankful for in the role I see you've played in helping us, and *especially* seeing Josey changing the way she clearly is, around you. That was, and is, special, just as you are, and are *unquestionably* becoming in our lives. I mean..."

Pausing, he took a moment to reflect the openness of his thoughts, and while taking a sip of wine, he looked at Maggie in a way she had not seen him look before. Pleased, nervous and loving his openness of conversation, she took the moment of silence between them to interrupt, share a point of her own. She, too, had a need to talk, to be honest.

"Why, thank you, Steve, you're so adept in your flattering me with your honesty, however, allow me to indulge, although I don't mean to..."

"Please do, we have an open forum," he interjected, expressing jest in his voice of vocal decorum.

"Well, I wasn't going to say it but now I will, given your words, but interestingly, Josey actually mentioned Angelic, her mother, to me, today, and what she had to say about her was *so* loving it almost made me cry, and yet, somehow, as she spoke, I got the feeling she was never sure *why* it happened so fast, her passing I mean. There was an obvious sadness in her voice that seemed to show in her eyes, too, especially when she told me *'Mommy was sick, I knew it, and Daddy tried hard to help her, but she didn't seem to want it as she kept saying, 'soon I have to go, Josey, and I'm truly sorry'.*

As Maggie's voice faltered relating her experience, a hint of tears were also evident. Emotionally touched, she continued, she had much more to say."

"I never quite knew what that meant, except to believe, Angelic must have been sicker than she, a little girl, could comprehend, hence the doubt. I told her that her Mommy would never want to leave if she didn't have to. Actually, I wanted her to understand that sometimes a disease can be harder and harsher than any of us might realize, before adding, that she should *never* think it was because of *her*, or Daddy, referring to you, or anyone else. Do you know, Steve, it was a poignant moment between us, one that sits not only in the back of her mind, but now, indelibly, mine also. And then, strangely, she snapped right out of it, and to my surprise, placed her little hand in mine and quipped, *'c'mon*

Maggie, there's lots to see yet', Steve, I'll tell you, that became another special and beautiful moment. Josey has a wonderful mind and spirit with a lust for life I'd say, and something else that bears repeating, you and Angelic, and especially *you,* now, have both done a marvelous job with her and if I may, allow me to add, I *love* little Josey, but love her in my *own* way, and yes, to me, too, she's special, *very* special."

"My, my, my, Maggie. *That's* a *beautiful* story. It's amazing, I *love* it."

As it turned out, they had chatted a little longer into the night than either one realized. With their wine glasses empty and another full day planned for tomorrow, Maggie decided to take the lead, offering her heartfelt thanks for this day ending before bidding her softly spoken, *'goodnight.'* Without the hint of hesitation, she slowly turned toward the door, to leave. Steve touched her shoulder as she did. Maggie stopped dead in her tracks. He took her hand, lifting it, to give her fingers a light brush of his lips, as if a kiss. He then looked directly into her eyes and with a smile offered, sincerely, *'thank you Maggie, you are quite a lady.'* She responded, *'and you're a good man, Steve',* before she motioned to leave, again. Unexpectedly, with a seeming caution, he put his arms out to hold her. Maggie, loving the welcome, eased easy into him, reaching around his body as she did. For what might have appeared to be the longest moment, they held on to each other as if it were a *final* goodbye. It wasn't, there was still tomorrow. Seconds later, his emotions in check, Steve released her from his arms, lightly kissing her cheek, avoiding her lips, before offering his absolute, *'Goodnight Maggie, sleep well, let's agree on eight-thirty in the coffee shop, okay?'* Closing the door behind her as she left, Maggie sighed, her room seemed a million miles away. Steve, meanwhile, stood for a moment as if gathering his thoughts before turning around to head for the girls' room, expecting, as he checked them, that they would still be sound asleep. They were. He retreated to his own room flopping immediately down on the bed, closing his eyes, murmuring, *'something's happening, Maggie, something happening, and it's all good, I like it, and strangely, I'm not scared anymore, I don't think.'* Not opening his eyes, his head spun in thought, of so many things. Maggie first, then, should he stay where he was or get up and get changed, then, Maggie, again, then…she was still there…then. Within the minute, he was asleep.

~~~~~~~~~~
~~~~~~~~~~

CHAPTER EIGHTEEN

If Steve Frankston, last night, had been slowly drawn to Maggie McConnell, then as she walked into the coffee shop next morning, wearing a most eye-catching light blue cashmere sweater hung lightly over dressy black denim jeans that were tucked into small healed boots, he almost gave himself away completely as he fixed a look on her every move toward them, his eyes never blinking at all. Looking stunningly beautiful, it wasn't that she was any different from any time before, it was more, that, in sharing their late-into-the-night conversation, it had allowed him to broaden his perspective of her and not view her through what might have been traditional *'rose-colored-glasses.'* So much more now, he saw the tender, warm, loving side of a lady who had grace and style, one that loved children as evidenced in her every day, in her store, a doll store that was like a magnet to little girls especially. Also, he wasn't oblivious to Josey's reactions to her, about the trip they were on, or to the doll show and the numerous fun-loving stories they were able to share. It seemed, Maggie McConnell had, in one weekend, achieved in bringing out in Josey, and indeed, if not, especially in him, a sense of freedom to move on, to make more of their life and to break away from the staid, predictable way the last many, many months had been. There was no question in his mind; she was a remarkable woman. Within himself, he was quite in awe of her. As she approached their booth, with a warm and inviting smile, he stood up to not only greet her, but also, to pick up with the last action they'd shared the night before, a hug, however, this time, not so tantalizingly close. Josey and Amy both followed him with hugs of their own.

"Well, good morning everyone, did you sleep well?" she asked of the girls, specifically. There was a resounding '*yes*'. "And what's for breakfast, dare I ask?"

"*Pancakes*," the girl's said in unison, as if they were twin sisters on the same wavelength.

"And *Steve*?" she asked, with an unintended lilt in her voice, looking directly at him almost playfully. He loved her little smile. The girls giggled to each other, noticing.

The waitress arrived and breakfast was underway. There were last minute things to do and little to no time to do them in. Not a second of what was left of their weekend could be wasted. Within half an hour they were gone!

First, close by, they visited The Hermitage, home to Andrew Jackson the 7th President of the United States from 1804 until his death in 1845, and today, his historical plantation and museum. As part of the tour, a story Steve particularly liked, linked heavily to the image and notoriety of Nashville, was the 1998 near-disaster F-3 tornado that almost ended the existence of The Hermitage when many trees toppled narrowly missing the building. History recorded, President Jackson probably planted most of them some 200 years earlier. Making the most of the devastation that followed, from the fallen trees, the world famous Gibson Guitar Company produced an equal number (years) - 200 Limited Edition 'Old Hickory' guitars, today, collectors items. Added to the glory; the Legend of Davy Crockett, King of the Wild Frontier, the 1955 Disney movie used The Hermitage as its film location and setting. None of them had actually seen the movie!

Passively interested, as the girls were, Steve was kind in his interpretation of history and what it might mean to Josey and Amy, who both, graciously shared, *'it was a very nice house'* and *'yes, we've heard of the President at school.'* Maggie smiled, understanding! Before everyone's time, The Hermitage was a wonderful visit, nevertheless.

With so much available to them, and so little time, the best remaining thing to do was undertake a casual, typical touristy drive around, simply looking at…whatever? Music Row, The Parthenon, and the newer Grand Ole Opry including looking in on a well-touted Country Church across from the site that was in session. From there, it was back to downtown Nashville enjoying The Walk of Fame Park and Music Row, the historic RCA Studio B Recording Building and the final stop, The Hard Rock Café where Josey and Amy spent, forever, looking at all the pop star and country star memorabilia on the walls; guitars, clothing, vinyl gold records (CD's, too) and photos. Later, they claimed it as the best stop of the Sunday tourist attractions. However, it was getting later than originally anticipating, and with it, Steve feigned being chagrined, nicely, though, at having to miss the newly opened Johnny Cash Museum; the Man in Black was one of his all-time favorites, musically. Regardless, the three-o'clock deadline time had arrived. Sadly, they all agreed, but accepted, it was time to say goodbye to Maggie who had the much longer drive home to Dunbridge.

Unexpected, Josey burst into tears as she turned to embrace Maggie. Falling into her open arms, hugging her like a little girl possessed, it was all one could do to tear her away. And of course, Josey's tears brought tears to the eyes of Maggie. All a helpless Daddy could do was stand by and watch, an emotion of his own building as he did.

"C'mon, Josey, Maggie has to be on her way."

Josey heard the order. Turning her head to look at her him, as she withdrew, her only words were "thank you, Maggie, I'm going to miss you, please call me, won't you?"

It was all Maggie could do to answer, however, she, too, knew the rules.

"I will, Josey, I will, I *promise,* but only if Daddy says it's alright."

Josey immediately looked at her Father, not saying a word. He remained his usual self, nodding his head.

"It's alright, Maggie. Of *course* you can call her because I *do* believe you might also have a new best friend. So get used to it, huh? She's latched I think!"

"Thank you, Daddy. Don't forget, Maggie, will you?" she cheerfully double-checked as Maggie hugged Amy goodbye, giving her an extra squeeze.

"*No,* Josey, I *won't*. As I said, I *promise*."

In her heart she meant it, but…? Swirling in her head was the thought she could also be letting herself in for an emotional crash, too. Conscious, in the back of her mind, there were the miles, the out-of-sight, the, the…then Steve came toward her, his arms outstretched to hold her.

Finally, sad as it felt, it was time for the *real* goodbye. Maggie loved the idea of him holding her again, but dreaded the thought of a farewell, not knowing when their next meeting might be? Their adventure together had gone all too quickly, however, without the doll show, she accepted, who knows what ever may have happened between them? Thankful for small beginnings, for the little water that had so far flowed under their bridges, the best she could hope for was, that soon, they'd see each other again. Another adventure maybe? With tears welling in her eyes, she looked at Steve. Happy, yet forlorn, she moved to step into his open arms.

"Thank you, Maggie. What a wonderful time, a wonderful weekend and as for the girls, you couldn't have made them any happier. We all have loved every minute of being here and for me, especially, being with you. Thank you, thank you."

As a momentary silence prevailed, his arms held her tighter. Clinging to him equally, Maggie could feel the strength, the warmth, loving particularly his *'especially being with you'*. Simple as the words may have sounded, they spoke volumes. She was a happy woman, however, she knew the need to hold back a little, not to show her true feelings, or say the words she longed to in front of the children. She'd save them for another moment in time, hoping it wouldn't be too long in the making, realizing, the next time, the what, where and when, would have to be *his* move. Hers had worked miracles; maybe his can match or better it.

"I've loved every minute, Steve, and thank you in return for sharing your time, and Josey, with me. Timely, but in the words of that Jerry Lee Lewis country song *'Another Place, Another Time'*, huh?" was all she managed to get out, glad that she had been able to extend an open invitation as part of their goodbye. About to pull away, thrilled, she felt the extra momentary hug to hold her exactly where she was, wrapped in Steve's arms. She felt her heart skip a beat. But all too soon, it was over. Reluctantly, under prying eyes, he released her. Josey and Amy had watched their farewell from inside the car. Amy quietly giggled, while Josey smiled, turning, whispering to her, *'see, I told you he liked her.'*

Minutes later, they were pulling away from Nashville, heading back home to Memphis and reality. Thankfully, as it turned out, the girls had suddenly gone quiet, as if worn out, exhausted, from reveling in their excursion. In the solitude of the drive and as the miles ticked by, Steve Frankston had time to think, and wonder, and reminisce a little of his own *'change of scenery'* and life. And Maggie McConnell was top of mind, their time together, their friendly chats, all moments to remember. He recalled one conversation vividly.

"Actually, not that I talk about it much anymore, and in fact, mostly choose not to, but in answering your question about my family, Steve, given you've been open with me, I guess I start by sharing, that my Father died just over three years ago now. The biggest blow was that he wasn't sick as such, and didn't have any ailments, and yet, without a warning in any way, he just doubled over one day, a massive heart attack we were told later. It was all so fast, at first I couldn't comprehend it, but as time went by, I began to realize, accept I suppose, maybe that's the *better* way to leave, if one is going to. Nothing prolonged, nothing tied to agony or watching a person fade, slowly. *That,* I believe is more cruel and without going there, now that I understand it all more, it's *why* I have such empathy to you, and Josey. As I've mentioned before, I can't imagine the agony of losing someone the way you, both of you, did."

Steve heaved a huge sigh, his upper body lifting as he did. Hearing another pose the thought of loss the way Maggie had, her Father in her case, somehow, in her very own inimitable way, she made it all sound so special. Maggie, he wanted to believe, totally understood – him!

"Anyway," she continued, "on a much *brighter* note, my mother is still alive. She lives close enough to me, up in Chattahoochee, on the Florida side of the Georgia borderline. We see each other often and she comes to Dunbridge to help me, usually in the busier season, which I love. Thankfully, she really enjoys my store, just as Josey appeared to and that, dare I say, was quite a thrill to me. I *love* seeing the glow on little girls' faces when they enter my store. Same product, or new, they always seem to find something that captures their attention. Actually, I have a wonderful clientele and I never tire of going to work. I love people and if I think about it now, having you and Josey come in, maybe I can count you as my *'new clientele'* because I *am* looking forward to when you bring her back, someday, and of course, with her little doll that I *will* take care of. We *will* make her new again."

Steve Frankston had relived, in his mind, more of Margaret 'Maggie' McConnell, her life story. Not one to dwell on any subject, clearly, the loss of her Father was hard, just as losing Angelic had been for him, and yet, for different reasons, she talked easier about the subject than he had managed so far. Was there a lesson in that, he wondered? Expanding his thoughts, to a girl, a woman - a Father will always be a Father, an important link, while with a wife, he assumed, the contrasting difference is quite remarkable. And to have a child between you, can you *really* compare?

Immediately, he knew, there was *no* point; to lose a dear loved one, whatever the relationship, is devastating. Angelic, again, flooded his mind and from it, a truthful somber sadness. Oddly, two thoughts sprang to mind. First, something she had told him – *'anyone can be a Father, it takes a special person to be a Dad.'* Could it be, then, that Angelic knew there would come a day he'd have to move on. How incredibly right she was. Both scenarios were playing out.

He glanced back at the girls, still playing their iPod's; listening to music. All was quiet in the car. In *their* eyes, he assumed, with the anticipation of the trip now over, returning from, anywhere, was never as much fun as getting there and at this moment they were doing nothing more than passing time away. He guessed they were happy enough, anyway, although he did plan on stopping to gas up somewhere off the freeway, and while they were in there they'd probably want something to eat, too. Satisfied, for now, cruising at the regulated 65mph, all was well with the world. With little else to do, except think as he drove, *again,* his mind wandered.

"Getting divorced was too easy, I regret to say," Maggie had told him. "To be honest, naïve at the time, or maybe we were too young, both of us, in hindsight, I doubt that he wanted to get married in the first place. I did, then, and someday I'd hope to again, but with James, that was his name, with James, he got lost along the way, in life I mean. I tried to help him as I wasn't prepared to let our marriage die, to end, for no other reason than, in his words, *'marriage isn't what I thought it was'*. Although, thinking about it now, talking about it, it's sad really, because before you knew it, soon, there were other women and with that, it's why I say the end came easy. I was shattered, of course, as I believe in marriage and always have, but you know, you can't help someone who doesn't want help which is why it was easy to walk, to end the marriage and then get about getting on with my life, which I did, and so far, so good."

Steve recalled asking her why she hadn't remarried, jokingly adding, *'you're not sworn off men, are you?'* They both laughed at that, however, Maggie quickly reassured him, if and when the time came, and it was right, to her, then she'd definitely get married as the one thing missing in her life, apart from a good man, is a child, or children. She had added, Josey, of all people, had brought a little more of that feeling out in her and had brightened her life immensely citing her immediate enthusiasm for dolls, which translated to her personally, her profession, her job.

"I qualify about not being sworn off men, Steve, by admitting I came close once to re-marrying, however, thank goodness I saw the light early of what was coming and frankly, I couldn't be bothered playing the games. I *am*, after all, in my thirties now, *low* I might add…" Steve butted in quoting he was thirty-five at which Maggie responded, *'close enough.'* She continued. "…Anyway, I was so much more secure in myself, immaturity wasn't something I wanted to deal with so I simply applied myself to what I do best, and so far, as I've said, I'm happy and life is good to me. There *are* things I miss, though, of course, we *all* do at some stage, anyway, that's it, *enough* of me now, *that's* the Maggie McConnell way of handling life these days and, truthfully, there's little I regret, really. And then I met, *you*."

Steve had been quite moved. In recollecting the life of this woman he had met by quirk of fate, piecing the bits together, he was slowly discovering the sheer depth of passion and love that existed quite naturally in her, to realizing, also, from adversity comes good in life. How it's handled, how it's dealt with in the broader concept of the picture, often, from it comes the better ending, the better result. Indirectly, idly chatting, Maggie had unwittingly taught him many things he hadn't really thought much about before. And the part he really began to like, Josey had taken to Maggie like her *'long lost friend'*, one who was returning after being away from her life for too long. Josey, he was sure, would welcome more of Maggie in their lives. His problem; was he ready to travel down that road? Shaking his head and frowning at the thought, *'it's not as if it's a bad problem to have'* he told himself. An easier smile followed.

Memphis, 87 miles, was the next highway marker to grab his attention, also an exit from I-40 straight into the upcoming gas station service center. A refreshment stop for Josey and Amy gave them a chance to stretch their legs, something they were most anxious to do. It also became the perfect spot to alert the Quartermaine family their second eldest, Amy, was within the hour to being home again. Unfortunately, Amy wasn't ready to end her adventure and leave Josey but as Mr. Frankston had earlier reminded her, *'all good things must come to an end, Amy, my dear.'* As he said it, her bottom lip dropped. It was a ringing endorsement of success; something Steve Frankston was prepared to make sure he'd never forget when it came to raising Josey, in making her young life, one to remember. Did he need help?

~~~~~~~~~~
~~~~~~~~~~

CHAPTER NINETEEN

Opening the store at 11am on Tuesday morning was harder than Maggie McConnell ever thought it would be. The past weekend was so vivid in her memory, so emotionally still front and center; clearly, she was now sure, Steve Frankston had managed to do the once unthinkable, he had haunted her mind, body and soul. She was euphoric. But…he hadn't called her! Her late departure from Nashville on Sunday afternoon, beyond happy to have been delayed, she was forced to do an overnight in Tuscaloosa, Alabama. And Monday morning, expectedly, saw her dragging her feet no matter hard she tried to motivate herself. Feeling so terribly alone that next morning in a hotel room that literally depressed her, even a *'hard-start caffeine kick'* couldn't make her brain function. Her mind was so Steve Frankston driven; Steve this and Steve that, she wanted to scream, but not screams of *'go-away'*, but more, *'what have you done to me, Steve Frankston?'* The remainder of the drive from Tuscaloosa to Dunbridge turned out to be so emotionally draining, she even by-passed a quick visit to her Mother coming through. Everything was a blur, and no matter what, nothing looked remotely familiar, which left her with her thoughts, and all were constantly running wild, hither, thither and yon, mile after mile. Thoughts that did nothing but frustrate her! Finally, pulling in to her driveway at four-thirty in the afternoon, all she could do was turn the motor off, grab her pocket book and head straight for the bedroom where she tumbled, still dressed, straight in to bed. Sleep was her overriding thought, the only thing that would allow her mind to rest, allow her to get her away, albeit in a positive sense, from Steve Frankston, and their memory moments. There were so many of them, and she loved them. Sleep would turn out to be, futile! Her mind wouldn't stop racing

Karen Kartney wouldn't take no for an answer, or *'I'll tell you later, I don't want to talk about it right now.'* It was written all over Maggie McConnell's face that she'd had the *'time of her life'*, except, whatever the time of her life it might have been, Karen was totally in the dark of the facts. She was of the belief; it had to be positive! That was, at the least, the good side of it all; she wouldn't have to deal with *'disastrous'* or *'what was I ever thinking?'* By twelve-noon, their conversation was quite different.

"The part that really worries me, Karen, is I believe I'm in love. I can't stop thinking about this man. He crowds my mind, every second, every minute, every hour, and that's unhealthy, *isn't it?"* she queried, wondering what her friend might think. Maggie wanted her endorsement, but then again, Karen was an honest and straight shooter, she might suggest something else. She'd hate that. She didn't!

"Maggie, from your one-sided observation, I can see how you'd feel that way. He's obviously a very charismatic man, and Josey; she sounds like a sweetheart in every way. A father and his daughter will be close, always, however, if a woman can gain the confidence and attention the way you have said it is with Josey, and she has been *that* clingy, emotional, in her own spontaneous way, girlfriend, you have cut through a barrier that many times takes years, or *never,* for many. Josey has clearly formed a huge attachment to you. And *she* came to you, *voluntarily*. That makes you *quite* the woman, Maggie McConnell; by now, I'd say, you have entered a man's heart, *and* thinking, for sure."

"*Really*, Karen, really, do you *believe* that?"

"I *do*, although, as you say, he hasn't called, yet, which I don't see as a real problem, so the only question remaining must be, is *that* what's really bothering you?"

"It is, and I admit it. So, good as you are at observing, and knowing things, what does *any* of it tell you and why shouldn't I be worried, yet?"

Apart from keeping her eyes firmly fixed on Karen, there was also a slight quiver in her voice as she spoke. She hoped the answer would be what she wanted to hear.

"*Why*, Maggie, *here's* why. Remember, he's raising a girl, a big weekend is over, there's school to get underway, then there's his own job, too, of course. You know, I'd believe that he's maybe a bit like you. Trembling, wondering, thinking, when is too soon, too soon to call, although don't forget, you *do* have an open line to Josey if you choose to go that route. There are options available, open ended one's."

"I wouldn't do that, Karen. I *couldn't*, much as I want to, however, there's the possibility she might call me, now that would be different, wouldn't it?"

Maggie McConnell needed reassuring in every way. Grown woman or not, aware of love, it's highs and lows, of men, of winners and losers, this time, it was all quite different. Today, this moment in time, psychologically, she had a need to talk and Karen, as always, was her ever-faithful lifeline. She hung on her every word!

"Yes, I realize that, Maggie, and I can feel what you're going through, however, the nicest part, to me, finally, someone had captured your attention, has brought you out of the *'I'm not so sure about a man in my life anymore'* to a new feeling, one where you obviously would *love* a man in your life again. That's healthy and good for you, and I pray, this time, it might be real. Honestly, I could think of nothing better for you."

Maggie McConnell, true to her feelings and past modus operandi, was conversationally transfixed. She wanted to hear more, but not quite what came next.

"But, Maggie, a small word of caution."

This was always the part Maggie hated. Choosing her words, Karen continued.

"Be cognizant of one thing, *small* one way, *big* in another and we've been down this road before, in a different sense, *then*! Memphis is *not* Dunbridge. Memphis is a city, a *big* one, it's where he lives and his child goes to school. Memphis is also where he works, whatever his line of work is, his position, situation, with whomever? Love is love and can jump the biggest of hurdles, move mountains as they say, *but…*"

There it was again, *'but'*, the one word that never fails to raise ire, having the uncanny ability to confuse – *infuriate* might be the better word! And it affects everyone, anywhere.

"*But*…you may have to face dealing with distance, remembering, it's the one thing that can bring a romance to an end, quicker than one ever thinks. Guessing, here to Memphis would be certainly more than the drive you made to Nashville and *that*, dear Maggie, makes it a haul. I say it for you to be aware of it, because if you and Steve do connect, I mean, *really* connect, those hundreds of miles will become an issue. It's never going to be *'I'll pick you up for dinner'* or *'let's go to the movies'* and the like. Maybe someone has to move, *think* about it, would *you*? Have you ever *thought* about that?"

Maggie was almost worn out, already, with the practical side of getting to know more about a relationship with Steve Frankston. *'Was it all going to be this hard,'* she wondered? Karen, of course, was right, the miles between them speak volumes and in all seriousness, they couldn't have a normal life as it stands right now. And the next question would be; could we handle the challenges yet to surface and even if we could, would they be for *'a while'* or would it crumble in trying to go the distance? Her head began to hurt.

"I don't want to talk about it anymore, Karen. I need a break, too many questions and while you make sense about it all, for now, I don't have a relationship with him, he hasn't called and I don't even know where I stand, so I don't have an immediate problem, either, *do I,* so enough already? We'll talk more about him when there's a need. I'll keep my memories for now, they were fun, and I'd do it all again, okay?"

A Steve Frankston truce was called. A Josephine Frankston truce, too. Maggie went back to work, people needed attention, and her workweek had begun.

Swiftly, and without warning or consultation, the school had implemented new rules. Uniformed security guards were at the gates, parking zones were monitored, students showed cards that had been printed and issued indicating they were enrolled, and the final *'assault on children'* as it was termed by parents; random searches of their backpacks which ultimately meant nothing. The number of books, homework and lunches, for those that packed them, indeed, the heavy weight they carried on a daily basis, made a mockery of random checks. It was a total imposition to students more than a deterrent for supposed weapons and instruments capable of doing harm! Parents were horrified that their children were disadvantaged; to the degree they were, over a *'supposed'* threat against the school, serious as it was, at the time. Some *'common sense'* had to prevail, they argued, against the school board. All of their protests fell on deaf ears. Steve Frankston was incensed, and showed it, along with plenty of outside support. He took a stand. Calling the TV Channel that had interviewed him during the *'siege'*, they, in turn, took up the cause with a stance that mirrored the parents; *'what kind of a message does it send to our children, the youth of Memphis, indeed, America?'* Pundits of all things terrorism and the affect it was having on America chimed in, and before Steve knew it, a storm had brewed to the extent; he and his fellow angry parents could not believe the support levied. He feared for the way political correctness was overtaking his country, his rights, and his freedom, even the Constitution! He was now well aware, Bill Williams, the Police negotiator on the day of the siege, of how he was being *'crucified'* for his actions taken, and yet, as Steve Frankston had repeated, over and over, his own daughter, his flesh and blood, could have been sacrificed that day, and for what, as it turned out? Too much was being made of *'rights'*, especially those two that day who, as it was portrayed, didn't have a chance to a reasonable reaction, to talk, they were, instead, *'gunned down'*, it was claimed! Finally, Memphis had, had enough! The irony of the stand Steve Frankston had taken and in being a chief spokesman for his selected group, surfaced when one TV channel sent out a not so cryptic challenge that was quickly picked up by others, finally spinning off as editorial in the Memphis Courier Mail; *'Frankston is in the right place at the right time to run for office. Memphis could do with a politician of his standing'*, it was claimed, and with mid-term Congressional Elections looming they proposed, *'he would be a stellar candidate.'* Steve Frankston shuddered! *What* had he started, he wondered, stemming solely from wanting to protect his own child, to now, it seemed, the city's, the county's, and the State's children, en masse!

Primarily a State's issue, and to many pundits, Memphis's problem, nevertheless, school security leapt quickly onto the national stage, again. Network's had already shown tremendous interest re-hashing many other security situations around the country in and on all Government's property, citing a more recent blunder; the Washington DC Naval yards. However, Memphis took front and center stage based primarily on the *'related news'*, the rights of the *'alleged'* slain terrorists, a direct and lingering fall-out from the siege. It was through these combined circumstances that Steve Frankston found himself in the spotlight, a place he did not want to be. Anxious to shun the media, he withdrew, as best he could, from the onslaught of those seeking interviews, only to be tracked down and annoyingly hounded!

Expectedly, Maggie McConnell suddenly realized, having seen the Memphis news report on a Cable News program, *why, maybe,* she had not heard from Steve. Initially, caught well off-guard, stunned, her immediate dilemma became, what to do about it, and how to handle it. She had choices, and clearly knew it, however, it wasn't that simple to her way of thinking. She had always wanted Steve to be the instigator, to contact *her* after their Nashville trip together. Making life more difficult, this time, Karen Kartney and her approach that she termed simple was; *'call him, you have every right!'* Maggie deferred, deciding, again and again to wait at least one more day, which always became, one more day, and then another!

Casting her doubts aside, she was, however, very impressed, not only with the way Steve Frankston had handled himself on television, and the various reporters' lines of constant questioning, but also, in the supportive calls implying implicitly that he would make, unquestionably, an excellent Tennessee Congressman. She doubted it was his personal calling, concluding therefore, maybe she didn't know him as well as she thought she might, accepting that he may have latent views of all things political, after all, the reason it was suggested in the first place was based on issues that were very political, and one that certainly affected his daughter Josey. And then she thought of Josey. How was she handling all this attention her Father was getting? Was she affected at all, did it bother her, was she, too, being singled out, in school maybe? Many scenarios rushed through her mind to finally accepting; maybe she should call him, to show that she cared for them both, and that maybe, this time, she could help in some way. Unintentional, immediate doubt clouded her thinking, remembering; she had asked if he might need help once before and was turned down, repeatedly! Could she take the same rejection the same way now, especially after sharing all they had? Regurgitating the thought, she doubted it, which left her with no alternative but to revisit her own question, again. She did; and found no immediate answer. Her indecisiveness bothered her. Would Steve think it was *she* who didn't care, that *she* was detached, that *she* could have called? Her inner quandary was one she didn't want, the thought of it all, without result, hurt!

That night, with three self-aborted attempts behind her, Maggie McConnell lay in bed wondering why she found such difficulty, in seeing through, a simple phone call to Memphis. Belatedly, she agreed with Karen Kartney, in too many ways she had every right, however, facts were, her reasoning for not following through was based solely on an internal fight she was having with her own mind. Why *hadn't,* or why *wouldn't,* Steve have phoned her? *What,* indeed, she asked herself numerous times, were his expectations of *her*? Also, *what* differing rights would he have, as opposed to *hers*? The part that hurt the most was the unknown factor of little Josey. Had her Father issued instructions for her *not* to call, as he had suggested they might, or could, and that he had no problem with it, then, or was Josey of the belief Maggie would call her, for no reason at all, even just to say hello, maybe? Questions, questions, and questions - they all had the ability to torment, and Maggie McConnell's mind was being overly tormented. So internally torn apart as she had become, and plainly realizing it within herself, in a moment of inner anger, taking it out on technology, she threw her cell phone, hard, across the room. It slammed into the wall narrowly missing the 42" flat television screen attached to it, then, fell to the floor, and by the sound of it, probably, in more than a few pieces. Maggie knew, instantly, that was about to become her first very big mistake. Call or no call that she might have made, versus any call she might receive; now, it was impossible for either! Quietly, emotionally drained, she cried, knowing she knew better, and that she had been totally foolish. To make matters worse, having finally composed herself, turning on the television, to the news, was probably her second mistake. Three stories in, a political reporter introduced Steve Frankston. *'Damn!'* she uttered out loud. Drawn to the reason why he was featured, at least it brought the slight inkling of a smile to her face, her immediate thought being, how handsome he looked, and surprisingly, wearing a suit and tie. She had never seen him in a suit before, only causal clothes. Again, it made her realize just how much she really didn't know about the man, against all she thought she did! Regardless, mesmerized, she hung on his every word until it was over, then, embracing every reason she could think of, in putting all of her up and down, positive negative, smart and silly thoughts together, she finally reached a real and concrete decision; in the morning, she would get a new phone, and call him, no matter what reaction he may inflict, or that she might be subjected to. There was no doubting it; she *so* needed to talk to him, *so* needed to let him know that she cared about all he was going through, with and for Josey, and that she'd seen the political overtures thrust his way, and that, if he needed her, anytime, she would be there, in Memphis, if it were the request, no questions asked. She would stop short, though - well, she thought she might - of telling him…what? *'Oh, God, what's happening to me?'* she said to no one.

For all Maggie McConnell mulled over, little remained clear, except, she finally admitted what was probably the stark truth of reality, that all of it could only ever be for one reason; that she was totally, unquestionably, never intending but glad to be; head-over-heels in love. And if it was a one-sided love affair, then so be it! Her inner voice repeated what she'd heard before, *'I love you, Steve Frankston.'*

Frustrated, feeling sad, alone, bewildered, she pulled the covers over her head to block the world out for a little while. Tomorrow would be a new day, when she'd grant herself a self-imposed brand new start. Somehow, she was convinced, her action would be well worth it!

Love has no bounds and when needed, it could move mountains. Maggie had prepared herself for…she wasn't exactly sure anymore?

~~~~~~~~~~
~~~~~~~~~~

CHAPTER TWENTY

His cell phone rang incessantly. One call after another, *'Do it Steve' - 'We're with you Steve', - 'You can count on my support and I have many who will join me.'* It was relentless, to the point, when Josey came home from school, the first thing she said to her Father was not dissimilar from what he'd been subjected to all day, all week, wherever he went, and in his mind, he was sick of it! Nevertheless, how Josey asked it, did drive home the message; he couldn't escape it!

"Are you going to be a Congressperson, Daddy? The teachers at the school said to me Tennessee needs you. What do they really mean by that, Daddy? Is that because of all the things that have happened since the school shutdown problem we had?"

Flattered in many ways, not so in others, Steve Frankston was equally annoyed, to think, politics from afar has entered his little girl's life. He wondered, also, are teachers fuelling the flame a little, too, through her? It was all a new revelation, of sorts. Never, in his life, had he ever thought that a career in politics was for him, or that he even cared that much about politics in general, except for the major issues that affected his everyday. To a point, though, he did concede that he'd been drawn into the fold because of exactly that; current matters that realistically were very much in his everyday; the school siege issue, children, security rules and measures, and more. It didn't matter! Mildly content as he was in most things, he was not prepared, yet, to change anything about his overall life to appease any political party for the sake of *'names on a ballot.'* To his way of common sense thinking, he already had a very important job; to love and raise his daughter. He already had a most satisfying, rewarding job in Graphic Design, with a Company that was growing rapidly. Why let politics make an entry into his life?

Remembering, as a young child, his own Father who he believed he loved, then, it would be during his teens, after his mother perished in a boating mishap, that he could never forgive him for the way he, cruelly, turned on him, and the life from thereon in he was forced to lead. For too long, too many times, Steve recalled, he was left alone, abandoned, to fend for himself in every way because his Father, who wallowed in self-pity and misery, chose instead, to drift from what seemed, one woman to another. Inevitably, at odds with each other, their relationship drew further and further apart, until one day, at sixteen years of age, he up and left to make a life of his own, believing, his Father had left him with little to no choice. Five years later, sadly, he would learn that he had died of pneumonia, contracted while sleeping under a bridge, somewhere in Georgia, amidst a number of other homeless people. Buried in a commune plot, in a pauper's setting, his Father had been reduced to a name only. In grasping the magnitude of such an end, Steve Frankston vowed to make something of him and his life and although fate had dealt him his own unexpected bitter blow along the way, the loss of his wife, too, he vowed with a vengeance, despite being alone again, he would *never* subject, or allow his little girl to ever experience the fate he had endured. He would protect his little Josey with every ounce of love and energy he could muster. And so far, they were doing pretty good. An irony, the lesson from adversity had taught him plenty; from recollecting a Father who achieved nothing in life, dying a sad and lonely, homeless unknown, to himself, being courted to a position of legislative power; Tennessee Congressman. The only satisfaction he gathered from it all was the platform such a destiny provides. Steve Frankston now had one, a strong one if chosen, however, a crucial decision was yet to be made; did he want it, the scrutiny, the commitment, and what did he want in his private personal life? And what of Josey? Stepping back, it hit him, full force.

Margaret 'Maggie' McConnell came immediately to mind. It was at that moment, a glaring truth realization returned, with extreme clarity. So wrapped up in his *own* thoughts, his *own* life, his *own* bewilderment of other people's needs of him, of the much adulation he was receiving, and more, he had jettisoned a part of him that he immediately recognized he had been negligent in. Maggie McConnell had not deserved his inattention. One of the nicest and brightest people to enter his life in the longest of times, clearly, self-aggrandizement and selfishness had taken over. He had let her down. Maybe, he believed, he might have let Josey down, too. Making it abundantly clear, then, as he had in Nashville, that he and Maggie would stay in touch, openly sharing that they were friends, Steve chastised himself for being so incredibly careless toward another; not even an email, a text, if that was all! Casting her aside, forgetting, had he also forsaken the *'something special'* Maggie was going to do for them, especially for Josey; her offer for his little girl's 'Angel' to be placed in Maggie's caring, loving, gentle, hands in her doll hospital? Steve Frankston was disgusted with his inactions toward someone who had been the epitome of generous and self-giving to him, to Josey. Quickly experiencing bouts of personal remorse, and absolute regret, he questioned himself; had he made the ultimate, terrible mistake, committed the largest of cardinal sins in a burgeoning relationship between friends? Was it too late to make amends? He reached for his cell phone, about to send a text, the easy way out, then, stopping himself, he reconsidered…not a good idea, a coward's way, maybe? Scrolling his contact list instead, when 'Maggie McC' came up, he tapped the screen. With trepidation, he waited for her voice on the other end. Initially, there was nothing, not even voice mail. *That* bothered him! He checked the number. *No voice mail?* He tried a second time.

Looking at the new cell phone she had purchased, Maggie wondered why she had kept the one she had for so long. Accepting she was bound by annoying contracts, this time, avoiding the pitfall, she bought her phone outright, a Samsung Galaxy 4 with a huge screen. Immediately, she was thrilled to hold it in her hand and watch the animated screen-saver showing white puffy clouds drifting through clear blue skies, indicating another perfect day was in store for her, weather-wise. A positive start, she thought. With her saved contacts and whatever else the Agent was able to transfer from her battered phone, when she checked her messages; the one that hit her hardest was the one that read, 'Steve Frankston.' Slightly annoyed on one hand, she was gratified on the other, gratified that she had not gone ahead and made the call to him as she was seriously contemplating last night, before she threw the phone at the wall almost annihilating, but fortunately, not entirely, its inner workings. She coded in her password, hit voice mail, and then put the phone to speaker. Anxious seconds later, she was riveted to the message.

'Maggie, its Steve. Please forgive me; I owe you deep, deep apologies for not calling earlier. I have no excuses and believe me, if it weren't for my own selfish actions with all that is going on here in Memphis, maybe I wouldn't have to be apologizing, however, that's not the case. I did get wrapped up in some things I don't think I should be and yes, it does affect Josey indirectly, however, not specifically. The fault is all mine and again, I apologize, you deserved much better from me. If you can accept that for now, I will call you again later tonight and explain. I trust that'll be okay, that you're not going to be too mad at me. Thanks Maggie. Stay well, till later, I'd guess, hope.'

Realistically, the only thing Maggie could do was smile. Yes, she was mad at him, a little, however, she was madder at herself. Karen might have thought she had rights and maybe she did, to a point, but in the overall bigger picture, no one has rights over anyone, she deduced, and certainly not her over Steve Frankston. She also knew, in part, exactly what the issues had been in Memphis, and that he would have been unaware the news had spread beyond being local, that it had reached even her neck of the woods, Dunbridge. Happier now than she had been over the past, too long, Maggie could more easily accept, when she and Steve speak, when he calls, she would share all she had seen on television, and hopefully ease the obvious guilt he appeared to have for not calling, the very reason she had unnecessarily *'beat herself up'* about! *That* part she would *not* share. Unable to contain herself, she replayed the message. Not for the content, but to hear Steve's voice again. As it ended, a slight smile formed; she couldn't wait for tonight, to talk to him again, and on her new phone, too! For all the right reasons, deep within, she had already *'forgiven'* him! She cared too much for something so slight, yet important, to ruin a relationship over, what…a lack of pragmatism! That's not who she was!

"Daddy, *why* haven't we heard from Maggie? I thought she said she was going to call. I wonder if everything is all right, do you know at all?"

It was an innocent question from a little girl. Her Father knew precisely what to say.

"It was because of *me* sweetheart, *that's* why. I have been *so* busy and *so* involved in all the things that have been going on here that I neglected to call her, however, just so you know, *I did*, today."

"What did she say, Daddy, what did she say? Is she going to visit us?"

"No, Josey, of course not, well not yet anyway. She lives a long way away as you know and she can't simply drop in, and nor can we, to her. Anyway, she didn't answer so I left a message, but I *will* be talking with her tonight, *later*. And in the morning I'll tell you all she had to say, however, so you know, not chatting wasn't because she had forgotten or anything like that, it was *me,* my fault, but it'll be all fixed later, okay?"

"Okay, Daddy, but I hope we can see her soon. But you do still like her don't you?"

Another innocent question, one he wanted to answer truthfully, and under the circumstances, did.

"*Like* her, Josey? Of *course* I do, what's *not* to like about Maggie? She's a wonderful lady and to be honest, I believe your Daddy wants to see her again as much as you, and we will. But *why* did you ask, did you think your Daddy might not like another lady in our life, or especially, Maggie?"

"Not at all, Daddy, no. But I do know Mommy's been gone a long time now and we both miss her and she won't be here for my birthday in two weeks time, but that doesn't mean Maggie can't share with us, does it? I'm bigger now and I understand things, too, and do you know what, even Amy asked me if you still like Maggie? She wants to see her again too. Oh, and if you do become one of those Tennessee Congresspersons as lots at school think you should, I'd be very proud of you, but if you didn't, you'd still be important, to me, I mean, you're my Daddy, and I love you!"

Despite jumping from one place to another, he was amazed how the mind of his young Josey was able to process things, and how fast she was growing up, already, almost too quickly. Accepting that adults sometimes underestimate children and their perception or knowledge of many things, Josey was cleverer than he had previously given her credit for. Congressperson, her word, Maggie, then her acceptance of her Mommy gone, and so much more, he was in awe of her and the way she articulated her thoughts, all in her very own, growing up, young girl way. He was particularly aware of her attraction and adulated friendship toward Maggie, and suspected, even, she was encouraging him toward her. The very thought of it gave him an inner glow; however, he realized, realistically, there might be some fence mending that had to be undertaken along the way first. In fact, he wasn't sure, if through his inattentiveness, if he, *they*, were still a part of anything Maggie McConnell thought about anymore! With Josey about to go to sleep, he'd soon find out.

"Thank you, Josey, and you're important to me, or to be more precise, you *are* my very world and *everything* I live for, and I *love* you and don't you forget it, young lady."

"I love you, too, Daddy and goodnight. Now, kiss on my cheek please." She projected face forward, with a smile.

A kiss and a hug later, partially closing her bedroom door behind him, Steve Frankston prepared to gather up his tools and *'go mend a fence.'*

Setting the weekend up came easier than expected. A *'getaway'*, some *'you and me time'* a chance to *'mull over some differences'* were aired - all made sense. It would also be a time to gain some insight help with a few concerns he had when it came to many outside overtures being made of him, along with his own, every day vocation, his life in general, and Josey, especially. With so many things happening so fast, going it alone wasn't as easy as it might appear, or as many might believe. Unquestionably, Maggie McConnell was the right person at the right time to be able to talk one-on-one with, and gain different perspectives, especially from a female point of view. In a mostly positive way, there were many issues at stake! And as Maggie had offered, willingly, *'I'll be there for you, Steve, anytime, anywhere.'* Faithfully, anxious even, she had waited for his call, when it came, they had talked at length, and when it was all over, she was as happy as she felt she could ever be. Through laughter, many times, and through seriousness on a couple of issues, overall, it was a wonderful conversation between two people who obviously had, she felt, a common interest, a growing bond. The next hour and a bit, whatever it was, seemed to fly by.

As they said goodnight, Maggie would sleep well, she knew, being able to allow her mind to hear all over again Steve Frankston's tender side, his love of life, his love for Josey, and to savor his last few words, *'I can't believe I met you, Maggie, and I freely admit, you bring out in me a new way to look at the world, and life, that's pretty special. Anyway, I look forward to us being together, soon, I'll call you again in the morning, okay?'*

Tomorrow wouldn't come soon enough for her, nor would the weekend, if, what they had planned could be pulled together. Maggie willed it to be, hoping, just as it had been with Nashville, that he felt the same way, in every way. Her redeeming thought, *'this adventure,'* was *his* idea, but then again, she, willingly had said yes, realizing instantly that the temptations toward each other would magnify. It was a thought that sent not only a shiver right through her body but an anticipation that made her feel quite nervous, too.

Both, had accepted, they were heading into unchartered territory, and from it there were bound to be consequences? Both, also knew, they were at liberty to choose their own destiny - continue to move forward, or turn back - before it's, maybe, too late?

~~~~~~~~~~
~~~~~~~~~~

CHAPTER TWENTY-ONE

A quaint little hotel on the banks of Lake Pontchartrain, in Louisiana, was as remotely pretty as any spot could ever be. Nestled among tall trees, the edge of the lake was no more than twenty-five yards away, the perfect place to sit on the jetty and dangle one's feet in the water. The only two on the jetty that evening were Steve Frankston and Margaret 'Maggie' McConnell.

"Ya know, Maggie, I always knew in my heart this day would come never guessing it would all play out the way it has, but I'm mighty glad it did, I have to say."

"Well, *me, too,* Steve, although for a minute there I had some doubts, not about *you,* more about whether what's happened along the way, *how* it might affect everything and if it could have a good ending."

She glanced at him as she said it, not wanting him to misconstrue it in any way. *That,* she was wary of!

"What'd, ya mean, Maggie, that I would *falter,* that maybe I wouldn't find a way?"

"*No,* not *really,* more like, when I saw you on television, not that you knew it was all over the news outside of Memphis. More like the pressure you must have found yourself under to get more involved, to be a major player, even all the running for Congress chatter about you that was everywhere in the press, and probably there was a whole *more* of it in Memphis, of course."

"It's a *crazy* world, Maggie, that's all I can say. I mean, what's happening is *frightening* in many ways, and all this political *'crap'*, as I'd call it, that's everywhere, when does it end, or does it? We're all losing ourselves, aren't we?"

"We might be, yes, and it *doesn't* end, I doubt, but anyway, more importantly, when I grasped *what* you were going through I could see *why* you were side-tracked in thinking about me, *or* what we'd shared in Nashville, especially when you said you would call." Sighing at the thought, it didn't go un-noticed. She continued. "And Steve, I have to admit it, because that's who I am, but seriously, I *really* thought it would be a while before I jumped back into your mind, or that you'd remember little ole Maggie McConnell from Dunbridge. Was *that* so silly, really, *was* it?"

"Oh, *Maggie,* how could you have thought *that,* I mean…'c'mon!"

"Steve, *think* about it! I can't be *too* wrong because it did take a while and after all, apart from phones, what about an email, a *text*? There was nothing but silence."

"Yeah, I know, and I'm ashamed, and again, I'm sorry, but you know, when I realized it…" he paused a moment as if gathering a thought, "…in fact, like you, in being perfectly honest as we are, it was Josey who jolted me somewhat along the way."

"It was?" she asked, surprised a little, wondering how.

"Yes, it was *Josey*. She *actually* asked me if I still liked you. Now *there's* a killer question from your own daughter, *that's* how much of an impression you've made on her. In fact, I think she thought she might not see you or hear from you again, because of me."

"Well, *bless* her little ol' heart, *what a girl!* To think, she thought of me, how nice. Okay, a confession. I actually thought about her many times, too, and even wondered if I should call her but then, I was worried that might be an imposition on you if I did, so I erred on that. I mean, your silence was deafening. And scary, too, for me, I admit."

"I wish you *had*, Maggie, in *hindsight* that is. It would have snapped me out of it way sooner, to double-checking just where some of my priorities were, or should have been. I shudder to think of the way I let you out of my life longer than I should have because it was possible, after a while you'd have to start thinking differently of me and that would have been *horrible*. I would have *hated* the thought of losing you, and I could have, for being so *incredibly* thoughtless. I was kinda crazy, really!"

"I'd hate to have lost you, too, Steve, and over, *what*? Believe me, I did want to see you again, hear from you, and in fairness, maybe I should've had the confidence to make the call, but you did say *you* would, so, *patiently*, I waited, but look, we're *here*. That's all behind us now. Let's leave it alone; it's ancient, counter-productive. Being with you, now, around this lake, all I can say is, *wow*, and Steve, you *excelled*, look at the surroundings. A recipe for our well being, I'd say."

Lunch was down by the Marina. A seafood restaurant that served the best of Louisiana in every way; Cajun and Creole cuisine; crawfish, gumbo, jambalaya, shrimp, etouffee', their choices were endless. Sunshine abounded, boats came and went endlessly, the sound of the water from the bayou, the birds, everything seemed to drift in and about everywhere, or as the mind allowed one to take in the best of southern hospitality, complete with trees laden with Spanish moss. Over a fine French wine, their conversation continued.

"My life's changing, Maggie, and you know, it's all because of you. You're to blame, in a nice way, of course."

"Well, I'm pleased, *thrilled,* too, and I love it, because *mine* is as well, Steve. I didn't think someone like you would come along quite the way you did, not that I'd change a moment of it and to think, there's Josey, too. Truthfully, though, in you feeling that way, I *have* to tell you, honestly, I feel the same way, so we must have something rather special in common and I don't know of a better way to have shared much of what we are, quite like being *here*. Different is an apt word. By the way, *tell me,* how'd you *ever* dream this one up, anyway, 'cause you've struck togetherness gold!."

Recollecting, Steve Frankston had moved quickly that next morning. Sharing his conversation with Josey first, when she went off to school, he immediately doubled checked with the Quartermaine's, Amy's folks, who were only too happy to have Josey stay the weekend with them. In fact, they told him they were off to the Memphis Fairgrounds to take in, primarily, a Marty Stuart/Connie Smith concert, plus, of course, all the fair had to offer and Josey would be marvelous company for Amy, a win, win all round. Steve was thrilled, as was Josey when he told her of the plans in play.

"But why don't *you* come with us, Daddy?" she had asked, innocently. "You like all that country music, you said?"

When he broke the news to her that he and Maggie were going to see each other, her first reaction was, *'but what about me, Daddy, am I coming?'* before she quickly understood, with the hint of a smile, kid-smart smirk even, what he might have been saying really, adding, *'but I'd love to go the fair, too.'* He promised her they would all get together as soon as possible and do, his word, *'stuff.'*

Next, he went to the Internet and sourced a common place that he and Maggie might meet, a place that was easy enough to get at, however, not on either of their respective doorsteps; Memphis or Dunbridge. Sharing the distance apart, driving, Louisiana and Lake Pontchartrain became an easy pick. Finding the exact spot to stay was a challenge but when he did, he also booked two separate rooms that adjoined. With respect, he had anticipated, *nothing*!

"You know, Maggie," he confessed. "*Once,* I doubted I'd ever get over Angelic, believing that she'd stay in my life forever, but, with the help of Josey, when we talk about her Mom, she seems to know, accept, even, that she's never coming back, and therefore it's all right that I like someone else, and believe me, interestingly, she has said to me, *'Maggie's nice, I like her and I think you do, too, Daddy, and you know what else, she'd be good to you.'* Can you *believe* that, how *smart* she is? She knows I like you and she's okay with it. And by the way, she and Amy talk about us a lot, too."

"Well, this Maggie *does* like her Daddy, she's absolutely right, and as I've confessed all along, I certainly think the world of Josey, too, but you know Steve, it's *not* through the children people should ever *like,* or *want,* or have a *need* for someone else. To me, it's always been about those involved, like in *this* case, you and me. Josey will grow up and leave someday, to live her own life, while others, say, you and me; we go on as normal, and strange as it may seem, having met by sheer chance, I've often wondered what would my life be like if I didn't know you, hadn't met you and by that I mean, *you,* the *man,* the *person.* You've struck a *huge* chord with me since I've known you that's for sure, so much so that now; I'd hate the thought of *not* seeing you again, to *not* hear your voice, to *not* see your face, to *not* know of your life. Such is the affect you have had on me; Steve Frankston…and I *love* it by the way. But anyway, as a sort of one on one, people, people, thing, my thoughts only."

"I think you took the words right out of my mouth, Maggie. How astute of you! And I doubt I could roll though the next, however long, and *not* see or hear of you, either, and *that's* the honest truth, and *not* simply to copycat you! I love the thought of us sharing some more quality time, and we *will,* promise, and I'll *keep* it this time, or not let time get away if I was to be more precise, I've learned that lesson."

"I hope you have," Maggie fired back, jokingly.

"But seriously, Maggie, I do wonder what our next set of moves might be and by that I refer to the road ahead. Memphis is quite the distance and Dunbridge, well…"

"Well, *what?*" It was a fair question.

"Well, Maggie, I don't know yet, however, for now, let's choose the higher more positive road, because somehow, I am quite sure we'll work it out."

What started as lunch was fast becoming mid to late afternoon. With so much to say and share, their hands often moving across the table, touching one another's, electricity had begun to build, and ignite, between them. Convivial and light, harder edged at times, many quite personal topics were discussed, and yet, through it all, an amazing similarity about life and living became evident. Common goals in where the future might lay found a rightful place between them. If either had ever suggested that their weekend together, so far, was time well spent in a growing relationship, then the agreement would be unanimous. Leaving the restaurant, their walk along the Pontchartrain shoreline was all they had anticipated. Hand in hand, light hugs here and there, the sound of rustling leaves in the trees everywhere and rippled waves caressing the waters edge, Steve Frankston and Maggie McConnell began to wish time might stand still, even for just a little while. They had *so* much to share, together. As dusk fell, and the sun slowly began to set, it was time to meander, aimlessly, back toward the hotel and plan their evening, wherever it may take them. Time waits for no one.

The nervousness that existed was mutual. The room service Court Bouillon, a thick fish stew served over rice, preceded the perfectly brewed Café Au Lait, its chicory coffee aroma strong and lingering. Over a homegrown semi-sweet Louisiana Blanc Du Bois wine, somehow, both knew, and maybe expected, before this evening was over, a little more than walking and talking, eating and drinking, laughing and sharing each other's company through a most glorious day would take them into that unchartered territory they'd anticipated. Was the cliff's precipice up ahead?

For the longest time, Maggie lay in Steve's arms, content, happy, protected. Words of love came easy. Then, as in the blissful togetherness they had shared earlier, slowly, he shifted from the position he was in and leaned forward to kiss her again. Willingly giving in to him, their arms wrapped around each other, he moved his body, tighter, closer in toward hers. Gently caressing her, moving from her back to her side, his fingers glided gently over her soft skin leaving her with an all-over tingling feeling. Cupping her breast, Maggie sighed, deeply. Instinctively, his head moved downward, his mouth taking in her nipple standing taut, hard, which he softly licked, his tongue flitting everywhere. It was all she could do to not moan, but quickly, it became too much, and without fear, she gave in to the sensation that overwhelmed her; she, he, wanted more of each other. Slowly, again, Steve moved to lift his body over hers. By instinct, and need, Maggie slid her hands over his back down toward his thighs, holding him for a moment longer, before giving in to guiding him, selfishly, to where she yearned for him to be. For too long, she, like him, had not enjoyed the pleasures they were now sharing in each other. For the second time that evening, as he entered her, becoming one, together, they moved in rhythm, in harmonious rhythm, their sensations building with each move, each push, each thrust. Nothing could be more beautiful than to share one with another, especially when love is the driving force, as they both wanted to believe. Consummating a union that could only conclude in a euphoric place, one where they longed to be, together, they reached a crescendo of such intense satisfaction, their reactions were natural. Clinging tightly to each other, one never wanted to let the other go. Her next words came easy.

"You know I'm in love with you, Steve, and I feel so…" Maggie gladly shared as once again she lay in his arms, loving the moment, the serenity and feeling of being so complete.

"And what are we going to do about *that,* Miss McConnell?" he interjected in open reply as if fishing for a direction of her thoughts for a tomorrow.

"I *don't* know, *truly*, I *don't* know, Steve, and it bothers me a little, too. Equally, though, what about *you*?"

"Well don't fret, darling, we'll work it out, because I'm *not* letting you go now," he reassured.

"Why, thank you. You don't know how that makes me feel, however, we *are* adults, and you know, love like tonight is one thing, but, where we go from here, practically, is another and *believe* me, you will get *no* pressure from me along the way, except, my love will grow, I'm sure, and no matter what, *no one* can take that from me now, *ever*."

"You're a *beautiful* lady, Maggie, and together, we have something that's yours and mine alone, *never* to be taken away," he willingly confirmed. "All we have to do now is harness it, and we will, no matter what."

Warm, loving, and contented as they felt, for what seemed like the longest time, they rested into each other. With a sigh here, a gentle touch there, light kisses, smiles or a gentle squeeze from each other, intermittently broke their satisfyingly magical tryst. Finally, it was Maggie who posed a thought that brought them back to the reality of the *'real world'* moment.

"Steve, something that intrigues me. What was it that first day? What made you change, or, what was it about me that you felt there might be something, in us, *me*?"

Strange as it was, eerie as the feeling instantly became, yet, able as he was now to accept the question, innocently as it was asked, Steve Frankston's very silent mind reminded him, with reverence, to a similar question asked of him once by Angelic in an equally most wonderful and tender moment. He loved the memory, however, Maggie was now very much in his *new* life. And yes, a man *can* love two women for very different reasons, and he did. Regardless, he would have no trouble expressing himself in reply. Truthful as he was, then, he would be obligingly equally so, now. But first…!

"Easy, *too* easy," he told her, "Your *unbelievably* good looks, your *staggeringly* beautiful, *incredible* body, plus your candor and charm, they *all* won me over in an instant to say nothing of your impact on Josey, of course. *My God, woman,* there are *too* many reasons!"

Maggie knew, right there and then he wasn't serious. Not for one second.

"Oh, *sure*. A predictable answer and flattering, now *really* tell me why," she counter challenged.

"I *am* serious Maggie. How could you doubt me?" he offered in swift jocular reply knowing he wasn't!.

Seconds later, not expecting her reaction, after throwing back the sheet that covered them both, Maggie's naked body was straddled over his. Slowly, in a tantalizing way, she brushed her breasts over his chest before settling in closer, propping herself up on her elbows, looking directly into his face. He was momentarily trapped, and loved it.

"Because I *don't* believe you were, *serious* that is," was all she said, knowing she'd forced his reply.

"All right," he countered, before gently kissing her lips, then likewise, unexpectedly as a retort, he tipped her back on her side followed by a gentle but loving hug.

"*First,* it was something in your easy and layback, almost non-caring, not meant that way of course, but nonchalant approach to something that comes easy to you, and yet, you did it so well, handled it so sensitively, and I'm referring to Josey, naturally. I thought at the time, in your store, *what* a lady, what a *wonderful* way to treat a little girl. It was obvious, you *meant* all you had said, all you showed and shared, every inch of the way. *Nothing* was too much trouble, and I posed to myself, *'unbelievable, is she for real?'* And let me add, I saw, also, a very beautiful lady, and in my eyes, a mere male, a simply *gorgeous* one at that – *you!* All I could think, then, watching you, your every move, your every action, was how I'd like to get to know you, know more about you. And for the first time in so long, with you having spurred the thought, I began to realize I should probably accept that there *are* other people out there, because before then, that moment, I'd never been sure, or wasn't ready. As I said at the outset, Maggie, truthfully, *that* day you made and left a huge impression on not only a little girl, but also a grown man - *me!* Now, there, does that explain it all, and don't ask me to repeat it," he laughed.

"*Wow! I can't believe it*. So eloquently put and yes, I really think you meant it."

"I *do*, Ms. McConnell, I *do*, can't you see that?"

"I can, Mr. Frankston, and my next request. Please, hold me close as I can't bear the thought of not having you near me, always, in your life." She paused. "But only if you *want* me, of course," she lightheartedly added.

Many a true word is spoken in jest!

The challenge was no contest! Deliriously happy, the call was answered as Steve moved to lay close alongside her, and together, with love, they looked into each other's eyes. As he brushed her lips, Maggie responded. With ease, shifting momentarily for comfort, moving his right arm slowly down her side before placing his hand well below her tummy, pressing lightly as he did, he gently began to caress her. Unable to control her feelings, from the touch of the man she loved, Maggie quivered before gently beginning to writhe. Instinctively, her hand moved down his body. Expectedly, when she touched him, his first reaction was a very light sigh, causing her to look into his face. Noticing his boyish grin, she couldn't help but smile.

'You're the devil in disguise Steve Frankston,' she told him, as her lips met his. Anticipating, wanting, needing, seconds later, Maggie couldn't resist; *'You **can?'*** she asked.

He snuggled his head into her neck, whispering in her ear, '***Watch me***!' A confident reply?

It had become a day and a night to remember, forever.

No matter what happened in the hereafter, from what they chose to declare, *'Lake Pontchartrain onward,'* Maggie and Steve became, gladly, inextricably aligned. A future together, a parting of the ways, either, for whatever reason, only time would answer the question.

~~~~~~~~~~
~~~~~~~~~~

CHAPTER TWENTY-TWO

The police came to the school today, Daddy, they were everywhere, it was real scary! We all thought bad things had happened again, like before, until we were told, why."

Josey related to her father, why; *'a kid had a wooden gun in his backpack and when they found it, the Principal called the police.'* It was school policy, a mandatory requirement, after affects of the recent Memphis Siege. Steve Frankston was horrified, knowing he, or any parent, was powerless to do anything about it. *'Safety of the children comes first'* was the message drummed home in the official school letter sent home via children to their parents. Josey also shared, Mr. Jones, their teacher in class, warned all children that afternoon, knives, scissors, blades of any kind, anything that might look like a weapon, wooden or metal, or otherwise, would all be confiscated and those who carried them in their gym bags, backpacks, carry-bags and the like, *'might'* be given a warning, *'once'*, after which, depending on the relevant circumstances, students might then be suspended from school. Stark reality became, as Steve Frankston chose to determine, *'officialdom'* at school, indeed, in many ways, in the workplace at large, was *'coming off the rails!'* There was no way he and many of his supporters would not attend, in droves, the next school board meeting. It had been the Police all over the school that had inflamed the incident. Was simplicity becoming draconian in execution?

Again, Channel 9 News, asked him for an interview, again, Steve Frankston agreed, stating, in general he understood, and was pleased certain issues were being taken seriously, however, in pleading for common sense in punishment to prevail when dealing with children, asked, in reference to the current event, *'was it really necessary to handcuff the eleven-year old and escort him, crying, from the school grounds to a waiting police squad car?'* He called it over-kill and abhorrent as the stigma was sure to stay with the child forever. As if only to appease him, the reporter offered that most of the other parents agreed with him before switching the line of questioning from school safety to one of politics.

"Your name has been mentioned, too often, for me not to ask you, in light of your stance and statement here, today, are you contemplating putting your name forward to run for the mid-terms and Congress, Mr. Frankston?"

Facetiously, Steve grinned in reply, "Was *that* why you wanted to talk to me in the first place, Sir, to get more into *politics* than caring for the children?"

"*Never*, Sir, *never*, however, many want to know, and you *are* qualified it appears, also, you haven't said no and the people, our viewers, would really like to know, I mean there are many issues at stake and you have been more than vocal, so, *are you*, Sir?"

"Put it this way…" Steve Frankston began in reply, "…given *you've* changed the subject. There are *many* issues that interest me, and they are as *real* as they are *serious*. That said, with some of them, I've come to believe *too* many politicians are not prepared to get their hands dirty, especially when it comes to combating *terror*, when it comes to taking care of *us*, the American people, and often, like today, there is *never* enough due consideration of the children. Then there's political correctness, pandering to those who mean harm, and not embracing the why they do, what they do, and then allowing them *far* too many rights, as we've seen recently, Texas, Boston, to name a couple. How many of these are we starting to have to comprehend are actually *'homegrown?'* It's a *real* issue and *all* need attention, but what, also, of accountability, or the lack thereof? I'm *sick* of it, as are most Americans, and *that's* where I believe more attention should be paid, but anyway, to answer your question, to consider what I might think about getting into the Congressional race ahead, frankly, I *don't know, yet!* Simple as that, and you can ask me as many ways you might choose, the answer will be the same, okay? I don't know…*yet!* Now, what's next?"

"So you *may,* is that what you're saying, I mean, you *do* have a stake in all of this according to your espoused agenda, and I say that, respectfully, to you as a sole parent, raising a little girl by yourself as I unders…"

To say Steve Frankston was infuriated with the reporter would have been a gross understatement. He was livid to the core with such an invasion of privacy, his audacity to bring Josey into the picture, as if it were his given right.

"How *dare* you, how *dare* you involve my family, a small child into this conversation. She has a right to be protected, however, by me, and you, Sir, have NO right to even head into that territory for whatever gains you think you might have a need to secure. If I choose to run for election, for the Tennessee Legislature, or school board for that matter, even for little league membership, it would have *nothing* to do with you bringing up my daughter because that's another story completely. So I repeat, *please,* leave her out of it; *don't* go there, *ever,* and frankly, right now, I'm more than done talking with you. Respectfully…" he looked directly into the news camera lens, "…by all means, as news, *deal with the issue* and *stay focused,* but do NOT take advantage of parents and small children's privacy while framing side issue questions, *especially* when the child is mine! Thank you."

Stepping immediately behind the camera after speaking was his way to avoid any lingering footage TV channels were notorious for filming, and using.

"*Whoa*! I never meant it *that* way, Mr. Frankston," the reporter immediately offered. "I just thought I'd take it to more of a human side of tryi…"

"*That's* the problem, you all try too hard and go off on tangents, and in the process, *miss* the very point of what you thought you needed to know in the first place," Steve said, in virtual retaliation, " and *don't,* is the best advice I can give you, okay?" Disgusted, he walked away.

For all the right reasons, as he saw them, that night, Steve Frankston sat with Josey to have a *'kid-to-dad-talk'* about whatever she wanted to ask, say or listen to. It lasted for almost an hour and the little things, the big things, to whatever degrees, regardless of who brought the subject up; they were shared, honestly, and with *'a whole lotta love'* between them. It was such a nice time, he wondered why, he, they, hadn't done it before, but then again, he accepted, Josey *is* only eight, but nine next week, he smiled about. It also reminded him, nine would have to be an *'extra special'* event given it's only one number away from double digits, and from there, the teenager arrives way quicker than any parent would want, especially him, a Daddy alone, dreading those years, inevitable as they were. How does a little girl, he later began to think after their chat, come up with such a broad array of, in her mind, simple, innocent, questions;

Was what the Police did that day, right?

Amy said her parents said that you'd be a good man, Daddy, if you went to Washington.

The teacher, Mr. Jones, asked me how long you had lived in Memphis and if you liked living here.

What happens, Daddy, when two people like each other a lot, does that mean they'll get married?

Maggie's cool, isn't she?

Why hasn't Maggie come to see us?

Do you like the job you do Daddy?

Those, among many, were a total pot-pourri of subjects that constantly chopped and changed, but all was from the mind of a little girl who asked questions as they bounced into her head. Tonight had been their best family type chat, *ever*!

Later, this time in conversation with Maggie, he pontificated a few thoughts at a different level. Talking, it seemed, was a form of therapy, a release, and with so much building all around him, his mind was literally racing.

"You know, Maggie, I think the world is not only going crazy at a rapid rate of knots, I also think we've all capitulated in such a way to it that the very framework of our lives, society itself, is changing, and *far* too rapidly, and much of it, like what's happening here in Memphis, is turning ourselves against each other. Sometimes we have to stand up and fight, take a stand! Am I *wrong*, or is it just *me*?"

Maggie wasn't quite sure which way to bounce on a subject near and dear to Steve given his very local circumstances, aware, as she had become of his interaction with a TV reporter. Passionate, almost fiery about the past events and how they had affected him, personally, she wanted to agree wholeheartedly to support him and give him reason to continue pontificating his rhetoric, however, she felt strongly, how it might be counterproductive to his overall well-being. Time, in one's life, is a precious commodity and Maggie felt too much time, expended mental and physical effort spent on issues, or causes by a sole individual, in this case, Steve, might ultimately be, overall, all too consuming. Given Josey needed him, she was torn on how to give an honest *'boots-and-all'* supportive answer. Having listened already to his take, his side, on the heart-to-heart chat earlier with his daughter, she was abundantly aware not only how he felt overall but also, he was taking his day-to-day far too seriously, and some of it was becoming counter-productive to his well being, maybe? Cognizant, and with due consideration of everything tabled and the fine line she'd have to walk, Maggie felt it might be better to taper their conversation while there was still an opportunity to remain calm, concluding, the light of a new day will hopefully bring a slightly different, more varied approach to his direction ahead, regardless of what he might choose to do, and after all, she *did* now figure in to it all, she still believed. *'Proceed with caution'* she told herself before expounding her next thought.

"Well, whichever, or whatever way you take, Steve, at least it's for the best part, positive, despite the heavy-lifting that might be involved, too," she suggested. "Thinking a little harder, or longer will be the secret to the end result, however, no matter what it turns out to be, we can deal with it, together, and where I can support you, especially with Josey in mind, you know I'm never really that far away."

"Yeah, Maggie, and thanks, and I've gotta say, I enjoy our talks, I *really* do and I value your opinions, not that I agree with them all, of course..." he laughingly threw in as if propelling his ideas more to reality, "...but I've digressed, too. Actually, I have a couple of ideas to run by you, but if you come up with a better one along the way, make sure you shout and let me know because Josey's birthday is next week, and she'll expect her Daddy to come through."

"I will, you can count on it, but relative to the other matter before we finish, my parting thought, Steve. *Please,* don't despair, life's to enjoy in the best possible way we all can, and remember, for what any of it's worth, money, power or position, *none* of them measure up to happiness, family, and for *you,* Josey. Think about it, I'm sure the overall picture is clearer than what one imagines."

Cryptic, philosophical, timely, he shook his head, construing Maggie's parting words, indeed, *'shot'*, was aimed directly at him, but for all the right reasons. Strangely, he thought, she's actually right! Unoffended, he saw it more as female logic, intuition and something maybe, he should embrace?

~~~~~~~~~~
~~~~~~~~~~

CHAPTER TWENTY-THREE

Being the CEO of Visual Communications and Head Graphic Designer for the Web and Software, incorporating Entertainment and Film, meant a lot, and certainly more than simply overseeing a competent staff and delegating duties. Both were an integral and actual part of Steve Frankston's everyday. The demands made on his position usurped all the hours in a day he could logically facilitate, however, because all were micro-managed to perfection, he was always able to accommodate his personal needs; raising an about to be, nine-year old daughter. Fully prepared, and ready to embark, tomorrow, the weekend, on his latest *'birthday adventure'* with Josey, and others, his excitement was tempered, badly, when an unscheduled Friday lunch meeting was called. Sitting with the President of Visual Communications at the downtown Memphis Peabody Hotel, a bombshell was dropped. Orville Greenspan didn't mince his words, supportive, as they were on one hand; they were equally difficult to listen to on the other. Caught off-guard, Greenspan informed him, with all the talk and media attention he was getting about being courted to run for political office for the State of Tennessee, if he were to accept a nomination, then Visual Communications would have to release him from the company as it would present a severe *'conflict of interest.'* The Company, as he knew but was reminded, does much graphic design, Internet and media work for both major political parties, Democrat and

Republican, also, although infrequently, Independent candidates, too! Greenspan added, proud as he is of him, claiming also that he'd be an excellent choice wishing him well in the process, if he nominates, regretfully, he concluded, a parting of the ways would be inevitable. Not expecting it, Steve Frankston, was shocked! With no room for commercial maneuvering, his decision cards clearly and openly on the table, friends as they were, their casual conversation moved quickly to family, philosophy of life, and given the topical interest of the very reason for the lunch meeting, state and national politics. Time, eventually, would get away from them both. With their extended convivial lunch over, before departing, with understood, little alternative, Greenspan reiterated to him a clear cut political ultimatum in decision; not to run at all and stay, a position he would welcome and prefer, or, nominate and vacate Visual Communications. When asked if a possible *'leave of absence'* was a viable proposition to be considered, the answer was an unequivocal, *'No!'* Watching the Peabody Ducks do the second of the programmed twice a day ritual walk to the fountain was not something either men stayed for. Duty and decisions were calling!

'Happy birthday to you, happy birthday to you, happy birthday, dear Josephine, happy birthday to you…' everyone sang along. On completion, Josey leaned down to blow out all nine candles at once with one breath, and did, easily! Smiling faces abounded in a crowd of about sixteen and while her biggest fan in the midst might have been her Father, hiding well his inner struggle, he didn't disappoint joining in the fun and laughter, watching his daughter about to cut and hand out

her huge double layer chocolate cream cake. Surrounded by Amy, Tiffany and Mary, three of her best friends, none was more *'extra special'* this day than the one she had hoped would be there with them all, and was, Margaret 'Maggie' McConnell. Standing in the huge open expanse area of their backyard, site and setting of the tented *'birthday bash,'* she couldn't help but notice the beautiful flowers in bloom everywhere, the thick, lush lawn mowed to perfection, the small hedges trimmed and the landscaped stylized concrete step pathway meandering in between the huge selection of varied shrubs and plants. It was a gardener's paradise, something else she never knew about Steve Frankston, his very green thumb. She was impressed, and had told him so!

Maggie had flown to Memphis for the special occasion, implicitly expressed, and asked, by Steve, who had implored upon her, Josey so wanted her at her party. Thrilled, there was no way Maggie could, or would have ever said, no. She would, however, have liked it better if Steve had said that, *he,* not emphasizing Josey, would love for her to join them, but then again, how could he, she realized, fairly. In the bigger scheme of things, to see him, again, and share some time, she couldn't wait. And to be with Josey, the opportunity that had already been too long in happening, none of it mattered. More important was to be, finally, in the close living environs of the man she now loved, and his little girl who she absolutely adored; it was all very much like, a dream, finally coming true. Her only lingering, small concern for him, not that it would ever have stopped her, was the dilemma Steve had shared with her, in advance, and his apparent negative tone of *'fair play'* and *'what am I going to do now?'* referring, as he had, about Visual Communications and his choices of a future. Maggie knew, this very subject was going to be very much *'first and foremost'*, after Josey's party. They would have three days, actually, a rapidly diminishing two-and-a-half, for them both to put their heads together and talk. It was the one *'downer'* on a long weekend, for her, that should have been, in her mind, one of joy, joy and more joy! She surveyed the crowd. Josey was obviously, deliriously, happy. Again, another occasion, where Dad had taken every moment of just the two of them to higher levels, where family life showed its true colors, its beauty and happiness. It was a subject playing very much on Steve's mind.

By six o'clock, the early evening, the day was over. Josey's ninth birthday party was a fabulous hit and everyone had a most wonderful time. The Quartermaine's, Steve's closest friends, graciously allowed Amy to stay overnight with Josey, a fitting end to her party and a chance for the two to watch DVD's and chat and do their normal little girl things together. They were always a happy twosome! They also left an open invitation for tomorrow night; dinner at their place, or a restaurant, whatever Steve chose given his most *'delightful guest,'* their words, referring to Maggie who they had spent considerable time with, *'adoring her personality, outlook on life and vibrancy,'* again, their words. Steve wasn't quite sure just *how* to take their parting remark - *'a very attractive woman, in fact, beautiful and when you're standing together, you make quite a striking couple.'* It was said with conviction. Were the Quartermaine's trying to tell him something, he considered.

"I'm not so sure I want to talk about it right now, to be honest. It was hard enough getting through the party to now have to take on board a decision that has far reaching ramifications and in what could be, many different ways, it's kind of mind-numbing, if you know what I mean. Frankly, I never expected, *ever,* to be in this position, and that's the truth, Maggie. It's not a place I want to be at my time of life."

"Steve, you're only, what, thirty five or was it six, you told me."

"Five" he enlightened her, "Thirty five."

"Okay, thirty five..." Maggie continued, "...that's a *great* age and if you really think about it, your decision, dilemma, call it what you will, it allows you to move in directions you may never have thought much about before."

"What do you *mean,* Maggie? Am I *missing* something here because I didn't think I was, at all?"

"You may well be, Steve, and *that's* my point. Mid thirties is a wonderful time in life, a wonderful age, and let's face it, I *know* what I'm talking about here, I mean, I'm only three years behind you and I love life, in every way. There's so much more to do yet, for all of us that is, and surely, life and living must have huge interest to you, too, whether it's politics, staying with Visual, moving on to something else, or even to *some-where* else? Goodness me, you could even switch entirely and totally re-invent yourself if you wanted to. The world's out there and as much as you love Memphis, it's *not* the center of the universe for you, or *is it*?"

"*Memphis,* are you *kidding* me! Let me tell you something, Maggie, and it's the truth. To be perfectly honest with you, I'm beginning *not* to like Memphis anymore, well, *much* anyway. Lately, I've actually thought of getting away from here, totally, to somewhere other than here and the only reason I haven't, maybe, is Josey. With all that's happened, the turmoil of sorts, the hounding I've been getting about running for office and *now,* the Visual threat, my future. Maybe Memphis has run its course for me, and *yes*, believe it, you've *actually* headed into territory, conversationally, where I've been in my thinking for a while, and if that makes you mighty perceptive, then Maggie McConnell, that's *exactly* what you might be, which begs the question, how do you do that, with me, be so perceptive, almost ahead of me, I mean?"

Finally, Maggie realized she had found a link. Perceptive she did not claim to be, however, many thoughts *had* crossed her mind over the past many days, and certainly since their romantic weekend getaway, their making love. She in fact wanted him right now, at this very moment, as they sat and talked in the outside patio. Unintended, lust had now entered her thoughts. Her only hope, indeed, wish, in that department was, under the circumstances, but *not* under the same roof where Josey and Amy were, that the clandestine midnight rendezvous that Steve had alluded to might still be something they could share. Where, was the mystery? But if not, she'd understand. Casting wishes aside, for now, conversation was their only shared interaction.

"No matter your decision, Steve, I *know,* and *you do*, too, *Josey* will be your number one deal breaker in any direction in *every* way. Her well being and safety, her school and future, her life and what's ahead, and what might be best for both of you at least until she is of age, whatever that turns out to be scholastically, after high school, *that* will be your priority, and believe me, with no insight in having children, I've seen and heard plenty, every day, in my doll store. It's a big old wild and wonderful world and I've seen many a child grow up right in front of my eyes, including one's from happy family life, to divorced, to temporary split ups and so on, even in another's passing, and do you know what, they *all* make it for the best part, and *especially* the parent's. Let me add, owning a store, especially a destination store such as doll stores are today given there are so few of them, I have been exposed to more than I can recollect, and the *nice* part, it's a feel-good to share in so many people's lives. And Steve, another point, and think about it, that's *precisely* how you and I met, and Josey. As I've said, my doll store is a destination, you all came to me, remember? Having said that, whether you see it as pontificating, grandstanding, preaching, or simply talking, the truth is, for me, I'm so glad we met and I must say, equally true, I *love* sitting here, sharing with you so many things about a future, *yours*, a direction, an overview about life…it's exhilarating to me and I can only thank you for thinking of me, inviting me here for Josey's birthday. Did I tell you that yet, already, today, I really don't remember, and it would be awfully remiss of me if I didn't?"

Steve Frankston was momentarily, without words to respond. Absorbing all Maggie had said, he knew one thing for sure, for the most part; it was all basically true and carried with it a lot of common sense. He doubted he could have expressed it any better when it came to the place and position he was currently in, accepting, also, it would take a little more time to embrace it all, however, in his mind, he was prepared to, unequivocally. Clearly, without intending to, in the subtlest of ways, Maggie had also made him very aware that he was falling for her more and more each time they met.

Sitting as they were, in momentary silence, looking around and about him, his eyes always coming back to her, little did she know how much he wanted to take her in his arms to hold and kiss her, and let her take him to places he longed to be, to help him cast aside the many thoughts of doubt in his mind, about where he, *they,* might go from here. He so wanted to make love to her, right were they were, outside, under the stars, in the glow of a hazy yellow half moon that shone its light over them both. However, it could never be; they couldn't; but for the children. Devilishly, a slight grin began to spread across his face. Maggie noticed.

"You're *smiling,* Steve! Would you like to share it?" she asked inquisitively.

"*Two* things, Maggie. *One,* you being here for the party, I couldn't have wished for a better person to be with me and to be here, for Josey, and *secondly,* if you actually knew what I was *really* thinking a moment ago, I mean, the smile I guess that gave me away, you might *actually* want to slap my face, so I'd best leave that answer alone."

"*Really,* Steve Frankston, *slap your face?"*

"Yes, *really,* Margaret 'Maggie' McConnell, *slap* my face, *yes,* that's what I said!"

"Then maybe we've both had the same thoughts I might believe, and maybe you might need to slap mine, too, *so,* when do we begin the slapping?" It was a moment of fun and frivolity that brought forth much laughter.

Steve moved from his chair toward her, and with his hands and arms outstretched, motioned for her to take his embrace. Willingly, she fell into him. Pulling her closer, harder into his body, they kissed. Wonderful as it felt, safe as she felt, as Maggie knew she was, without hesitation, quickly, she also pulled away.

"I hate the thought of it, Steve, but I am *so* aware of our surroundings and I know how a little girl might feel, or react, if she happened to walk into this right now, I'm sorry, but I think it's the right thing to do."

"It's *me,* really, Maggie, *I* was the problem, the instigator, and you're absolutely correct! More of that female logic I fear but also the sensitive caring in you. I love it!"

They retreated back to their chairs, both looking at each other, both smiling *'the naughty person'* grin that immediately turned into more carefree laughter.

"Ain't life grand? Two grown ups acting like teenagers. I never thought I'd feel it again, or see it, *well,* that's from *my* side, anyway."

"Me neither, Steve, but I *love* it, and I love…" she paused. He looked at her. "…And I love…" she blinked her eyelids rapidly, "…And I love you, being here with you. There, I've said it again, and I *do,* it's true!"

She hoped he might have grasped her *real* meaning about love and not of their implied *'lust.'*

In that same moment she instantly flashbacked back to her arrival in Memphis, coming to the party, seeing Steve and Josey at the entrance gate, where they had waited for her to deplane. Josey was all smiles, running up to her after managing to get into a clearway from other passengers. Instantly, her arms reached out for Maggie, who in turn, embraced her, lifting her high into the air before gently guiding her back to terra firma, *'I've missed you Maggie'* were her first words spoken. Steve could see, again, the immediate connection, as if mother to daughter, and yet, this time, he was able to handle it better, accept the link, and marvel at how his little girl could embrace another, as if second nature, and maybe it was.

To say Maggie was nervous, initially, it would have been true and she felt it. Unsure of what to expect, in every way, there had been a degree of trepidation in her coming to Memphis, as this would not only be the first time on the Frankston's home turf, but also, the first time she would see, and share, first hand, *where* and *how* Steve and Josey lived, and in many ways, it could be perceived as, *'hallowed ground'*, a place where Angelic once walked and shared. *That*, in many ways, would, or could, not only be difficult, but also cloud her thinking about reality, and past life. But in fairness, wisely, Maggie had already reconciled and mulled over, correctly, someday it had to happen, and that maybe sooner than much later was the better way. She had no qualms in making the trip, that was a given, believing passionately she also had the ability to handle it, however it played out in real terms. She was about to find out!

"Let's go home, shall we, and Maggie, *'welcome to Memphis,'* our town this time and as you'll see, not *quite* Dunbridge."

It had been a beautiful welcome, after too long, one she'd remember always. Next came their home in Whitehaven. Simple enough in a very spacious way, rambling as a first visual, Steve's low set home was surrounded by Sycamore trees that looked spectacular, full of sundrenched shiny green leaves. The grounds, in every direction, had a landscaped look that gave the property a postcard picture view of *'welcome'*. Four bedrooms, three bathrooms, a living room area that was simple and functional, it was the kitchen that brought the *'wow'* factor to the initial walk through. With the finest of granite for bench tops and the all steel kitchen appliances indicated, maybe, this was a man who either loved to cook, or, it was standard equipment when he bought the place. As Maggie recalled, the former might be more the reason; Steve had already endeared himself as a self-proclaimed chef extraordinaire, almost, as he helped prepare Josey's birthday party. Portraying the way it would, or should be, Steve had not only been the *'guide'* as they wandered through the house showing Maggie around, he had also motioned, carefully, and with the utmost of consideration, *'Maggie's room'* for the weekend. Josey, meanwhile, as *'guide assistant'*, went to great lengths to show Maggie how bouncy her bed was while telling her, much to her father's delighted horror, that they had bought a new comforter only yesterday, especially for the occasion of her visit. It was a matching *'flowers and leaves'* color to complement the wall, a very light green texture, and the lampshades, also a subtle green. As Maggie told Josey, *'I'm impressed, thank you.'* Josey hugged her as she jumped off the bed, *'you're welcome Maggie'* she replied, with a light giggle. Steve looked at Maggie, who looked at Josey, who looked at Daddy. "C'mon you two, there's plenty of time to see the rest of the house, I've got chores to do."

"But, Daddy," Josey almost demanded, "You forgot to tell Maggie that you picked the flowers in here from the garden this morning, especially for her, remember? You said ladies love flowers and Maggie should have some of the ones you grew, remember?"

Maggie had noticed the beautiful roses in a vase on the bedside table, also two huge hibiscuses in the bathroom, one red, one yellow. She loved them. They certainly added to the beauty of the overall decoration. Knowing what she now did, they were immediately *'extra'* special. Steve, meanwhile, caught off guard, looked at Maggie, and while lifting his shoulders as if in a shrug, with a smile seemed to explain, "Why, yes, I did, but that was between you and me, little Miss troublemaker!"

"Thank you, Steve, that was very sweet, and touching, too," Maggie shared, truthfully, "and thank *you*, Josey, for telling me, they're quite beautiful."

Exposed big time, Steve steered them both for the back-screened patio where the Quartermaine family and others had already gathered, ready to help with the move outside for the days event, under the decorated tent. Amy and Josey, meanwhile, headed elsewhere; there was a need for Josey to share with Amy her birthday presents, the best one being; her very own iPad tablet.

Quiet for the past few moments, as Steve had noticed, he released Maggie from her wandering trance with a simple question.

"Would you like another glass of wine?" he asked, low key in tone.

His voice almost startled her. She shook her head, wondering how long she had been in what might have seemed *'another world.'*

"Oh, sorry, but aaahh yes, I would, actually," aware now her mind had obviously been elsewhere, but then noticed immediately, what was *his* almost vacant look.

"Steve, are you okay? You're *staring,* do I sense something, like *serious* thoughts. Are *you okay*?"

Again, he saw just how perceptive this lady was with him, as if she could read his mind, and yes, serious thoughts were running through his mind. Was it time, or more important, was it the place, even, for him to be brutally honest with her, to share some inner held *'guarded secrets'*. Or should he reserve for a different time, although, maybe, not place? He wasn't sure, and yet, she knew, instinctively, something was on his mind. He weighed his odds!

From Maggie's point of view, always, she felt she could handle anything, anytime it came at her, and yet, this time, she belatedly believed, it may *not* be the case. She erred on the side of extreme caution, given the circumstances. Quickly, she answered her own question, circumventing, what might be. But then again, maybe, a few of her own observations might be timely? She proceeded anyway.

"Steve, if there's *one* thing I've learned in these thirty-something years of mine, it's that there comes a time to *seriously* contemplate where one might want to be, and what one might *want* out of life. I *hear* you right now, and I sense, or see, melancholy, which I *love* in a man, however, melancholy can be a substitute for holding back, being reticent about expressing oneself out of fear, an unknown. Accepting that, if *that's* the case, quite simply, *because* I am so happy and content right now just to be with you, I have a need to suggest that maybe tomorrow would be the more perfect time for us to pick up where we left off a short while ago. Today, and now tonight, has been *so* nice, and *so* pleasurable, I'd rather it remain you and me. And I say it for no other reason than I sense, as I've said, a brooding melancholy in you. With *so* much that was *so* incredibly different today and so well done, clearly, you excelled in putting together a celebration. With no offence intended, let's take it for what it's been, a truly marvelous day, and for now, evening as well. And yes, now that you've asked, going back to your original question, yes, please, I would like another wine. Is that okay?"

"*Yep!*" Steve responded, matter of factly. "*Yep!* I'll go get it! I'll be right back."

With an obvious frown, a sense of admonishment, a scowl, even, and a heave of apparent frustration from being, nicely, he felt, *'shut-down,'* he moved from his chair heading straight for the kitchen. Maggie, not missing the body language, could only sigh. *'Oh dear! That didn't go down too well, I fear.'*

Sitting alone, looking up at the heavens and seeing the same stars in the same black velvet sky, the same moon and its glow as they both had only moments ago, now, a slight sense of despair began to overtake her. *'What is it,'* she wondered; *'this man, who is so charismatic and delightful one minute, how is it that he can be so shaken or distant, the next? And tonight of all nights!'* She accepted, what he'd been through in life already was enough to challenge any man, but the man *she* knew now, and had come to know so far, who seemed to have so much more drive, gusto, and inner strength, left her asking, *'what was it, what is it, that has the ability to allow a display of mild disagreement to overwhelm?'*

She felt she wasn't far away from finding out!

Inside, pouring the wine, Steve Frankston thrashed all he had just listened to over in his head, concluding, there's always a time and place. Unquestionably, he loved the fact that Maggie McConnell was with him, in his home, *that,* he was quite sure of. Since the day they'd first met she had never failed to brighten his every moment in thought, his every moment in wonderment about where life might lead, and it was amazing to him, how new love can lift a spirit when least expected. Today, and tonight had been no different. Maggie had been exemplary in every way amongst what had been, mostly, strangers, to her. Nothing had fazed her in any way. Unquestionably, she was very much a people person and he loved her being in his very presence; she was, as always, a joy to behold. Which brought him full circle in his head of what he was thinking. Was it painfully clear?

Upset, miffed, hurt, and more, he may be in what Visual Communications might *want* or expect of him, and angry as he may be in why there might be a selfish motive for *'others'* to want to lure him in directions he wasn't prepared for, or even wanted to go, referencing politics, but why was it in this very instance… in his own home, immersed, in a most beautiful way with a most gorgeous woman who clearly loved and cared about only him, and little Josey…that he was steering toward harsh words, even an argument, and over, *what*? What was he thinking and what is his problem? Everything he wanted he was surrounded by. Why, then, had he acted, reacted, as he did, that could bring forth obvious repercussions, in a peripheral sense, to another, Maggie, now sitting alone outside on the patio and probably wondering the exact same thing? What had *she* done, or what had *she* said, to trigger his actions moments ago? He didn't know, however, there was one thing he did, and that was, he was definitely *not* going to destroy any of it through basic stupidity…his!

Placing the wine back in the fridge, he headed outside again to the one person that had the ability to not only lead him in directions he actually wanted to head and might prefer, the one he and Josey had been traveling, but also, to logically, in conversation, help find the real deep-seated reason for his attitude, just displayed. He accepted, probably, he had a little immediate *'back-peddling'* to do. Maggie was exactly right; life's way too short, not to take chances.

Time for some male recognizance he told himself, and as for chances, he was considering taking one. Well, maybe…in the morning…or some other time?

~~~~~~~~~~
~~~~~~~~~~

CHAPTER TWENTY-FOUR

So, Maggie, as you did the traveling to Memphis, this day is yours. Josey's yesterday, yours today, what would you like to do, see or otherwise? Josey and I are at your beck and call and no stone will be left unturned to make it memorable. Okay? Fire away!" As fast as Steve Frankston had made the offer; the two *'girls'* in his life looked at each other and smiled. Instantly, he realized, they had probably already talked. He was right, they had!

Very aware that it was earlier than what might be considered right, Josey took her chances anyway, gently knocking on Maggie's bedroom door in the hope she would be invited in. Seconds later she heard, *'Come in, Josey.'* Instinctively, Maggie knew. Closing the door quietly behind her she told Maggie, *'Daddy would not be happy with me, I don't think, if he knew that I woke you up to come and visit.'* She was reassured it was okay. Inviting her to sit wherever she liked on the other side of the bed, Josey propped herself up on the pillow she had fluffed up before placing it against the headboard. For the next, almost hour, they talked about, everything! The party, Josey's presents, Amy, her best friend, what it was like at school these days, Dunbridge where Maggie lived, and much to Maggie's delight taking care in her responses, Josey's Daddy, Steve, and how nice he is and the many things they share together, to the obvious; that Josey loved him. Strangely, although Maggie had expected it, no mention was made of Angelic, her Mother. Under the circumstances she decided not to venture there not fully knowing, if she had, how it might affect Josey, or in whatever way. She also did not want the ire of Steve given he might frown, or react adversely on it if it were instigated by her in the first place. Without having to worry about any negatives during the time spent together, Josey became, to Maggie, especially, precious and heart-warming. If two people had a time to bond, unplanned, the past almost sixty-minutes were invaluable. However, Maggie was cognizant of one very special subject not raised by Josey. Either an oversight or untimely, she brought the matter up on an absolute *'need-to-know'* basis. It was important!

"So, Josey, while I'm here, you know we should take a look at 'Angel', don't you agree? She needs to be mended and you told me many times you couldn't wait, so maybe today will be the day, if, of course, it's possible. Unfortunately, I didn't bring my *'Doll-Doctor'* hospital emergency bag with me so I mightn't be able to, but we should try, *shouldn't* we?"

"Yes, Maggie, and thank you. I was hoping you would ask me to be honest because Daddy said I was *not* to, while you were here, as this was a special visit for my birthday, but he *did* say it was all right if you brought it up, and could do it, so *yes*. I've been *so* worried she'll never be fixed. I miss not being able to pick her up and hold her and play with her."

"Then we'll do that after I get up and shower and get ready for today, for whatever we, your Daddy that is, might have planned for us all. Do *you* know what we're doing or if there's something in mind already in play, maybe?"

"No, I don't, Maggie. Daddy says that he'd let you decide whatever you want to do and I agreed with him.

You've come a long way to be here so he wants to do what *you* want to. That was the plan, the way he said it, that's all I know. He did say you'd probably thought about a little."

"Oh dear, that might be a little hard because I don't know what's here in Memphis except the second most visited house in America, Graceland, but you've probably seen that a hundred times living here, unless you don't know about Graceland, being so young. It's funny really, I never thought much about that before."

"C'mon, Maggie, of course I know about it, everyone does who lives in Memphis. But to tell you the truth, no, I haven't actually been there. Daddy has and he's always said, someday, he'll take me but so far he hasn't and anyway, it doesn't *really* matter, I mean, I don't *know* his songs 'cause he'd be pretty old. What about you, though, do you know any of the songs, or know *who* Elvis Presley is?"

"Truthfully, Josey. When I was born, he had already died. I didn't know his music or films, but everyone's parents did, and that's how I found out about him. And of course, still to this day, everyone hears about him and the radio plays his music, and the TV his movies and people come to Memphis every year to visit his house and his grave, and all that, so we all know *something,* and having said that, maybe now I'm here, and you haven't been to Graceland, what say we go there, Graceland? Would *you* like that, maybe?"

"Yes, Maggie, actually, I think I would, with you. Then we'd be going somewhere together, both us for the first time, that's pretty *exciting,* I think!"

"Okay, but Josey, listen to me, we'd better let your Daddy ask us first, don't you think, and when he does, then we can agree with him and then it'll be like, spontaneous."

"What does *spontaneous* mean, Maggie?"

"It's like, er, an immediate, fast reaction to something, like both of us saying to Daddy *'yes'* when the idea about going to Graceland comes up, especially if he mentions it first. Then we both simply agree, together that is. That's what spontaneous is, what it means."

"Oh, okay, that's fun, like a game. We'll do it that way and then we'll all go to Graceland, it'll be a nice day, I bet." She paused a moment. "Hey, Maggie, you said Graceland was the second most visited house in America, *what's first?"*

"Josey, how could you ask that? I thought they'd teach that to you in school, but obviously not. Anyway, instead of me telling you, why don't you guess instead?"

Now lying flat on her tummy from the bottom end of the bed with her head propped into her clenched hands, under her chin, Josey frowned, as if thinking hard. She was staring at Maggie who was still under the covers, the sheet pulled up and over her. Staring back at her, "C'mon, it's obvious…" she chided playfully, "…you *must* know it."

"Maggie! I've got it!" Josey sat bolt upright on the bed. *"The White House."* Maggie nodded her affirmative.

Preparing herself for the day ahead, the shower was the perfect place to think, to reflect last night's self-inflicted torture. Trying to say good night and part from one another from the idyllic atmosphere of where Steve and Maggie had spent almost the entire evening, talking, became a battle, fueled by two bodies who longed for each other. Safe as Josey was in her room, separated as they were from one side of the house to the other, still, under the same roof, in the same house, neither of them wanted to put Josey through what might be *'a difficult mome*nt', if she were to find them, together, compromised by position. They knew the wrong message would be sent and the mental strain of not understanding might be the outcome, and finally, importantly, her Mommy might be gone, but Daddy and Maggie weren't married. To a little girl; shock, horror, difficult to comprehend; they didn't know! Steve led the charge.

"Sorry, Maggie, great as my plans might have been, but you know, it was futile, really. For all the right reasons, we can't, and it tears my heart out, selfishly."

Maggie knew and despite hoping, as expected, common sense and sanity between them prevailed.

"Steve, even if you had felt it to be right and said we'd take our chances, I think I would have said no, anyway, and I'm *glad* you feel the same way. I could *never,* in any way feel comfortable, and I doubt you could either, so we'll do what's right, however, like you, and I freely admit it with all my heart, I *so* want you, again, and yes, it's a kind of torture which makes us *more* than bad, *doesn't it?"*

Both managed a light laugh, not only of the comment, but also the predicament.

"Too much going on, Maggie...well, many things anyway, and I feel good about them all, however, there is one thing you should know apart from my already huge appreciation for your coming to Memphis."

Maggie looked at him, sheepishly, hoping that whatever it was, it would be nice.

"Unquestionably, you were a *highlight* in every way," he told her, "not only Josey, but to *me,* especially. And to my friends, they *loved* you and thought you were a sweetheart.

The Quartermaine's actually hope we can catch up again but I've already said no-go!"

Maggie was thrilled. Not that it was difficult being surrounded by strangers at a function, but more, that she was accepted so readily, it was a nice feeling.

"Thank you, Steve, I'm touched, and pleased, too. I liked them but there'll be another time, hopefully."

Holding each other in an embrace that was the epitome of careful *'friendship'* only, Steve could still feel the electricity of excitement and anticipation running through his entire body. The closeness of Maggie, to him, was a thrill beyond anything he had known, lately. And the silent bonus: his mind was telling him, *'You love being with her, she's contagious. Maybe you should never let her go again, ever.'* Difficult as he thought it might be, he agreed. He chose his next words with care, knowing, honesty had to prevail.

"Every time I *see* you, or *think* of you, and *every* conversation we have, more so lately, together, or on the phone, I feel you *consuming* me, and today, tonight, I doubt we could get much closer, in mind and soul at least. You're making me mighty happy, Maggie, to a level I doubt we'll escape from, and soon, we'll reach a bigger crossroad than the one that's already ahead I'd believe, and all I can say is, I hope you feel the way I do, because things are getting tougher, Miss *'Magnet'* McConnell…" they both smiled, corny as it was. He hadn't finished, "…without a doubt, Maggie, I want more of you in my life, so the question is, do you think you can *handle* it, or *me* for that matter, and Josey too? *Can you?"*

Every word spoken was music to Maggie's ears, she couldn't have been happier.

"If you *only* knew, Steve Frankston, if you *only* knew!" she confirmed in answer to his direct question. "If *you* think I'm a magnet to you, then let me qualify; I am *so* drawn to you it's like I *can't* see your face soon enough. You make me *so* happy and believe me when I tell you that I want to share me with you in every way, and I can only say in absolute honest reply, I am *so touched, thrilled,* to know you feel even *half way* similarly about me, and *yes,* as tonight might confirm, we might have some talking to do, whether it's here in Memphis, Dunbridge, or on top of the Empire State Building. And *one other* thing, when it comes to Josey, *please,* let me tell you, I *so* adore her, *so* love her in my own way, she single-handed helps make me one *incredibly* happy lady and *nothing* will give me greater delight than to share in her growing up, as friends, or…or…*whatever*?"

"I think, somehow, Maggie, the feeling is mutual in *her* to *you*. And that's nice. And *that* sure makes me feel good."

But now, it was time. The night was over. Their short and simple goodnight kiss, after all the lights were turned off inside the house, could only ever have been witnessed by *'anyone'*, if that *'anyone'* happened to be around, and even then it would have been in the soft glow of the night-lights that came on automatically. And Josey, they knew, was in bed. Sweet, caring, loving, the final words spoken as their hands left each other's touch; 'Goodnight Maggie and thank you'. 'Goodnight Steve, you're very special; you know that, don't you? Sweet dreams.'

Graceland was an unbelievable experience, for Josey, for her Father, but especially for Maggie. Having heard about the iconic landmark for so many years, to be there, to walk the grounds, to be inside the house, to see all the trophies, awards and finally, the gravesite where Elvis Presley and his mother, Gladys, and father, Vernon, and his twin brother who died at birth, Jesse Garon, who most had never even heard about, were buried; it was mystical, ethereal, and somber, all wrapped in one. How could one man have achieved so much, to have been such an icon, a changer of life itself for a generation of impressionable youth; it was unimaginable! Josey's mild fascination for the man and his achievements was for no real reason at all other than to be with her Father, and share with Maggie, who was mesmerized by Graceland, and the individual, which in turn, actually made her pay more attention on where they were and all they were experiencing for the bigger picture of how Elvis and Memphis were forever interlocked. Steve, meanwhile, had a closely held silent reminisce of being at the much visited home once before, with Angelic. Her many shared Elvis Presley stories, her parents, too, all came back to him. But that was then. He chose to play it all down, to share with genuine enthusiasm, Maggie's wonderment of the historic venue in its entire splendor. Regardless, it was eerily de'ja'vu for him.

Elvis Presley bought the home in 1957 at the height of his early career and paid, it is documented, approximately $100,000.00 for the property. Located nine miles south of the city of Memphis, Graceland, sits high up on a hill on 13.8-acres at 3764 Elvis Presley Boulevard (Highway 51) and a mere four miles from the Mississippi border, the State he was actually born in. It was once, the home of S.C. Toof, a former pressroom foreman for the Memphis Daily Appeal newspaper. He named the grounds, then, a 500-acre farm established during the American Civil War (1861 – 1865), for his daughter, Grace who later inherited it. In 1939, Grace Toof's niece, Ruth and her husband, Dr. Thomas Moore, rebuilt the mansion to the Colonial Revival Style, as it stands and looks, currently. Today, a museum, enjoyed by millions, Graceland, a large twenty-three room white-columned mansion, built of Tennessee tan limestone with two large lions placed on both sides of the portico, was opened to the public in June, 1982, listed in the National Register of Historic Place in November, 1991 and declared a National Historic Landmark in March, 2006.

By the time Maggie left Graceland, a whole new appreciation for her, of the man, his life and times, was realized. Openly holding hands as they left the guided tour, Josey loved to see her Father happy, and if it took their trip to Graceland to bring a little more out in him when it came to his overall happiness and sharing, *she,* more than anyone may have ever suspected, was feeling the day was already a winner. Josey, of course, really liked Maggie, too, and being a part of going where Maggie had wanted to, as they had surreptitiously talked about earlier that morning, she asked the obvious question, not truthfully telling her or her Father, that nice as it was, she'd had enough!

"Did you enjoy coming here, Maggie?"

"Oh, Josey, let me tell you, I *did,* I *really* did. It was so much more than I ever expected."

"And the highlights?" Steve queried of her, seriously wanting to know.

"Simple. The beautiful chandelier in the dining room, the gold trimmed furniture, the incredible stained glass windows featuring colorful peacocks in the design, the painting of Elvis at the foot of the stairs and *whoa,* wasn't he one handsome young man back then?" she added with a smile, looking directly at Steve. "Shall I go on?"

"I don't *think* so, Maggie," he replied, nicely.

"*Oh,* but let me say one more thing, apart from that I could have stayed there much longer if it were possible, but I would liked to add..."

Josey looked at her Father, who looked at Maggie.

'Okay, Maggie, what *else,* now you're on a roll."

"...I just wanted to say the Meditation Gardens, how *beautiful* it all is, and how *wonderfully* touching that they all, as a family, can be together in such an idyllic surrounding. I *loved* it, a *definitive* highlight, for me!"

Understanding fully, the gushing adoration of the many people they shared the tour with, the Music Room, the walled waterfall in the Jungle Room, the kitchen and his parents bedroom, then on to the Trophy Room, ahead of ending up in the Meditation Gardens, it was, to Maggie, an eye-opener of sheer delight. Gold records by the seeming hundreds, a wide variety of general memorabilia including guns, badges, suits, awards, posters, the displays, all of it, was nothing short of incredible. Then later, back outside, across from the wrought iron Music Gates at the front entrance, to conclude their day and time at Graceland, they all went on board the $250,000.000 private Convair 880 jet, the 'Lisa Marie' that Elvis named for his only child. Small, in many ways by todays current crop of entertainers who travel exclusively in privacy and comfort, the Lisa Marie was a bit of a let down. Nice, the walk through ended rather quickly.

Finally, exhausted from all the walking, stopping, standing and staring, Josey asked *'when do we eat Daddy?'* The answer was *'now'* as they headed off toward their car, preparing to head for the city and downtown Memphis where Steve had promised to take them; their destination - The Peabody Hotel. Dismissing his personal thoughts of it being the location where he was delivered his employment ultimatum, The Peabody Hotel in all its splendor and luxury, was embedded Memphis, and he wanted Maggie's visit to be forever memorable. Also, in walking distance from there, she could see and enjoy another side of Memphis, one that spelt, music and tradition - Beale Street. If there was one thing Steve was going to do, it was to pull out all stops for Maggie, in the hope, if need be, that she could embrace *'all things Memphis'* as in his heart of hearts, he knew, at some stage along everyone's highway in life, a day of reckoning arrives and too many times, when you least expect it. Preparation might be one thing, expecting the unexpected, is another! For now, though, their day of traipsing around as tourists was beginning to wind down.

~~~~~~~~~~
~~~~~~~~~~

CHAPTER TWENTY-FIVE

Josey's highlight of the day had been watching the ducks at The Peabody Hotel. Having never heard of it, let alone see, the twice-daily 11am and 5pm ritual, she and Maggie were enthralled watching the five North American mallards strut their stuff. Brought from the rooftop by elevator, to be released and walk the ground floor carpeted runway to the lobby fountain was quite a sight. Josey, in her element, echoed her delight *'Oh, Maggie, they are soooo cute, so cute. I love them.'* Maggie agreed. Daddy knew he had done well, again. Happy to see his *'girls'* loving the atmosphere, he took photos on his cell phone camera, for posterity. They did, for the record, also visit the famous Sun Recording Studios on Union Avenue, site of where Elvis Presley made his first recordings in 1954, and in particular, the first demonstration acetate he made as a birthday gift for his Mother, Gladys, titled *My Happiness.* Maggie insisted on a photo outside with her and Steve, never knowing when she may be in the city again, if ever! The very thought of *that* becoming a reality sent a *cold* shiver right through her entire body. She shook it off immediately!

Back home again, becoming déjà vu as if it was meant to be, sitting, talking, reminiscing and sharing the quiet downtime over drinks outside, Steve and Maggie were extremely content and easy relaxed comfortable in each others company. After Josey's heartfelt, sincere, and long *'goodnight'*, especially to Maggie, they couldn't help but smile at the fun-filled and loving interaction she had displayed, both agreeing whole-heartedly, when her Father offered, *'I think it's safe to say, she really likes you.'* As she left them to head for her bedroom, Josey looked back, to ask if Maggie would come and say goodnight again before she went to sleep. Incredibly touched, her rapid answer was a very reassuring *'of course!'*

"What *have* you done, Maggie?" Steve asked, with Josey now gone. "*You're* getting more attention than *me* lately. Do *you* two have a secret pact or something?"

"*Oh,* Steve, she's being a girl, that's all, you should *know* that! Little girls like other *'girls,'* me for now albeit older, or maybe she misses not having someone to share with, here at the house, I don't know. To me, though, I *love* it and I'll shower her with whatever I can give and whatever she likes all day long with your approval. Children *deserve* happiness in life and you *certainly* live up to that part of the deal, from what I've seen. And to *reassure* you, Steve, a Daddy will *always* be Daddy, no one will *ever* take that away, and *certainly* not from Josey, as I see it with you both, so don't worry, I'm just a temporary diversion this weekend, she'll settle into her routine again after tomorrow."

The words *'temporary diversion'* hit him as a hurricane might. Simple as they were in conversation, many a true word is spoken in jest and Steve heard it loud and clear. Maybe there was an element of *truth* in it, as Maggie sees it, or might believe, he thought. It didn't matter, though, he knew he had to, for his own sake, dispel the thought as it was suggested and bring some clarity to her of his true feelings. She deserved it and equally important, he was *not* about to let her out of his life, period, *that* he *knew*! Something had to give and maybe it was time to set some new wheels in motion, and unlike yesterdays, or last night's interaction, if tonight was as good as any, then…then…he was in a quandary. Accepting that Josey loved this lady, a situation that was becoming painfully clear, then she, too, would *hate* for Maggie not to remain a part of her life, innocent as she might be to the feelings of adults when it came to mutual attraction and matters of the heart, or a more than burgeoning *'love affair.'* He turned to look at Maggie. Oblivious as she was to his inner thoughts, as he did, she couldn't help but think to herself, as she had many times before, how far they had come since that first day in her store, to this moment, and all the water that had flowed under those same respective bridges. There was no doubt in her mind, every day, she loved him more, and as Steve looked her way, if it were possible, his boyish smile melted her heart that much more than yesterday. Having shared the most entertaining of days with him, and Josey, Maggie's nagging thoughts reverberated in her head; *'What's going to happen when I have to leave him, again? It gets harder each time, and I hate it! And then there's Josey, too.'*

"What is it, Steve?" she asked.

There it was again, he marveled; Maggie's female perception of him. Deflecting his momentary real thoughts in his answer, he spoke from the heart.

"I was just thinking how beautiful you always are," he replied, trying to be nonchalant. "And *what* a day, one of the *nicest* I've had, and shared in a long time, well, here in *Memphis* anyway," he added, not forgetting Lake Pontchartrain that reminded him instantly of their tryst and how memorably beautiful that time was also. "You're *incredible* and to be honest, I find it hard to believe I ever found you, and now, I'm finding it harder again to think about you leaving me, tomorrow, it's awful! My heart may even break a little, I fear."

Maggie McConnell couldn't believe what she had just heard. Was that Steve Frankston telling her that he felt *exactly* the same she did of him? If yes, she wanted to hear more. Totally unaware, he obliged

"Just thinking about taking you back to the Memphis Airport almost makes me want to…shudder," he confessed. "To say nothing of Josey and it seems to me…"

Suddenly, Maggie's hand went into the air, her index finger protruding firm. There was something she had to do.

"Hold the thought, Steve, speaking of Josey, I have an appointment, remember, and I *can't* let Miss Josey down?"

Not really wanting to, terrible timing, she knew, Maggie jumped out of her chair to head inside and Josey's bedroom. It was too late! Josey must have been more than tired, and after the hectic day they had all put in she was probably quite exhausted. In the less than ten minutes of '*goodnight*' to now, she was sound asleep. Maggie straightened her top blanket, moving it away from being too tight under her chin, then leaned down to kiss her cheek wishing her a *'sweet dreams little girl.'* Before leaving the room, she turned to look back at her, silently making her own wish as she did. The soft pink nightlight was just bright enough for her to glance around the room, and with a smile, remember, the joy of being a little girl, who is loved.

'I don't *doubt* it,' was Steve's reaction when being given an update of why back so fast.

Long as the day had been, or appeared to be, it was still relatively early by the time they had arrived home, and with

Josey fed and off to bed early, for Maggie and Steve, the night was still young. First, though, a light snack for them; a chicken-avocado club sandwich was the verdict and with that thought, Maggie headed for the kitchen insisting it was her turn to be the culinary chef!

In her absence, in the silence of sitting alone, Steve had time to get his head together and process all he felt he wanted to say and share when she returned and with a myriad of thoughts rushing through his active mind, the period of solace was long enough for him to decide that tonight was as good as any to reveal a little more of what he was thinking, wanted, and, *maybe, where* he was going in his life, especially with the choices he was soon going to have to make; politics or graphic-design? Maggie, in his life, had become a high priority, he knew it, however, torn inwardly, the nagging voices in his head constantly led to one thing; if Maggie was the best thing to have happened to him in such a long time, then what could pose any problem between them? His deepest concern was not so much Maggie per se, her feeling toward him, it was the oft times talked about, time and distance – Memphis, Tennessee and Dunbridge, Florida. He silently wished she lived in Memphis; it would be all so much easier, while Florida, could he live there, *again*? Did he *want* to, even? And my job, such as it may turn out to be, what then? And Maggie has a retail business, a highly successful one, so what of Maggie and *her* concerns? *All,* were fair questions. Selfishly torn might have been one way to describe his personal feeling, his jumbled, muddled mind; torn twixt and between might be the other more accurate, apt way.

Confused, looking toward the heavens and the many stars that twinkled brightly, suddenly, a huge, fast moving shooting star made a rapid-fire streak through the already picturesque night sky. Was that an omen, he wondered, a sign, *my* signal to wish upon a star, wanting its blessing, confirmation? Taking a positive stance, he closed his eyes, and did, anyway.

Seconds later, Maggie came through the screen doors with a cheery, bright smile and a double plate of…whatever it might have been she had finished up making. Placing the plate on the patio table, as promised, chicken-avocado it was, along with two beers. It looked sumptuous!

"*There,* Mr. Frankston. Dinner for two and liquid refreshments to wash it down, and *yes,* I'm going to join you in a beer this time, I feel like one, I hope you do, too!"

"You're *quite* the chef by the looks of it, handy in a kitchen also, nice!"

Maggie looked directly at him, tipped her head to one side, lifted an eyebrow and smiled. She took the remark as he might have intended it to be, a compliment.

Making light idle conversation while they enjoyed their snack came easy. Memphis, its attributes and pitfalls, the Mississippi River and how long is it, as in, where does it actually start to ending in New Orleans, the blues musically and the origins Memphis gave the world with it, to finally, what is it with all the damaging storms and tornadoes of late? The topics were simple, the interaction, equally stimulating. They had much in common, their conversation flowed, their comfortability with each other, a given. Taking a moment to excuse herself Maggie went inside, returning a few minutes later. Sitting back down, she surprised him, *'Josey is still sound asleep, hasn't moved at all.'* Her words, her actions, impressed Steve big time. *'How thoughtful'* he silently acknowledged, *'thinking of Josey, checking in on her, concerned.'* Again, he marveled at the lady sitting with him, she truly was, a gift. Moving from his seat, without a single word he leaned down and kissed her lightly on the lips before withdrawing. Maggie looked up at him, pleasantly surprised. Not one to miss the moment, he leaned down again and repeated his actions only this time lingering longer and with a little more passion. To her dismay, he then returned to his chair.

"*Wow*! You can do *that* anytime given the small rush I feel…" she told him, adding, "…but what brought *that* on, Steve, and *don't* tell me, my *stunning* good looks or whatever it was you said last time when the unexpected happened? *That's* redundant!"

"I love you, Maggie, and somehow, right now, I wanted to show you, a kiss was my only option."

"*Steve*! Do *you* realize what you're saying, I mean, has that beer gone to your head *already*? The romantic in you is bursting through, but don't get me wrong, I *love* that you love me, you can tell me as often as you want to, okay?"

"Then I will, I love you, Maggie McConnell, and I'd say it again if that were your wish."

Maggie's reaction was instantaneous. Following his lead, this time it was *her* turn to move from *her* chair to sit in *his* lap and while wrapping her arms around him, she had no compunction but to kiss him, with guarded passion, directly on the lips.

"I love you, too, Steve, and have for so long now, it seems and I couldn't wait to know if you felt the same way or how much and I can't begin to tell you how you've turned my world upside down, but I like it and I love you, too, I *do*!"

Withdrawing slightly, Maggie chose to stay sitting right where she was. Something told her Josey would not be walking in on them anytime soon or at least she hoped not! Tantalizingly playful, her loving smile contagious, beaming from ear to ear, he kissed her again, but on the cheek this time. As he did, expectedly, he felt a surge in his body. Difficult to do, he contained himself, regardless.

"I guess we have to chat, huh?" he suggested.

"We said that last night as I recall," Maggie reminded him, "but we knew it then, and still do, and we can, anytime. I'll always be ready because, believe me, being with you, Steve, for a while, at least, my life seems more settled, and for that, thank you. You've brought a peaceful calm to me."

It wasn't a question, or an answer, it was an emotional feeling, and for Maggie, it had been mounting for so long, it seemed, tonight was meant to be. Knowing now, how Steve and Josey lived, and where, and seeing how their daily lives are handled, the closeness of everything they do, alone or together, it was a thrill to be able to put it all in the one so called *'pot'* and see how it all mixes up. Coming here, Maggie told herself, to Memphis, had been the icing on the cake, Josey's birthday weekend would never be forgotten. Their love, from being contained to emerging from slowly to more and more, was now, seemingly, out in the open for the world to see. Even to Josey! The next three hours flew by.

While physical and emotional interactions were held in check, head longing to the forefront from both their points of view, the time honored; what, why, when, and where questions, emerged, and with them, degrees of complication.

The *'what'* was simple; what brought them together, what are they thinking – fate, and they love each other. Let's work it out was easy to declare. The *'why'* was a no brainer! When two people love each other, it's irrelevant and therefore becomes a *'why not?'* With so much in common, in so many ways, why *wouldn't* they share more, together? The *'when'* was a two-fold? When did they know, or when do they share a life with each other, permanently? They agreed, they knew pretty quickly when the chemistry started - the day they met. Much else was left open-ended, to another time. Finally, the *'where?'* That was a conundrum of magnitude that never found a resolve. There were huge plusses and negatives that pulled in every direction. The main thing agreed on, an open dialog was in play, and early as it might be in the game of love and happiness, a resolve could be found, and would? However, it *did* cause the most consternation of the night.

"Steve, I love you and happily say so, but allow me to say something I feel is important. You see, I'm *very* conscious about Josey, and she can't be *'sprung'* about this. *How* we go about telling her, getting her involved in a direct or indirect way is very important, I don't have to tell you *that*. Bottom line is, you're her Father, and to me, the whole thing, to the biggest and best part is your call, the *how* you want to tell her, and the *right* way you think it will be handled. Believe me, I will bow to whatever and will get only as involved as you choose for me to be, is that okay, agreed?"

"It *is*, Maggie, and thank you, but then again, here's *my* take on it given I've already thought about it. The way I see it is, we either *low* key it short term for now only, or, alternatively, *find* our solutions first to the challenges we have, and *then*, embrace her from there. That said, we can, of course, have a conversation about it as early as tomorrow, with Josey, and share openly with her our feelings, some we've declared tonight, even. My instinct tells me she'll be happy no matter what or how we put it, and frankly, it wouldn't surprise me if she doesn't have more questions, some we mightn't have thought of, she is nine now, remember, and young kids have plenty on their minds."

It had sounded to Maggie as if Steve supported talking with Josey immediately, and as much as she would like that, her female logic was still very much in play. Heart over mind was easy, common sense and reality was harder to come by. She was *equally* aware; Josey's first and maybe prime concern would no doubt be, *where*? Her future was at stake, also. Another important point to consider was, *how* vocal would Josey be about it, if at all?

"Yes, I know, she's getting so grown up now and in her own inimitable way it's lovely to see and interact with her, but Steve, it's kind of *scary* too, *don't* parents *always* want kids to be kids for as long as they can keep them there?"

While nodding his head, agreeing, other issues, big ones, sprang to mind.

"Something *else*, Steve," Maggie continued. "*Odd* as it may sound, not to be taken the wrong way, but let's be specific, almost *blunt* if you will about a couple of things, and believe me, it's *all* relevant, maybe, even, *paramount*."

Maggie was hoping she wasn't plunging headlong in to dangerous waters, but more, heading in the right direction of conversation, in reality, of common sense communication. What she and Steve had undertaken tonight was as serious a pathway as two people could *ever* walk down, but clearly, there were flaws, personal issues that had the potential to become explosive, in time, if not dealt with, now, or certainly in the very near future. As she saw it, an awful lot was at stake for both of them, all in the name of love, and as openly declared this very evening, building day by day. Also, two *other* decisions were getting crucially, if not already, critically close to *'high priority'*. He had *not* decided, yet, whether to stay with Visual Communications, a Company that not only paid exceptionally well but also had a future he was secure in, including stock and profit sharing. Then there was the so called *'pending'* decision to be drafted, through increasing pressure being placed on him, to a career in politics, to stand for a seat available in the Mid-Term elections in Tennessee for the House of Representatives, to Congress. His personal aggravation; choosing a political run through a major conflict of interest, he would be immediately released from Visual Communication, his employer. Adding to the woes of decision-making, going the political route, a failure to be elected by the people of Tennessee, he would then be *out* of a job, *any* job, *period*! Then, what?

Not by calculated design, however, wittingly, or otherwise, Maggie McConnell had, in all fairness of their transparency, placed his two-folded dilemma, his *personal* challenge, honestly and openly back out on the table. '*Was that a good move,'* she wondered? Would she live to regret it, maybe? It didn't matter. It was too late!

Emotionally, long after midnight, they said their heartfelt and gut wrenching *'goodnight'* to each other, the same way they had the night before, although this time, there was a little tension in the late night air, too. Finalizing nothing of real substance, they had agreed, for now, the first and major point of the long night's conversation, low key it a little longer, tomorrow was a new day and who knows, they may have a change of heart, and if so, *then* would be the more apropos time to announce their more concrete plans.

In parting, nothing felt as euphoric as their relationship did twenty-four hours ago, in fact, less than even twelve hours ago. As she closed the door to her room, after their quietly spoken '*good-night*', Steve missed the look of sadness on Maggie's face. In the soft glow of the night light and the four walls that surrounded her, from what had been happiness abounding in a house full of love, with regret, it had now become, *'a lonely place to be.'*

~~~~~~~~~~
~~~~~~~~~~

CHAPTER TWENTY-SIX

Ever so quietly, Maggie sobbed herself to sleep. Tossing and turning, she was more than overwhelmed at all of the events that had taken place. The day had been so perfect, in every conceivable way, and the evening, one to be remembered, but now, maybe, for all the wrong reasons! She knew, in her heart of hearts, she may have single-handed, sunk the most wonderful ship she was sailing on, with her one, hashed over in her mind time and time again remark; *'let's be specific, almost blunt, about a couple of things, and believe me, it's all relevant, even paramount.'* From that very moment onward, courageous as they both had been in discussing their possible planned future together, a degree of futility had reared its head. Until difficult key issues were resolved, their love would have to withstand much harder personal challenge, scrutiny, even, if politics became an issue to contend with. Not that Maggie had any *'skeletons in the closet'* she knew. Her life had been, so far, exemplary, and to many, maybe, staid, boring! How easy it would have been, she accepted, to have taken the easy route and gone along with Steve. Talk with Josey in the morning, tell her they were in love and wanted to get married, and they would live…*where*? *That's* when the problem started and when it all got too hard!

In the darkness of night, in a strange room, in a city far away from where she was comfortable, where she knew only two people in the world, Maggie thrashed over in her mind, that very question…*where* would they live if they shared a life together? Would Steve give up all *he* has, with Josey, blindly, to move to a little place in Florida called Dunbridge, to be with a doll lady? And what would *he* do, if they did? And would Josey *hate* leaving her friends, would she *resent* her as fast as she had come to love her for changing her life so dramatically? In the darkness, while Maggie's tears continued to fall, her mind stayed active.

But if she *had* gone along with Steve, after they had talked with Josey, would that mean the onus would fall on *her* for decisions, only to find that the mountain was too high to climb? Would *she,* could *she,* leave all she had built, her doll store, the doll hospital, the security of her very life, and move to Memphis…and if so, to then do…*what*?

And if she and Steve couldn't agree on either direction, would that mean *all* they had shared these past many weeks, or planned for a future, would be cast aside becoming the final straw that ends a beautiful love affair? Would that, then, have been *her* fault, would *she* be the *'spoiler'*, the one who said *'no'*, and by indecisiveness become *'the evil one?'*

The once peaceful harmony and proposed love that had filled their past days and weeks had, seemingly, now, turned to unexpected sorrow, and Maggie had *no* idea how she was going to face Steve Frankston in the morning. And as for Josey, innocent in every way, how would she *ever* understand why Maggie was different? Could she do, as he had suggested, *'low key it a little longer'*, act as if they had never had the conversation and wait for their phone interaction over the next few days, weeks if it turned out that way, for *him* to conclude what *he* wanted to do? Emotionally drained, Maggie drifted in and out sleep, conscious of one thing extremely important to her; the procedure needed to *'repair'* Angel, Josey's broken doll. Immediately, she resolved, first thing in the morning she would go out and secure the necessary materials, if she could find them, and complete the task at hand, and if not, then she would take it back with her to Dunbridge and her hospital and mail it back to Josey within the week. *That* would be a priority, something she *could* do, and with all her heart, dearly wanted to. She also realized, maybe, in full-filling her mission it could also put the makings of *'the beginning to an end'* in play, something, in the bigger picture, she did not want to happen. Casting negative points aside, she remained adamant, wanting nothing more than to honor her pledge to Josey, to her Angel. A little girl needed peace in her life, and small as the issue might seem to many, it would always remain, *huge,* to her. *Why, why, why* was the one word that spun in Maggie's head, over and over, and yet, for all the why's, everything stayed the same; there *were* no simple answers. And with the sun rising tomorrow, that same word would still be there – *why*?

Amidst her sorrow, her heart told her, start the way you plan to finish. She had been right to pose the questions…what was needed now, tomorrow…the next day, whenever, was the right answer. She prayed they'd find one.

~~~~~~~~~~
~~~~~~~~~~

CHAPTER TWENTY-SEVEN

It wasn't the same, Karen, it just wasn't the same," Maggie started. "In *fact*, to really understand it better you *had* to be there and of course, you weren't, and could never have been, but I had to wonder, I mean, *really* wonder, what *was* it about Steve, what *was* it that made him become so indecisively directional down one road, because it made no real sense to me, like, that wasn't *him*, as I *knew* him, and yet, there I was, the way I felt…hung out to dry a little, maybe a whole lot!"

Maggie McConnell, again, was having a one-on-one about the heart, heartstrings, love, and more, with her near and dear friend, Karen Kartney. If one thing remained always consistent about Karen, it would be her ability to listen, and to say nothing, until she either felt she *had* to, or, in this case, until Maggie had talked herself out! Right now, she was rambling along, trying to make sense of how a love affair that was so *right*, so *beautiful*, so *special*, could have, as she now felt, have the potential to go so wrong? She just didn't understand it! None of it made any sense to her, at all.

Steve Frankston, clearly, had disappointed her, just when she was at her most vulnerable and so dizzy in love with him. Hard as it was, deciphering the good from the bad, the wheat from the chaff, with *him* and *his* line of thinking, the even harder part to come grips with concerned his daughter, Josey. To see the look on her face, the angst in her body language, to finally, the tears in her eyes, it was devastating. It took all of Maggie's hard earned courage to keep from joining her, knowing, instead, *someone* had to be strong. She had already gone into a small degree of damage control, urging Steve to stay levelheaded, and to *think*, long, hard, and serious about what he wanted in life, and what his expectations might be of others, specifically, as Maggie had pointed out, not only *she*, but *others*, too, who were also looking for answers. He hadn't addressed *any* of them, and soon, time would run out. She urged him to consider the Company that employed him and seriously wanted him to stay, versus, the fickle, cruel and pathetic way political parties conduct their business these days, citing the IRS, the AP scandals, the Benghazi investigations, Syria, the controversial health-care system, the debacle of the Memphis siege *'and there's more if you want them'*, she added. Power was nice, many craved it, and being able to strut around for the rest of your life being called *'Mr. Congressman'* might *sound* important, however, she begged of him, consider with caution, first and foremost, what *exactly* was it that he wanted out of life?

She asked, *what* gave him satisfaction, adding then, from every day reality, what was actually *wrong* with obscurity, and being able to live in a world where you can lead your life the way you want to, in peace and anonymity? And finally, family, *especially* Josey, and never having to consider day in and day out what is expected or dictated of one, because public life demands higher levels that often are abused, anyway. Life's happiness topped everything, she had driven home, suggesting, having choices in life is fine, however, decisions made had to suit the end purpose. In her mind it was all absolute, common sense, pure basic logic!

Josey had knocked on Maggie's bedroom door again the next morning, although, with today being a Sunday, she thought she should wait at least until just after eight. When Maggie heard her, she again beckoned her in, however, as fast as Josey bounded into the room and climbed onto the bed, ready to talk as they had yesterday, Maggie clearly dulled Josey's euphoric moment by asking her if she could sleep an extra hour as she and her Daddy had sat up so late talking. Noticeably quite disappointed, without choice, Josey agreed, asking if she wanted her to bring her coffee when she came back, promising not to until 9.15, designating the exact time, qualifying, *'would that be all right?'* Maggie agreed, adding *'yes, please'* to coffee. Josey slinked away, with grace.

With little else to do and very wide-awake, she went from Maggie straight to her Daddy where she received a totally different response; a smile and big hug.

"*What*, young lady, have you and Maggie engineered for today, as you did yesterday."

Bewildered slightly, Josey wondered; *'How would Daddy have known that?'* It didn't matter, she confessed to him anyway! Moments later, when Steve learned Maggie wanted to stay in bed longer, he wondered something entirely different; aware he might have erred slightly last night. Josey had provided the clue!

At nine-fifteen, when Maggie and Josey *did* sit and talk over the coffee she had delivered as promised, Josey noticed, quickly, the happy-go-lucky laughter of Maggie had all but gone, and she was quite different. Saddened, innocently she sought the reason why.

"Is everything okay with you, Maggie, you don't seem as happy today? I hope nothing is wrong."

Her question hit Maggie hard. Never intending, she had given herself away, which meant, emotionally, she was an open book, even to a small girl. She feigned the real reason the best way she knew how.

"Of *course* it is, Josey, everything's *fine*, it's just that this morning, I'm quite tired. Yesterday was a big day and then, last night, well…it was a late one with Daddy as I said, *plus* I had a couple of wines more than I should have, I think, so I am a little slower than I'd like to be this morning."

With only the hint of a smile, plausible, Josey nodded her head as if she understood. Maggie continued.

"Now, *today*, we can do whatever we want, *but*, first things first, because one of the things I am going to do, with no if's and no but's from you, *we, together*, are going to look at the real plight of Angel, okay, 'cause remember, we did have a deal, right? Are we still on for that?"

"Yes, yes, Maggie, that'd be great. I was *hoping* you would say that."

Maggie knew immediately she had defused part one of the problem at hand. She had yet to face part two, Steve, unaware, at all, how he might be thinking, feeling.

"All right then, now, after my coffee and then my shower, we'll have to arrange with your Daddy that we go to a store, if the right one's for materials are open, to pick up what we might need. That will be a priority, so what say *you* chat with Daddy and get it all in play, in advance, while I get ready, okay?"

Josey was gone in an instant. Maggie, meanwhile, headed for the shower.

With soap everywhere, and the hot water casting off a light steam, while running her hands over her body, her thoughts became a wish; that Steve could join her. She could remember too well his firm hands caressing her at their Lake Pontchartrain hideaway only weeks ago, she wanted to return to a time when their love was uncomplicated, when time seemed to stand still, as she wished it could, again, now. Last night was necessary, yet sadly it had become potentially destructive. Uttering a soft mournful sigh, all she really wanted in her life was the love and laughter they had only a day ago. Again, her mind wandered as she pictured Steve, naked as she, in the shower, both, ready to devour each other, as they had, often. Her mind was still in Louisiana. With her hair rinsed, her head tipped back to clear the last suds of soap away, when she turned off the faucet; she looked herself over, imagining how wonderful it would be, if she could, unabashed, walk back into the bedroom and the soft warm bed she had left only minutes ago, to where Steve would be waiting, and who would have had no power at all in resisting her. Rubbing scented moisturizing oil over her body, with each stroke, again, it was Steve, making her feel, *'all woman.'* Not knowing why, uncontrollably, she heaved a huge sigh. *It was not to be*; he wouldn't be there.

Dressed, ready to greet the new day, short as it would have to be, when closing the bedroom door behind her a grim reminder sprang to mind; the 3.15pm flight back to Florida. Josey's birthday celebration weekend was soon to be over.

When Maggie came into the kitchen where Steve was sitting, scouring the Memphis Sunday newspaper, he looked up at her offering a simple and pleasant *'good-morning'* smile.

His immediate thought; *'how naturally beautiful this lady is.'* "How'd you sleep," he threw in. Friendly, yes, however, very low key, monotone, as if expected to say something!

"Under the circumstances, quite well actually, and you?" Maggie had lied while answering the question!

"Not quite like a log, but close to," he shared, his voice lifting a little this time.

"There was a bit of thinking to do" Maggie reminded him, referring to their conversation late into last night, "and for a while, my head spun a little, unfortunately."

"Mine, too," he declared, honestly, "and Maggie, I *promise* you that I'll get it right between us, *quickly*, but I *can't* afford make a bad or wrong decision, you *know* that!"

"Are you referring to work, or politics, or *me*?" she asked, her small degree of sarcasm obvious.

"Oh *dear*, is *that* how it is?" he queried, this time with obvious attitude.

"I don't *know*, Steve, I *really* don't because the *'getting it right between us'*, your words, *that* call belongs to you right now, and I guess we have a little time to kill I'd believe on the subject, unless you know something different, already. Regardless, you won't get any pressure from me making the *'bad or wrong decision'*; your words again. But I'll wait for you, for now. *Believe* me, I have *plenty* to get along with."

"Are you *mad* or something, Maggie? And if so, *say* so."

"*No*, Steve, in fact, *surprisingly*, I'm not mad at all. What we have is a waiting game, one that *you've* called, *not* me, as I see it, so take it for what it is, that's fair, isn't it?"

"I guess, if you put it that way, anyway, we've got the morning," he suggested, casually, "so *what* have you and Josey figured out today, if anything, apart from getting some parts for her doll if we need to?"

Immediately, Maggie knew Josey had done her job before she started hers.

"Nothing, Steve, *nothing,* except of course, as you now know, I did plan to look at Angel so that's my first port of call. That said, I think Josey is in her room right now so maybe I'll head there to re-evaluate my earlier diagnosis to see what we have to do."

Shifting from the planned rigid stance she'd held, she motioned to walk away.

"Maggie, *before* you go." Steve moved from his chair to be alongside her. "Look, I'm *sorry* about last night, the way things ended in conversation. You're *right,* in many ways, and in a few, maybe not, however, I sense a tension this morning and we shouldn't let it be that way. *Agreed*?"

In an attempt to defuse the frosty air that appeared to exist, he motioned to put his arms around her but as he did, Maggie instinctively, not planned, drew back her shoulders. Realizing an immediate futility of his action, sensing a barrier, he, instead, decided to back away completely.

"Oh, I see, then we *do* have a conundrum, an issue, that's painfully clear, to me."

"A conundrum, *maybe,* but not one of amusement, sadly," Maggie was able to officially inform him. "And we *do* have to talk some more, but Steve, no games, *please*. Love you, yes, but don't leave me hanging based on what *you* alone might want to do. I have a life, too, and while it's a yes, that we're finding common ground right now, I *don't* want to headlong into something where I can't at least have some input, and I'm not talking about control. I've *been* there, *done* that, as *you* no doubt have, but I have a life and a viable one at that, so, what we really have here is a need to settle what has the makings of a *serious* situation. Until *you* work *you* out, I'm on the sideline, surely, you can see that! Anyway, for now, let's agree to the decision of last night, take time-out and utilize the time ahead to determine *where* we're going, but specifically, *you*, okay? Now, I really should go and see Josey, she's probably waiting for me and I did promise her."

Steve watched her walk away. He shook his head, a little confused, unkindly thinking, *'women'*, and yet, he knew, for the most part, Maggie was right. It *was* more about him! And yes, their future, if there was to be one, was now entirely up to him!

Maggie went on to explain to Karen, as part of her extended *'I need to know everything'* from her friend, that when she finally looked at Angel, and saw the problems, fixing Josey's doll was *not* the slam-dunk she expected it to be. A composition doll, not only was she quite badly chipped in some areas, she was also in need of some restoration to return her to her original sweet self, also, unquestionably, she would need complete re-stringing. Her clothes, too, would need some TLC, but that was the easy bit! She then proceeded to tell her how it all played out in real time.

"Josey, it's a little more than can be done *here,* this morning, and in fact, with the extra attention I'd like to give her, to be honest, it's going to take me, probably…"

She could see the tension on Josey's face, the disappointment. Always, it was a doll doctor's heartbreak, knowing how much little girls love their precious dolls. Josey seemed to hold her breath, waiting for the final verdict. Then, her jaw dropped. The not-so-good news was delivered.

"...it's going to take me," Maggie repeated, her head spinning, knowing her schedule and the turn around factor of such surgery on a doll of this type, and not wanting to upset Josey any more than was absolutely necessary, "...about, let's say, a week."

"A *week*, Maggie, a *week*, oh dear, oh dear, what *now* then, what am I going to do, I mean, I..."

Nothing, to her, sounded good.

"All right, this is what we'll have to do, the alternative..." Maggie began to tell her. "Let's wrap her up in her blanket in the basket, and wrap her good, then, I will take her with me, on the plane and when I..."

She never got to finish her plan.

"*No, no*, I can't do that, you *can't* do that, Maggie. A plane, take her *away* from here, from *me*, I can't do..." Maggie interrupted her.

"Josey, Angel will be in *good* hands, *my* hands, I'll take *good* care of her, you know that and I can have her back to you, in the mail, in about a week."

Angel's diagnosis delivered, to Josey's ears, had gone from bad to worse, upsetting her badly.

"In the *mail*, Maggie, *no, no way, I can't!* She could get *lost* in the mail and I'd never see her again, *no*, I can't do that!"

No matter what, Maggie could not convince Josey to allow her to take Angel away from her, from the safety of her room, her very possession. To Josey, it was unimaginable and *nothing* would change her thinking. Emotionally, it was *'game-over'* and Maggie realized it was futile, therefore, not to labor the issue, not try to change her mind. Her strong willed nine-year-old mind was set! Angel was *not* leaving, and *not* going to Dunbridge and Margaret 'Maggie' McConnell's doll hospital. Another arrangement entirely would have to be undertaken. What, though, and under the circumstances of all she and Steve were going through, it remained to be seen.

"It must have been hard for you Maggie," Karen Kartney proffered, "extracting Angel from Josey's clutch would have been a miracle."

"It could never have been, and sadly, Steve was of no help. He, actually, missed the point entirely, suggesting Josey was *'being silly, it's only a doll'*. I was *stunned* that he could have been *so* insensitive, to his Josey of *all* people, and honestly, with him, too, she was *not* a happy camper. In fact…" Maggie went on to magnify the impact, "…Josey was *so* upset, she stormed out of the living room where we had moved to for better light, back to her room, Angel in hand, and slammed the door behind her. It was *awful*, believe me!"

"My, oh my, I hear you, what a mess that would have been." Karen was horrified.

"A *mess*, here's the *rest* of it."

Unquestionably, there was a need to talk.

Continuing the story, when Maggie told Steve *'that was a cruel thing to say to a little girl,'* he reacted equally snappy, suggesting that she herself could have been more tactful, and *never* have said that she would simply, *'mail the doll back to her.'* He thought *that* was more insensitive in the bigger picture. Maggie explained it was an every day occurrence in her store when it came to doll *'patients'*, Steve's only reaction was *'well Josey's not* ***anyone*** *and you should* ***not*** *have said it.'* Clearly, to Maggie, the morning had started badly, degenerating somewhat, to the point, at her suggestion, what they did together between eleven and two, after which she had to be at the airport, would be of no consequence. In fact, she said outright, *'I don't mind at all if you get me there early, I'll wait the time out. In fact, being around an airport full of strangers might be a little more civil.'*

Sadly, innocently, all that had been previously wonderful, fell apart completely. Josey, Maggie explained, came to the airport, sensing, it appeared, the obvious tension that existed between her and her Father, but chose to be chatty and smiling as they rode along, pointing at everything and nothing as if it were part of her farewell to Memphis, *'until the next time'* as she so openly chose to say, more than once. Fortunately, when it was time for the final farewell, Josey hadn't changed her feelings in any way; Maggie was *still* special to her. Apologizing for the tact she took about Angel, totally understanding Josey's thinking, Maggie told her they'd talk on the phone and work something out that suited, a simple suggestion, readily accepted by a child.

"I'm going to miss you, Maggie," Josey had blurted out, along with a few tears. And then, surprise of surprises, she whispered, "And don't you worry, *I'll* talk to Daddy."

'What!' thought Maggie, floored! *'Out of the mouths of babe's!'* Josey had taken her aback, almost literally. Also, unintended as it was, even her Father took a quiet deep breath, learning, as he now had, Josey had heard, or picked up, more than either of them thought possible, despite being careful, as they believed they had been in their conversations. Disappointed at the turmoil Steve might have created, and a goodbye in play, there was little he could do about it all on an airport sidewalk. Accepting he had some soul-searching to

do, regardless, finally, he turned to hug Maggie, closer than she thought he might. For now, bygones were just that!

"I'll get it right, I will..." he reassured her, "...and Maggie, apart from always a huge thank you in my life, Josey's too, I'm sorry about a few things, I know I should know better. Before you, *long* before you, I thought I was an oak, strong, ready, and could tackle anything, but now, my dear sweet lady, I'm beginning to think that maybe I'm more a willow, that I should bend, and somewhere in there, betwixt and between, lies the answer, I *know* it."

Profound words, indeed, Maggie thought, and if he meant them, already a big step in the right direction. They were also enough to make her saddened heart lift a little.

"And Maggie, before you leave..." he went on to say, noticing the look on her face showing clearly her low spirit, the pain he had inflicted "...take with you, and know, that in my life you are special, *very* special and I love you."

Confused, just a little, Maggie knew, her parting words had to be the right one's. After all, she loved him, too.

"It's okay, Steve, believe me I *am* trying to understand but it's not coming easy. Look, whatever it is, whatever you decide, *make* it all really worth your while in the long run We've said it *too* many times, and it'll be forever true, life's *way* too short, it needs to be lived, and love; on a vine it withers, and I don't *ever* want that to happen to us. I love you dearly, too. Unfortunately, from a most memorable weekend for which I can only thank you, a wind blew in and Steve, we just ended somewhat badly, I fear."

Minutes later, Maggie was gone, through the doors, into the terminal.

"So, there you have it, Karen, my weekend and more, in Memphis. Different huh? Can you top that one?"

"Oh my God, no, it reads like a movie, Maggie. So who plays *you,* Jennifer Anniston?" she laughed. "But let me say something else, my dear," she added quickly, her tone moving from lighthearted to more serious, "From what I've heard, and can *clearly* grasp, you've been honest, *brutally* honest, and the next move in this play is *not* yours, and please, hear me again, Maggie, *not* yours. So take it easy for now, take your time, and proceed with caution because never have truer words been spoken, as was the admittance of Steve himself. Having said that, heed them, *let the willow bend.*"

~~~~~~~~~~
~~~~~~~~~~

CHAPTER TWENTY-EIGHT

Openly admitted, for everyone to know beyond any shadow of any doubt, Steve Frankston was politically a registered Independent. More difficult as it can sometimes be, running for Office as an Independent raises other problems; money! The *'party machine'* is not in place the same way the two major parties are, therefore, politicking is much more demanding. Regardless, as reported by the Memphis newspapers, both the Republican and Democrats unashamedly urged Steve to switch, to join their camp, however, the overtures were not forthcoming. It would be revealed, initially on the Internet, his interest in politics was waning, to the extent, as one had already predicted, he would not run at all. It turned out, *'rogue bloggers'* and the Memphis Courier Mail were right!

To quell the media, Steve Frankston crafted his own press release and fired it out to every news media outlet he knew, print and electronic, that existed in the Greater Memphis area.

'Regretfully, I will not be putting my name forward to run for office in any capacity, or party, in Memphis, Tennessee. I have thought long and hard about the offers made and appreciate the incredible ground swell of support that existed for me to seek nomination for The House of Representatives in the soon to be, mid-term Elections. To serve as a Congressman for this great State would have been an honor, however, with respect to all, especially already named Candidates, my personal commitments to my family

must, and will, take precedence over any position I may seek, and certainly the one referenced. Recent events, locally, may have propelled me to levels unexpected, and I am appreciative of the impact I may have made, however, it is imperative that I stay true to who I am, as an individual. Should the opportunity arise again, in the future, and they suit my directions of the day, then I do not and never will, close any door behind me, especially at the political level. America will always need new blood in the Halls of Congress and in The Senate. To all who nominate, I wish you well, for those who supported me as a prospective candidate, thank you, sincerely. For the record, I remain, to this day politically, still, an Independent. Respectfully, Mr. Steven Justin Frankston Citizen, Memphis, Tennessee.'

Covered extensively, and with many news organizations seeking follow up comments and explanation, Steve Frankston turned every one down. He chose to *'retire'* from no position he ever held, with one request only; *'respect my privacy'*. He had made his statement; politically, he had nothing more to say – period!

Immediately following the release, he returned to the offices of Visual Communications and its President, Orville Greenspan, to confirm, not only the reported press articles of his non-acceptances, but specifically to confirm his intention to remain with them for as long they needed him or as they, and he, felt he could *'do the job.'* He then requested an immediate two weeks furlough, *'to clear my head.'* Understanding, it was gladly given! Visual Communications were delighted; they had never wanted to lose one of the Company's most valued employees.

"Daddy, what's *happening*? Things seem to have changed lately and I wonder why, *have they*?"

Josey had been confused, also a little sad. Ever since her party and after Maggie went back to Dunbridge, lately, whenever she brought her name up for whatever reason, her Father seemed a little distant or more silent about her than he had ever been, or she had known.

"Don't you *care* for Maggie anymore, did I do something *wrong*?" she added, "and if I did, what should I do now? To be honest, Daddy, I *miss* her, I do."

Josey was referring to the self-claimed *'tantrum'* she threw when she had told Maggie she could not take Angel on the plane with her. Laboring under the belief that it was *she* who had upset her Father, who in turn probably upset Maggie further; Josey was ready to say she was sorry for causing so much trouble. Having harbored her thoughts a little too long and letting it get the best of her, finally, she had plucked up enough courage to ask him *'if it were true'*, and if it was, then she would tell him she would change her mind. She'd let Maggie have Angel, and would send her in the mail, and that it didn't matter anymore.

Josey's questions had been heartbreakingly simple, however, this time, Steve Frankston knew; this Daddy would have to lay all his cards on the table. Totally unnecessary, with Josey believing *she* was the cause for his reticence or mood swing, and then looking to take the blame, suddenly, unwittingly, he realized that he had allowed his personal, internal struggle, to fester, dragging *her* into the quagmire along with him. Within his slightly troubled mind, and with Josey now having come to him, he felt he had let the greatest love of his life down, and for that, he felt almost ashamed; a nine year old had *not* held the key, or been the reason for his failures in earlier decision-making. Indeed, this nine year old depended on her Father's decisions, good, bad or *'otherwise'*, and in her eyes, forever so far, her Daddy had made all *good* decisions, *no* bad ones. The *'otherwise'* was probably where she didn't have the wherewithal to understand what it might even mean - *he* did! It was time to act, *now*. And in time, he would owe his Josephine a debt of gratitude; not that she'd comprehend the - *why*? After giving her a loving friendly hug he set out to right his wrongs.

"Sweetheart, *none* of this is your fault, *none* of it, not one single thing, and *that's* the absolute Gods honest truth. *You*, like your little doll, your Mother's very namesake, are an Angel, and to me, your Father, *my very special Angel*. And I love you. In fact, you'll never know how much you've actually helped me see the light ahead."

"I *have*, Daddy, *how*?"

Another simple question, again, to the point.

"Well, it's like this..."

No sooner did he start he would immediately hesitate. He needed to frame his message in plain easy to understand words and not get too complicated in all he wanted to say.

"The situation between Maggie and me is simple. Our position is not as..." he stopped again. "Josey, *before* I share the between me and you stuff, *remember*, amongst other things, we *will* be talking about Maggie, too, and I *know* how you both are when you get together, so *before* starting, I'll ask you something first and you have to agree, all right? *No spilling secrets or what we say together, okay?"*

His daughter looked at him, smiling her always *'I love you, Daddy'* girl grin.

"Okay, Daddy, I *won't*, but I *still* want to know first, how me, a little ol' nine years old helped *you* see the light, whatever that means, I don't get it!"

"What you *did*, sweetheart, in explaining that light, it means you helped bring out my real, *bigger* problem, and here's how and why."

Josey shifted in her seat, her eyes firmly fixed on her Father. He grinned, and then continued.

"It's like this, I've been *so* wrapped up in my own problems of the day, and *all* the people that wanted me to be a politician, and *then* all the calls I kept getting, a lot of them when you and I were together as you know, *well*... I'd have to talk to them. *That* all took me away from you much more than it should, and *then* there was my regular work, and I *haven't* told you this before, but Josey, if I did do the political thing, you know, run for Congress, then, with my job at Visual Communications, unfortunately, I wouldn't have been able to work for them anymore which meant I had to make a choice; *the elections or them!* It's been *hard* and truthfully, it's messed my mind up a little along the way. Which brings me to Maggie. With us getting close, the things that were happening, the being with her, all of us, *together*, I just wasn't sure *which* way to turn, *which* way to go, with *anyone*. *Everyone* wanted answers, and it's been pretty tough. So you see, Josey, there was *so* much on my mind I began to lose sight of all the things that were, and *are*, important to me, with *you* being number one and I *have* to say, Maggie being, *well*, number *two*, maybe, through it all...I, er I..."

"*Wow, Daddy,* what are you going to *do* then? Is it all *still* a problem for you? *What's* going to happen?"

Her Father smiled, an acknowledgement of how really perceptive his daughter was becoming. He loved it. His answer was simple.

"*Good* question, Josey, *clever* little you, but *this* is where *you* come in and *help* me. But *tell* me this first, what do *you* think? Now that you know what I'm wrestling with, let me know what *you* think about it all, and *don't* hold back, ask *anything* you like, okay? I *promise,* I'll answer you."

For the next few moments he watched his daughter ponder the points he'd confessed. First a large frown ran across her brow, then an upward movement of her mouth, then her lips curled a little as if wincing before she placed her hand under her chin to look at him with a small grin on her face. Then, a mini *bombshell*! Yes, she really *is* smart!

"Daddy, do you *love* Maggie?"

Her Father took a deeper than normal breath, clearly not expecting a question so loaded at the start of their in-depth dad to daughter D and M (deep and meaningful).

"Maggie and I have become very close, Josey, you already *know* that," he told her.

Flat voiced in his delivery, he'd immediately deflected the question, but Josey wasn't having any of it.

"I *do* know that, Daddy, but when two people get as close as *you* have, sometimes that means you might get married someday, *doesn't* it? *I've* seen the way you hug her and to be honest, I've seen you *kiss* her, too. It was nice, though, I *liked* that! You still didn't tell me, though."

Steve Frankston was realizing very quickly it was time to move on and explain a few of the other important matters he wanted to with his daughter, who was herself beginning to tell a couple of secrets of her own. Clearly, Josey was way more aware about what was going on in their house than he had ever given her credit for. He wondered, for a moment, what else she knew, had heard, or had seen, even?

"You're *right,* I *have* kissed Maggie, in fact, Josey, I've kissed her a *few* times, however, let's *not* go there, let's go where I need to and what I want to share with you, okay?"

"Yes, Daddy, but you *still* didn't say if you loved her. *Do you*? Do you *love* Maggie?"

Bam! She'd cornered him. Again, his delaying tactic hadn't worked, straying from her original question.

"Okay, Josey, *yes, yes* I *do* love her, so *there,* but *look,* I've got much more to say yet and we haven't even *started* our little chat, however, knowing you and your questions, you'll have to *promise* me, *again,* that it'll all be *strictly* between me 'n you, as we agreed, *okay*? Got a deal still, huh?"

"*Yep*!" she confirmed and to make her point, she projected the little finger of her right hand out, posing it to stand clear, the rest of her fingers turned tightly inward. Steve, with a broad smile of going along with her did the same. As their little pinkie fingers entwined, together, they gave them an extra squeeze as if bonding tight.

"So, our Josey, Daddy, chat will be safe?" he checked.

"Our Josey, Daddy, chat will be safe," she confirmed. "*Truly,* I mean it. So what else, what's next?"

Between serious and not so serious, funny and not so funny, up and down, over and under, and to places they never thought they'd go; the next hour or more flew by. Dad and daughter had enjoyed a time not shared quite this way before. And all of it, their heart to heart, remained a pact between each other, their pinkies having been entwined!

Ten Days Later

When the plane touched down on the tarmac on the runway of the John Wayne Airport in California, three of the happiest people in the whole wide world were on board. Josey, sitting between her Father, and in her mind, one of the nicest ladies she had met so far in her young life, Margaret 'Maggie' McConnell. Loving the fact her Daddy really thought so, too, *nothing* could have been more perfect. Having never been on a plane before, Josey was amazed how quickly the world could change. Memphis was very cool, almost freezing when they left, while in California, stepping off the plane, the first thing she felt was the warmth, which left her no choice; she took off her sweater.

The ride in from the airport was an eye-opener. Traveling down the 405 Interstate to San Juan Capistrano to arriving at the Capistrano Swallows Hotel, a most wonderful surprise, it looked so…luxurious! Close to the beach with facilities that were superior in every way for the needs of *'vacationers'*, the adjoining rooms they were led would extoll luxury and every expectation Steve Frankston had been promised when he made the arrangements. Wanting for nothing, their stay was guaranteed to be, at the least, memorable.

"Steve, this is *extraordinary* in every way, anyone would think you'd won the lottery, although I must say, you've always had good taste, it's just that *this* time I think you may have outdone yourself."

"It's all for my two favorite girls," was his simple reply to Maggie. "If *ever* you both deserved my *undivided* attention, then from here on in, you've *got* it…*oh,* and I meant to say it when we walked in the door, *'welcome to California,'* our home away from home for the next full seven days, can you take it, I mean, *can* you?"

"Yes, and thank you, Daddy, I love it already, *don't* we, Maggie?" Josey asked, speaking for both of them.

Smiling, Maggie glanced immediately toward Steve.

"That we *do*, Josey, *that* we do, and we're going to have fun. I can't wait to see the pool either, can you? Oh, you *can* swim, can't you?" she double-checked. They laughed. Obviously, there were still many things to learn about Josey, as it seemed every time whenever they were together, a new revelation would surface, but it was all fun.

The next few minutes were spent wandering in, out, and around the rooms, checking everything as they went, including Maggie's, interconnected with an adjoining door, for ease in staying close by, together. The procedure was maintained – for Josey's sake, although Maggie had said to Steve, well in advance, *'Leave it to me this time; I'll work it out. I'll talk to her and explain it,* ***somehow****. You know, the female side if you will, she'll understand.'* He easily agreed, adding that it might sound a little more credible coming from her. Simple as the exchange was, the subject matter did raise a smile.

Shocked yet happy in so many ways as to where they were, in sunny California, Maggie considered for a moment their circumstances and the tables that had turned for all the right reasons. Then she had a flash revisit as to *how* it all came about; readily accepting, it could *easily* have fallen apart!

Ten Days Earlier

When Steve Frankston had called Maggie, because of the lengthy delay in not even a word of *'hello and how are you'*, she had been openly quite ambivalent about not only taking the call, but also in not talking to him at all, period! She had been furious, mostly at herself, for what she was beginning to think; what once was a beautiful new entrée into the world of love and romance, it had, over the past few days degenerated somewhat into a game – one she called *'mind games.'* Equally, the part that really hurt, she was sad for Josey who she had come to love, and maybe, in view of her feelings, just a little too much! Maggie had begun to believe that she had, through her own making, set herself up for what was about to be, a major let down, one she could well do without in her life! With the comforting help, *or not,* of Karen Kartney, right or wrong in her analysis of the past chain of events in her whirlwind ride in all matters of the heart, sadly, she had also considered it had all the earmarks of – *total disaster*! *Nothing* felt good! Accepting that thought, not really wanting to, to then secretly disregarding her inner feelings, Maggie hadn't, by choice, forgotten Karen's wise words of wisdom either; *'the next move is not yours, let the willow bend.'* It had remained, sound advice. Then, it happened!

Maybe, Maggie thought when her cell phone screen read Steve Frankston; *maybe,* she wouldn't answer him at all, that she'd let him squirm a little. But then, she quickly tossed around in her head, *'what was the point,'* and furthermore, would that be nothing more than childish, after all, this could also be the very call where the willow *does* actually bend, and maybe more than she might ever expect. Her other choice was to let the call go to voice mail and give herself the privilege of hearing what he had to say first, to let him qualify his silence, his perceived ambivalence to talk before this, thereby, she would allow herself to make a calculated decision in which way to bounce with the message, as it suited her. Reply, or not! She *hated* her next very silent thought – *'would that be female cunning?'* She physically shook within, *never* wanting to be categorized that way, *ever*!

"Hello Steve, or should I say, *stranger,* maybe?"

It was an easy decision, gladly; she'd taken the call.

"Hi, Maggie, and yeah, you're right, I suppose, and I *get* it. Seems like I've said sorry a couple of times too many, lately, huh? And here I am again with another one."

Maggie was ready for an apology and ready for an excuse, however, straight out of the ballpark, she was going to get what *she* wanted to say out first. Then let the chips fall.

"*Well,* maybe you should have thought about that earlier, Steve…" She began with a tone that was *meant* to sting. "…I mean, *what* is it with *you,* with *men* per se, maybe? *What* is it that you mess us women around sometimes, thinking it's all going to be okay when you say a simple, *'I'm sorry?'* Frankly, I'm getting a little too old for this as you might be, too, Steve, and maybe you should *also* think about what you *do,* the *way* you act, and *how* you go about it all as you go forward, the *very* subject we talked about in Memphis, that got you bent out of shape a little, *remember*?"

Maggie was on a verbal roll not wanting to miss a single subject that was on her mind in airing her feelings, believing, sometimes, that's what you've actually got to do to be heard, to be understood. She continued, uninterrupted.

"You *know*, maybe the heels we've cooled should *stay* cooled a little longer…" she chanced in saying, "…because I have *so* much to do, and *so* much on my plate, *work* plate that is, and *don't* forget, I have a business, people actually *depend* on me, Steve, and to be open and upfront about it all, I've got a fair bit behind on some of it because I've gone along with *you*. Well, from *my* point of view, *my* way of looking at from where we've come, and where we so far *haven't* got, fragment of a dream or full blown, yours, mine, *whoever's*, maybe its time you started to go along with *me* a little, and let me mess *you* around for a while, huh? At least the playing field might be more level, and maybe, also, you might understand better what it's like for the shoe to be on the other foot a little better, too. *Pissed* somewhat, *yes*, and I feel I have a *right* to, but one thing's for sure, that you can *count* on, I *won't* labor it. Talk, yes – we need to, and I *will*, if *you* still want to. Anyway, *that's* my take on this, aaahh…*what* should I call it, *charade*, possibly? Dreams are beautiful, Steve, and I've had more than a few, however, what's *left* of them, *sadly* right now, they're a little mixed up, if not, a *lot*!"

Chance or no chance, she'd taken it. Too many? A momentary silence prevailed. She knew he hadn't hung up, the seconds still checked active per the call-timer on her cell phone screen. She also heard a deep breath. Was it for wasted breath, his, mine, she wondered?

"You *got* me, Maggie, you *got* me in one, I *admit* it, and for what its worth, *yes*, I'm *sorry* again, that was hard to listen to, however, if you're willing to hear me out, maybe there's a chance we can get this show back on the road again."

"*Show*, Steve! Is *that* what you call it, a *show*?"

Maggie didn't like the connotation at all!

"Bad choice of words, Maggie, that's all…let me explain, *please*! But if it's too late, say so, I'll leave you alone."

Maggie knew, time to lighten up or pay the consequences, after all, there's a price for everything.

"I'm *all* ears, Steve, I've got *all* the time in the world for this, although, let me make one more thing clear before you start, *please,* no lame excuses, or dressed up stories, maybe this, maybe that, I'm not *ready* for it, *any* of it, *okay*?"

"Okay, Maggie, but I will say, what I have to tell you, what I have to share, is from the bottom of my heart, and for what it's worth, Josey and I have already talked and if there's one thing I have grasped in the inaction of my actions, I've done a pretty poor job by two girls, *you* and *her,* and I won't say sorry again, it gets redundant, I know, also because you *detest* that word right now, but I *will* declare this to you, I've been to the mountain to coin a phrase, and I've *seen* the sights in the valley below, okay? If I was *ever* ready to talk, it's *now,* so, bear with me, *hear* me out, that's *all* I ask of you. When I finish, whatever you *say,* whatever you *think,* whatever your decision, *that's* the way it'll be. *Fair*? I'll heed your reply, *win or lose,* as there can be *no* draw, I'd doubt!"

For the next, almost an hour, they chatted.

Nine years old, smart as a tack, underestimated, unwittingly, Josey had brought a truth out in her Father she never could have known. From their shared sit down chat and many words spoken, innocently, the proverbial penny had dropped! In his life, so far, the years had been a test to Steve Frankston, starting from the day he had first met Josey's mother, Angelic. He doubted there wouldn't be a mountain he couldn't climb to make his and her world, their time, their life on earth, one of the greatest love stories ever told. Nothing had ever stood in their individual ways to achieve happiness beyond imagination. And when Josey joined them, their future became even rosier. She was such a joy, such an inspiration and together, they couldn't wait, hopefully, for a little brother for her to make their family complete. But it was denied, and when Angelic fell sick, battle as she did, all too soon, the beautiful dream that was, fell apart. It was a shock they could never have seen coming! She and Josey, together, had a mere five years. From there on in, Steve, Daddy to Josey, they were both on their own and nothing could have prepared him for the road ahead. And so the struggle began, however, no stone was left unturned to be absolutely sure Josey knew love abounded, even though it was one-sided – her Daddy. Lonely too often, offers of help, invites by many, nothing could ever make life the same. Josey's school friends, their parents, some of them tried to match make, there were even times when Josey herself, unsubtly encouraged by others, suggested to her Father that they might join up with – whoever? For three years now, Steve Frankston had lived, worked and shared his life with one girl only, Josey, and he'd have it no other way! He never once waivered, that was, until he met Margaret 'Maggie' McConnell. *Why, how, whatever* it could have been, he had no idea! However, in a doll store, in Dunbridge, Florida, there she was. What made her instantly different, he had no real idea, except; her sheer beauty did make him turn his head, for the second time ever! He smiled momentarily for Angelic and New Orleans, his first! That aside, beauty, he knew, was one thing; it could be skin deep – but no, with this woman, Maggie, immediately, it was more her charm, her most positive approach to life in general, her demeanor, her aura of care, and so much more…it was all wrapped up in one, not superficial. And if beauty came with it, then it was a gift. Had God finally smiled down on him, with Angelic's approval? Maybe, he thought, but probably…it didn't matter, he took his chances and chose - *Yes*.

Unquestionably, there had been a reason, a fate of sorts? It tied to the moment, and to Angelic. He remembered her words, spoken with conviction, sincerity, and with all the love she could muster, despite what she had to say - *'…so please, Steve, go on with your life, I'll understand. It wouldn't be right for you not to find new love, someone else to take care of, to love, and I mean that for both you, and for Josey. Believe me, I would.'* Words never to be forgotten they recurred, often – Angelic reassuring him that it was okay. In a very odd way, with all that currently prevailed, even Josey, indirectly, was endorsing her Mother's very thoughts and wishes.

Finally, with the help of two very special people, Steve Frankston, slowly, had begun to find his way back. Unfortunately, though, in stumbling along the way as he had, he'd also let danger enter the fray. And now, unfortunately, it was distinctly possible he had not seen the light soon enough given his proverbial *'moment of truth'* had arrived, his oft times quoted, *'day of reckoning,'* too. Amazed, but ready to reconcile his selfish concerns, through and after Josey's helpful *'chat'* and intervention, his cell phone was the only tool left in his arsenal that had the ability to become the conduit to inner peace - his own, and hopefully, others, *one* especially. He picked up the weapon of choice and tapped the screen.

~~~~~~~~~~
~~~~~~~~~~

CHAPTER TWENTY-NINE

Maggie had no real problem accepting his explanation of all that had happened, not only between the two of *them*, but also for Josey, the one they both mostly wanted to protect. Upset as she was, and had been, it was never her intention to allow an incident, an oddity difference, to end their relationship. She was far too aware, silence can be deafening, two wrongs don't make a right, or stubbornness is probably more destructive than most ever believe. Adults might make silly moves and say silly things now and then, in fact many times do, but for all that prevailed in the on-going lives of the three of them at this moment in time, the biggest thing was, with responsible communication, they'd be able to overcome the differences of the circumstances from whatever side one chose to look at them. Factually, Maggie felt she had made her point by *not* calling and making demands, and if she was ever going to become a victim of a change of heart, Steve's, then she was prepared. She had steeled herself to bow out gracefully. However, deep down, she hoped it would never come to that. Thankfully…it didn't! Back then, those ten days ago, when Steve Frankston's name on her cell phone screen lit up, it became the first step of allowing them both to move forward. They did! And had!

The Capistrano Swallows Hotel catered for all ages, all events and all types of special needs, as requested, and for their first activity, Steve had arranged a trip to the San Juan

Capistrano Mission, where he, Josey and Maggie would take a Docent guided tour. Founded on All Saint's Day, November 1st, 1776 by Spanish Catholics of the Franciscan Order, it was marvelous. The Docent, dressed in historic attire, took them around the ten acre mission explaining the folk-lore, showing them the building and its architecture, the fountain, the Catalan forges and sacred Garden, the museums, all the magnificent splendor of its Mission's history that dated back centuries.

From the tour, they would learn, as legend would dictate, where they were staying, The Capistrano Swallows Hotel took its name from the American Cliff Swallow, a migratory bird that each year makes the 6,000-mile flight from Argentina to, primarily, Southern California. Nesting between the San Juan Capistrano Mission's eaves and archways, protected within the ruins of the Old Stone Church, they inevitably became a *'signature icon'* between spring and fall. The *'las golondrinas'* popularized in song *'When The Swallows Come Back To Capistrano'*, as folk-lore tradition thrives, the first of the swallows arrive faithfully on March 19th, Saint Joseph's Day, then fly back south on Saint John's Day, October 23rd.

Despite missing the celebrated annual event, Fiesta de las Golondrinas, their tour culminated in the tiny Serra Chapel. After they both lit a candle, standing at the alter, their heads bowed, Josey held Maggie's hand. Maggie had explained, this was the time to say a special prayer, suggesting to Josey, her mother, Angelic would be most appropriate to talk to and for. A solemn tradition, it was not lost on Steve who never ceased to be amazed at the little things that seemed to capture the moment, especially when it came to Maggie. He knew, there and then, unequivocally, while watching them both, he had made a very right decision about the future, as he believed it, moving forward. Moved and touched, wanting to share the religious feeling of being so very thankful for so much in his life that was good, he stepped toward the alter to join them, to light his own candle, to make his own silent prayer. With a smile of obvious tenderness, looking at Maggie as he finished, he felt truly blessed to see that she had been looking at him. Happier and thankful, more than he could ever wish to be, taking both girls by the hand, they left the San Juan Capistrano Mission, their most wonderful visit complete. Walking back out into the warm West Coast sunshine, unable to contain her true feelings, Maggie felt a strong need to share her thoughts.

"Thank you, Steve, that was truly *beautiful,* mind altering, almost. I haven't experienced something so incredibly moving in far too many years, and despite not being a regular in church, I do have my inner beliefs, and today, in the chapel, I was deeply touched, thank you again."

Agreeing with her, Josey looked at them both and smiled, *'me, too, Daddy, I thought the church was really nice.'* Unlike the Graceland tour, this time she really meant it. Unquestionably, the Capistrano Mission visit would have far reaching affects, and linger longer as a memory.

"So let's go to the beach, shall we?" Steve suggested to Maggie and Josey over breakfast. "It's time we put our feet in the sand, watch the waves roll in, feel the water between our toes and maybe look for some sea-shells, who's in?"

In unison, Maggie and Josey responded most favorably, *'Me!'* Minutes later, with their shoes off and their jeans rolled up as far as they would go, they headed for what they hoped would be the warm waters of the Pacific Ocean. They were not disappointed and for the next hour it was all they could do to contain their frivolity of splashing one another, kicking the waves as they rolled into the shoreline, aiming the water as high as they could to land on whoever was closest at the time. Josey collected as many shells as she could carry, pleading, *'Maggie, could you hold some of these for me?'* for the one's she couldn't. They finished up starting a little seashell pile, near where they had placed their towels. Next, Steve began piling sand up in a mound, Josey joining him, wanting to know if he was going to build sand castles. When he told her he was going to make a ship, with two decks and three funnels, she was excited, asking, *'can I help you, Daddy?'* It was no contest; *'of course.'* Maggie, meanwhile, scurried around looking for anything that could enhance the ship's appearance as it came together, using shells for portholes, a twig for the flag pole, and whatever else was handy, particularly little pebbles for general decoration. It was a team effort and when it was finished, photos were taken on cellphone cameras to remind them of a special day at the beach, the first of what they hoped would be many, together. Smiles abounded.

While taking time out to regain some energy, Steve and Maggie, in a quiet moment, were more than content to sit in the sand, legs stretched out, watching the white caps of the water breaking at the shoreline. Josey, meanwhile, a ball of energy, jumped up to begin running in and out of the water, kicking and splashing, laughing and smiling, having what could only be, the *'time of her life.'* Tiring of that, she then began writing, whatever, in the sand. Moments later, not allowing for the oceans ebb and flow, a breaking wave would rush in washing away her words, taking them back out to sea. She laughed, they laughed. Not to be defeated, she moved a little further away to write, whatever, again. Happily, this time, the tide couldn't repeat itself.

"Come and look, Daddy, Maggie' she called. They did.

'Daddy loves Maggie.' Three simple words crafted by a nine year old.

"Oh *really*?" Steve said. "And is that what *Josey* thinks?" he added.

"It's *true*, Daddy, you *know* it, and yes, I do."

Maggie raised her eyebrows, glancing at Steve.

"You've loved her for a long time, Daddy, I know that, too. Tell me I'm wrong!" she challenged. *Another* no contest?

Slightly uncomfortable, but not showing it, Maggie looked at Josey who smiled a big wide grin at her. Sensing why, she held her hand out to take the twig she had used to write her message. She then bent down to write hers, *'Maggie loves Josey.'* Without hesitation, Josey bounded toward Maggie wrapping both arms around her giving her the biggest squeeze she could muster. Maggie returned the gesture. To Steve, it was another of her tender moments, and as always, he loved them. Releasing her, Maggie kneeled down to be at the same level as Josey, their faces, close.

"You *love* the beach here, don't you, and you're really having fun, too, huh?"

"I *do* and I *am*, Maggie, I *am*. I haven't really been at a beach before and it feels so, so…so," she was stuck for the right word. *'**Different**, might be what you're looking for'* Maggie told her, finishing her sentence, knowing how exhilarating the beach can be, the sand, the water, the ocean air, the incredible visual expanse that makes the world seem so big, especially through the eyes of a little girl, who lived in a big city, in the center of America where there *are* no oceans, or beaches, only rivers. She was aware, of course, the mighty Mississippi that runs through the heart of Memphis wasn't just *any* river, and yes, it *is* majestic. But it wasn't a beach, with sand, or an ocean reaching back to the horizon, or a shoreline with breaking waves. Josey was clearly in her element, enthralled with every moment of where she was.

"You know, Maggie, I'm so happy we came here and I'd love to stay here, forever, with *you*, and Daddy, and me. We could do this every day. I'd love that, a lot."

"That would be nice Josey, but you know…" Maggie countered, before double-checking where Steve was. She was considering that this might be the opportunity she was looking for, that they might take a short stroll together, down the beach a little, to be alone. She had not forgotten she was yet to explain how the next few days, and nights, might play out between her Father and her, and the real possibility they might be compromised, more than a little, maybe! Before deciding, she again looked his way. Surprised, they both noticed he was finishing writing his own message in the hard sand, far enough away that any breaking waves could not wash it away? She would have her girl-to-girl chat later, she decided. Together, hand in hand, she and Josey headed in his direction. Approaching him, within a step or two, she was able to read the message. Then, it hit her, Josey, too. Emotionally and by natural reaction, Maggie's hands went straight to her mouth that dropped wide open in disbelief. *'Maggie, I love you, will you marry me?'* - his love letters in the sand. Steve watched Maggie, without moving. Frozen where she stood, her legs wouldn't move. She looked up, trembling, barely managing to blurt out her excited reply.

"Yes, Steve, *yes, yes,* I *will* marry you, and I love you, too, but you already know that."

As he took the three steps needed to be with her, Maggie fell into his arms, almost knocking him off balance that could have sent them both down into the sand.

"Daddy!" Josey called out. *"Daddy,* she said yes, I *told* you she would, didn't I?"

Maggie instinctively turned her head to Josey and in a mildly firm voice, asked, "Did you *know* about this all the time Josey, *did* you, and you *never* told me? Did you two collude to get me here, to have me where you wanted, down at the beach, so you could set up and do what you've both done, you more than guilty conspirators, both of you?"

"Yes, Maggie," Josey admitted, without hesitation, "and I *told* Daddy you would say yes, and Maggie, you love Daddy so why *shouldn't* you marry him, then we'll all be together? That'd be so cool, I'd *love* that!"

"We *should,* Josey, and we will, but *how* did you do it, *how* did you manage to keep it all such a secret? You and I have shared lots of things before, I mean, how...how...you're *such* a little devil, you know that, don't you?"

Sitting in the sand, just the three of them, plus a few seagulls and numerous passers by walking hand in hand in the sunshine, the idyllic setting, the joy of the moment, and the love they all had for one another, when Steve openly declared to Maggie, in front of his daughter, Josey, his love, and the hope for a future together, expectedly, but maybe not, unashamedly, Maggie's tears of joy finally began to fall.

Caught up in their declaration of love for each other, and sharing in the happiness all around them, Josey succumbed to the moment and began to cry, too. Dad's arms went out to comfort her and willingly she responded, hugging his neck, squeezing tight, almost too tight! Sensing Maggie kissing his cheek, Josey lifted her head beaming her big wide nine-year-old grin. "I'm happy, Daddy, *really* happy."

"Me, too, sweetheart, and I'm a *lucky* man, aren't I"

For a split second, his mind went back to the Mission of San Juan Capistrano and the quaint little chapel where they had all stood, with candles. Steve recalled his wish; happy to know that it had come true in the very way he planned it, and that Maggie had come to him in the way he had asked that she might. Watching only, as he had at the time, he was thankful that he had heeded the message in his head, that he join Maggie and Josey at the chapel alter and light his candle. And then, with a hint of intrigue, he wondered what Maggie's thoughts and prayer might have been. He could only believe they were brought together for a reason, and the first one for him was love, love in every way…for the love of Josey…for the love of Maggie…and for the love of Josey's little 'Angel' the *real* and underlying reason for *everything* today, and soon, was readying to find new life in a little girl's world.

Under bright blue skies, in a seeming world of his own, with the two *'girls'* in his life he loved dearly, Steve Frankston could ask for no more than the blissful peace and joy he felt in his heart. Finally, now able to recognize and release his inner heartfelt feelings, he was thankful…thankful for the second chance, thankful he could again, share love.

~~~~~~~~~~
~~~~~~~~~~

CHAPTER THIRTY

How could Maggie have ever known? If she'd been caught off-guard once, she was soon to be caught off guard, twice! After their sojourn to the beach was over, they quickly cleaned up ready to head out to the local shopping mall where they could not only wander at leisure, but also, be assured they could find the necessary, and badly needed, *'change of clothes'*, accepting, a visit to the beach required one to be very casual, and certainly in more minimal attire than their earlier visit. They needed swim costumes, shorts, loose fitting tops, sandals, too; all agreed, *'we need to be and look, more Californian.'* Expected, while at the Mall, they visited many other stores, too, specifically dress shops, something Steve didn't mind, especially as Josey had instigated some of it! Maggie actually wondered why; Josey was never a big shopper, as she understood it. Regardless, it became the perfect way to spend a long lazy afternoon, topped off, for Josey, with ice cream. Getting back to the Capistrano Swallows Hotel just after five, dinner was already set for seven they were told. For Maggie, the timing was perfect. While Steve excused himself to double-check with the booking office in the lobby about what they might do for the next few days, tourist-wise, she would utilize the time he was gone to maybe have that impromptu girl-to-girl chat with Josey, it was still necessary, she thought, but then again, it might have to be after dinner, she *did* have to *'ready herself'*, for their big dinner reservation, of course. Just before he closed the door, Steve glanced back at Josey, and with the coast being what he determined as *'all-clear'*, he gave her thumbs up and a big wink to match! She smiled in return while calling out, *'bye-Daddy, don't be too long, okay?'*

Maggie looked incredible! Steve could hardly take his eyes away from her. When she finally emerged through the adjoining door of their hotel suites and stood in the living room of Steve and Josey's suite, there appeared to be a glow, an aura, all around her, as if someone was shining a managed light on her…the vision splendor was all – Maggie! Stunningly beautiful, she wore a light green, long, gracefully falling dress that showed every contour of her body. With thin straps over her naked shoulders, and a hint of cleavage, enough to turn any mans head, the dress draped down to rest just above her ankles. Low high-heeled sandal styled shoes completed her intoxicating look. Even Josey acknowledged her glamor with a *'Wow, Maggie, you're soooo beautiful!'*

"Not that we're going to one" Steve chimed in behind her, "but, Maggie, my dear, you could be the *'belle of the ball'* and to think, if you were, you'd be with me, although I'm sure Rhett Butler might want to cut in, and me out!" he added with a lilt in his voice.

"And *who* is Rhett Butler, Daddy?" Josey asked, as if worried about an intruder! Maggie and Steve both smiled.

"Oh, no one important here today, or any day, Josey," he told her, "but Maggie *is* very beautiful, isn't she?" he asked, as if seeking even more approval of their both already declared astonishment.

"She's *always* been beautiful, Daddy."

The private room, off from the main dining area of San Padre's Capistrano Restaurant with views of the Pacific Ocean, was a surprise Maggie couldn't have anticipated. Visually captivating, the décor was very Spanish, fitting perfectly the imagery she already had of California, even the furniture complemented the architecture. Full-bloomed colorful Bougainvillea plants were everywhere. It was a setting, befitting the very reason Steve had said to Maggie as they headed from their room, *'I wanted us all to go somewhere special, to celebrate all we've shared today, that you and I will be married, and Maggie, I've already waited too long.'* She leaned forward to kiss him lightly on the lips. As she did, Josey reached up to take her hand. With a gentle squeeze and a smile as she looked down at her face, Steve issued the orders, *'Okay girl's, let's head inside and celebrate shall we?'*

Shocked, feeling as if her breath had been taken from her, the first face Maggie saw was Karen Kartney. Her faithful friend, her *'doll-doctor-intern-sidekick,'* her very own private and personal confidante, Karen wore a smile as wide as the Grand Canyon. Next, she saw Wayne and Annette Quartermaine and along side them, almost missed by her, given she was still seated, was Amy, Josey's very best friend in the world. Then, the *biggest* surprise of all, her mother, Eve, somehow lured by stealth away from her Chattahoochee home and *how,* Maggie did not have a clue! Later, Karen took all the blame.

Nervous, speechless and taken completely by surprise in every way imaginable, while still holding Josey's hand, she carefully made her way toward the table, afraid her legs might buckle before she got there. Eve, her arms open wide for *'her baby'* to come to her, embraced Maggie, who wanted to cry. Forcing herself to hold back her tears as she felt the arms she had loved around her, forever, as a little girl, as a grown woman, all she could bring herself to say would be; "Momma, how *could* you, and all the way from your river home, *how* did he do it, how did he *ever* get you away, but believe me, I am so happy, so happy…and to see you here today, tonight, in California, what a thrill, and Momma, I think I'm a lucky girl."

"I do, too, Maggie, he's a *good* man, someone I've so longed for…for you. Love him always, Maggie, good men are hard to come by, and Steve, he, he…"

"I *do* love him, Momma, and I *will*, and Josey, you'll love her, too, especially when you get to know her."

Pulling away from her Mother's arms, Maggie turned to Steve who was standing right behind her.

"How *could* you? How did you manage to do all this, and hide it all? What were you thinking, I mean, how ca…"

"Maggie, it was for *you*, me and Josey, we thoug…"

Maggie spun around to Josey who looked up at her, sheepishly, aware of what was coming next. She was smiling.

"You *knew* about this all along, Josey, all along?" Josey nodded a yes. "I thought the conspiracy between you and your Father was *already* over, the beach and all, but…but…there was *more*. You *knew* there was more and *still* kept it a secret?"

Josey nodded her head in the affirmative, again.

"Come here little lady, at least give me a hug you little perpetrator of all things wonderful, to say *nothing* of luring me to the Mall to shop, too, but *thank you, thank you,* Josey for…for…well, being, you!"

During the light interaction, Amy had rushed around the table to be alongside Josey thinking she might need her moral support, and fast as she arrived, Josey immediately reminded Maggie who she was, forgetting momentarily about the Nashville Doll Show and all the fun they had. Lovingly, Maggie hugged Amy. The Quartermaine's shared the light interaction offering their embrace and sincere congratulations. Soon, the small gathered group was ready to be seated; the evening had only just begun.

Next day, outside, as arranged to absolute perfection in how everything fell into place, the white archway, the chairs, the flowers, the music, when Margaret 'Maggie' McConnell said *'I do'* when asked by the preacher, *'do you take this man, Steven Justin Frankston, as your lawful wedded husband, to love, cherish and hold, forever',* she meant it in every conceivable way. She truly did plan to love, cherish and hold him, forever. And after the ceremony, when Josey tugged at her dress, the very special one they both had rushed out to find for the wedding ceremony, and told her, *'I'll love you and cherish you, too, Maggie',* no words could ever have been more sweet and heartfelt, than from a nine year old, who openly accepted Maggie as her *'new Mother,'*

"You know, Maggie, for such a long time, I always *hoped* you'd love Daddy, because I *knew* he loved you, he *told* me so many times. And I loved you, too. I always hoped a day like today would come and Maggie, I'm glad it did. Today is so great!"

It was all Maggie could do to hold back her tears. Instead, she scooped Josey up in her arms and gave the longest hug.

"Thank you, but you're a *'little devil,'* too, Josephine Lisa Frankston, you kept so much from me, and *amazingly*, hid it so well, but it's okay, I do forgive you…this time!"

Standing off to the side, Steve Frankston, witnessing it all, could never have been happier. Today, he felt his life might finally be complete, again. In a quiet moment, standing alone, his mind full of love, he looked to the heaven's above, to the blue skies of California and the small white clouds looking so perfect, so beautiful, over the Pacific Ocean and the beaches of San Juan Capistrano. In silence, he spoke the words he knew he must, and would. *'Thank you Angelic, thank you. I* ***know*** *you approve, and believe me; Maggie will love and take care of Josey, too. And always know, I still love you for all we shared, and you'll always be, to us, in our lives, our beautiful Angel'*

~~~~~~~~~~
~~~~~~~~~~

CHAPTER THIRTY-ONE

Josey hugged her Father, then Maggie, as she prepared to say farewell at the airport to travel home to Memphis with Amy and her parents, happy to stay with them until the newlyweds returned home from California. Josey knew her Daddy was in the very best of hands, just as *he* knew, Josey was, too. It was also part of the deal she was privy to long before all the events had played out the way they did, and to immaculate perfection. The part she had loved the most, and shared with Maggie, was how Maggie reacted when she discovered everything that had happened, that it was all part of the very secret pact she had honored with her Dad. Accepting it graciously, Maggie was not only impressed, but couldn't help telling Josey, *'I might have to keep a very careful and watchful eye on you, 'cause you're good, but I love you, and I can't wait to get back to, wherever we all end up!'* Pondering for a moment, a quality she actually liked, child or no child, Josey, had also proven beyond the shadow of any doubt, she could keep a secret. For her, though, this time and for all the right reasons, she was glad it had remained that way; the best kept secret in the whole wide world had become her greatest thrill…she loved her Daddy.

'Bye Maggie, I love you' Josey called out as she walked away, *'and **no**, I don't have any more secrets.'* Maggie smiled, believing her, implicitly. Suddenly, for no reason at all, she realized a reality of conversation that had not been resolved between her and Josey, however, in the spirit of all that had

happened, so fast, collusion included, it didn't matter now. Her suite had been cancelled; all part of Steve Frankston's grand initial plans.

That night, after making sweet, beautiful love for the first time as man and wife, as Maggie lay with Steve, content, happy and feeling forever blessed in every way, there was something she really wanted to ask, to know. It would be for no reason, except, intrigue!

"Steve, whatever made you go to such lengths to do all you did, and in such a well planned and executed, clandestine way, never to be sure if I would *really* say yes? That was *quite* a feat and gamble, really."

Steve looked at Maggie giving her the grin she loved to see in him. Instinctively, she kissed his cheek. Gazing at her, looking so gorgeous, his mind told him, on his road to life and all that might be ahead, he would always want her by his side, that he was lucky to have ever found her, and that, forever, they would be together. He dearly loved her, and how fortunate could he ever be that she loved Josey, too. His answer came easy. This lady was becoming, had become, his very life.

"Maggie, many years ago I did something, not on impulse really, but because I *knew* I was right, and time proved me to be exactly that, *right*! Just as it is, and was, with you, now. Frankly, I took my chances, betting the odds, relying on my feelings, instinct!"

Maggie had no way of knowing the memory of *'taking chances'* went as far back as New Orleans at the conference where he first met Angelic, when the guest speaker, Troy Hazelwood, spoke convincingly on that very subject *'taking chances'* followed by *'trust and honesty.'* The speakers words rang true today in the very events between them both, as they had played out. Just as it had been with Angelic, Steve knew, and his heart kept telling him, the once Margaret 'Maggie' McConnell, the very *now* woman in his life was the best thing to ever happen to him since his life was so devastatingly changed all those years ago. If there was *ever* a second chance in life, *she,* Maggie, was it, and never in his wildest dreams was he ever *not* going to follow his heart, and take his chances. In doing so, when Maggie said *'yes'*, again, finally, his life could be complete. He loved her.

"I always knew you to be a very perceptive man, Steve, and unabashedly, I'm glad you did. And here's something I'll share that I remember only too well. That very *first* day, the day you came into my doll store, *really,* I admit it, you almost took my breath away, not that you knew it, but you did! I was so taken by you it was amazing! Anyway, *that* was quite a day, one I've never forgotten, and now look at us both. Who could have ever known? In life, there is never any telling, the where, the how's, the why's, it's truly fascinating."

"*Well,* Miss Maggie, not to copycat you, or one-up you, but *this* is the truth, also. If I, *almost* took your breath away, let me tell you this, you *did,* you *truly did* take mine away, *completely*. Fact was, *then,* I could hardly speak at all!"

"You're so kind, flattering, too," she said, "but I *love* it, and don't stop, however, seriously now, here's my next question. How did you ever get Momma out of Chattahoochee first, and then get her to wherever she flew out of, to here, San Juan Capistrano? You obviously had help, Karen, however, that was quite a coup. Momma's a tough little cookie to move, anytime! You did exceedingly well."

Smiling at her, the inner devil in him took over as he made a suggestion that he wasn't going to take no for, as an answer. She'd have to concede but he'd keep it simple.

"When you've kissed me again, I'll tell you the whole story, *all* of it, *how* I did everything, the *lot*, but first, there have been *far* too many questions and maybe not enough lovin', so before I sta..."

He didn't need to say it. In tandem, with great minds thinking alike, without hesitation, Maggie threw back the lone sheet that covered them both to move her body over his, their nakedness, sensuous and cool on each others skin. Full, soft and all woman, in a tantalizing way, while lovingly skimming and caressing her breasts gently over his chest, she immediately placed her lips on his, then, with a slow writhe of her body, on and off, gently pressed down. Combined, their same in tandem mind shattering feelings led them both to places they loved and longed to be. As their tongues searched each other, and their hands moved over each other's body, soon, they were one. Together, in a pleasurable slow rhythm, with a crescendo building, one they couldn't control, finally, there was a joint cry that spelt pure ecstasy. With a sigh, allowing the moment to linger, holding each other tightly, breathless, they looked into each other's eyes. She heard, *'I love you Maggie'* and as he traced her face, her cheeks, her eyes, her mouth, with his fingers, he heard in reply *'I love you, Steve, I'll always love you.'* As her eyes welled with tears of happiness, she snuggled her face into his neck.

Steve explained, reminding Maggie, how she had told him that Karen Kartney was instrumental in the idea of them meeting up in Nashville for the doll show, and that, in her words, Karen was a Miss I-Can-Fix-Everything-In-Life. Unaware, Steve had phoned Karen at the store to thank her for being so astute in bringing them together, to wit, Karen replied, *'anytime you need any help, don't hesitate to call me.'* It was borne out, when Steve revealed, to help get the plans he had made for California and getting Maggie's Momma, Eve, out there, with that challenge, he needed Karen desperately. He had followed through on her offer.

Instantly, Maggie realized, Karen was not only a huge player in the overall game, but also, she had known all along about her impending proposal of marriage from Steve, too. She also remembered her *'let the willow bend'* analogy, thinking, how wise she was, then, not knowing if that was before, or after, their heart to heart conversation of all things love and romance? Not that any of it mattered, really!

Karen, for Steve, as the conduit to Maggie's Mother had explained to Eve, under veils of strict secrecy, Maggie would need her out on the Coast, sharing with her the marriage plans, and that she would desperately want her to be there for the occasion. Agreement, as it turned out, came easy and in getting Eve to fly, she never batted an eyelid! The on-going hardest part, Steve confessed, was two-fold. Swearing Josey to secrecy, at which Maggie laughed, amazed that she did, and so well at that, but also, in secreting everyone, Karen, Maggie's mother and the Quartermaine family to the Capistrano Swallows Hotel and keeping them under hidden wraps, hence, their lengthy stay on the beach and the excursion to the shopping mall. He added, the Hotel was magnificent about the simple wedding arrangements he'd asked for. Experts as they were, with large or larger, small or smaller when it came to weddings, setting up for the

3pm ceremony, and catering for it outside in the naturally colorful garden area, everything went off without a single hitch, even in securing a last minute photographer.

To lighten his story, a little, Steve then decided they should remember, not to forget, that both of them would, from here on in, forever be able to blame Karen Kartney for bringing them together and for the way their lives played out from that time on, after the Nashville Doll Show. Maggie agreed, grateful that she had a loving, faithful friend in Karen.

"I'm staggered, Steve. That was such an undertaking, I almost feel guilty for not helping, after all, I *was* the subject, with *you* of course, but really, when I think about what it all took to put in place, the people, the secrecy, it's mind-boggling! You see it in the movies but not in real life, but then again, maybe you do, because you did it, in *our* real life!"

"Maggie, the hardest part was putting *us* back together again after my admitted silence. *That* is where I almost blew the whole thing, after all, you were a little peeved at me, and don't say you weren't."

"A little, maybe, but I would have come around anyway, I loved you too much to ever let you go, or not be in my life. That would have been unbearable. I would have been miserable for the rest of my life, believe me. You are quite the man Steve Frankston, but tell me, because I'm not sure I'm totally clear on one thing yet, and after the revelation you have just unraveled, *this* question will come easy, I think, or hope. *What's* happening in Memphis? What *really* happened there, although I know you gained two weeks vacation time, which tells me something, but not everything?"

Before leaving Memphis for California, Steve Frankston met with Orville Greenspan, President of Visual Communications, again, to explain that he would not be resuming his position with them, on his return. Electing to resign his position as CEO to the Web and Software Division, incorporating Entertainment and Film, as truthful as he could put his position and situation into words, regretfully, he concluded; *'therefore, I will need to put my family and life into full perspective, and sadly, I will move on, it's the right thing to do.'*

As before, Greenspan would hear none of it! Valuable as he saw Steve to be for Visual Communications, he offered a counter proposal; Consultant under contract, also, accepting Web and Internet work can be done anywhere in the world, from home, *'so why should Dunbridge be so difficult to manage, plus, what's 450 miles when it comes down to it'* he suggested, offering his hand to shake it as deal, to confirm it.

The explanation took the new Mrs. Frankston, aback.

"Are you *serious* Steve, *seriously* serious, I mean, you aren't *kidding* me here, are you?"

"Why would I, Maggie? I told you I loved you and I've told you I can't ever let you out of my sight again, I need you with me, in my life, in Josey's, we *both* love you and what better place to start our lives together than in Dunbridge. You *do* have a doll store to run don't you, how would you *ever* do that from Memphis?" he jokingly, almost flippantly threw in. "Anyway, I'll base Visual Communications for me at home, and, oh by the way, you don't mind if we start looking for a new home together when we get back, do you?"

"Oh, my goodness, it never ends with you, does it? House hunting now? But yes, I love it, that'll be fun."

The excitement, the sheer thrill of all she had just listened to, the love she was clearly feeling in every imaginable way, the sacrifices that had been expressed, all to make her happy, suddenly, Maggie became inwardly emotional. Wrapping her arms around Steve, moving in closer under the sheet, hugging him tight, no greater joy could be imagined than for the serenity she felt inside at that moment. And to think, with the mountains he'd moved, he did it *all* for her. With tears still rolling down her cheeks she blurted out an inner emotion that had overwhelmed her.

"Why me, married to you? What did I do to deserve such a man like you, Steve Frankston? How could it have been that you came into my life, that you found me?"

His response was a kiss. And for the next few moments, all was still; all was calm as they lay in each other's arms. Deliriously happy, they were at peace, life was serene. Then, suddenly, unexpected, belatedly, and with an air of comedy, he lightened the moment with a thought.

"Why, *you,* you asked? *You, me, married*?"

Maggie nodded her head. It still amazed her.

"*Well,* my dear sweet, Maggie, *Mrs. Frankston,* have you *forgotten*? How *else* am I going to get Josey's doll fixed? *Marrying* the Doll Doctor was one way, for sure."

Instantly, both burst out laughing.

'Touché' Maggie finally managed to offer.

~~~~~~~~~~
~~~~~~~~~~

CHAPTER THIRTY-TWO

Steve Frankston's direct flight touched down in Memphis right on time. Thrilled for her Father to be home again, when Josey was finally reunited with him, and in his arms, she wanted to know…*everything*!

Margaret 'Maggie' Frankston's plane touched down in Panama City via Tallahassee, just over twenty minutes late. Karen Kartney, faithful friend, conspirator extraordinaire, and custodian of the Dunbridge Doll Store whenever Maggie was away, which had been more often than not lately, doing…whatever – she also, wanted to know…*everything*!

Within the week, Steve and Josey Frankston, with their Ford Expedition carrying precious cargo on board, started their journey from Memphis, Tennessee to Dunbridge, Florida where they would, excitedly; meet up again, with Mrs. Margaret 'Maggie' Frankston, nee McConnell. Departing on time, the exact 473 miles, according to the GPS, could not be traversed soon enough. With fervor and anticipation, especially for Josey who was finally able to bring her little doll, Angel, to Maggie, to be made whole again. Maggie, meanwhile, expecting a patient of importance, had prepared a special bed for her in the doll hospital. Even Karen Kartney managed to get involved. Responsible for all *'doll patient'* check-ins, listed as dictated by Maggie, 'Angel #1 VIP – AMW', she was to be placed in the inner sanctum area of the doll hospital. Karen was confused; there *was* no inner sanctum and the doll hospital had *never* used the code AMW before. Curious, she double-checked the information. AMW, it turned out, was the newly created *'Alongside Maggie Wing'*, which meant, she was so important, she was never to be let out of Maggie's sight. Karen loved it! However, best laid plans aside, what they needed and were really waiting for now was the patient herself! At exactly 4.15pm that same afternoon, the long road trip over, Angel, successfully admitted, could be found, resting gently in her bed in the AMW. Tomorrow, with love and care, she would be as good as new again, a very pleased and happy Maggie Frankston absolute guarantee.

That night, while Josey slept in her temporary home away from home, happy as any nine year old could ever feel, her Daddy and new *'Mommy'* sat together to ponder a future. Loving the way they had interacted earlier as they sat on the bed and chatted and before sharing a kiss goodnight, Maggie implored to Josey that she use her name, understanding and explaining, that she would never expect her to call her Mommy, and that her love could always be shared. Angelic she told her, would forever be her Mom, *'and anyway, I love it when you call me Maggie'*, she truthfully told her, *'so please, Maggie, it'll be, okay?'* Josey accepted it and in her own inimitable way shared the nicety of all the reasons why as Maggie pulled the bedroom door behind her. *'I love you Maggie, and you'll still be a Mommy in your own way, I know that. And thank you for everything, too, especially loving my Daddy.'*

Maggie couldn't believe her good fortune in life. Josey was truly, one of a kind. She vowed to be the best *'new Mom'* she could ever be - she loved her.

As arranged and by design, Maggie was gone early next morning, long before Josey woke. Steve had shared coffee with her before leaving, and then, after preparing breakfast for Josey, he woke her about an hour later. He had stalled for time with her, sharing, that they would meet Maggie for lunch, later. Daddies can't always fool their little girls, Josey thought, guessing why, all along, what was up. She was right! Calling into the doll store, before they were to ostensibly meet for lunch, sitting upright in all her splendor, for all to see, and dressed immaculately, Angel was the perfect doll. And Josey needed no coaxing to see, or know, where she was as she entered the store. Front and center, she sat in a chair, as if looking at all the other dolls in the store; a Queen of stature, with her loyal subjects all around.

"Oh, Maggie, she is beautiful, truly beautiful."

Before Josey even attempted to pick her up, she gave Maggie the longest, hardest hug, adding, "Thank you. I *knew* you'd never let me down."

"It was *my* pleasure, Josey, and I must say, I can see *why* she was so *special*," Maggie began to enlighten her. "Do you know that your Mom handed down to you, and from your Grandmother, *her* Mother, I believe you said, a *very* collectible doll? She is not only *spectacular*, but she's *rare* and *valuable* also. Not many of these dolls were made."

"She is?" Josey had never thought about money, value, before. To her, a doll was to love, to hug and share with, to talk to, and be your friend. As Angel always had been.

"Yes," Maggie reiterated, quickly, adding, "but money is *not* always the issue, remember, love and friendship is, even in a doll. Angel is very lucky to have such a friend in you. And I can understand *why* you think so much of her...like you; she's beautiful, too. A real little Angel."

It had been easy for Maggie to explain the importance of a doll in a young girls life. Just as boys love trucks, cars and the like, girls love dolls. Fads come and go, just like friends, but a little girls first doll in life, especially if they are handed down in the family, from either Grandmother or Mother, when they are, *that's* when they take on an even greater meaning. It's history, family history. Josey had such a doll. Angel was already third time loved, and hurt as she had become, Maggie had made her whole again.

Josey couldn't stop looking at Angel, holding her. And as her Father watched, the smile, the love, the sheer beauty of seeing his little girl at peace again with what had been quite stressful along the way, a Daddy couldn't be more proud. And he was, the same way as he had been in awe of how Maggie spoke, and told her stories, explained everything. And Josey had hung on her every word, taking in the importance of the message. It seemed, to Steve, every day there was a new reason to love Maggie more. When it came to children, to the sensitivity of so many little things in this world that make up what life is all about, in *their* eyes, she had a *gift,* a way to communicate, and the children *listened.* Josey was the luckiest little girl in the world, he believed, to have a *'Mom'* who would now help him guide her through life, with a love he could only begin to imagine. He, too, was a lucky man, in too many ways. And if there was one thing he was looking forward to in the future, it would be his life with Maggie, with both his *'girls,'* small and vulnerable as one still was. Now they could *both* protect her.

Maggie took the afternoon off. With 'Angel' now out of the doll hospital, safe at home again, she, Steve and Josey headed over to the popular Dunbridge County Lake for a planned picnic lunch. Idyllic, peaceful, all around them the huge trees covered in Spanish moss, offered shade, not only where they sat, but also to parts of the lake surface that gently rippled in the soft breeze, its waters lapping the edge, its sound, melodic and relaxing. Informed through Karen, as they munched on their sandwiches, that they had a date with the realtor tomorrow who had five properties for them to look at, all to the specs given, a conversation of anticipation followed, one they couldn't wait to be realized and brought to finality. Finding their new home together would mean the start of their new lives together. It was the perfect moment for Maggie to take the occasion in a totally new direction.

"I hope you'll like it here in Dunbridge, small maybe, but it *really* is a nice place."

"With you, Maggie, *anyplace* is a good place." Steve offered, meaning every word. He'd seen enough to be most happy. Small, he thought, was good.

"Amy has said her parent's would let her come and visit and stay with us, in the holidays, anytime," Josey added to the conversation, "and Daddy said I could go to Memphis to visit them, so I don't worry much about it, Maggie, however, I *will* miss Amy, though. I miss her already, and Tiffany, and Mary, and...."

Speaking her friend's names had a tone of sadness, causing Maggie to quietly shudder. It was the one area she was most sensitive to. Josey was leaving her friends and the only life she knew, although she had been most gracious in her understanding, happy, as she had declared often, to be wherever her Daddy was, and now, to be with her, too.

"I *know* you will, Josey," Maggie commiserated, "but maybe when we find our new house there might be some friendly neighbors around who have children. That'd be nice." She had elected to be philosophical, taking a positive, reassuring stance.

"Angel's my friend for now," Josey continued. "She's better again and she sits in my room where we can talk, and look at things, and she watches me while I sleep, too. She'll be my friend always, Maggie."

"Speaking of Angel, along with you, maybe she'd like another friend, too. You can always find her one in the store, Josey, you know that?" Maggie offered as she had before.

"I *do*, Maggie, and thank you, maybe I will. Maybe she *does* need a friend, *everyone* should have a friend don't you think?"

"Yes, and it's a *great* idea," Steve chimed in. "Angel was far too long without one so now is probably the perfect time, along with a new home, a new town, it's an *excellent* idea, Maggie. Maybe we'll check tomorrow, what say you?"

Agreeing with a nod to both of them, Maggie had something else to add to the conversation. All she could hope was, that her timing was right, wondering also, what both their reactions might be.

"About Josey needing a friend while we're talking about friends, that is," she started. "I think I might have *another* maybe *perfect* answer for that," she added, looking for a response, any response this time.

"You *do* Maggie, for me, *who*?" Josey asked, curious to what she was talking about.

"I'm *not* sure!" she replied, nonchalantly. "What about a brother, or a *sister* maybe? One or the other could be your very bestest friend, I'd believe."

Steve and Josey looked blankly at Maggie, then at each other. Maggie shrugged her shoulders, adding, "I think we have one, or the other, on the way."

"What?" Steve exclaimed, caught off guard. *"Seriously?* Are you what I *think* you might be? I mean that would be…"

"I do believe so, Steve," Maggie interrupted, hoping she'd handled the news the right way, although, judging by Steve's instant reaction, she guessed she had.

"So, Josey, what about it, a brother or sister? What's *your* choice here?" she asked, excitedly.

Josey didn't need any prompting. Young, she might be, however, she got the message immediately and quickly joined her Father's cheering line.

"Maggie, Maggie, is it true, is it true, because I'd *love* a sister, or a brother, whatever! *Wow,* that would be unreal. A *real* brother, or sister! *Wow!"* she repeated, her smile beaming from ear to ear.

It didn't matter. Maggie had hit a home run, it seemed. Immediately, thrilled, Steve and Josey hugged Maggie, then each other, their happiness, their unbridled joy, contagious, infectious, Maggie couldn't have scripted it.

"*Careful* now," Steve cautioned, "We don't need a problem. And Josey, we'll have to *watch* Maggie from here on in, *nothing* strenuous." He laughed.

The day, the moment, Josey, Steve, Maggie…a happier trio could not be found in the park no matter how hard one might have looked. Sitting, talking, eating, laughing, planning, sharing…to finally, new life, who could ever have imagined - a broken doll, now mended, had led them all on a long and wonderful journey, one they could never have believed would have ended the way it has. Angel, had performed, it could be claimed, *'a miracle.'*

Josey, Maggie, thought so!

Steve, obviously in agreement, smiled at both, the loves of his life. Placing a hand on Maggie's tummy, looking at Josey, then at Maggie, his words were simple, drawn from the depths of his heart.

"You know, my dearest of girls, but for the love of Angel, and her transformation that was needed and sought, *Josey*..." he then turned to look directly at his beautiful daughter, "it was *you* really...had we not taken our original journey to end up here in Dunbridge, who *knows* how our lives might have turned out? For the love of Angel, and by that I mean, *your* love of Angel, thankfully, we are now, all of us, truly blessed and God I love you both so much."

Now standing, he motioned them to take his hand.

"Let's go home shall we...this day, this life; all of it belongs to us, together. Let's go live it."

****

A NOTE FROM THE AUTHOR

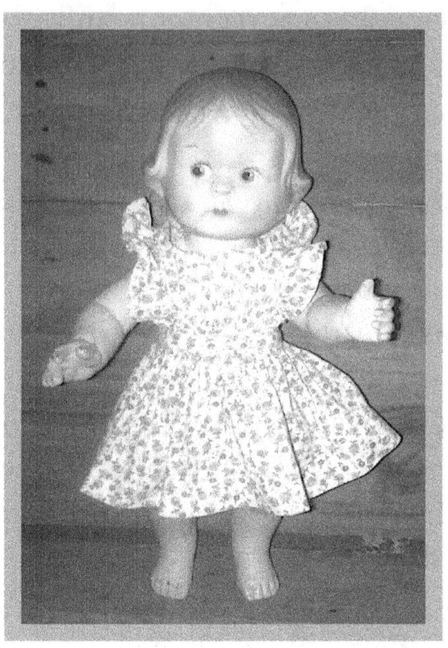

Named after Josey's Mom, Angelic, this is *'Angel,'* the little doll portrayed in this manuscript, the one Josey loved so much. She became - the story. To qualify, with added reason below, it was my absolute intention to create a fictitious storyline weaving, what is clearly, changing circumstances when it comes to dolls in this our more modern way of life and the way today's generation continue a much loved tradition that is centuries old. In this, the Internet driven 21st century, bricks and mortar doll stores are disappearing, rapidly, probably, most never to be seen again. So, too, are some of the most wonderful dolls created by onetime, master doll makers, particularly in 19th Century Europe (France and Germany, specifically). Today, in a more disposable society, what remains is a mass production of a variety of dolls, forced on the market to satisfy little girls with little to no consideration of artistic creativity. That's not to say it is wrong, it's just that with this new direction and approach, some of the most incredible dolls of a bygone era, some of the most beautiful creations ever, will be ultimately lost, destroyed or discarded, willfully, and with so few bona fide *'Doll Stores'* remaining to keep the art alive, someday, the existence of both will be lost to history. Thankfully, and very importantly, one should not dismiss the collector of which there are still, in the U.S. and globally, many thousands. And please, so you know, *'Angel'* is today in the hands of a true collector. Thank you, Paula.

And so…with due consideration of the premise outlined, unashamedly, with love, I crafted this story of fiction in tribute to my wife, Lynne Kristi-Harding, a double cancer survivor, who owns and operates, still, one of the largest doll stores around, including, yes…a real Doll Hospital, in the State of Florida (DeLand). Ten years hence, her doll store and hospital still thrives, as does her dedication to what she calls, *'the doll industry'*, and I suppose, for now, it can still be termed as such. In accepting her portrayal of dolls and doll collecting as diminishing, this story was my way to pay tribute to *her* profession – *her* passion and love of dolls - knowing, that what she does and how brings so much pleasure to so many in every conceivable way imaginable. Believe me, I've witnessed it!

Now, admittedly, crafting a full fictional storyline around a doll was interesting, indeed, in being perfectly honest, it was a challenge bigger than I expected, however, what better way than to use real situations, some of which, with license, did find a place within these pages. Regardless, ambitious or otherwise, I hope you agree that in this finished manuscript - I might actually have hit the mark. I hope so!

In summation, paramount, and of absolute equal importance, I also very much wanted to impart a belief with fervor and firsthand knowledge; that although one's loss in life (in varying ways) is sad, heartbreaking and personally traumatic - along the way, in time, there *can* be healing, there *can* be new life, and there *can* be, indeed *is,* more than believed, a second chance at love finding its place if one is open to such a course, and mostly, it is found in very unexpected ways...as Steve Frankston, Josey, and Margaret 'Maggie' McConnell, found, herein.

A Footnote - For those that may wonder about the little girl on the front cover, for the record, she is my beautiful nine-year-old granddaughter, Lulu, who lives in Australia. I trust you'll agree, she represents, to perfection, visually, the most wonderful and charming girl in this novel – *Josephine 'Josey' Frankston*. Like Josey, could this be the budding entrepreneur in her, the artist – it is, after all, her first paid assignment ever?

Thank you for allowing me a moment of indulgence and by the way, if you choose to, visit Lynne's store on he Internet – www.dollsofdeland.com

OTHER BOOKS AVAILABLE BY PETER L. HARDING

THREE DAYS LATER (2012)

LOVE SURVIVES THE DREAM (2013)

THE SLEEPING PRESIDENT (2011)

A short story synopsis of all book are on the following pages for your reading pleasure. All are readily available on www.amazon.com in paperback or as e-books on phone/tablet electronic files.

To communicate with the author about this and other releases; email – peterharding77@gmail.com

THREE DAYS LATER

'Decree Absolute' – two words that changed the life of Tony Thompson forever. Living the big city life in Hartford, Connecticut was one thing, meeting Chelsea Martin from Florida's small town DeLand on a Caribbean cruise was another. Both divorced *'forty-something'*, both successful in their own right, the Realtor and the Doctor had more than simply being single, lonely and free, in common. But cruises end! With a thousand miles between them and a need to be connected, the Internet with finger touch precision did its job. However, you can't touch your new best friend. Something had to give! Southern hospitality, sunshine never ending, and Spanish moss was quite the contrast to snow, sleet and slush.

Discovering with passion, the delights and differences of a lifestyle in the *'Athens of Florida'* on Main Street USA, in forsaking Connecticut, and the disconnect of divorce, Tony discovered in Chelsea's DeLand, a new and smaller world, one full of life and down home charm. As two worlds collide and north and south again battle, this time for lifestyle - three incidents of magnitude will test their resilience.

There are reasons why love endures, why life throws out challenges, and why we sometimes find difficulty separating the forest from the trees…and yet, with the right vision, looking in the right direction, in the end, it can all be painfully clear. Tony saw it, Chelsea accepted it. Pulling heavy on the heart strings - Three Days Later is a love story that never ends.

~~~~~~~~~~
~~~~~~~~~~

LOVE SURVIVES THE DREAM

Jody Nugent, the only child of an affluent New England family, secures work in Boston Television immediately after high school graduation. Content to be settling well into a career, unexpectedly, she makes a devastating personal mistake that brings with it inevitable choices. Soon, her life becomes hauntingly tormented.

Jennifer Wyngate moved from waiting tables in Los Angeles to the glamorous runways of fashion modeling and television commercials. National fame follows in the spectacular small screen series *'Street Dreams'* which head longs her toward a decision making career move, too good to refuse; a big budget movie to be filmed on the glitzy Surfers Paradise strip on the sun-drenched Gold Coast of Australia. As if decreed, fate enters the fray.

With timing being everything, the crossing of paths with the compelling and charismatic Sam Hunter, a roving Australian Photographic-Journalist from Brisbane who travels the world on contracted newspaper and magazine assignments, will turn out to be the catalyst to a life-changing, chain of events, never imagined or expected.

Amidst delight and dismay, the chance meeting of strangers from worlds apart, sets the scene for potential chaos as hidden secrets are exposed causing mind shattering highs and lows, plus everything in-between. What, then, for those embroiled that learn the shocking truth?

~~~~~~~~~~
~~~~~~~~~~

THE SLEEPING PRESIDENT

Threats of war shatter the idyllic wedding and dreams of young Mustafa Rahman and Shereen Taraki. Accepting offered escape from Khaimaad Village in Afghanistan to an unknown well planned destiny, a terrifying Khyber Pass *'flight to freedom'* into Pakistan follows.

Securing American refugee status in Karachi, the penniless immigrant's, befriended and mentored by New York based Afghans, over time, in their new country, amass personal wealth, unimagined.

First born Shawn becomes a successful media icon before entering elected public office. George, his tormented younger brother fights the new war on terror, in of all places, Afghanistan, while his twin sister, Kristen, a language translator, moves to Washington DC.

With the family gone, leading their own lives, against their collective wishes, when their Father, Mustafa, again accepts help, honoring a lifelong promise, he unwittingly guarantees *'Mission Accomplished'* to a once meticulously planned, sinister, evil plot. Love and survival, business and high stakes politics, patience and intrepid, masterful forethought, all culminate, when the ultimate price, originally expected, was finally, shockingly claimed!

A question, forever, will remain – Could it happen?

~~~~~~~~~~
~~~~~~~~~~

ABOUT THE AUTHOR

Peter L Harding, an Australian, lives in Florida with his American wife Lynne. The experienced worldwide traveler has lived and worked in five countries – his native Australia, New Zealand, Canada, Great Britain (London) and his current home, since 1995, in America. His childhood years were spent in a home for unwanted children where he was raised before being sent, alone, at age sixteen, into an unknown world. That world became his educational playground.

From a former car-park-jockey in England, to an on-air radio disc-jockey in Canada, to a successful broadcast industry executive in Australia, his passion for music became his chosen career path. Holding top managerial positions in both print media (newspapers) and the record industry (RCA) the world still beckoned. Travel, again, formed a huge part of his life including, tour guide, traveling exclusively by bus, through Europe. Then, from a stint in Sports Management, it led to his moving to the USA, his more recent home.

Settled, writing became a diversion and his growing catalog of work is enhanced with this latest release – For The Love Of…Angel, an inspired, fictional, love story.

In his words *'Every day is as exciting as yesterday.'*

His motto; *The world steps aside to let everyone pass – if they know where they're going.*

~~~~~~~~~~

All previous releases available at www.amazon.com Search/Books: Peter L Harding – for paperback or e-books electronic delivery. If needed, download the free Kindle app for all phones and tablets – www.amazon.com
~~~~~~~~~~

www.ingramcontent.com/pod-product-compliance
Lightning Source LLC
Chambersburg PA
CBHW062028170626
46813CB00001B/325
* 9 7 8 0 6 1 5 9 0 4 3 4 4 *